D0582283

THE COVENANT

The Covenant

PAIGE MITCHELL

NEW ENGLISH LIBRARY
TIMES MIRROR

To Abe, with love
Thank you, darling

First published in Great Britain by Secker & Warburg Ltd., 1974
Copyright © 1973 by Paige Mitchell

*

FIRST NEL PAPERBACK EDITION NOVEMBER 1975

*

NEL Books are published by
New English Library Limited from Barnard's Inn, Holborn, London, E.C.1.
Made and printed in Great Britain by Hunt Barnard Printing Ltd., Aylesbury, Bucks.

45002482 2

Book One

One

REUBEN WOKE to a memory:

The year he was twelve it had snowed. He had wanted a shotgun. His father had taken him out to the old Cosgrove plantation and taught him how to kill squirrels without a shotgun. Saying, *... a Buchman's gotta know how to survive on the land.*

Reuben stirred. The present claimed him – dawn, Saturday, the last week of February. Then came the familiar sense of vague urgency. Each day, like a beggar's parade, the realities filed through his law office in downtown Holmesdale – grief and anger and chicanery and despair, men who endowed him with the twin roles of father and god. He was in charge of his own fate, they were not.

Then he remembered this morning's particular urgency: John Tyler Higgins.

He came fully awake.

In the quiet, the white porcelain clock ticked loud and virginal. A pair of small, gold hands moved on past six.

Beside him, Mollie slept – a mass of tangled dark hair, a slender wax curve of back. He felt a quick burst of sexual desire which immediately slaked itself. He had no real need to touch her.

He got out of bed, naked, pulled on a blue silk robe, then headed for the window. A wall of mirrored closets gave him back the reflection of a sizable man without the flab of the ex-athlete, in spite of the fifteen extra pounds he was always swearing to diet away; but discipline wasn't his long suit. He lived by his instinct. He lived by his feelings. Like the case of John Tyler Higgins. Why the hell lay his neck on the block – for a stranger?

Why the hell?

Because that was his style.

5

He parted the drapes, held back a mist of French eyelet curtains. The first snow in four years had begun during the night: light soundless flakes still cobwebbing the pines and lacing the rose garden, coming to rest like a mass of white ash on three acres of wooded hillside. In any other place, it would have been an estate. In Holmesdale, Mississippi, it was simply a good hunk of land. The snow was a gift to it, dry and gentle and windless, not enough to damage the beech or the sweet gum or the pair of willows that marked the path to the greenhouse.

A squirrel hurried along the wrought-iron fence that enclosed the swimming pool, tail rippling in the air like an Elysian banner. It streaked up the trunk of a long-necked pine, shaking the branches to make its own miniature snow flurry, king of the morning. At that moment, the snow quit. The sky became instantly clear, the air phosphorescent. Then, a squadron of rats that had been nibbling away at the woodpile emerged and marched towards the woods, leaving the first set of tracks on the brilliant white land.

He left the drapes fall back. The moment of personal inventory was finished, the morning ritual of contact with land and self. The rest ran smoothly, by rote. Reuben didn't have to think about Mollie, asleep, under the white lace quilt; or Mollie's woman-day – coffee in bed, and mothering two sons, and tomorrow teaching Sunday school, and taking the countryside photographs that she developed in the darkroom he had built for her. He didn't have to think about whether or not he liked the pattern of daisies on the night-black wallpaper, or the carved teak nightstands, or the antique dresser she had painted Chinese red. Not even, anymore, about whether or not he could afford these things. He had been married to Mollie for nineteen years. She had been seventeen. Now, when he thought about Mollie at all, he thought about the fact that he loved her, but it had ceased to surprise him.

He went through her dressing room into the bathroom and showered. The bathroom, like the bedroom, was papered in midnight and strewn with daisies. The sun-yellow carpet went all the way through. He shaved by neon, thinking about Higgins and pulling the razor across the jaw which had become a gravel bed. He didn't look like a boy anymore. In March, he would be forty-one. A few silver hairs had appeared at the temples and in the bristly tan eyebrows. And lately he had begun to see his growing resemblance to the portrait of his grandfather that hung in the corridor of the Marville City Hall. The old man, at his age, had grown a few miles of cotton and owned a few miles of slaves –

though they weren't called slaves by then, tenants and croppers. It had been thirty years after the Civil War when Joe Buchman came from the Russian Ukraine and put down his seed. And passed on his face. As a sign.

It was Saturday. Instead of a business suit, he pulled on the gray mohair sweater Mollie had given him for Christmas.

Then he went down the hall, past the boys' rooms. Joe, named for the old man, was twelve – asleep with the covers over his head. Phil was six – asleep with the cat and the cage of hamsters.

Reuben thought about Higgins. What he knew about Higgins. Not much:

Ten years ago, in '58, the Higgins family had moved into Holmesdale from parts unknown – Higgins had been seventeen and strange-looking, a head of moonlight-white hair and shoe-button eyes and taller than a basketball player. Upon arrival, he had saved two young boys from drowning in the Pearl River and his photograph had made the front page of the *Holmesdale Clarion*: JOHN TYLER HIGGINS, HERO.

People forgot him. There was a mother who had been pensioned off at Webster Asylum for the senile and the insane; and there was a sister who had married a man named Stimpson from New Orleans; and Higgins had gone off for a couple of years and come back calling himself a Practitioner of Dentistry. After that, Higgins had lived in old Mrs Parsons' boardinghouse on Second Street, his dentistry equipment set up in the front room so his patients went past the veranda filled with old women stitching in rocking chairs and old men straddling the rail and reading the Memphis newspaper. By that time, Higgins had become a familiar figure on Main Street, in a crumpled white linen suit and an old Panama hat which he wore even in winter, always walking alone, and moving slow, like he had nowhere to go and nobody waiting for him when he got there.

But that didn't make Higgins a queer.

At the end of the hall, Reuben came down the curving staircase, letting his hand slide along the smooth, polished surface of the bannister rail.

Why fool with it?

He remembered last spring, when he and Attica had taken Mollie's station wagon after some fertilizer, and he had seen Higgins, pale as a ghost, ambling along on Main and talking out loud to himself, and Attica had said, – *looks like a swamp devil*.

What the hell's a swamp devil?

Born to make trouble, Attica said, and that's all he'd say. Veteran of more than fifty years as a black man in Mississippi, Attica had learned not to talk too much.

Later, he had come to learn what Attica meant. By summer, the rumors had started, stories of Higgins hanging out with the Snick workers trying to register black voters. And when old Mrs Parsons kicked Higgins out of her boardinghouse, everyone knew the rumors were true. Then damned if Higgins didn't move into the Holmesdale Bank Building and set himself up a fancy office, and after that he committed the unforgivable: he hired himself a female assistant black as ink, and then he began taking in black patients. M. K. Taylor, the cop who had arrested Higgins, had said: *A goddamned white man workin' on nigger teeth.*

M. K. Taylor had picked Higgins up on a morals charge with an underage transient boy who died three days after signing a confession.

What are you going to do – let a man be framed? Kornfield had thundered. Daytime rates from New York.

Because Higgins had copped out on the bond posted by the A.C.L.U. and fled to New York – and three days ago the call had come in from Kornfield, asking him to take the case for the sake of legal conscience, Jewish psyche inheritance, and identification with the underdog.

Reuben had said no to all three.

Finally he had agreed to think about it, let Kornfield know. On Saturday. Today was Saturday.

He hit the bottom of the stairway. His heels rapped across the marble-floored entrance beneath a massive crystal chandelier. He stopped long enough to pull his overcoat from the hall closet, then went through the swinging doors to the kitchen. The kitchen was empty, Leila and Attica not in yet. A big country kitchen of whitewashed pine and brown brick, iron and copper pots hanging from the ceiling. He pulled on his overcoat and went out the back door.

His breath frosted the air. He went past the patch of King Alfred jonquils which had thrust and blossomed through the thin layer of snow. Insisting on an early spring. In less than a month the dogwood and redwood would bloom, and Attica would set out the tomato plants, and the moccasins would begin to crawl out of the Pearl.

He went past Mollie's station wagon, the back stacked up with camera equipment, and climbed into the navy-blue Cadillac he had collected last month as a legal fee. Payment for representing Honest Dick Duggan in a state income tax case.

A Cadillac was a *fee*.

8

What the hell was the Higgins case? Five hundred flat from the Civil Liberties Union in New York. Not enough to pay for his time and he'd have to turn the money down anyway. He didn't want any checks from the A.C.L.U. going through the Holmesdale account of Buchman & Woods.

He started the motor. Then he saw the brown paper sack – four jars of muscadine jelly, also a legal fee, a note signed 'Annay.' Payment for getting Anny Bowden's black son, Clyde, out of jail for the third time; the charge: disturbing the peace – a cutup party at the Atlas Cafe which was a questionable black hangout raided with regularity by the local police.

Between cases like Anny and Higgins, he'd end up a saintly pauper.

He left the motor running. He set the muscadine jelly in the snow outside the back door.

What he needed was a trip to New Orleans. A twenty-four hour bout with a bottle of Scotch, and a wild, crazy lay.

He backed the car down the hill past the row of gardenia bushes that Attica had wrapped in plastic. Nobody had known it was going to snow, but Attica had read the signs. In the new generation of blacks, there were those who went north and those who stayed to box themselves in with impotent disdain turning their angers against each other. But the older generation did what they had always done. Attica's wife, Leila, tended the children; Attica tended the gardenias.

At the bottom of the hill, across the road, were the woods that guarded the lowland of the Pearl. Through the stripped winter trees, the first rays of sun glinted on floating slabs of ice. If it didn't snow again, by midafternoon it would all be slush.

At the edge of his land he halted the car and looked back at the fluted columns of the antebellum house rising from the snow. He saw the house as himself. A little damned big and a little damned arrogant, hard-built from sweat and anger and commitment. Structured to withstand the onslaught of changing seasons, the pilings went deep into the hillside. Built only four years ago, it might have been built in his grandfather's time, every detail authentic, true to the heritage the old man had established. He saw the house as a statement of his life.

Then, in his mind's eye, he saw his father, just before Jesse died, right before the house had been completed. He saw his father, short and stocky, and picking his way through the framework, and pointing with old Joe Buchman's cane. And saying, *You sure think you're somethin' now, boy, I guess you think so, don't you?*

9

Two

THE CITY LIMITS began a mile away.

It was an ordinary Saturday – no traffic yet on Morningside Drive, the key artery of the upper-class section of town. Holmesdale, once an Indian trading post, had become a city laid out like a three-leaf clover. The business section at its heart, the three leaves marked off its caste system. Eighty-five thousand blacks lived in the section called the Oyster Bar, on narrow unpaved streets, in two-family shacks owned by white landlords. A hundred thousand whites inhabited the Westdale leaf – neat miniature ranch-style houses with barbecue pits – blue-collar workers and school-teachers, those who made less than thirty thousand a year. The Morningside leaf belonged to the old families, the nouveau riche, and the Jews – Reuben fell under the heading of all three. The rewards were membership in one of two country clubs, a private swimming pool, more than one servant, and the right to drive past the expensive, well-spaced houses lined up in the quiet of the snow.

He had worked his ass off. He had earned it.

It took him five minutes to reach the intersection of highway where two shopping centers faced each other. The encroachment had happened in the last fifteen years; he had watched it take place. Holmesdale reflected the way the entire state was going – land receding and concrete highways coming in, the lure of cheap labor and natural resources bringing in factories; the dream had changed shape. Fifteen years ago there had still been land; there had still been the law on the books that insisted on an equal plot of land and gardens for every building; there had once been crape myrtle trees blooming everywhere. Now the dream had become shopping centers, high-rises, urbanisation.

His grandfather would have cursed it.

As he pulled into Morningside Heights, he saw Monk Levitt hadn't arrived yet. Twenty years he had known Monk – since 1948, since the days of the Sigma Alpha Mu handshake in a broken-down fraternity house on Audubon Street in New Orleans. Back when Reuben had been the only Jew on the Tulane football team and the only Jew flunking out of pre-med. Back when Zack Rosen had nicknamed Milton Levitt 'Monk,' saying: *Every girl wants to fuck an ape.*

He parked in front of the Williamsburg, a delicatessen, gourmet shop, and restaurant. A bay window sported a copper hood and an assortment of Danish hams, Italian salami, English cookies, and Israeli pizza sauce. Nothing southern in any of it.

He stood for a moment in front of the window which represented the final straw in the pack that had broken his father's back. Then he wondered why Jesse had invaded his head twice already this morning. Bringing back all the years in Maryville, back when he was a kid, back when his father had owned the only general store in Rose County. Selling seed and supplies, and molasses and fatback, everything on credit and sometimes years to collect; three thousand blacks to every thousand whites. Why today? Why the memory of Jesse, and Jesse's old store, out on the windy highway where the roads made the sign of the cross? His father had been maybe his age back then, the age Reuben was now, cutting up a side of beef with strong, bold strokes. Then Jesse had rolled up his sleeves and washed his hands at the yellow-stained sink; Reuben could remember the soapsuds foam in the curly black hair of Jesse's knuckles and hands and forearms, thinking then that was the mark of a man.

What had happened to that?

At thirteen, Frieda had sent him off, the military academy down on the Gulf Coast. The upperclassmen had beat the hell out of him, and a homosexual professor with a bulldog had tried to seduce him, and he had prayed every night he would die from the mosquitoes. He had blamed Jesse. But it had gotten him into Tulane alright, into pre-med which he had hated and which had defeated him. And he had blamed Jesse for that too. Then the chain stores had moved into Maryville, and Jesse couldn't compete, and everything had fallen apart. He had blamed his father again; and by that time the anger had turned into contempt.

Five years ago, his mother and father had finally left Maryville and moved to Holmesdale. Jesse had tried to sell real estate, but the freedom had kept him drunk on fresh air and there hadn't been enough connivery in him. Then his mother had come up with the idea of the Williamsburg. Reuben had backed her up. And a year after it opened, Jesse was dead.

There was guilt in the memory, and anger, and the sight of his own reflection in the bay window reminded him how little he resembled his father. Jesse had been small and wiry, the runt of the Joe Buchman litter; Reuben was six feet, a throwback to his grandfather Joe, as ragged and burly as the old man had been, and Reuben had been told he was as dogged and intractable. But the frontiers his Russian grandfather had confronted were gone; and the frontiers that had killed his father had no size; and the frontiers left to him had not been given names except by northern journalists who named 'issues' without understanding any of it – and that included the case of John Tyler Higgins.

He went through the door of the Williamsburg. A bell tinkled. His mother looked up from behind the meat case without missing a beat on the slicing machine. Frieda was wearing a butcher's apron over a forty-dollar dress, and her hair was freshly done from the beauty parlor, and the bones of her face had left her with dignity, if not youth. She was attractive enough to have married again, but he knew she wouldn't. The idea of a man offended her. She had been married to his father for forty years.

He said, 'What the hell are you doing up this early ?' – beginning the morning ritual, protective and angry. The protectiveness had been part of his training. The source of the anger had never revealed itself.

She quit slicing and began to weigh the meat into sandwich-size portions. 'Syd closed up last night.'

'Screw Syd – he's younger than you are.'

'He needs his rest,' she said. A lie. Syd Kaminsky was a horse. Right after Jesse died, Frieda had gone to Chicago – from delicatessen to delicatessen until she had finally found Syd Kaminsky working at the Nosh Box. Like a horse. For a hundred a week. Reuben had made up the contract. A draw of a hundred and a quarter against a piece of the net. It was business. The contract gave Frieda control. Syd had arrived with a wife and a baby. A burly, pock-marked man with a wry humor and the ability to work fourteen hours a day without dropping. Eventually he had acquired a mortgaged house in Westdale and a new Chevrolet. Frieda had come to depend on him, Reuben had come to like him. Once, prompted by guilt, Reuben had asked him: *Why the hell don't you get out of here ?* Syd's answer had been: *You don't understand. It's easier here. It's still 1945 around here. A man's still got a chance.*

'Goddamnit,' he said, 'when are you going to quit being a martyr ?'

'When you quit shouting.'

'I'm not shouting!' Every morning he shouted. He knew it. She knew it. Round One.

She stooped and uncovered a pan of blintzes in the meat case. She sold blintzes as crepes, she sold chopped liver as pâté, she sold kreplach as chicken ravioli. Jewish dishes rechristened with French and Italian names had made his mother the gourmet expert of the Morningside cloverleaf.

'The lox is fresh.' She began to spread cream cheese on a bagel.

He took a seat at a corner table. Mirrors reflected knotty pine walls washed down with green, wooden tables and ladder-back chairs, shelves loaded with gourmet items. From the kitchen came the sounds of mixing and grinding, oven doors closing; Frieda was famous for her cheesecakes.

'You look tired.' She set the lox and bagel and coffee in front of him, then sat down.

'I'm fine.'

'I hope you're not going to get involved in that Higgins case.'

'Why not ?'

'It's not good for your career.' From '61 to '66, she had fought integration with the best of them. Yankee newscasters in search of mothering and a pastrami on rye had always been startled to find a Jew lined up with the rest. It hadn't been principle, it had been business.

'I'll handle my business, you handle yours,' he said.

She bent towards him and lowered her voice. 'I heard they took over the land outside of town.'

'Who's they ?'

'Black militants.'

'Where the hell did you hear that ?'

'I pay a little extra to the help.'

'It's not enough to pay income tax, you have to pay extra for *trouble*.'

'I hear they have shotguns,' she said. 'I hear they're calling themselves the African Republic.'

'They don't have shotguns.'

'How do you know ?'

'I *know*,' he said. She suffered from fantasies of retribution.

'We don't need any more trouble.'

'Then don't pay extra for it !'

'Don't shout,' she said. Round Two. A black boy with a bucket came out of the kitchen and began to mop the brick floor. Reuben concentrated on the lox and bagel. Frieda pulled a letter from her apron pocket.

'I got a letter from Willie. Aunt Elena's terribly ill.'

'I'll send some flowers.'

'It's not like the other times for Elena. I can tell by Willie's letter.'

'What do you want?' He knew what she wanted. She wanted to remind him that she was concerned about his father's relatives in Maryville. Jesse's three brothers. Jesse's only sister, Elena. Back when they lived there, his mother had considered them gross and uneducated and incompetent. Which they were.

'Maybe we'll go to Maryville?'

'Maybe.' He had no intention of going to Maryville. A visit with Elena, and with Jesse's three bothers, and having to listen again to the story of how old man Joe had named his father for Jesse James; and how the four brothers had once been known across the Mississippi delta as the wild ones; and how Elena had once been the most beautiful girl in the cotton belt. All the unreconciled things lay in Maryville, most of them buried, like his father, his grandfather. No thank you.

'I hope you mean it. We're a family. We're still a family, you know.'

'Old man Joe and Papa,' Reuben said. 'That's all I claim and you're the one who taught it to me!'

'Don't shout,' she said. Round Three.

She rose and went back behind the meat case and began to cut pickles. In silence. She always retaliated, finally, with silence. *None of them are any good*, she used to say. *Except Jesse*. And Jesse had spent a lot of years proving he wasn't like the rest of them.

He finished the bagel in silence. She kept hers. He kept his. Finally the Levitt Construction truck pulled up outside the window. In the back of the truck a Chinese chow guarded a pile of lumber and some dynamite which was on its way to the site of the new temple. Monk swung down from the truck and came through the door, a Sephardic-dark man dressed in a wool plaid jacket, jeans, and cowboy boots.

Frieda said, 'The water pump isn't working right.'

Monk kept walking. 'Call a plumber. I ain't responsible.'

Five years ago, Monk had built Morningside Heights, an imitation of a Virginia village. Monk had gone all the way to Charlottesville to get the plans. He had laid it out: the British colonists who had come to America had set up an imitation of England in Virginia; then those who came afterwards to Mississippi wanted an imitation of Virginia; so what you had to sell was an imitation of an imitation. But what the hell, it made money. And Monk needed money. Twenty years ago, Monk had married Sheila Fisher; Reuben had been best man. The wedding had been held in the Holmesdale Hotel, the flowers had cost three grand, the food and liquor twice that, and a hundred doves had been set loose in honor of love. Nobody learned until afterwards that old man Fisher had lost everything the night before – a retail store, a used-car lot, and a bonding company – on the turn of a poker card. Monk had been supporting the whole damned family ever since. Southern style.

Monk lowered himself into the chair Frieda had vacated.

'Ugliest damn dog I ever saw.' Reuben swallowed some coffee The coffee was cold.

'It's a mean bastard. Picked him up yesterday in New Orleans. Cheaper than a night watchman. Somebody's been stealin' dynamite.'

'Who ?'

'How the hell should I know ?' Monk said. Frieda came around the counter carrying a cup of coffee. 'I called Chief Simmons. He said, *Don't you worry about it, boy*. Screw him. I picked up the dog when I went down to see Papa –'

Frieda set the coffee in front of Monk, gave Reuben a fraudulent smile, then disappeared into the kitchen.

'– Papa's gone crazy!' Monk said. 'Where the hell do you think I found him ?'

'Where ?' Noises came from the kitchen. Frieda banging around. Screw it. He'd send Elena some flowers. He'd send Frieda some flowers. How did he always end up with guilt and flowers ?

'Remember when Papa came up right after Mama died and we thought he was cuckoo with grief on account of he burned cigarette holes in the furniture, and Sheila was havin' a goddamned fit – ?'

Reuben nodded. He lit his first cigarette of a two-pack day. Then he swallowed the last of the cold coffee. Screw it. He had enough on his mind. Higgins. Screw Higgins.

' – so I had to send him back to New Orleans and then I had to buy all new furniture and after that I didn't hear a word from him ? Well, yesterday I drove down there and you know where I found him ?'

'No,' Reuben said.

'In the goddamned French Quarter! Livin' with a bunch of freaks. Readin' *poetry*. An old Sephardic Jew with a yarmulke on his head.'

'They're all crazy,' Reuben said. 'That whole generation.'

'I said, *Papa, you're almost seventy years old, for God's sake*. You know what he said to me ? He said – *Milton, I like it here*.'

'What did you do?'

'What could I do? I wrote him a check.'

Three

HE LEFT MONK in the parking lot outside the Williamsburg, took the highway downtown, and headed across the railroad tracks into the Oyster Bar. He didn't know how the name originated, but he presumed that oysters meant sex and Negroes were reportedly obsessed with sex; and a matter of sex was the reason for his presence.

Except for Lincoln Avenue, the streets were all named after fish. He went past Mullet Street and Catfish Avenue and Bass Row, a series of streets crammed with dilapidated two- and three-family dwellings, all looking alike and badly in need of paint and repair. Screens rotting and windows broken and walls bulging out from too many inhabitants.

He turned into Brim Street, no wider than an alley, an old rutted blacktop curving down to a dead end which was a weed-impacted cemetery. He was looking for 872½. It turned out to be the last house at the end, close enough to the moldy headstones to spit on them. The house didn't look any different from the others, except somebody had planted jonquils, coming up through the snow like those outside his own kitchen window. And the car parked in the dirt outside was a new red Mustang. As he went up the steps he could see the back of the car was filled with boxes of household goods, lamps and blankets and pots; somebody was moving.

He knocked. The porch was sagging, but the door had been painted a bright red.

In a moment, it was flung open, wide, like she wasn't afraid of anything. Then she stood there looking him over through the rotted screen, trying to make sense out of a white man on her doorstep, not even yet eight in the morning. She was fully dressed, wearing jeans and a lavender sweater and her hair tied back in a print kerchief. In her early twenties. If she had been white or even café au lait she would have been a knockout. But the phrase that came back to him was *chocolate to the bone*.

'Are you Eula Williams?' He tried imagining her in a technician's uniform.

16

'That's right,' she said. 'But I ain't buyin' nothin' today. No life insurance. No cemetery plots. No bathtubs for butterflies. No stew pots big enough to cook a missionary. They don't make good eatin', all bone and no truth.'

'I'm Reuben Buchman,' he said. 'John Tyler Higgins' attorney.' He had never laid a black girl. He hadn't thought about that omission in years.

She flashed a lot of white teeth. 'Well, ain't that somethin',' she said. 'What the hell are you sellin' ?'

'I'm buyin',' he said. He heard what it sounded like. He heard, also, that he had slipped into her dialect.

'Buyin' *what* ?'

'Talk,' he said. 'Information. All I want is a simple interview.'

She pushed open the screen. 'I'm packin',' she said. 'Ten minutes. No charge.'

He followed her through a parlor that had been cleared out. In the bedroom, suitcases and boxes were piled in a corner. The bed had been stripped down to the mattress. Two empty suitcases lay open on it. He didn't go any farther than the doorway. She began taking things from bureau drawers and folding them into one of the suitcases. Lingerie.

'Where are you goin' ?' He felt the need to take charge.

'Route sixty-six. As far as it goes.'

'Why ?' He was questioning her as if she were on a witness stand. It made the situation more viable.

'What's here for me ?' she said. 'I had the bad luck to be born here, that's all. I'm too smart and I'm too educated and I'm too *sassy*. And I'm too black to open a whorehouse.' She looked him in the eye. Then she made another trip to the bureau and back. He cleared his throat.

'How long did you work for Higgins ?' he said.

'Three months. About.'

'What do you know about him ?'

'I know he was framed.'

'How do you know ?'

'I know.' She folded a flimsy nightgown and laid it in the suitcase. He realised she wore no brassiere under the lavender sweater. He reminded himself this was a simple interview.

'How ?'

'I ain't gonna take no witness stand. I'll be long gone.'

'Then you might as well tell me the truth,' he said. 'You've got nothin' to lose.'

'What's to gain ?' she said.

'Don't you want to help Higgins?'

'I told him it was his neck when he hired me.'

'Look,' he said, 'I'm tryin' to help the man.'

'Why?'

'I don't believe in a helluva lot,' he said. 'But I believe in justice. I don't like frames.'

'What kind of shit is that?'

'There are people who don't run,' he said pointedly. 'There are people who stick around and fight because they love this place.' Somehow she had turned it around, taken charge.

'All bone and no truth,' she said. 'Missionary shit. Is that how you get your kicks?'

'No –' It came out defensive. He busied himself lighting a cigarette, then looked around for an ash tray, wondering how he could turn it around again.

'Use the john.' She snapped the suitcase shut, set it on the floor, and went to work on the second one. He went past her, into the bathroom. Somehow he had lost control of the interview. Smoking, he went over who he was and what he was doing here. He believed in justice. He thought of himself as a realist which he felt was a lie; he thought of himself as a Jew which he felt was a half-truth; he thought of himself as a southerner which was the whole truth – heir to the legacy of his Russian grandfather who had staked the claim. He flushed the cigarette down the toilet. He wondered if the old man had ever laid a black woman.

When he came out, he said, 'I get my kicks in the courtroom.'

'Maybe you do.' She laughed. 'I guess maybe you do.'

'Did you have an affair with him?'

'You want to get me for miscegenation?'

'You'll be long gone.'

'If he laid me, then you know he ain't queer. Is that it?'

'That would follow.' He wanted another cigarette but he didn't want another trip to her john.

'And you wanta know even if you can't use it in court?'

'It's for my own information.'

'What about all the queers married to white women? Layin' white women? With children even. Does that "information" make 'em not queer?'

'I'm only interested in Higgins,' Reuben said.

'He laid me,' she said. She snapped the second suitcase shut and set it on the floor. 'He ain't queer. Everybody knows a white man don't lay a *nigger* unless he *likes poon-tang*.'

Reuben cleared his throat. 'Thank you for the information.'

She picked up both suitcases and held them out to him. 'On your way out, put these in the car for me.'

He drove back downtown.

There was no one in the streets. Not because it was early and not because it was Saturday, but because it was February. The tempo of Holmesdale reflected the rural areas that still made up most of the state. For the farmers, the year began in March with the planting of cotton and ended in September with the picking of cotton. The months between were the intangible ones, the months of hog killing, barbecues, church meetings, a feeling of idleness, nothing pressing or important. For the city the farm calendar was obsolete, but the tempo of his grandfather's time prevailed.

He parked in front of his office. Across the street was City Hall, a piece of classic revival architecture on the land that had once been a muster ground and marketplace. There had once been a municipal garden around it. That was gone. Left were a half-dozen token oaks and a small patch of snow-covered lawn.

The clock in the tower bonged eight. His footsteps left prints on the thin layer of snow.

He stopped in front of the small copper plaque that read BUCHMAN & WOODS. In smaller letters was the name JAMES SANDIFER – a young, eager, respectably intelligent, newly graduated Ole Miss law student. He and Justin changed them like underwear. Buchman & Woods was the base – solid, unchanging, a team. Still, he hadn't yet told Justin that Kornfield had approached him – waiting until the last minute because he knew Justin would raise hell; knew, always, the things that Justin would raise hell about, and Higgins was one of them.

He had known Justin since law school. They had been moot court partners – Reuben, the romantic; and Justin, the pragmatist – and it had worked. Graduation had been the time of Korea. Reuben had gone into the air force, first lieutenant, judge advocate. Justin had gone into the F.B.I. While Justin had been tracking down Mexican wetbacks in Riverside, California, Reuben had been in Norman, Oklahoma, where he had been nearly court-martialed for his unorthodox courtroom methods and for generally raising hell about the military system of justice, which presumed a man guilty until proven innocent. Reuben had come back first. A year later, Justin had joined him. Reuben had brought energy and drive and the instinct for success. Justin had brought the status of a pre-Civil War family and the political connections inherited from his father, who had been lieutenant governor in the thirties. Ten years ago, they had built the office together. It had been an old store. Monk had metamorphosed it into a replica of a New Orleans slave quarters: a narrow, two-story old brick building with tall, arched windows and wrought-iron balconies. It had worked. They were emotional opposites, but it had worked. It still worked. Justin would raise hell. Then he'd take the case anyway.

The door was unlocked. Inside nobody waited on the red velvet Victorian sofa, but Olive deLucca, his senior secretary, was already there at her typewriter. It was barely eight in the morning and he had already dealt with three women today counting Mollie, who had the good sense to sleep.

'Good morning,' Olive said, brisk and cheery. She was a bony forty, a compulsive efficient, and a motherly nag. She watered his plants, took care of his personal bills, and reminded him of details he wanted to forget. She also got out enough work for two. Olive had once been married to a shoe salesman who had run off with a Barnum & Bailey bareback rider, but nobody ever mentioned it. The accepted story was her work was her life; that's how she had wheedled the key.

'What the hell are you doing here this early?' He reminded himself Oliver wasn't his mother.

'There's a lot of work.' She pulled a sheet from the typewriter and tucked a hairpin into the bird's nest at the nape of her neck. 'And Luanne's not coming in.'

'Why not?' He hung his overcoat on the brass tree that stood next to the picture of Lincoln: *A lawyer's time is his stock in trade.*

'She's sick.'

Luanne Pepper was eighteen, pretty, and infatuated with him. Hired for her legs. One secretary for maximum efficiency, one for maximum decoration. Something to make every client happy. 'What's wrong with Luanne?'

'I don't think she'd want me to talk about it.' Olive adjusted her glasses, cranked another sheet in the typewriter, and typed up a bill. It was the end of the month.

He started for the stairs. At the bottom, he stopped. 'Call the florist,' he said. Olive picked up a notebook and began to scribble. 'Gladiolas to Elena Buchman Caldwell in Maryville, Mississippi. That's all the address you need. And send a dozen roses to the Williamsburg to my mother.' That took care of that.

'What do you want on the cards?'

'Get well soon for Elena and love for my mother,' he said. 'And while you're at it send a bouquet to Luanne.'

Olive looked up. 'I don't think you ought to do that.'

'Why the hell not?'

'It's her *period*.' Olive turned bright red.

'For Christ's sake, why the hell can't you find me a secretary with good ovaries?'

'You hired her.' Olive's look would have cowed an African chief. She turned her chair and began to clack away at the typewriter. Then she stopped. 'Kornfield called from New York about Higgins,' she said, brisk and businesslike. She started typing again. A damned one-woman fortress.

He made the adjustment. 'It's ten o'clock in the morning in New York.'

'Nine,' she said. 'He said he was trying to catch you. He tried all day yesterday.' She kept typing. Bills.

He came back to her desk. 'I'll talk to him after I've seen Mr Woods. And not before. Do you understand that?'

'Yessir.' She didn't look up. She kept typing.

'Buzz me as soon as Mr Woods gets in.'

'Yessir.' She kept it up.

'For Christ's sake, what do you want me to say about *periods*?'

She stopped typing. 'I don't belong to women's liberation,' she said. 'I hope you're discussing punctuation.'

'Luanne Pepper,' he said.

'You hired her.'

'Fire her.'

'I couldn't do that.'

'Why not?'

'I couldn't fire someone for illness,' she said.

He climbed the stairs to the second floor where he and Justin each occupied offices decorated by their respective wives. Caroline Woods had paneled Justin's office in rosewood, laid crimson carpet on the floor, and hung strands of black, crystal, and ruby beads at the window. It looked like a Moorish whorehouse.

He went past, down the hall to his own office. His office was paneled in swamp timber, the carpet was mustard, the fireplace was old brick.

Over the fireplace was an oil painting of Mollie done by an eighty-year-old French Quarter artist with enough memory left in his genes to fall madly in love with her. It showed in the painting.

There were women who didn't age; Mollie was one of them. She looked hardly different than she had at seventeen. A mass of dark hair, a fine-boned body, a cameo face, big black eyes. He had grown used to the painting, but there were times, like now, when he looked at it and was swept by old memories. Mollie at seventeen. The prize, the beauty, the prodigy, the enshrined Jewish virgin nurtured in the dingy fringe neighborhood of New Orleans Italians and Catholics.

They had fought for each other. That was the memory: Mollie and her sister, Zoe, had been reared like divas. He had been a Mississippi bumpkin flunking out of pre-med. But Frieda had become their ally. Jesse had been recovering from his first heart attack in Maryville. Frieda had arranged a late summer garden wedding. The two families had met like adversaries. The Singers had hated these people who had spawned a son who had stolen their only daughter at seventeen. The Buchmans had hated these people who presumed to judge their only son not good enough. The wedding had taken place anyway. Afterwards there had been the scene between Frieda and Edith, glaring at each other across a kitchen table at two in the morning, adding up wedding figures and shouting about coercion and manipulation and broken promises and responsibility for children. *How much did one pay –* Jacob Singer had shouted – *for the loss of a daughter?*

He and Mollie had moved directly to the University of Mississippi where he had enrolled in law school. *You should have what you want, Reuben. You can do anything if you really want to,* Mollie had said. It had seemed true. They had moved into a portion of an army barracks that had been converted to student housing. She painted the walls black. They paid thirteen dollars a month for a galvanised shower and a kerosene stove. She took a job with a local photographer, taking Annual pictures for twenty dollars a week. Once a month they drove to Maryville in the rattletrap car they had bought for fifty dollars and filled the back up with groceries from Jesse's store on the highway. Two years later he had graduated third in his class.

He looked at the portrait. She looked the same. He didn't. He wan't. Life hadn't touched her. He had seen to that. For himself, he liked being in the middle of it.

Olive had built him a fire. She had opened the drapes across the French doors leading out to a patio that had once been a rooftop, now filled with pots of azaleas sitting in the snow. He never used the patio. His time was spent at the massive cluttered desk dealing with the conflicts that were indigenous to this territory that he loved; and sometimes dealing with the rare moments of clarity when he perceived the insanity of this territory that he loved. But he believed the so-called madness was life. He believed that what was now called sanity had become sterility – he saw it in the faces of men when he traveled, in airports, in streaming city hubs, the dead pale faces of those who were *sane*. Because sanity, around the country, had become a rational approach to death and to loss, an acceptance of helplessness. Madness, for him, was an alignment with this place that was still a frontier, still writhing, still unconquered by computers, pulsing with the contradictions of struggle and committed to the idea that it was better to die a violent death than an empty one. In those things still lay the possibility of hope; he believed that.

He looked at the portrait. He sometimes wished for a woman who understood life as he did.

That was a lie. What he wished for, sometimes, was Lea.

He picked up the Higgins affidavit and read it again:

AFFIDAVIT

Personally appeared before me, the undersigned authority in and for the jurisdiction aforesaid, M. K. Taylor, Deputy Chief of Police, who being by me first duly sworn, on oath, states:

. . . that heretofore, on or about January 3, 1968, to and including January 27, 1968, that John Tyler Higgins, an adult male person, did willfully and unlawfully contribute to the delinquency of Thomas Petry Hampstead, Jr, a minor male person of the age of 16 years.

. . . in that he took and harbored said minor child in his home, thereby aiding and encouraging said minor child from returning to or communicating with his parents, Thomas Petry Hampstead, Sr and Peggy Hampstead, then residents of Cleveland, Ohio.

. . . and further, by willfully and unlawfully seducing and persuading said minor child to permit him, the said John Tyler Higgins, to gratify his lust by indulging in acts of unnatural and perverted kind, including unnatural intercourse by the commission of acts of sodomy per anus and numerous acts of sodomy per os.

. . . and further, by subverting the morals of said child, and keeping said child in clothing, food, shelter, and medical attention, with the express purpose of causing said minor child to continue participation with him in said unlawful acts, contrary to Section 8172–17, and against the peace and dignity of this sovereign state. . . .

It was the fourth time he had read it. This time he saw that the voyeuristic quality hadn't originated with the affidavit, but from his own internal processes. Each time he read it, he felt a combination of peeping-tom curiosity and revulsion. And he knew that's what a juror would feel. That was why they had picked an accusation like this one. It was emotionally charged. Perspective got cloudy, the issue got lost, and the protection of the courtroom system of justice got canceled. Because a man framed on a simple charge of embezzlement didn't have to prove he *wasn't* an embezzler. The burden lay on the prosecution to prove that he *was*. A homosexuality charge turned it all backwards. It got to be more like the military courts back in Norman, Oklahoma, in 1950. A homosexuality charge precipitated the feeling that a man was guilty until he proved himself innocent. Hadn't he, himself, gone to see Eula Williams ? And wasn't the sight of her body the thing that satisfied him it was truly a frame ? And wasn't he, even at that, more enlightened than the average juror ? He didn't know a hell of a lot about homosexuals, had never had any dealings with any except the professor at the military academy whose memory inspired more pity than ire. He felt sorry for men who weren't men, who were intimidated by women or who wanted to be women, whichever it was. He wouldn't take a case to defend a real homosexual, but neither did he share the Yemenite view that all homosexuals should be thrown from the highest point in the City to their death. They were cripples, for God's sake. At least that's how he figured it. But now he was doing it again, preoccupying himself with the sexual nature of the case, instead of zeroing in on what it really was. A man had been framed on an erroneous criminal charge. An innocent man. How he felt personally about one man screwing another had nothing to do with it. And he'd damned well make that clear in his speech to the jury.

The buzzer interrupted him. He pushed the button.

'Is Mr Woods in ?'

'No,' Olive said.

'What is it ?'

'I wanted to remind you you're having breakfast with Jake Gorman at the Hunt Club.'

'I didn't make any appointment like that.'

'I did,' Olive said. 'You were gone all day yesterday and Mr Gorman was frantic, and I remembered he'd had that heart attack, so I – '

' – made a breakfast appointment at the Hunt Club.'

'Ten o'clock,' she said.

'Did you make any other appointments I ought to know about ?' Reuben said, with sarcasm. The sarcasm was lost on her.

'No,' she said 'But I thought I'd better remind you about the dedication of the Auditorium tonight What about your tuxedo ?'

'It's at the cleaners,' he said.

'Kornfield called again from New York.'

He cut her off.

Then he dealt with his irritation. She had done the right thing, she always did the right thing, that was the most maddening thing about her. He *had* forgotten the tuxedo he had dropped at the cleaners on Thursday. Jake Gorman *was* a twelve-grand-a-year retainer and Jake *had* had a heart attack, and yesterday both he and Justin *had* been unavailable. But he didn't want to be reminded of yesterday's fiasco. He and Justin had spent the day with Isadore Rabin of Ko-Bee Metal Parts out of Youngstown, Ohio. Manufacturers of ballast and metal parts for fluorescent fixtures. Justin, by gubernatorial appointment, was head of the A. & I. Board, balance agriculture with industry; and Isadore Rabin was considering the financial advantages of a factory in Claymont, Mississippi. He had gone along because, handled right, Ko-Bee might become a sizable retainer client. But everything had gone wrong. It had begun with brunch at the Mansion – white-coated convicts serving local grown products from silver chafing dishes. Then, in a burst of Mississippi chauvinism, the governor had proceeded to pour Mississippi molasses all over Isadore Rabin's scrambled eggs. After that, they had gone out to the factory site where Fred R. L. Watson, a local novelty salesman, was leading a group of rednecks in a protest against Yankee industry coming down to hire blacks. The trickiest parts of the deal had never been the ninety-nine-year land lease or the floating of bonds, which were set – the trickiest part had always been public relations. The state wanted and needed the factories; the blacks wanted and needed the factories; but the rednecks consistently raised hell about the equal-employment policy that was necessary for all factories with government contracts. Justin had finally pacified Fred R. L. Watson by taking him aside and promising to sponsor him for a foreman's job. Like magic, the men had dispersed. It always amazed Reuben how easily, and for how little, unpropertied men could be bought. It hadn't amazed Isadore Rabin. He and Justin had spent the rest of the day reenumerating the advantages of free land rental, revenue bonds to cover building construction, and non-union labor. Rabin had gone back to Youngstown, Ohio, to think it over. He wouldn't be back, with his decision, until the end of March.

He closed up the Higgins file and buzzed Olive.

'Call my wife,' he said, 'and ask her to pick up my tuxedo.'

'I already did. She's not there.'

'It's eight o'clock in the morning. Where the hell is she?'

'I'll get the tuxedo myself,' Olive said.

He cut the connection. Then he swiveled in his chair until he was facing the portrait. She looked out at him. Mollie. In the portrait she looked pale and translucent, the way she had on the late September day that Phil was born. He had brought her red roses and a diamond bracelet he couldn't afford. It was the aftermath of his affair with Lea. Sometimes love and guilt looked like the same thing.

She looked out at him. Mollie. He had known her since he was sixteen. Sometimes, not often, he wondered if he knew her at all.

Sometimes, not often, he wondered which woman the old man would have chosen.

Four

'A *nofki!* Jake said. 'From nowhere! In *Miami*, he met her.' He pushed at the chicken livers and scrambled eggs, making a mess on his plate – sixty-three years old and recovering from the massive coronary, but the damage hardly showed. Jake was stocky and broad-chested with the look of a small aging bull hung with a lot of gold jewelry. And a red flag.

'Maybe she's a nice girl.' Reuben forked a liver. He had been Jake's attorney for thirteen years, chosen simply because there were only two Jewish lawyers in Holmesdale and the other one worked for Standard Oil. Jake didn't trust gentiles. Periodically Jake didn't trust Reuben either.

'Are you crazy?' Jake said. A black waiter in a white coat and a red sash came over and refilled the coffee cups. The Hunt Club was a bar, a dance floor, and a restaurant which occupied the entire top floor of the Holmesdale Hotel. It had originated as a place to have a drink in a dry state, then the state had gone wet two years ago – no more need for bottles in lockers, but the Hunt Club still maintained its patronage on a membership basis.

'I think you're jumping to conclusions,' Reuben said.

'*Gina*,' Jake said. 'What kind of name is that? I ask you? She says she's Italian. Italian, my eye! She looks like a damned *Arab*.' He did everything but paw the table and snort. The waiter left. Jake glared.

26

Reuben said, 'Don't get so excited.' For Jake it was a rare outing. He spent most of his time at home being coddled by his wife Rosalie. Since the coronary his two sons, Mickey and Leo, had taken over the running of Gorman Steel. But it was Jake who still made the decisions. Because it was Jake, during World War Two, who had ballooned a junkyard into a million-dollar business that was Gorman Steel. 'You're a sick man,' Reuben said.

'Sick! I'm sick in the heart. In the heart I'm sick. Where is Max sick? In the *kup*. Sick in the head he is! He comes back from Miami. With *her*. This is *Gina*, he says. My *fiancée*. A fool he is, my brother-in-law. All these years, Rosalie trying to make matches. No, no, no, he says. He's a bachelor. Alright. A fifty-seven-year-old bachelor. We'll get used to it. Alright, we *got* used to it. Then what does he do? He comes back from Miami with a –'

' – a *nofki*?' Reuben went after the eggs.

'A gold digger,' Jake said. Back in the junkyard days, Max Nathan, Rosalie's brother, had operated as the outside man. Which meant Max had collected the junk and Jake sold it. Which meant, today, Max had a piece of a million-dollar business. Which made Max a rich man.

'Maybe she's not.'

'Listen,' Jake said. 'Okay. So Leo is married to Beda, a nice Jewish girl from Vassar. Is she anything like Beda? No. Beda's Jewish for one thing and *American* for another. From Idaho. This country. Okay. So Mickey, my youngest, he married a goy. But didn't Mickey at least go off to Europe for three months to think it over? And Bonnie was from *Mississippi* at least. And before they got married, didn't Bonnie take lessons from the rabbi? Is she anything like Bonnie? No. You tell me – what does that make her? You think Max is a movie star? With an accent yet? Almost sixty years old and *she can't keep her hands off of him*. And all Max wants to do is take out more life insurance.'

'I'll talk to him,' Reuben said. 'Eat your breakfast.'

'She'll kill him,' Jake said. 'All she does is make sex with him. For all that insurance, she'll kill him. With sex. And who'll be my partner then? Tell me? Who? *Her*?'

'I'll talk to him.'

'When?'

'Tomorrow. It's Sunday. I'll talk to him.'

'What's wrong with today?'

'I've got other business today,' Reuben said.

John Tyler Higgins.

* * *

27

When he got back to the office his tuxedo was there but Justin had come and gone.

'He said to tell you he'll be back at two.' Olive was sealing the stack of bills to be sent out on Monday.

'Where the hell did he go?'

'To the Mansion. He drafted a letter to Isadore Rabin for the governor to send off. He said he'd likely have lunch there.' Justin covered all bases. Pacifying Isadore Rabin and bucking for lieutenant governor. All in one lunch. Either one meant money for Buchman & Woods.

'Did Kornfield call again?'

'I guess he gave up.' Olive sealed an envelope.

'He's not a man who gives up.'

'There's nine thousand dollars in accounts receivable and Vernon Powell's waitin' in your office,' Olive said. Nine thousand dollars was a lot of money and Vernon Powell was Justin's client.

'What the hell did you put him up there for?'

'It's not good to have a colored man waitin' down here. A white client comes in and sees him and thinks that's the kind of lawyer you are.'

Reuben bristled. 'What kind is that?'

'You know what I mean.' She sealed an envelope.

'No,' he said. 'I don't.'

'One of those credit lawyers,' she said.

'You mean the kind who garnishee paychecks?'

'No.' She sealed an envelope. 'The kind who work on credit. You know you live over your head. We've got enough trouble gettin' the money in around here.'

He had an old rule of thumb for psyching a man out; he had invented it himself. If you want to know what a man is, you ask three questions: Who's his God? Who's his boss? Who's his woman? For a woman it was simpler. You ask: Who are her children?

Vernon Powell's God was Jesus. His boss was the white man, any white man. His wife had been dead for twenty years and he obviously had no need for a live one because he hadn't replaced her. By himself he had raised two sons on Horatio Alger – both had gone through Holmesdale State College for Negroes, then north.

Justin had a few black clients. Powell was Justin's client because he was one of the few blacks around who owned sizable acreage. An establishment black. A good nigger. His legal needs were

28

usually contracts, and he paid cash on the barrelhead. One of those blacks who wanted everybody to know he was the model and so deserved his portion. He had one of the most productive farms in the area.

Upstairs, in the office, Reuben found him sitting in a leather captain's chair, mesmerised by Mollie's portrait. It took a moment before Vernon realised he wasn't alone, then he jumped like a guilty trespasser. He wore a circle of white wool hair like a halo over purple chipmunk cheeks, and he was stuffed like a pork sausage into a black preacher-type suit with a high collar, string tie, and pointed black shoes polished to a mirror shine. It was the getup of a black hustler concerned with propriety, of a juggler who balanced servility and affluence. If Powell had been white, Reuben would have disliked him on sight. Because Powell was black, other instincts took precedence. The Yankees gave it names like paternalism and guilt, but it went deeper than that.

'What's the trouble, Vernon?'

'I ain't accountable for what they're doin',' Powell said, 'and I want you to know that.'

'Who's they?' Reuben said. 'And what are they doing?' He crossed to his desk and sat down and picked up the telephone and dialed his house.

'Brendon Hollyhoke,' Powell said. He came over to the desk. 'He told me it was for a *hospital*.'

Reuben held up his hand. Then he talked into the phone. 'Is she there?' he said. He made a gesture at the chair. Powell sat back down.

'Nossir,' Leila said, at the other end of the wire.

'Where the hell did she go?' He lit a cigarette. He saw Powell's eyes stray to Mollie's portrait again.

'I don't know, Mr Buchman. She don't always tell me where she goes.'

'Where are the boys?'

'Out with Attica. They're tryin' to build 'em a snowman before it's all gone.'

'As soon as she comes in, have her call me.'

'Yessir.'

He hung up. 'What was for a hospital?' he said.

'Twenty acres,' Powell said. He had begun to sweat. 'Everybody knows how hard I worked for that land. Everybody knows I wouldn't sell not *one foot* of that land. Not for nothin' – ' He pulled out a handkerchief as big as a surrender flag and wiped his face.

'Are you telling me that you sold twenty acres of land to a man named Brendon Hollyhoke?' Reuben said.

Powell nodded. 'He said it was for a hospital.' They were back where they started. 'It ain't for no hospital. They're gonna use it for – '

'Do you have a contract?'

'Mr Woods drew it up. There's a copy in the file. But that ain't – '

'Let's look at it,' Reuben said. He buzzed Olive and asked for a copy of the contract. Then he held up his hand and picked up the phone again and dialed Max Nathan's apartment. Powell fidgeted, mopped his face, and kept sending scurrying looks at Mollie's portrait. At the other end of the line, a woman with an accent answered. The accent might have been anything. He asked for Max.

'Max has gone out for champagne,' she said. Gina, he assumed. He had a quick vision of Max Nathan drinking champagne from her slipper. 'Who is it?' Gina said.

'Reuben Buchman.'

'Oh yes. Max has told me much about you.' She had a bedroom voice alright, Jake was right about that. 'Would you like champagne?'

'I'm busy at the moment,' he said. Olive came in with the contract and laid it down on the desk. Powell dragged his eyes from Mollie's portrait and bobbed his head at her.

'Shall I give Max a message?' Gina said.

'I'd like to see him tomorrow.' Reuben nodded at Olive. Her view from the rear had as much sex appeal as Powell's string tie.

'Come for lunch,' Gina said. Olive disappeared.

'Thank you.' He picked up the contract and started to read it.

'*Pasta*,' she said.

'*Ciao* – ' He hung up and finished looking over the contract, thinking that maybe it wasn't such a bad thing that had happened to Max.

'The contract looks in order,' Reuben said. 'Two hundred dollars down and the balance to be paid in bimonthly installments of a hundred apiece. It doesn't specify what the land's to be used for.'

'A *hospital*,' Powell said. He mopped his face again in agitation. 'It's three weeks now and they ain't startin' on no hospital, and they ain't paid me not one more dime and they won't even let me *near* – '

'What the hell is this signature ? – Brendon Hollyhoke, *President*.'

'I been tryin' to tell you,' Powell said. 'Brendon Hollyhoke says he's president of the *African Republic*.'

'What the hell's that ?' But it sounded familiar. Then he remembered his mother had asked him about it this morning. Damned if she hadn't had her information right.

'There's about a dozen of 'em,' Powell said. 'Yankee militants. They're holed up out there on *my land* with shotguns and dynamite and they're sayin' they're citizens of the African Republic and they're gonna *secede* –'

'Secede ?' Reuben had a mental image of a group of angry blacks imitating the tactics of pre-Civil War whites. But the humor and irony was lost. Vernon had said *shotguns and dynamite*. He remembered the Chinese chow in the back of Monk's truck: *Somebody's been stealin' dynamite*.

'They ain't in their right mind,' Powell said. 'They're talkin' about how they got a *beachhead*. On *my land*. They're talkin' about they gonna take over a lot more land for their republic. Three southern states! I don't want no truck with 'em. I ain't got no use for Malcolm X. I'm a Christian. They ain't in their right mind, and *I want 'em off my land !*'

'We'll file an Injunction to Quit,' Reuben said.

'What's that ?' Powell said. 'What's that mean ?'

'It means the sheriff goes out and serves a complaint and they get off your land.

'They ain't gonna go that easy, I'm tellin' you that.'

'If they want a blood bath, they'll get a blood bath.' Reuben hoped not. They didn't need any more Yankee headlines, or any more invasions by cameras and questions. Black men and white men alike, who couldn't handle the problems in their own back yard, were the first to appear and tell the South how to run its business.

'I ain't accountable for them and I want everybody to know that,' Powell said.

'We know that,' Reuben said. 'But there's somethin' else I need to know.'

'Anything,' Powell said.

'How come you keep on lookin' at my wife's portrait ?'

'I used to be an undertaker,' Vernon said. 'She's got the mark on her.'

'What kind of mark ?'

'How long's that junction-quit take ?' Vernon said.

'What kind of mark?'

Vernon shook his head, then passed the handkerchief over his forehead. 'She was beautiful alright,' Vernon said. 'But it sure was there when he painted that picture. The mark. How long since she passed away . . . ?'

By two o'clock the snow was gone, leaving dirty puddles in the downtown streets, and muddy tracks on the stone bas-relief of Moses at the peak of the courthouse roof underneath the slogan JUSTICE FOR ALL.

Reuben walked back from lunch.

The reception room was empty, but Justin's overcoat hung on the brass tree. Olive had left a note on her typewriter: *Kornfield called about Higgins. Again.*

One of these days he'd fire her.

'*Hell no* –' Justin said.

Justin sat behind his desk. Reuben paced the crimson carpet. It was their usual manner of arguing. Reuben was the bull elephant, Justin the fox – freckled skin, sand-colored hair, a pair of small bright eyes that never missed anything.

'It's a frame.'

'Maybe it's not.'

'He's no goddamned queer. He screwed the black technician. Eula Williams.'

'You can't use that in court.'

Reuben stopped pacing. He leaned over Justin's desk. 'They think he's a niggerlover so they went after him in a way that won't stir up the Yankee press. Hell, that kid was a runaway. Blind as a bat. All Higgins did was buy him a goddamned pair of eyeglasses.'

'The kid signed an affidavit, didn't he?'

'The kid's dead. He jumped from a second-story window trying to escape from a Cleveland Delinquent Home – died from concussions.'

'That's great. You don't even have a witness to break down on the stand.'

'The kid had a delinquency record – there's a good chance of discrediting his affidavit.'

Justin picked up a dead pipe, lit it, sucked life into it. Justin was making him wait – like any damned good lawyer. There were women clients who thought Justin was Solomon. Women liked waiting for men to light pipes.

'What about Sergeant Taylor's affidavit?' Justin said. 'The law says Taylor had to catch Higgins in the act.'

'For five dollars, M. K. Taylor would swear Jesus screwed Mary. You know he's a goddamned sadist. Once a week they catch him doing a rubber hose act. You know what the hell he is.'

'He's Simmons' chief deputy, and Simmons is –'

' – our client.'

'Nice of you to remember.'

'Goddamnit, I'm not going to let a divorce fee from the chief of police make my decisions for me.'

Justin knocked out the pipe, then smiled carefully. A good lawyer, but he telegraphed his punches. 'Then why let Kornfield make them for you?'

'Screw Kornfield.'

'There's not another lawyer in town who'll touch this case.'

'I like lepers.'

'Sometimes I think I don't know you at all,' Justin said. His face closed like a steel trap.

'What the hell does that mean?'

'It means we've got enough on our hands. You come in with the Vernon Powell thing for me. We've got the Rabin factory. That's enough playing around with political repercussions. I'm not taking Kornfield on as a closet member of this firm.'

'Leave Kornfield out of it.'

'Have you?'

'Don't cross-examine me, I taught you how.'

'Higgins couldn't get a local lawyer, right? So Higgins took off to New York and got hold of Kornfield. Right? So it's Kornfield who wants you to defend Higgins. That's right, isn't it?'

'That's right,' Reuben said, 'you've got it right.' He left the desk and moved to the window and jangled the bead curtains. Out on the street, the garbage cans had been put out for the Saturday evening collection. Glory Christmas, the toothless black crone who sold afternoon papers on the corner, was systematically going through the cans and piling the stuff in an orange crate on skate wheels. It was a picture Kornfield would have gloated over.

'You're a fool,' Justin said. 'At least the Vernon Powell thing is good for us politically. At least the Ko–Bee factory is good for us financially. What the hell is this good for?'

Reuben turned. 'Did you ever make any decision in your life that wasn't *expedient*?'

'I'm a survivor, not a proselytizer.'

'Maybe you don't know me,' Reuben said. 'Maybe I don't know you.'

'You want to discuss our fifteen-year partnership or you want to discuss Higgins?'

'I'll get Bill Thatcher to appoint me. That'll cover your god-damned neck.'

'And yours,' Justin said.

'And mine.'

'What's Kornfield's leverage?'

'None.'

'What the hell is he to you? Some kind of surrogate father-figure?'

Reuben came back to the desk. 'No.'

'I don't like it,' Justin said. 'I don't like homosexual dentists and I don't like crazy Yankee radical lawyers. I haven't had any use for Kornfield since '62, and you know damned well what I'm talking about.'

Reuben knew. In '62, the freedom riders had begun to come. It was the year Mollie was pregnant with Phil. They had come by the hundreds. Boys in shaggy beards and girls with long, straight hair. Idealists and pawns, begetting violence and becoming martyrs. So many of them that the D.A. had needed help. Three law firms in town had been appointed to prosecute. A political plum. Buchman & Woods was selected. Reuben was the courtroom powerhouse. It was his chance to make a state-wide reputation for the firm. It was Reuben who had ended up in the courtroom on the side of pro-secution against Kornfield who had come down from New York to defend. Reuben had been thirty-five. Kornfield had been in his late forties, craggy and honed, with a mass of flyaway hair turning gray at the temples. On a theater marquee, Kornfield might have been billed as the Great White Jewish Father of the Court-room.

'You're wrong about Kornfield,' Reuben said. For three months he had fought Kornfield in the courtroom. Kornfield fought like a hawk in a windstorm with the anger of a martyr and the seasoned ability of twenty-five years in a courtroom. Each day Kornfield lost to a jury of Mississippians. Each day he returned with renewed passion as if it had not occurred to him that he might lose again. Reuben had known he was up against a pro. Admiration and respect had set in. Eventually they had even become quasi-friends, adversaries with a mutual admiration for a craft well done. There had been drinking sessions and ideological arguments. Then Kornfield had gone back to New York. And two months later, Reuben had abruptly switched sides and got himself appointed to defend the same agitators he had been

34

prosecuting. Justin had always been certain it was Kornfield who had changed Reuben's mind.

'If it wasn't Kornfield, who was it?' Justin said.

It hadn't been Kornfield.

There had been a girl. Lea. Lea had changed his mind.

He hadn't been looking for a love affair. Sometimes things changed, turned upside down. A Yankee girl with a cause. They had locked her up behind the barbed wire that had been used to fence in the fairgrounds. Six years. It was a long time ago.

'When I change my mind, I change my *own* mind,' Reuben said. He had, in fact, changed Kornfield's mind. A little. Though it was tough to explain it to men who hadn't been born to pine and magnolia, to southern sunlight, or to earth heat that baked through to the soul. But he had tried to tell Kornfield that it wasn't a black thing or a white thing; that both races had been birthed by the same mother, the South, and it was the land that bound them; and that those who left felt themselves exiles. And if it was going to be worked out anywhere, it would be in the South. *I've seen your cities and they stink!* It would be worked out in the South by the people who lived here.

And now Kornfield had called him on it.

'Why the hell do you want to fool with it?' Justin said.

'I don't know.'

It was after five when he left the office. An early February dusk. The snow was gone.

At eight o'clock the audience assembled. Most of the residents of Morningside and visiting dignitaries from around the state. The opening of the new Holmesdale Auditorium was a black-tie affair.

The governor's wife cut the ribbon. Catholic Bishop Frank O'Hara and Episcopal Father Benjamin Farnswell and Rabbi Harris Greenblatt each gave an appropriate benediction to bless the event which had gathered a crowd of more than two thousand.

The program that christened the Holmesdale Auditorium was a Beethoven concert. The concert was over at eleven o'clock. Reuben drove straight home.

It was midnight by the hands of the white porcelain clock when the phone began to ring beside Reuben's bed. He had just taken off the tuxedo. Mollie was closed in the dressing room. He stopped to put on the blue silk robe and light a cigarette. Then he crossed to the bed and picked up the receiver.

'Reuben Buchman,' he said.

An unidentified voice at the other end of the line began to crackle. Phrases strung together without meaning:

' ... Synagogue of Satan ... seed of the serpent ... Satan's children ... '

'Who the hell is this?'

'We bombed your rabbi. Eleven forty-five. Nine-oh-eight Maple. Count your days, you dirty Jew.'

Reuben smashed his cigarette in the ash tray, which had once been a bone plate on the dinner table of some long dead southern aristocrat. China, fragile, it cracked, then split. He realised that the door to the dressing room had come open, and that Mollie was standing there, wearing the blue fleece robe he had ordered from Neiman-Marcus last Christmas. He heard her say, 'Who is it?'

He stared at her. He realised he was still holding onto the receiver. *'We'll get you bastards!'* he shouted.

The line went dead.

Five

THE FIRST THING she thought of was the rabbi. This afternoon Harris Greenblatt had sat in the leather chair of his study, playing rabbi. She had said: *Goddamn you.* Now it had happened.

'It's a crank call,' she said. 'It's midnight. It's got to be a crank call.'

'Suppose it's not.'

Mollie could feel them kick off, all the old terrors, the nightmares of her childhood. They, the *Nazis*, had finally arrived.

'It's a crank call,' she repeated. She felt herself smile. Like an uncontrollable tic.

'Is that all you can say?'

'I'm sorry.'

He dialed hurriedly. 'It's busy.'

'What?'

'Harris' line, for Christ's sake.'

'Maybe it's out of order.'

'Goddamn you,' he said. 'Maybe the bastard's telling the *truth*.'

'I'm sorry.'

'What the hell are *you* sorry for?'

He opened the closet and snatched a pair of trousers and began to get into them. She could see he was beginning to believe it. He was getting dressed for it. She watched the anger congeal on his face. He was a gladiator. He tested himself on the crises of others. This one was different. What she saw on his face was different. Then she knew what it was. The anger masked fear. She didn't want to look at it.

'Get Monk on the phone.' He pulled on a sweater.

She went over to the bed and began to dial Monk's number. She watched her fingers. She had known damnation would arrive when she had gone beyond the fingers of one hand, that was the standard. Last night she had still been able to count her lovers on one hand. It had still been acceptable. Beyond that, her life would become shocking. It was a private reasoning born in the ashes of a cremated sexual morality. This morning Jean Aucoin had changed that. Now damnation had come.

'The line's busy,' she said.

'Goddamnit –'

'Do you want me to try someone else ?'

He came back to the bed, carrying his shoes. He took the phone away from her. He sat down on the bed. She watched him pull his sox on with one hand and dial with the other.

'Is Chief Simmons there ?' he said. Then, 'Where the hell is he ?' Then, 'What's the address ?' His face turned to chalk.

He hung up. 'It's true.'

'No,' she said. The image of the rabbi came and went.

'Bastards.' He pulled on his shoes.

'Is anybody hurt ?'

'I don't know.'

'Don't leave me alone,' she said. She hadn't meant to say that. She had meant to remind herself she no longer needed him. She had meant to remind herself she had once tried to leave him.

'Go to sleep. I'll call you.'

He went through the door. She watched his back go down the hall, then vanish. She hurried down the hall and stood at the top of the stairs. She watched the top of his head move across the marble floor of the two-story entrance hall, then disappear beneath the crystal chandelier. She felt her blood turn to ice. In a moment she heard the back door slam.

She came back up the hall to the bedroom and crossed to the window. His headlights blinked up at her as he backed down the driveway. Inside, the ice cracked and slid away. Beneath was the cauldron of fear. She heard the sound of the car speeding off. Then the sound vanished suddenly. She was left with the silence. In the silence, the tears came.

Not enough tears to wash her away.

The tears freed the panic. Set it loose. As if someone had turned off a light and her fears came scurrying out from their hiding places like mice. . . .

. . . The rabbi sat in the leather chair, wearing pipe and slippers, big tortoise shell glasses and a spry moustache. *What is it, Mollie?* he said. This afternoon. 908 Maple. A yellow clapboard Cape Cod with white picket fence and roses. Frances had answered the door carrying Cherry, the tiny white poodle, under her arm.

In the study, she set the Sunday school books down on a table near a struggling African violet. *I can't teach Sunday school any more . . .* , she said. Looking at Harris. He and Frances had come here ten years ago. From Brooklyn. They had come to change the ways of the South and had been seduced instead. They were no better than she.

Harris peered through his glasses. *Oh − ?* He was wearing a green velvet smoking jacket with patches at the elbow. He looked like an affluent professor. He looked like an aging violinist gone tone deaf. He looked like a man who had learned that a southern Jew was one who sang 'Hatikvah' translated into English. He looked like none of that. He looked like her father.

I'm sorry, she said.

What is it?

I don't want to discuss it.

He said, *Mollie −* But she was already on her way out. She stopped in the doorway. To her back, he said, *I forgive you, Mollie, for all your sins. . . .*

She turned then. *Goddamn you*, she said.

She went into the bathroom and threw up. Then she washed her face. The face in the mirror told her she was still a woman who could enter a room and hear that small, invisible moment of silence while everything stopped. Those moments women measured and from which they made a life. Her life.

Maybe it was over.

She had wanted it over. Knowing it would happen, she had tried to make it happen. End it. Two years ago. She had told Reuben she was going to Switzerland.

Thirty-four years old then, and she had never been out of the South. But she had made appointments with the pediatrician to give the children their shots, and she had made rational phone calls inquiring about passports. Didn't she know – Reuben had said – he would give her anything, everything he had ? What did she want ? *She wanted her life back, that was all.* . . . He had refused to accept it. The loss of a wife, two sons, the blowup of a seventeen-year marriage that had been patched like an old rubber tire gone to many miles on a treadmill. He was oligarch of a vest-pocket empire, consort to a southern Jewish princess; one required the other. She had been made to understand the facts of divorce in a state where women were chattel. She had been made to understand she had no idea of what she might be going to, or what she was running from. She had been made to understand it was a madness that had come over her. In the end she had been paralysed. They had never talked about it again. She had been ill and now she was well. It was as if it had never happened. She had taken another lover instead.

Number five. She could no longer remember his name.

Today, Jean Aucoin had become number six.

Before noon. He lived on the edge of the Oyster Bar. A room in one of the old Victorian houses that had been turned into sleazy rentals. One of the few streets in Holmesdale that was *mixed.* . . .

. . . *There was a ceiling fan. Static. A crack in the ceiling like an intricate cobweb. The sputtering flames of a space heater which gave out a faint heat and a meager light. An unfinished door perched on bricks which served as a desk – littered with papers and textbooks and a gray crookneck lamp, and a bright red dimestore clock ticking away like a woodpecker.* . . .

She had that female faculty for small details, the shallow skill of an observing eye, refined by the conditions of a gilded constriction. When she turned that eye upon herself, she culled the cold, clear details of her life, each isolated act, but – like soldiers – they added up to nothing beyond an army. Where the real battle was, or what it was about, eluded her. There was simply the thing that drove her into affairs with unlikely men – like Burke, the first one, two years after her marriage to Reuben, too old for her and too alien, and yet, still, periodically, he invaded her dreams like a ghost from the past. After Burke, she had evolved some intricate system of weighing male clues, geared to decide if this one, the next one, the one after that, had the thing she needed, was looking for, whatever it was, she could not name it.

She came back into the bedroom.

Then she went down the hall and looked in on the boys, found them safe, asleep – remembered this morning, at seven, taking them out in the snow, giving them cookie sheets to use for sleds. Wearing the black coat with the mass of fox at the hem and a knitted white cap, she had crouched at the bottom of the hill and photographed Joe and Phil skidding down the icy driveway. The wind had rustled the pines. Sparrows pecked at the breadcrumbs Joe had scattered in the snow. Phil had come running, his orange scarf flying. She had stopped in the snow and hugged him. . . .

. . . *No, baby,* Martin Gallagher said. *You can't come here to learn. This is a black college.* Holmesdale State College for Negroes. She had seen his work. She had tracked him down. This morning. A tall, bearded Mississippi black, educated at Xavier in New Orleans and returned to his roots to teach. Photography. In the exhibit there had been a white artist's photograph of a black boy shining shoes, called 'Nigger Shine.' Next to it was Martin Gallagher's retort: a photograph taken in New Orleans of white men collecting garbage on mule-driven wagons; the caption read 'Mules and Garbage.'

Xavier's integrated, she argued. She watched him appraise her, a steady engaging eye that focused itself through the gold-rimmed glasses that were his private lens. Evaluating this white woman, Mollie Buchman; who had come seeking something she could not give a name to, but knew it was there, and knew he had made a pact with it, this thing called art but was not art, was something else; an alliance with life.

We don't want you here. We don't want to integrate. When it happens we want an exchange. We're claiming our own.

As if he knew she wanted to take. As if he knew she had nothing to give.

I'm sorry, she said.

You won't find it here, baby. Maybe you'll find it somewhere. Maybe with your camera.

I don't know . . .

Listen, he said, *it's simple. Money's nice but it's not home.*

She came back to the bedroom. She crossed to the nightstand and shook a cigarette from Reuben's pack. She lit it. The ash tray, the bone plate, had split. Into pieces. In the sight of it was the real fear. The fear of coming apart. Sometimes it happened. Sometimes she flew apart. An explosion of self. Nobody noticed.

Now it had happened. Now it was real.

They had finally arrived. *They* had been halfway around the world. She had always perceived them as imminent. Waiting. Now they had come.

She had once worked it all out. Sex was gentile; virtue was Jewish; innocence was southern. Violence was gentile; repressed anger was Jewish; lying was southern. Eating peanut butter was gentile; genteel poverty was Jewish; affluence was southern. But the lists could not reconcile what had been irreconcilable. It had taken her too many years to figure it out. By the time she understood any of it, she also understood that she had trapped herself.

Now there was a message in it: *You can't hold it all together*. Not the earth, not your life, not even your own frail psyche which has been informed finally and once and for all that *you are doomed*. A first-class cabin on the *Titanic*.

She swept the pieces of the ash tray into a Lucite wastebasket.

Six

A WIND HAD COME UP. The wind didn't help. Three blocks away, he could see the smoke and the hot orange light from the flames of the Cape Cod at 908 Maple.

He parked as close as he could. A crowd had already gathered; tragedy pulled spectators. He plunged into the middle of it, through faces he had never seen before, saying 'Let me through' with an authority accustomed to having its own way. Nobody argued.

He felt like a stranger.

His grandather had come in 1892; his grandfather had staked the claim; *nobody could destroy that*.

They had tried.

In a minute, he was close enough for the heat from the obscene bonfire to crawl through his blood like the invader it was. The flames were leaping around, sparks shooting off and spiraling like fireworks against the night. Two fire trucks had already arrived and a dozen burly men were hauling snakelike hoses around.

It was seventy-five years at stake. There had been Jews in New Orleans, and Jews in Holmesdale, but his grandfather had been the first Jew in Maryville. A damned pioneer. The old man had reclaimed the South from the Yankee – for his children, for his grandchildren; *nobody could destroy that*.

They had tried.

Suddenly, the water began to pour from all directions, converging onto the shingled roof ot the Cape Cod house. There was a gaping hole in the middle of the roof, and the flames didn't look like they were going to give up easy.

There were half as many cops around as there were firemen, blue uniforms sprinkled through the crowd. He recognised M. K. Taylor, the boiled-eyed cop who had arrested Higgins. The sight of Taylor's face brought back the sound of the voice on the telephone, both personifications of violence provoking an inchoate surge of rage. He reined it.

Then he spotted Simmons at the edge of the crowd, looking up at the blaze like he might be anybody – an overfed, mesmerized onlooker, his pajama bottoms hanging out of the cuffs of his trousers. But Simmons wasn't just anybody, wasn't just a classic beefy edition of southern justice; too many men had made that mistake and Reuben wasn't one of them.

He headed for Simmons, the ghost of his grandfather riding his back. All the legends. With twenty dollars, the old man had bought twenty acres, had traded a gallon of whiskey for a half-starved mule, had burned trees and grubbed stumps and built a cabin with two rooms and penned a place for chickens. He had made whiskey and traded it for seed. He had driven his plough into the delta soil that was rich from the washings of the river. The old man had built an empire of three thousand acres. The land was gone, but the Buchman mark was on the land; *nobody could take that away*.

'*Bastards* – *!*' he said to Simmons, in a strangled voice that told him something had been touched that had been buried for seventy-five years. The old man. And Jesse. And his own right to be what he was.

Simmons didn't answer him. Simmons wasn't a talker. Simmons was a drinker and a markesman and a womanizer, but he wasn't a talker. Simmons' cold blue eyes were buried in a flat pudgy face, and he had the body of an awkward rhinoceros, but women liked him; he was working on his third divorce – Reuben had handled them all.

'What happened ?'

'We're workin' on it,' Simmons said.

'For Christ's sake – '

'Blood all over the damn place,' Simmons said. 'You wouldn't think a goddamned little poodle dog like that would have so much blood in him. Little bitty damn thing. She carried it right in the ambulance with her. Wouldn't believe it was dead.'

'Ambulance ? What ambulance ?' Reuben felt the pop of cold beads of sweat, like spores sprouting out in a spring rain.

'Gone,' Simmons said. 'About ten minutes ago.'

'Who's hurt ?'

'What the hell's her name ? The rabbi's wife. What the hell's her name ?'

'Frances – '

'Frances,' Simmons said.

'How bad ?'

'I ain't no doctor, I'm a cop.' Simmons frowned. 'You don't look so good.' He pulled a flask from his pocket. Reuben drank. It was bourbon. The liquor cut through and exploded into something Jesse had once said to him; the old man had said it to Jesse and Jesse had passed it on: *We ain't got to worry about bein' Jews in the South, they got the nigger to lynch.*

'Bastards – '

'Calm yourself.' Simmons took the flask back. Simmons' face blurred. Reuben lunged back through the crowd, pushing his way like a bulldozer. But the crowd had gotten thicker and they didn't want to part for him.

Suddenly a head reared, baneful and ugly, face bared, evil revealed, a match for the voice on the telephone coming out of the crowd like a scrawled obscenity. 'Hey! Where the hell do you think you're goin' ?' The voice crackled.

Reuben's fist shattered the face.

When he looked down, he saw who it was. M. K. Taylor was sprawled out on the ground like a deposed potentate.

Reuben turned and kept going.

When he reached his car, Simmons was standing there. 'You can't do it that way,' Simmons said.

Reuben climbed behind the wheel, slammed the door, and rolled down the window.

'It ain't you and it ain't your church and it *ain't your goddamned grandfather – !*'

'It's my job,' Simmons said. 'You stay out of it.'

Reuben drove off.

Sinai Hospital had been built in the French chateau style of the thirties. Lights twinkled from windows which undulated around turrets.

Reuben pulled into the parking lot.

Then he cut the ignition, lit a cigarette, and reached for his bearings. The cold sweat broke again. The signal of violence too close to the surface. He had gone off like a goddamned land mine.

It was a situation he couldn't control. A feeling of helplessness triggered hothead reactions.

It went beyond that. Way beyond that.

What came back to him was the barefoot kid in overalls who had torn off his knickers. In Maryville. He was eleven. He had gone after the kid with an ax. That kid today, a grown man, walked around with a piece of his ear missing.

What did he feel stripped of tonight?

He got out of the car and crossed the parking lot and went in. He checked at the desk and took the elevator to the third floor.

The hospital corridor was empty. He despised hospitals. The best of them were dictatorial inviolate worlds. There were the authorities and there were the helpless. For the well-being of one the other took charge. The nurse on the desk was a colonel in the doctor's army.

'Frances Greenblatt,' he said.

The cold sweat was gone, but he was beginning to shake.

'I don't have a report on her condition.' The nurse wore a name-plate: Mrs Sanchon. But she wasn't wearing a gold band and her hair was dyed strawberry and she had the look of an efficient widow. He realised his mind was working hard on minor details, holding something at bay. His fury.

'Where's Dr Schraft?' Jack Schraft was the best surgeon in town, one of the few honorable, dedicated doctors left in the world. He spent most of his life at Sinai – he was always around.

'He's with Mrs Greenblatt,' Sanchon said.

It took a moment. That meant surgery. 'What kind of surgery?'

'He operated on her arm. A beam mangled it.'

'Bastards.' He felt the shaking grow visible. From somewhere Sanchon produced a glass of water. He drank it. The trembling subsided. 'Where's the rabbi?'

'In the waiting room.' She made a gesture down the hall.

'You know what happened?'

'I'm only a nurse.'

'They bombed him,' Reuben said. 'They bombed his god-damned house.'

'Who?' she said.

He turned and went down the corridor.

Harris, devoid of his glasses, and still wearing his tuxedo, was sunk into the green plastic divan like an ink blot. He looked up.

'Cherry's dead,' he said. 'Frances loved her. Frances loved that dog.'

44

'I'm sorry. I'm goddamned sorry,' Reuben said.

Harris shook his head dolefully. 'I'm a rabbi. That's the price a man sometimes pays for what he believes.'

It was a symphony of sorrow and defeat and a loud note of something else Reuben couldn't name. Then it came to him through that trained lawyer's sense that could pinpoint the source of another man's emotions. Vindication. Harris was vindicated. Hanging on to his virtue like a thief to his loot.

'She's going to be alright,' Reuben said. He bridled himself into a plastic Danish chair. What he wanted to do was run.

'I hope so,' Harris said.

'When they bring Frances back, I'll take you home with me,' Reuben said. It was a penitent offer. He had seen Harris' soul and was ashamed of its size, and the pretense now said he was blind. 'You shouldn't be alone.'

'We've had our differences,' Harris said, 'but they don't matter now, do they?'

'Damned right.'

'Frances loved that house. I would have gone back to Brooklyn a thousand times. But she loved that house.'

'Monk'll get it back like it was.' Reuben felt trapped in a collusion of hollow sentimentality.

'It'll never be like it was.' Harris managed a fragile smile. The smile ended at the doorway where Jake Gorman was making his way in like a barefoot man walking on nettles.

'It's terrible.' Jake nodded like a coronary patient who had been gotten up by a nurse with a flashlight. He had put himself together in a suit and an overcoat, but the bluish color of his skin betrayed the effort.

'You shouldn't have come,' Harris said. 'You're a sick man.'

'I'm president of the congregation,' Jake said.

It struck Reuben that everybody was identifying themselves tonight. Simmons had said: *I'm a cop*. Sanchon had said: *I'm a nurse*. Harris had said: *I'm a rabbi*. Now Jake: *I'm president of the congregation*. As if nobody knew who they were unless they said so.

'Cherry's dead,' Harris said. 'Frances loved her. Frances loved that dog.'

'I'm sorry,' Jake said. 'I'm so sorry.'

Like some kind of damned funeral. Everybody mouthing words and saying nothing. Reuben had once seen a wild raccoon trapped in a pit of netting and pine straw. He felt that same sense of suffocation. He needed to take a leak and he was beginning to sweat again.

He got up and gave Jake his chair, though there were plenty of others in the room. 'I'll see you later.'

'Reuben – ' Jake called him.

He stopped in the doorway. He knew what was coming. It came.

'Don't forget,' Jake said. 'About talking to Max tomorrow.'

'Screw Max,' Reuben said.

The corridor was empty.

The desk where Sanchon had been was empty too.

When the elevator arrived, Leo Gorman stepped out, pale as glass under a Bermuda vacation tan.

'Where's Papa?'

'Jake's in the waiting room.' Reuben stepped into the elevator. Leo held the door.

'This isn't going to do any of us any good.'

'We'll deal with it.' Reuben studied Leo. In the last couple of years, Leo's wife – Beda – had gone heavy; Leo had gone mod. Longer hair, sideburns, a full moustache, and lately had taken to riding around town on a motorcycle. He was a new generation man and the beast of fear was having a heyday in his eyes.

'How?'

'I'm a lawyer, I'll figure it out.' Reuben removed Leo's hand. The door closed.

He was halfway down before he realised that he, too, had identified himself. It was catching. Whatever it was. He knew what it was. Fear. And the cold sweat had come back.

The elevator door opened. In the lobby, on a Moroccan striped couch, a balding man in a Hawaiian shirt with his feet propped on a plastic free-form table was reading a paperback: *The Power of Love*. He looked up, saw Reuben, then beckoned with the imperiousness of a man who had inherited three million dollars and turned it into one. With effort.

Reuben came over. 'Everybody's upstairs.'

'Not me – I hate that bastard.' John Abrahmson grimaced, like a rubber Kewpie doll being squeezed in all the wrong places.

'That's not news,' Reuben said. Harris, periodically, gave a liberal sermon. John Abrahmson, periodically, wrote a letter to the *Holmesdale Clarion* disowning him. 'So what the hell are you doing here?'

'My grandpaw started this congregation, didn't he? And he built the original temple, didn't he? And my papa built this damned hospital. I've got a right.'

'We all know you've got a vendetta with Harris,' Reuben said. 'But this isn't the time for it.'

'He got us in this.' John rummaged around in a folder and came up with a paper. 'What about his Yankee mouth? He asked for it. They ain't never bombed nothin' but niggers before. He *asked* for it.' He waved the paper around. 'I'm gettin' signatures. I'm gonna impeach him.'

'For Christ's sake, go *home*.'

'You're my lawyer. I want you to sign it.'

Reuben reminded himself that John was five grand a year. Retainer. Then he said, 'Shove it up your ass.' Then he walked off.

The hospital was on two acres of ground. The wind had gotten stronger and was blowing around the pines. The cold air cleared his head.

He went across the grass and took a leak in a plot of azalea bushes.

Then he lit a cigarette and started to walk.

But he couldn't think. Something kept him from thinking. Something. His perspective was cloudy. His instincts were off. It nagged at him. Something. He couldn't get hold of it.

He went over the facts. His facts. He had punched M. K. Taylor, a deputy chief of police. He had provoked Simmons. He had offered the rabbi his house out of penance for anger. Then he had proceeded to curse Jake Gorman and alienate John Abrahmson, two of his best damned clients.

He knew now, without question, that his anger was out of hand. If he had been his own client, he would have reamed himself out. He would have said: Go home. Go to bed. There was nothing he could do. What the hell did he think he could do?

He reached the edge of the grounds. He saw he had been heading somewhere. Back to the parking lot. Back to his own car.

He climbed in and sat there a moment wondering where it was he wanted to go and who it was he wanted to see. It wasn't home. It wasn't Mollie. That much he knew.

Then, through the windshield, he saw Max Nathan hurrying across the parking lot. Waving. Max had spotted him. Holding something by the hand. He assumed it was Gina. A head of black curls buried in a mass of red fox and teetering along on high-heeled suede boots.

'*Reuben.* Reuben, my boy!' Max shouted.

Reuben took a vow to remain in charge of himself. Then he got out. He watched Max come along, a short man in a tweed overcoat, and bobbing a tiny Rex Harrison hat up and down. Max was an

47

innocent. Attacking Max was like shooting quail. Too little meat to bother.

'A terrible thing,' Max said. He paid his dues to the immediate situation, but his heart wasn't in it. It was clear that Max had deserted earth for some other planet.

'Terrible,' Reuben said. That was over.

'This is Gina,' Max said. An incipient grin broke through. 'This is my Gina.' Back to business. And pleasure. Back to that place where couples walked into sunsets.

'How do you do.' Gina put out a suede-gloved hand. Reuben took it. It turned out to be pleasure. He could see the thing that had terrified Jake. Next to Rosalie, Gina was Cleopatra. She looked far from mindless, but not conniving. There were a lot more years than Jake believed on that earth-ravaged face which had been artfully replastered with theatrical makeup. He could see the thing that had got Max out of the dungeon of celibacy.

'A little happiness I deserve,' Max said.

There were worse ways to kick off.

'They think I want his life insurance,' Gina said. 'You're his lawyer. I want you to tell them. No life insurance. I want him to live. I want to help him live.'

Reuben climbed back in the car. Max poked his head through the window. 'You see?' he said.

'A little happiness you deserve,' Reuben said. He pulled off.

He drove back to Maple Street. He didn't get out of the car. The fire was under control and the crowd had dispersed. M. K. Taylor was gone, but Simmons was still there, giving orders to a couple of cops with cameras and flashbulbs.

The clock on the dashboard told him it was one o'clock.

He drove back to Morningside Drive. At Elmwood Avenue, he turned off. He went past darkened houses big enough to be orphanages, surrounded by gardens and moss-covered trees and pieces of moonlit Greek statuary. At a stop sign, a jackrabbit scurried across in front of his headlights, then vanished. A moment later, he pulled up into the driveway of Justin's Federalist house.

It looked like the rest. Not a light on anywhere. No one had telephoned Justin. It wasn't his business. Justin wasn't a Jew.

The word had never been mentioned. *Jew*. In fifteen years. Maybe it was testimony to the fact that it didn't matter or maybe it was a denial of something that mattered too much. And maybe it was time to find out.

He got out of the car and went up the walk. He knew he was

48

exhausted and paranoid and looking for trouble. He knew what he wanted from Justin. A statement: *It doesn't matter; it doesn't matter if you're a Jew.* He knew Justin was his partner and they had been through the gamut. Fifteen years. Who the hell did a man turn to if he didn't turn to his partner ? He had always come through for Justin and Justin would always come through for him. He knew that. Why did he keep reminding himself tonight of all the things he already knew ?

He rang the doorbell. He kept on ringing until Justin came to the door. Justin had taken the time to wash his face and comb his hair and dig the loaded pistol out from under the mattress.

The forty-five was pointed right at Reuben's abdomen.

'For Christ's sake. Put that thing away.'

'It's two in the morning.'

'I know what the hell time it is.'

Justin dropped the gun into the pocket of his terry-cloth bathrobe. Reuben came in. Justin closed and locked the door.

'What's the trouble ?'

'I need a drink,' Reuben said.

In the living room, crystals jangled as Justin turned on a lamp. The light hit the blood-red carpet which crawled across a thirty-foot span. The rest was antiques and Italian provincial except for a big black baby grand piano. At the end of the room, a pair of gold and white doors hid the bar – for the benefit of Justin's mother, a tiny obsessive Baptist who came to visit twice a year from Harrisburg. Reuben opened the doors and poured himself a shot of Scotch from a crystal decanter. In the mirror beyond, he could see his own image. He looked like a man who was running from something.

He drank the Scotch down, then poured another one.

Then he crossed the room and faced Justin. Something grotesque in it; two men who had shared their lives for fifteen years and now he had to worry about how to put it.

'What's the trouble ?' Justin said. Again. Quiet.

Then Caroline's voice floated down from the stairway. 'Is everything alright, Justin ?'

'It's Reuben.'

Reuben heard the diffident rustle of a dressing gown as Caroline ascended again. Mollie would have come down and made them some coffee. Not Caroline. Who the hell did she think she was ?

A bitch.

'What's the trouble ?' Justin said. For the third time.

'The rabbi's house was bombed.'

It echoed. A long moment went by. Sixty seconds of corruption and mistrust. Finally Justin said, 'When?'

Not an emotional reaction anywhere. Justin did what he always did. He asked for a fact. That echoed too.

'Around midnight.'

Justin crossed to the marble fireplace, stooped, turned on a jet, and put a match to it. A half-burned log flared up, lighting his face. His face had closed in.

'Goddamnit, his wife was hurt.'

It doesn't matter. Justin refused to say it.

'It's an emotionally charged situation,' Justin said. 'We both know that doesn't help anything.'

What had he expected from Justin? Loyalty? Sympathy? The offer of Justin's capabilities? Now he saw it for what it was. Justin was the enemy. Justin was the goy. He could suddenly see that his partnership with Justin was like a bad marriage. It worked publicly, socially, economically – but what he needed, Justin withheld. He felt stripped down by the combination of violent insights he couldn't afford.

'You're an old F.B.I. man,' Reuben said. 'Where do I start?'

'Start what?'

'I'm not going to sit around and do nothing.'

'The F.B.I. has its own office here. You know that.'

'Get Tom Barksdale on the phone,' Reuben said.

Barksdale had been sent down by Hoover in '64, the summer the three civil rights workers were killed.

'I hardly know Barksdale,' Justin said.

That was true. Barksdale represented bigotry to the blacks and integration to the whites; both steered clear of him. Neither Reuben nor Justin had ever established anything with Barksdale beyond southern cordiality.

'Get to know him,' Reuben said.

'It's two o'clock in the morning.'

'There's been a bombing.'

'Why don't we deal with this in the morning?'

'There's been a bombing.'

'Look – the F.B.I. doesn't come into something unless a federal offense has been committed, or unless they're called in by the local authorities. You know that – '

'You don't give a damn, do you?'

'You're wrong about that.' Justin shook his head.

'Who the hell would do such a thing?'

'You want theories? Maybe the militants on Powell's land,

50

maybe the whites who don't want Rabin's factory, maybe some-body who knows you're thinking about taking the Higgins case, maybe none of it.'

'I don't want your goddamned theories – '

'What do you want?' Justin said.

'I'm going to see Simmons,' Reuben said. 'I'm going to see Simmons because I know how to handle Simmons. You know how to handle Barksdale. I want whatever information he's got and I want it by tomorrow morning.' ·

'What makes you think he'll give it to me?'

'You're both F.B.I. men.'

'Ex – ' Justin said. '*Ex*-F.B.I. man.'

'Are you telling me you're not going to do it?'

'I'll do what I can. You know that.'

'That doesn't satisfy me.'

'What would?'

'Nothing you know how to do,' Reuben said. It would never be the same again; not because it had changed, but because it had al-ways been what it was, and now he could see it. Still, the cry persisted. Say it: *It doesn't matter*. Say it. Screw him.

'I'll talk to Barksdale,' Justin said. 'I don't know what good it'll do, but I'll talk to him.'

'When?'

'Tomorrow. He's an Episcopalian. I'll see him in church.'

He drove back to Maple Street. The spectators had cleared out. Simmons was gone. There was a policeman on duty, a burnt-out wall, a hole in the roof, and a six-foot crater where the rose garden had been.

He stopped at his office and picked up a bottle of bourbon. Like an animal, he went from room to room, claiming his territory. Then he left and drove to the police station.

Simmons was in his office. He went in and set the bourbon down on the desk. Simmons looked red-eyed and blue-jowled.

'I came to return the drink.'

'You're lucky I didn't lock you up.'

Reuben nodded. 'I appreciate that,' he said. 'I guess we've been friends a long time. Three divorces is a long time.'

'I don't know nothin' about women,' Simmons said, 'but I know how to handle bastards. This time I'm dealin' with bas-tards. You let me handle it.'

'You're a good cop,' Reuben said. He went over to the water cooler and pulled off two paper cups. Then he came back to the desk and filled them with bourbon. 'What have you got?'

'A couple of leads.' Simmons opened up.

'Like what?'

'A 1963 light blue Ford sedan. Rose County license plate. We're checkin' automobile registrations.' A straight answer.

'Who saw the car?' Reuben sipped at the bourbon.

'A couple of witnesses,' Simmons said. Straight enough.

'Anything else?' It was too easy. Something was wrong with it.

'It was dynamite. Definite. They used dynamite,' Simmons said.

'How can you tell?'

'You a munitions expert?' Simmons swallowed some bourbon.

'Hell no.'

'Then take my word for it. It was dynamite. Your friend Levitt had some dynamite stolen on Thursday. We're checkin' out his crew. Mostly niggers.' That's what was wrong with it.

'You think the blacks did the bombing?'

'I got no thoughts,' Simmons said. No more straight answers.

'When do you think you'll have a couple?'

'I got no calendar either.' Simmons finished the bourbon. Then he got up, pulled on his overcoat, and put the bottle in his pocket. 'That's good bourbon.' he said.

'I've got the rabbi staying at my house,' Reuben said. 'Maybe you ought to send out a cop.'

'What for?'

'I like my house. I don't want anything to happen to it.'

It nagged at him. All the way home through the predawn streets. When he pulled up in the driveway, he let it go because he knew he was too damn tired.

He let himself in the back door and went up the stairs. The door to the guest room was closed. He cracked it and looked in. A figure was asleep in the canopied bed; he assumed it was Harris.

He closed the door. Then he stood still a moment looking down the hall to the darkened doorway of his own bedroom. For that moment the anger and violence became a desire for sex. But he didn't want Mollie. His wish was for a headless woman, simply a body. No talk. No questions. A simple, thrashing, mind-blowing *fuck*.

Like Eula Williams.

He came down the stairs, stopped in the bar, and picked up a bottle of Scotch and a glass. Then he went through the dining room into the study.

It was a small room. Three bookshelf-lined walls and a window looking out to the woods. He sat down at his desk and started to drink. The night's events went past him again, something in it leaping out at him, but he couldn't get hold of it.

He had punched M. K. Taylor. For a start. He had cursed two clients. He had put his law partnership up for grabs. It was time for a cold, clear analysis. He had obviously believed the bombing had challenged his right to be what he was. He had felt stripped. The bombing had set off a chain reaction of inner violence. Now it was time to quit being victimised by his own emotions. It was time for the lawyer to take charge.

It was his case. The case was seventy-five years old. In his shadow was the old man, his grandfather, who had sloughed off the Russian and Judaic heritage in favor of earth hunger. It was his case and his history. He knew the history. The old man had come in 1892. Only fifty years after the first settlers – those men who had just got their hands on the plantation dream when the Yankee snatched it away. For thirty years after the Civil War the real battle took place. Then the Yankee gave up and went home. That's when Joe Buchman arrived, with his bushy Russian beard and *shtetl* boots, and his thick Yiddish accent that blurred the few words he had picked up in the East Side New York ghetto. He found the South setting about to rebuild its old traditions. Joe Buchman joined in. Slavery had disappeared, but the dedication to cotton and the plantation system remained; a place for men who could subdue the land again remained. Joe Buchman was a foreigner and a Jew, but Joe Buchman was white. He knew how to handle a crew of niggers; he knew how to get 265 pounds of cotton to an acre; and he knew how to make the best corn whiskey in the whole damned state. He started with twenty acres, and he ended up with three thousand. On the day the old man died, in the flood of '27, there wasn't a man, woman, or child in the Mississippi delta who didn't know the name of Buchman.

The heritage remained. That was his case. He was a man of two pieces, a Jew and a southerner, and the two pieces had cleaved together for three generations. But tonight he had felt a tearing apart, as if the bombing had torn apart seventy-five years. And he had reacted. Anybody else would have reacted. As simple as that. He finished the Scotch.

He rested his case. Poured another Scotch. Any questions?
– I have a few questions.
Fire away.
– What happened tonight? The fact. The simple fact.

You know what the hell happened. The rabbi's house was bombed. He swallowed some Scotch.

– But you took it personally.

Damned right. It *was* personal. I'm a Jew.

– Maybe it didn't have anything to do with that. Maybe it was a mistake. The wrong house. Maybe Simmons was right. Maybe it's a black with a personal grudge. Maybe Justin was right. Maybe the red-necks are still mad about the Rabin factory.

Sure. And maybe it was a nut. Or maybe it was a drunken kid. Or maybe it was *anything*.

– Exactly.

What the hell are you trying to tell me?

– You didn't react. You overreacted. You'd better watch out for that. It's touchy territory. You're more insecure than you thought about being a Jew.

Screw you.

– Think about it.

What the hell have you come up with? Justin's theories? Simmons' theories? What about the most obvious one? What about the one nobody mentioned? What about the goddamned Klan?

– You finally got hold of it?

Damned right. It was right there. All the time.

– What about the thing *you* didn't mention? You let it set you off and then you buried it, didn't you? Why didn't you tell anybody about the phone call? *Count your days, you dirty Jew!*

He downed the rest of the Scotch and poured himself another one.

Seven

FOR TWO YEARS Buster had worked for Levitt Construction. For two years he had kept his mouth shut, picked up his nonunion paycheck, and made payments on his rattletrap pickup. Then, on Thursday, he had known it was time to bust out again. But he hadn't said anything to Eula. He wasn't going to be run by a woman.

Brim Street was dark as a mud hole. He ground the truck to the end and quit in front of 872½. Then he got out into the wind. It was blowing through the cemetery stones like a banshee, worse than an hour ago. Now it was no longer Saturday night, it was Sunday. Eula had said she was going on Sunday, no matter what. And he could see the red Mustang was loaded up like a garbage truck.

At the bottom of the steps he pulled off a half-dozen jonquils. Then he went up the steps to the porch. The screen door was open. The red painted door was unlocked.

Inside, the parlor was empty and dark. The door to the bedroom was closed, no light coming out underneath. When he opened it up he could make out the shape of her on the mattress, wrapped up like an Indian in a blanket.

'Eula – ' he said.

The blanket stirred. He crossed to the bed and looked down at her. She had her back turned.

'Eula – '

She turned over. 'What the hell are you doing here?'

He reached up and switched on the bulb that hung down over the bed. He could see she'd been crying. He could see she didn't like him seeing that. She had been born in this place. Like him. Leaving was like tearing up the roots of a tree from the ground. She had torn her roots up with hatred, but the dirt was still clinging there.

'I brought you some flowers.'

'Go to hell,' she said. But she took the flowers. He got out of his jacket. She pulled the heads off the jonquils and threw them at him, one by one, all the time he was taking his clothes off.

'Who do you think bombed Whitey tonight?' she said.

'Who the hell cares?'

'Cricket Yallowby told me. I called the Atlas Cafe. Lookin' for you. You weren't there. Clyde neither.'

'I was out gettin' laid.' He grinned at her.

'You bone-black bastard – '

He laid down on the mattress. 'Give me some blanket.'

She opened the blanket. Her skin gleamed in the light of the hanging bulb. 'Turn off the light,' she said.

'Uh-*uh*. I like to see what I'm doin'.'

'It's the last night we got,' she said.

'I'm gonna make you remember it,' he said. 'You gonna make me remember it.'

'Go to hell.' She pulled away from him.

'We been all through that,' he said. 'I ain't goin' with you.'

55

She sat up and wrapped the blanket around her. 'You didn't have nothin' to do with that bombin', did you?'

'Give back that blanket, I'm freezin' my balls off.'

'I'm crazy,' she said. 'I been lyin' here. Ever since I talked to Cricket, I been lyin' here. I been thinkin' about how maybe you done that bombin' and maybe now you gonna have to *run* –'

'I don't run,' he said. 'I don't run from nothin'.'

'You gonna stay here and rot.'

'Listen,' he said. 'I ain't tryin' to keep you from goin'. Maybe it's a good thing for you. You got schoolin'. You got sense. I got nothin' but what I can do with my hands. I know what I got, I don't fool myself none. I ain't gonna go up there and work in no plant. And I ain't gonna live cramped up in no room with six other strangers and I got to climb six flights of stairs to get there. And I ain't gonna sit on no fire escape to get hold of no sun.'

'It ain't like that,' she said.

'You ain't never been. You don't know.'

'You ain't never been neither,' she said.

'But I *know*.' He thought about the men who came through the Atlas Cafe – the shantytown box on the unpaved portion of Catfish Avenue, a quick spit from the I.C. tracks where the freight trains started rumbling at dusk and didn't quit before sunup. The Atlas Cafe served as a way station for the men who hopped a freight in Chicago or Detroit to come down – broke, on the run, angry, hungry – to visit some great-aunt of grandmama not laid eyes on in twenty years. And Cricket Yallowby gave out cots and meals, his own 1968 backwards version of the underground railroad. The men told how it was up there. How a black man wasn't free for nothin' up there, except free to starve. How there was no way to change nothin' up there. And how here, down here, there was still a chance to fight.

'No more talkin' about it,' he said.

'What you gonna do when I'm gone?' she said. 'Every Sunday you gonna go out and look at that forty acres that somebody said your grandpaw used to own? And think about gettin' it back when you ain't never gonna get it back? All you got here is what *used to be*. And what *used to be* was nothin' but worse than what you got now.'

'Don't bitch me,' he said. 'And don't bitch my grandpaw.'

'You bone-black bastard –'

'I lived on the land 'til I was eight. I know what it feels like. You gotta fight your way up there. I gotta fight *my* way down here. Don't bitch me.'

'Just like the man said,' she said. 'You're one of them people who don't run. One of them people who 'love this place.' You talk just like Mr Charley – '

'I done warned you – ' he said. 'Don't bitch me.'

'Buchman – ' she said. 'Ain't he *the man*? Ain't he the one your mama and papa work for? Ain't he the one got you your job?' Her voice rose, shrill and angry.

'What about Buchman?' he said.

'He was out here this morning'.' Her tone goaded him.

'What for?' he said. 'What the hell for?'

She laughed. 'Tellin' me what a good nigger Buster Jackson is.'

He hit her. She fell over onto the bed. He pulled the blanket off her. 'You ain't gonna be fit to go nowhere tomorrow,' he said.

'*I'll cut your balls off* – ' she said.

He wrapped himself in the blanket. 'No,' he said. 'You won't do that.'

She lay there, naked and glaring at him. He knew it would take her a minute. He knew just how long it would take her. He hadn't hit her hard. He didn't like to hit her. But she always kept on until he did. First telling him how to be a man, her way – but he had his own way of being a man. And she couldn't understand his way, so she always kept on until he hit her, and somehow that turned her into a woman again.

She crawled over to him. He opened up the blanket and wrapped it around both of them. Then he rocked her, until he felt her come back to herself again.

'What was Buchman doin' out here?' he said.

'He says he's gonna defend Higgins.'

'What for?'

'For kicks,' she said.

He had hold of her now. She was with him. 'What'd you tell him?'

'Turn out the light.'

'What'd you tell him?'

She laughed. 'I told him what he wanted to hear.'

He reached up and switched off the bulb. 'You're a bitch of a woman,' he said. 'You watch out for yourself up north. . . .'

The Atlas Cafe was packed like a cattle pen.

Just inside the threshold Buster stepped over a mangy long-haired dog asleep on its side, heaving a bloated mottled belly and pawing its legs in the air like it was dreaming of running somewhere out in the country.

He pushed his way through the crowd to the oval pit where Cricket Yallowby pumped a bellows at the coals, the rocks turning white hot under the grate where the ribs and chicken sizzled. Cricket waved, then turned a slab of meat with a devil's pitchfork, a gargantuan man dripping sweat from a pomaded head, while the smoke found its way out through a trapdoor in the ceiling. When the cops arrived, the trapdoor would slam shut, and a bucket of water poured on the coals made a getaway screen. Cricket had it down to a science.

Ritzy, the only black midget in Holmesdale, sat on the edge of the pit, his short legs dangling. 'You heard about the bombin'?' he said gleefully.

Buster grinned. 'I heard.'

'Halleluyah,' Ritzy said. He did an imitation of white parishioners on Sunday morning.

Cricket rolled his eyes like a pair of gambler's dice and forked over a half-dozen split chickens in one deft motion. 'They after white meat tonight,' he said.

Buster cut through the packed tables to the musicians' stand. A scarred upright piano was going crazy, and somebody was playing a washboard, and a fat man was whipping the drums; Clyde was going at his father's old slide-guitar and singing:

'. . . They arrested me for fo'gery, can't even sign my name,
They arrested me for murder, I ain't never harmed a man . . .'

It was a song Clyde's papa had taught him.

Clyde's papa had died at Parchman, the penitentiary out in the delta, one of those progressive prison farms where the convicts built highways and grew cotton and made their own clothes and were allowed monthly sleepover visits from their wives. And children. Clyde had seen his papa once a month on Sunday for fifteen years; once a month, on Sunday, Clyde had learned how to sing and play the slide-guitar. His papa had been camp musician. Before he died from pneumonia because a white doctor ignored the fever of a black man who'd been sent up for beating a pawnbroker in Gulfport. The pawnbroker had offered him two dollars for the slide-guitar so he could go home to his wife and baby for Christmas.

All that was left of him was the slide-guitar. And Clyde's singing. It was all there in Clyde's singing.

Buster stood at the edge of the stand until he caught Clyde's eye. Clyde nodded, small and wiry like a bantam prizefighter; wearing purple pants and a silver vest, like a black snake in rainbow colors. He knew how to strike like one, too, when a man wasn't looking; but he hadn't learned that from his papa. He had learned that from being undersized.

Buster went past the pool table; past the clacking balls, and the cracked Coca-Cola light shining down on the grimy green felt, and some raucous cursing, and the satin rump of an easy lay kicking up one big heel. Then he ducked through a door that led to the broken-down supply room and kitchen.

The sound of the music pumped through the walls from outside. At a table, in the center, an old black woman with a rag-tied head and pendulous breasts sat picking out black-eyed peas into a basin. She grinned and nodded with the cheery wordless croak of the deaf. In the corner, on one of the two cots, a refugee from an IC freight punctuated the air with a periodic snore like the honk of a goose.

There were cartons stacked everywhere, labeled Pork N Beans, and Mustard, and Lard, and big tubs of flour and molasses and sugar and rice. The floor hadn't been swept in a year.

He went around back of the deaf woman and poked around in the barrel of rice until he felt something hard and firm at the bottom of it. He cursed under his breath. Then the door opened and Clyde came in, the guitar slung over his shoulder and carrying a bottle of beer. He went over to the sink and set down the guitar and the beer and splashed water over his face. When he turned around the beads of water hung there like he had just broken out with smallpox.

'They didn't come get it,' Buster said. He jerked his head towards the barrel of rice where the dynamite had been buried since Thursday. Then he had sent Clyde with word to Brendon Hollyhoke: *When Vernon Powell sends the sheriff out, you blow his ass off* 'What kind of goddamned African Republic they runnin' out there ?'

Clyde slugged at the beer, then wiped his mouth with the back of his hand 'They sent word. It ain't no night to be out in the streets. Not with no afro. Not carryin' no load around.'

'I copped the fuckin' load in the daytime,' Buster said. 'That was fine, I guess. Fine for me to take all the risk. Then they don't even pick the stuff up – '

'What you want to do ?' Clyde said.

'I got a good mind to take the goddamned stuff back where I got it. Fuck Hollyhoke. Let Powell get the land back.'

'You ain't gonna do that,' Clyde said. 'You know you ain't gonna do that.'

'Why the hell not?' He thought about Eula. He knew why the hell not. 'Every damned Saturday night the cops raid this place. What if they find it?'

The deaf woman nodded and grinned.

'They ain't gonna find it,' Clyde said. 'They lookin' for *him*.' He pointed the beer at the sleeping man. 'They lookin' for panthers. Every black Yankee motherfucker's a panther to them.'

'What the hell is Hollyhoke? A black Yankee motherfucker,' Buster said. 'Maybe he's settin' us up for somethin'.'

'For what?'

'You gonna go out there,' Buster said. 'Right now.'

'I ain't goin' out there tonight.'

'You gonna go out there tonight and tell Hollyhoke he don't pick it up by midnight tomorrow we gonna blow *his* ass off.'

The wind was still blowing strong when Buster pulled up in front of the small clapboard church at the corner of Lincoln and Bass.

Light was coming through the windowpanes, painted with a water-base paint, smudged with black and blue and brown, but a clear pane here and there – enough to let him look through and see his mama still there, up on the altar, working away at the silver cross.

Never any money to give to Jesus, Leila said.

So every Saturday night, no matter how late she got off, she hied herself to the church to polish the cross and mop and wax up the ragged wooden floors.

Then, on Sunday, she could watch the light come in and shine on the cross and shine on the floors; and Buster sometimes heard her worrying about too much time spent looking up at the silver cross and down at the polished floors, taking the sin of too much pride in her own handiwork and not enough in the work of the Lord.

The last time he'd gone to church with her, he was twelve.

That was nine years ago.

It was the end of the summer he had helped Attica out at the Buchmans, not the big house they lived in now, but the one before that, on Oak Road, big enough, the yard filled with roses and crab-apple trees and Attica hauling the fertilizer around in a wheelbarrow. And every chance he got, the kid he was, he went around peering in the windows, trying to see what it was like, to be white, in a house like that. Cupping his hands and pressing his nose against the window screens, looking at all the rooms dressed out of magazines; a child crying in a painted white crib and his own

60

mama running with a bottle. He could remember the sight hurtling him into disorder, the inner confusion crashing around until a sound had come out of him, loud and terrible And Attica had come running. *Don't make no racket, Buster! Hush....*

That was the summer he quit going to church.

He rapped on the pane. Then he went around to the front door and opened it; he stood on the threshold, as far as he'd go.

'You ready to go home?'

'I been ready,' she said.

She came down backwards from the altar, looking up at the cross. Then she got into her old brown coat and came down the aisle, past the dozen battered pews, her face worn out with work and fatigue.

'Where's your papa?' She didn't come to his shoulder. Since he was twelve, he'd been bigger than she was.

'Asleep,' he said.

'Drunk, you mean.'

'He's got a right,' Buster said. He had been eight when the land they were renting was sold and all the tenants evicted; they had moved into town. Attica had got pleurisy and grief, and Leila had got a job as a bus girl in a downtown cafe. Then this fine white man had come in, ordering lunch, and asking her if she knew a couple. Handing her out a card, *Buchman & Woods*, a gold band around it and lettering that stood up under your fingers. The two of them had gone to work there. And Attica's soul had never got used to it.

She locked up the door of the church. He helped her into the truck. When he got behind the wheel, she said, 'In Heaven they got his name. Attica Jackson. He's gonna rot in purgatory.'

'He's got to make it through this life first,' Buster said. He thought about Eula. Eula saw how it happened when a black man took on a wife, and after that the children began to come, thinking they had the same rights as any human being – until they learned different. He couldn't raise children to look on him with the eyes he looked on Attica – with the love and the hate and the pity and the anger.

He was going to miss Eula.

The street was dark and empty when he pulled up in front of his house. He cut the motor.

'I gotta tell you somethin',' he said. He didn't want her to hear it tomorrow in church, with him not there to take care of her.

'Don't be talkin' to me about your papa, talk to the Lord,' she said.

'It ain't about Papa.'

'What, then?'

'The rabbi's house got bombed tonight,' he said. 'That ain't gonna make the Buchmans too happy.'

'*Oh my God —*' She closed her eyes and rolled her head around in a circle. Then she started to cry. Staring at him and crying. He knew she was remembering the Black Brotherhood pamphlets she had burned up in the kerosene stove a year ago. *We believe in the people's right to defend themselves in Vietnam as well as Harlem, New York, or Holmesdale, Mississippi, U.S.A.*

'I didn't have nothin' to do with it,' he said. 'Why would I have somethin' to do with it?' Because he wasn't a kid anymore, him and Clyde painting STOP SEGREGATION on all the stop signs on Lincoln Avenue, all through the section where James Meredith stayed before he went on to Ole Miss. He knew she was remembering all of that.

'Swear it,' she said.

'I swear it.'

'They got Jesus and they got Lincoln and they got Kennedy,' she said. 'You'd think that'd be enough for 'em.'

'It ain't so bad,' he said. 'Wasn't nobody killed.'

'You wait,' she said. '*You just wait.*'

He hoped she was right.

Eight

REUBEN opened his eyes aware it would be a hellish Sunday, but it took him a moment to remember why. Then it washed over him with the sense of a nightmare, and when that sixty seconds had gone by, he knew it had been another exercise in panic and fury and not one to welcome back for a return visit.

He had learned his lesson last night.

The bed was rumpled. Mollie was gone. The door to the hall was closed. The porcelain clock said eight o'clock. He had had four hours sleep, more than he might have expected. The phone hadn't rung. Then he saw that Mollie had moved it to the dresser and taken it off the hook. And left the newspaper beside it. Like it was any ordinary goddamned Sunday.

He got out of bed, put the receiver back, and rifled the newspaper looking for news of the bombing. There was nothing. He realised it had happened too late to make the Sunday home edition. Inside his head, a little man was working away with a jackhammer.

He turned on the radio and went past three Sunday Bible programs before he found a station with news. There was the Vietnam War, no better; and the weather, windy and cold. After that came the report. 'An unnamed spokesman for the F.B.I. has made the following statement: "Last night, around midnight, a home in the Morningside section of Holmesdale was dynamited. It is an event that has caused speculation and outrage among a number of citizens. As we are all aware, these are tense times in Mississippi. In such times there is the tendency to jump to false conclusions on the basis of little or no evidence. The F.B.I. has not been called in. We are confident that the local authorities are doing everything possible."'

He knew the 'unnamed spokesman' was Tom Barksdale.

It looked like Barksdale was busy with absolution. The question that came out of it was: Why?

The shower washed away the racket in his head. But the *Why?* kept pounding. Then an answer emerged by combining the events of last night with the deliberate evasion of the radio report. The answer was clean and hard and deliberately emotionless and it went like this:

The rabbi's house had been bombed.

The F.B.I., for whatever reason, would like to stay publicly clear of it. But the Jews had influence and would have to be pacified. That left it with Simmons, the local authority.

A culprit would have to be found.

Preferably one with a touchy image that was politically expedient.

How about a bad nigger who had stolen dynamite from Monk Levitt's construction job? From the site of the new temple itself? That would clean everything up, make it look like a personal vendetta, all neat and gift-wrapped.

Jews shouldn't be careless with dynamite and bad niggers should be locked up.

Maybe it was paranoia and maybe it wasn't.

When he got out of the shower, the phone was ringing. He bet

63

himself twenty dollars it wouldn't be Justin and it wouldn't be Simmons and it wasn't.

It was Leo. 'I'm calling for Papa.'

'Shoot.'

'Papa thinks we ought to have a meeting.'

'What for?'

'We've been talking. Suppose it's the Klan?'

'What if it is?'

'We need to talk about it.'

'What if it's not?'

'We need to talk about that too.'

'What the hell are we going to talk about if nobody's got the facts?' Reuben said. 'It'll be hysterics, that's all it'll be. You tell Jake when I get the facts, I'll call a meeting.'

'Who the hell put you in charge?' Leo said.

'You want the job?'

'No,' Leo said.

He was shaving when the phone rang again. It was Monk. Monk wanted the same thing Leo wanted, a meeting, more adamant about it and less easily put off. Monk could smell personal danger. He skirted around the truth of the dynamite but he couldn't put it together and Reuben didn't do it for him.

'No meeting now,' Reuben said.

Monk gave him some static but finally hung up.

He pulled on some clothes, then went down the hall. The children's rooms were empty, the hamsters twirling around in their cage and a rock poster half coming off the wall where it had been Scotch-taped. The door to the guest room was closed.

When he got to the kitchen, the wind was blowing against the shutters and Mollie was putting together some gumbo, chopping onions and tomatoes with a big French knife. Later, tonight, she would serve it for dinner. At the moment, it gave her somewhere to go.

She didn't hear him come in. He stood there a moment, his eyes on the slope of her shoulders and the graceful motions of her arms. There was a quick flash of guilt for a number of things, none of which he wanted to extract. He focused instead on minor remorse. He had played savior to would-be suicides, and confidant to irate husbands, and host to political bigots and visiting radicals and millionaire industrialists and drunks. Now he had the rabbi stashed in the guest room. Everybody got the guest room and the gumbo.

He saw her feel his eyes on her back. She turned around. There

64

were tears coming down her cheeks, maybe from the onions and maybe not. It was one of those times when he could remember clearly that they had once been as young as anybody had ever been, and the feelings between them as bright and painful. She looked hardly different than she had at seventeen, trudging across the campus carrying the photographic equipment, big-eyed and solemn, her dark hair blowing in the autumn wind. She had been small and determined, and he had sensed, even then, that the absence of size was a result of being condensed to double strength – but she had taken vows not to be diluted. The night they had told her parents they wanted to get married, Edith Singer had fainted and Jacob Singer had walked out of the house, leaving him to revive his soon-to-be mother-in-law. When Edith opened her eyes, Mollie had said with icy coldness, 'I will never set foot in this house again.' The next day he had received a telephone call from Jacob. A simple two words: *You win.*

'There's a policeman out there.' She wiped the tears with the back of her hand, a childlike gesture that touched him.

'I know. I asked for him.'

'Do you think we'll be bombed next ?'

'Hell no,' he said. 'Where are the boys ?'

'Talking to the policeman.'

'What'd you tell them ?'

'Nothing.'

He went to the window and looked out. Phil was on one knee behind a gardenia bush, peering out and firing at the cop with an imaginary gun. He looked happy and violent.

'Maybe you'd better get them out of here today,' he said.

'Where ?'

'Take them to the Williamsburg. Pack a suitcase. Tell my mother to take them to her house and let them spend the night. It'll be good for her. If she asks you any questions tell her you don't know anything.'

'I don't.'

'You don't have to know anything,' he said. 'I'll take care of it. Just come back here and answer the telephone.'

'Where are you going ?'

'To take care of it,' he said.

Mollie left.

Harris came down, dressed, and holding on to his martyrdom. Jack had saved Frances' arm, but she wouldn't be playing any concerts; with luck, she'd get fifty percent utility back. He didn't want any breakfast, coffee would do. The phone rang again. Jack

Schraft asked about Harris' health. Reuben said Harris was fine, he was on his way to his office at the temple as usual. The two hundred Jewish families that comprised his congregation deserved to be both served and reassured. As Harris had just said to Reuben: Religion, like show business, must go on.

He drove to the Oyster Bar. Leila's house was on Mullet. It looked a little better than the rest. He took care of Leila and Attica and they took care of their family. The family consisted of Buster and three bastard granddaughters sent back from daughters gone north. He had once bought Leila a first-class plane ticket to visit her daughter in Chicago and Leila had refused the champagne dinner because she hadn't known it was free.

He was parking in front when Leila came out of the house, with the three little girls who had been scrubbed and ribboned for church. Leila was wearing the fake leopard coat that Mollie had given her on her forty-sixth birthday, a hat with a veil and some velvet flowers that had once been Mollie's, and glossy white gloves and a big patent purse. He watched her come down the steps wearing the sum of Mollie's cast-off clothes, and he felt something stir in him, a synthesis of love and regret, the memory of some kind of warmth he could never recapture. It occurred to him that the black man was always called boy, but the black woman was known as mammy.

They reached the sidewalk at the same time. 'Leila,' he said gently.

'Oh my God, Mr Buchman,' she said. He could feel the fear spring up in her, but it wasn't fear of him, it was fear of his presence here on a Sunday morning, unexpected and therefore terrible.

'I came to see Buster,' he said.

'Buster ain't done nothin',' she said. Then he knew she had heard about the bombing. But she was black, and a black couldn't know anything about whites unless a white told them. That was the unwritten rule. She couldn't even say: I'm sorry. She couldn't even say: I'm afraid.

Reuben went up the wooden steps. Leila left the three girls on the sidewalk and hurried up after him. They faced each other on the porch.

'They're all sleepin',' Leila said.

'You'll have to wake him up,' Reuben said.

She understood that she had no choice. She went through the door. Reuben followed. He found himself in a combination parlor

66

and kitchen. Behind that, he knew, were two rooms and a bath. To his left was a lumpy divan flanked by two chairs he recognised as throwaways from his own house. To his right was an oilcloth-covered table and leftover breakfast dishes. There was the television set he had given them three years ago, and over it pictures of Christ and Kennedy. In the center of the room a stove pumped out excruciating heat and the smell of kerosene.

Leila disappeared.

A muted discussion floated in from the other room. Reuben didn't sit down. He stood. For twelve years, Leila had spent nearly every day of her life in his house; he had been here, in her house, maybe six times in all, and he had never sat down.

In a moment, Attica appeared, wearing a shaggy bathrobe and the prudence of a captive, his eyes red from Saturday night drinking.

'Good mornin', Mr Buchman.' He made an exaggerated display of atrophied manhood, bobbing his head and clasping his hands in front of him. In the best of times the obeisance was a game, used to extract five dollars for a bottle of gin or to distract from the cucumber patch not yet planted, but there was no badger game in it today.

'I'm gonna see Buster,' Reuben said. 'Now. Right now.'

'He ain't feelin' too well,' Attica said.

'Now,' Reuben said. He watched the marasmus of fear take over Attica's face. 'I ain't gonna say it another time.'

Attica left. There was another moment of hushed unintelligible voices. Then Buster appeared.

'What's the trouble?' Buster was wearing khaki trousers and a sleeveless undershirt that accented the muscles he had earned at Levitt Construction. Unlike Attica, there was no softshoeing around. Buster's face was composed, ready to parry.

'The rabbi's house was bombed last night.'

Buster didn't parry. 'I heard.'

'Where'd you hear?'

'The Atlas Cafe. Last night. They done it to our church just before Christmas. It happens regular.'

It wasn't audacity, it was simple truth. The simple truth told by a black should have equaled audacity. But it didn't. Buster was his nigger. Reuben had paid for Buster's shoes since he was eight, had even paid for Buster's appendectomy – Jack Schraft himself had done the surgery.

'On Thursday, dynamite got stolen from your job,' Reuben said.

Not a muscle twitched on Buster's face. He was facing a white man. Reuben knew he had been taught from the cradle how to face a white man. 'How come you askin' me about that?'

'I figured you'd know.'

'I do a day's work for a day's pay, that's all I know.'

'The rabbi's house was dynamited,' Reuben said. 'Dynamite. They're gonna try to pin it on you or one of your friends.'

'It happens every day,' Buster said. His stubborn defiance was canceled by the spark of fear that leaped up in his eyes.

'I don't want victims,' Reuben said. 'I want the bastard that did the job.'

'They ride free,' Buster said. 'They been ridin' free for years.'

'You want the rap?'

'Not me.'

'If you've got that dynamite, or you can get hold of that dynamite, you bring it to my house by four o'clock this afternoon. I don't give a damn why it was stolen or who stole it. That's the deal. If that dynamite's intact and if it's safe in my hands, then they can't pin it on you.'

'I don't know nothin' about it,' Buster said.

'You've got a choice,' Reuben said. He opened the front door. A rush of cold air blew in. 'You can take your chances with the cops, or you can take your chances with me.'

That was it. He left on it.

At the bottom of the steps he passed out one-dollar bills to the three little girls waiting for Leila. Then he got in his car. When he looked back, Leila was in the doorway, the veiled hat hiding her face, and the velvet flowers streaming in the wind.

When he pulled into Brim Street he saw the house was closed up and Eula Williams' red Mustang was gone.

On the phone, Mollie said, 'I don't know anything about the bombing.' She was gentle. The usual female gamut included guilt and compassion and insecurity, the alliance of the mutually subverted and the nationally misunderstood. Between Mollie and Frieda, Mollie knew there was that.

'I'll take the babies to my house,' Frieda said. 'They'll be safe. I'd never let anything happen to them.'

'Thank you,' Mollie said. They were women connected to the same man and therefore the same offspring. There was that too.

'Where's Reuben?'

'I don't know,' Mollie said. A woman mothered a son. A woman reared that son to become her own ideal man. A woman sowed and nourished the seeds of industry and responsibility and sacrifice and devotion to family. Then another woman reaped the harvest. There was that most of all.

'I hope he's not in danger,' Frieda said.

Mollie dropped the boys at the Williamsburg. She didn't go in. She didn't want to face Frieda. She seldom wanted to face Frieda anymore.

It hadn't always been so.

She met Frieda on March 22, 1948, Reuben's twenty-first birthday, the reason Frieda came down to New Orleans from Maryville.

It was in a hotel room, in the Roosevelt Hotel. Mollie had never been in a hotel room before. She had never traveled, at all, beyond the overnight train to Macon, Georgia. Each summer, she and her younger sister, Zoe, were taken by their mother to Macon to visit a small immigrant grandmother who put them, all three, in a big four-poster; and who baked small individual challahs each Friday for her and for Zoe; and who was married to a man everybody called Mr Steinberg.

A hotel room was something exotic.

She could remember the stars in the magenta carpet, and the mint-green wallpaper with its silver-leafed jungle and the faces of tigers sneering through, and the rococo cherubs holding back a pair of blue velvet drapes at a long window which looked down on Canal Street, everybody scurrying across the widest street in the world because the sky had suddenly turned dark and it had just begun to rain.

And Frieda said solemnly, *I wasn't born yesterday. I know how it is to be in love.*

The next day Frieda bought her a sea-blue silk dressing gown that went all the way to the floor. It had slim quilted cuffs with seven mother-of-pearl buttons, and a tiny collar, and it rustled in rich folds from a hand-stitched yoke. Her mother had once spent three weeks embroidering cross-stitch circles on a muslin dirndl for her to wear in a school play. And had once appliquéd flowers on a white sheath for her to receive a scholarship award. And for the first date she had ever had, had made her a suit with a brown satin bustle out of her father's old army uniform. But no one had ever given anything as wasteful and undeserved as a floor-length silk dressing gown.

It still hung in the back of her closet, faded and streaked.

＊ ＊ ＊

She didn't drive to 908 Maple.

She didn't want to look at it. *The bombing.*

She didn't drive home either. She went down to the Pearl River and parked and got out and sat on a tree stump and lit a cigarette and thought about the girl in the sea-blue dressing gown who had spent yesterday morning in Jean Aucoin's bed.

In the past six years she had spent a lot of time in bed with strangers. None of the strangers she had slept with had been Jewish.

Her mother had three reminiscences. Edith would tell these three stories on holidays, on Mollie's birthday, Valentine's day, and Chanukah. The stories, recounted in a loving tone, were indelibly stamped in Mollie's memory.

The first one was this: Mollie had been a premature baby, born at seven months, two and a half pounds. She had been *wrinkled and red like a monkey and covered with hair,* and when the nurse brought her in, Edith said, *Take that away, it can't be mine.*

The second one was: Six weeks later when they brought Mollie home from the incubator, *you promptly broke out with boils and nobody could touch you!*

The third one was: One day Edith walked into her room and found *you in your crib smeared all over with your own bowel movement.*

Of course she grew up to be beautiful.

She had always wanted to wear a white communion dress and be married to God. She was sent to Hebrew school. There were bright black hieroglyphic letters that moved backwards across the page. And a snaillike man in a skullcap who rapped her knuckles with a ruler. She spent most of her time in the basement bathroom scrawling sexual obscenities on the wall. *Fuck God.*

Jean Aucoin was a long way from *God.*

Put everything back, she had said to him.

Yesterday.

Mustering up the kind of authority she used with Leila and Attica, knowing it wouldn't work because Jean Aucoin wasn't black, and he wasn't all that young, and he wasn't frightened at all.

She had parked the wagon on an isolated dirt road outside of town, under a willow, near a frozen creek. *You won't find it here,*

70

baby. But maybe you'll find it somewhere. Maybe with your camera. Martin Gallagher had said. She had gone into the woods to take photographs.

When she came out, a strange man was crawling out of the back of the station wagon, loaded down with her equipment.

No one around for miles.

She expected him to run. He didn't. He stopped and stood there, waiting for her, dark-haired and muscular in a blue denim jacket and jeans, while she kept coming towards him, knowing that if she screamed, called out, no one would hear. With all of her cameras strung around his neck, he waited for her. Until she could see the color of his eyes, an electric blue, absorbing the sight of her, calculating and shrewd and possibly dangerous. When she reached the back of the wagon, she said, *Put everything back.*

He smiled. His whole face broke with the smile. And she knew he understood the situation, the isolation in it.

You might say please, he said. A strange lilt to his words. Familiar. She hadn't heard it since childhood. Then it came back to her. Then she understood the strange coloring, the dark skin, the black hair, the blues eyes. Louisiana cajun.

Please, she said.

He began to put the equipment back, one piece at a time, taking his time, not looking at what he was doing, but keeping his eyes on her.

I'm not goin' to touch you. You don't have to worry about that.
I wasn't.
Sure you were. Maybe you're disappointed?

She felt her face flame. Then, unaccountably, she started to laugh. It didn't feel like fear, or hysteria, the laughter was at herself. One hand over her face and peering through her fingers like a child caught in some forbidden game. Then he began to laugh with her, both of them laughing at the absurdity of the fantasized rape, which, of course, would never occur. Then, in the quiet that came after the laughter, it took shape, like a third invisible being holding out a hand to both of them.

I could use a ride back to town, he said.

She nodded. He closed up the back of the wagon. She turned the car around and headed for the highway. She kept her eyes on the road. On either side, the morning's snow was beginning to melt.

Do you take photographs? she said.
No, he said. *I take cameras.*

71

What else do you do?
I'm a doctor, he said.

She pitched the cigarette into the river.

Then she got back into the station wagon and drove home.

The policeman was walking his three-acre beat. Reuben's car was gone.

In the kitchen, the makings of gumbo were spread out on the sink. Wihout taking her coat off, she dialed Jean's number. She listened to it ring. Through the window, she could see the policeman. The concept of imminent disaster intensified a dread of the unlived life. The anxiety was familiar.

'Hello,' Jean said.

It took her a moment. 'This is Mollie.'

'*Chère*. How are you?'

'Alright.'

'I've been thinking about you all morning,' he said. 'I was afraid you'd be upset.'

'I'm not,' she said.

'What a crazy, freak thing.'

'Yes,' she said.

'Are you sure you're alright?'

'I'm fine,' she said. 'When are you due at the hospital?'

'I'm on the night shift. Nine to nine.'

'I'll be there this afternoon,' she said.

'You'll be at the hospital?'

'No. Your apartment.'

There was a moment of silence. 'Are you sure you want to come this afternoon?'

'How about never?' she said.

'Are you crazy?'

'That's possible.'

'I adore crazy women,' he said. 'It's just such a freak thing. I can't ever remember Jews bein' bombed in the South before. I was there when Dr Schraft operated on Mrs Greenblatt. I never sawn him so shaken. I figured you'd be – '

'I'm not,' she said.

'I'll be here all afternoon,' he said.

Nine

WHEN REUBEN came in the back door, the oversized pocket watch that hung on the whitewashed pine of the kitchen wall said twelve. Buster had four hours.

Mollie was stirring the stock for the gumbo.

'Did Justin call?'

'Yes.' She gestured at the counter where a yellow legal pad had been filled with messages.

'Is the rabbi back?'

'He just telephoned. He went to the Gormans' for Sunday dinner. I haven't written that one down yet.' She put a lid on the copper pot and turned the flame down.

He picked up the yellow pad. 'I'll be in the study,' he said. 'Maybe you could bring me some lunch.'

'What would you like?'

'I don't give a damn.'

'Where were you?'

'It's too complicated to explain,' he said.

'I'm sorry.'

'I don't want to fight with you.'

'It's my life too,' she said.

'Why don't you go out and take some pictures?' he said.

In the study, he went over the messages:

Long distance. New York. Kornfield. Please return call. Operator 27. Area code 212. He thought about Higgins. He had enough goddamned trouble.

Bishop Frank O'Hara expresses regret. Offers funds, if needed, from the Committee of Churches to rebuild rabbi's house. Nice and Christian. The Committee of Churches fund had been established six months ago to help rebuild a series of black churches that had been bombed. Because the blacks couldn't afford to rebuild themselves. It was a nice, Christian offer that lined them up with poor blacks. Screw O'Hara.

Max Nathan expects you for lunch. Pasta. Screw that too.

Dave Colman. Please return call. Dave was a Yankee who had

73

moved down seven years ago to manufacture cheap luggage with cheap labor. Dave Colman wanted to know what he always wanted to know: How does this affect me? Dave could wait.

Father Farnswell. Expresses shock and regret. Offers living quarters at the Episcopal rectory for the rabbi and his wife. Nice. He had a life-size image of Harold and Frances asleep under a plaster-of-paris likeness of Jesus.

Justin. Please return call.

He dialed Justin's house. Caroline answered. It took Justin a long damned time to come to the phone.

'What'd Barksdale say?' Reuben lit a cigarette.

'They're not officially in the case.'

'That's not news to me.'

'He said the local authorities are doing everything possible.'

'Goddamnit, I don't want to hear what I already heard on the radio.'

'Barksdale's a close-mouthed man,' Justin said.

'Go to hell. You know how to get information out of a goddamned stone.'

'Maybe you're not aware of it,' Justin said, 'but periodically you require declarations of loyalty that go beyond –'

'I've got a right.'

'So do I. But I don't require it of you. I trust you and I trust our partnership and I don't make up tests for you that have failure built into them.'

'You're telling me that you tried with Barksdale and you failed?'

'I'm telling you that you damned well know getting information out of the F.B.I. office isn't done off the cuff. You also know damned well that Hoover doesn't have a soft spot for agents like me who quit on him. All you get from a goose chase is a feather duster to tickle your ass.'

'Where the hell do you stand?' Reuben said.

'With you.'

'It doesn't look that way.'

'I can't help your eyesight,' Justin said.

'I've got twenty-twenty hindsight,' Reuben said, 'like everybody else.'

'It's right in front of your nose,' Justin said. 'It's been in front of your nose for fifteen years.'

'I'll take a long good look at it,' Reuben said. He hung up.

Then he put out his cigarette and took a long good look. One fact stood out. They both knew where each other's bodies were buried. He dialed long distance and asked for Operator 27 in New York.

He got Kornfield at home.

'I'll take the Higgins case.'

'I knew I could count on you,' Kornfield said.

'No fee.'

'What's it going to take for you to go all the way?'

Reuben had a mental image of Moses. In the six years he had seen Kornfield's picture in newspapers and on television, he had watched Kornfield's hair grow longer and his temples grow grayer and his drama grow more intense. Kornfield had gone from being a hawk in a windstorm to Moses, and was aiming at Jehovah. 'Don't sell me that radical crap – you know I don't make my decisions that way.'

'I figured you remembered a conversation we once had – about the Klan in the South. You said they don't bother the Jews down there. I believe your exact words were, "They've got the nigger to lynch." When I heard the news about the Greenblatt bombing this morning, I figured you'd remember that conversation.' A brief righteous silence hung for a moment.

'Stick to Higgins,' Reuben said. 'I need the records from the Cleveland Delinquency Home on Thomas Petry Hampstead. Also anything you can get from Juvenile Court – social worker's reports, parole officers, whatever there is on Hampstead. I've got to be armed when I try to discredit his affidavit.'

'I've got tapes of Higgins' version, and some comments of my own. I'll send those too,' Kornfield said.

'When do I get Higgins?'

Kornfield hesitated. 'The A.C.L.U. doesn't want to let him come back. They think it's stacked.'

'I'm not taking a case where the defendant won't show up so the Yankees can prove nobody gets a fair trial down here. Tell the A.C.L.U. to shove it, or find yourself another lawyer. Now when the hell do I get Higgins?'

'After the trial date's set. We can't have him hanging around there any longer than he has to. There's the possibility of more violence. It's all the same thing, isn't it? The Greenblatt bombing, the Higgins case – it's all the same issue.'

'Why the hell don't you look in your own back yard? What about the goddamned riots in Newark?'

'They're southern blacks gone north,' Kornfield said.

'Damned right. They may not like it here, but they know where they stand, and if they don't make trouble nobody starves to death.

We don't promise them anything we don't deliver. The ones that don't like it go north. It's all *equality* they're told. Then they get there and find out it's a goddamned lie. As long as they're here, they've got hope. Once they get up there, they've got nowhere to go anymore – and no hope. So they explode.'

'You're an extraordinary and contradictory man,' Kornfield said. 'The Jews get bombed in Holmesdale, and you telephone me to take the Higgins case, and then you make a speech about how much better off the blacks are down south.'

'You'll never understand the South,' Reuben said. 'Why the hell don't you quit trying ?'

'You're too close to it,' Kornfield said. 'You don't even know what you're dealing with.'

'This is my territory,' Reuben said. 'I know what I'm dealing with.'

He went back to the messages on the legal pad:

John Abrahmson. Wants the rabbi fired. He pictured Kornfield and John Abrahmson, face to face. The thought made him feel better.

Anny Bowden. Clyde in jail again. That could wait.

Long distance. Willie Caldwell. Aunt Elena died in her sleep last night. Funeral tomorrow in Maryville.

It hit him in the stomach. Death.

Another Buchman. One less.

A deep sorrow invaded him. Past griefs, past deprivations swept him. Jesse. After his grandmother, his father had been the first to go. His father's coffin image took shape. He had sat for forty-eight hours straight by Jesse's coffin. But it hadn't purged anything. Now it was Elena, Jesse's only sister. Gone. When Elena was young, she had looked exactly like Garbo. A sense of his own mortality rushed through him.

He shouted for Mollie.

He heard her footsteps come across the planked wood floor of the dining room. When she got to the study door, he saw she had a tray in her hand. On the tray was a western omelette and a pot of chicory coffee.

'Why the hell didn't you tell me about Elena ?' He vented his anger on her. Anger was life. Anger was a weapon against death.

She set the tray down. She poured a cup of coffee. The steam curled up like the ghosts of the dead. 'I didn't know how,' she said.

'You didn't know *how* ?'

'I don't know how to talk about death,' she said.

He got up and came around the desk. She came to his chin.

76

'Mollie – ' he said gently. 'For God's sake, Mollie.' He put his hands on her shoulders and looked down at her. He knew what her fears were, he had known her since she was sixteen. She had always taken refuge from life in some flower-strewn landscape of her own mind, and though she had her own self-guarding strength, she had never been able to deal with the outside world. Her sister, Zoe, was like that too.

'I'm sorry.' Her eyes filled with tears.

'Don't cry.' The phone began to ring. He let Mollie go and picked up the phone. It was Frieda. When he looked back, Mollie was gone.

'It's too much at once.' Frieda's voice was clogged with tears and he could hear the boys playing in the background.

'Damned right,' he said.

'I can't believe it. The bombing. Elena. It's too much.'

'I'll send Mollie after the children.'

'No,' she said. 'They're fine. Just fine. I can take care of them.'

'Are you sure?'

'I took care of you, I can take care of them.'

'Alright.'

'The funeral's at two,' she said. 'I thought we'd go early. I'd like to – ' Her voice cracked, then straightened itself out. 'I'd like to visit your father's grave. . . . '

'I don't know if I can go all the way to Rose County tomorrow.' He heard it echo. *Rose County.*

'Reuben – ' She sounded stricken.

'That's not going to do any good.' *Rose County.* What was it about Rose County?

'We're a family,' Frieda said. 'Even Willie.' Every family had its goy. Willie Caldwell was it. Willie was also a night marshal. In Rose County. Then he remembered. The license plate on the car seen near the bombing was from Rose County.

'You're right,' Reuben said. 'We're a family. We'll all go.'

'Thank you for the roses,' Frieda said.

The omelette was cold, but he ate it. The coffee was cold too. It seemed to him that all the women in his life served him cold coffee. He drank it anyway. Then he went back into the kitchen looking for Mollie. What he found was the copper pot of gumbo simmering away, and a note that said: *Have gone off to take pictures. Love, Mollie.*

The note was a relief.

The giant pocket watch chained to the wall said five after one. He had three hours to wait for Buster.

The shades were pulled. Jean's crookneck lamp threw a yellow circle over the litter of the desk, but the light didn't intrude into the violet dusk of the bed. From outside came the sound of a loose shutter as it banged back and forth against the old Victorian house in the wind.

'No,' Mollie said.

'C'mon. I want to know.' Jean lay on his stomach now, spread-eagled across the bed like a kid.

'I don't have dreams like that.' She ran her fingers lightly across his shoulder blades and down his spine. In a moment, his muscles came to life under her fingertips. She felt a mild sense of power.

'Sure you do,' he said. 'Everybody has sex dreams.' He reached over and touched her face. The gesture was gentle and reassuring. His touch was sure. He knew a lot about women, that was clear.

'What are yours?'

'I'm in a garage.' He closed his eyes. 'One of those big automobile repair places. And all around there are cars that have been taken apart. There's a dismantled engine, a disembodied hood, stuff like that. And I'm fucking a woman on the floor of the garage. And it's great.' He opened his eyes. He grinned at her. Everything about him was slightly too much. As if nothing in his face had been tamed or civilised. 'What do you think that means?' he said.

'It means you're a good mechanic.' She giggled.

'Am I?'

'Yes.'

'That's because it's a fine chassis you've got there, lady,' he said. He pulled back the covers and let his hand travel over her body while he crinkled his face into an exaggerated leer. 'I do believe it's a classic.' He tickled her. She giggled again.

'What about the mileage?'

'It was only driven by a little old lady on Sundays,' he said. 'To church and back.' He shook his head sadly.

'You're *crazy*.'

'Now it's your turn.'

'I dream . . . ' – she closed her eyes – 'of running off with a man named Mr Biggerstaff.' She opened her eyes. 'Now what do you think that means?'

'Not funny.' He turned over and sat up. 'You'll have to do better than that.'

'Making love in the bathtub?'

'You didn't dream that either.'

'Why does it have to be a dream?'

78

'Dreams tell the truth,' he said. 'I'm a truth freak. I dig for the essence of everything.'

'Sorry,' she said. 'I'm a congenital liar. But I tell marvelous lies. You'll like them.'

'Do you speak French?'

'Nobody gets out of a New Orleans high school without speaking French.'

'I'll sing you a song about lies,' he said. '... *Les maringouins a tout mangé ma belle ... Et y ont laissé les deux gros orteils ... Y les ont pris pou' faire des bouchons d' bouteilles ...* '

'Mosquitoes?' She did a rough translation. 'The mosquitoes have eaten up my sweetheart. They have only left two big toes. They took them to make corks for bottles ...?'

'The mosquitoes are lies,' he said. 'That's what lies do. They eat you up and leave two big toes. That's all they leave. Enough to make bottle corks.'

'You *are* crazy.' She sat up and lit a cigarette. She didn't offer him one. He had said yesterday that his vices didn't include cigarettes and they didn't include sexual guilts. Just to set the record straight. 'You believe in stealing, but not lying,' she said.

'I'm a primitive,' he said. 'Stealing is primitive. A man needs something, he takes it. That's survival. I survive. I survived the swamps and the sugar mills and the Vietnam War. Stealing's a positive act. But lying is cowardice. Fear. It's a negative act. It poinsons anything that lives. You throw a few lies into sex, you've got nothing.'

'I don't even tell the truth to myself,' she said quietly.

'But that's suicide.'

'Survival.' She shrugged. 'That's how *I* survive. I live in pieces. If I ever put the pieces together, I'd have to act. And there's no action I can take. I'm a *southern Jewish woman* – two passive adjectives and a passive noun. For most of my life, I've been legally chattel, physically frigid, spiritually dead, and emotionally strung out. I don't have sex dreams. I have dreams where I escape from who I am and what I am. So don't push me, and don't stretch me. I'll crack.'

'Is that a threat?'

'It's the truth,' she said. 'You wanted the truth, you've got it.'

'Alright. You ask the questions.'

'I don't want to. I don't want to know anything about you,' she said.

'Don't you want to know how many other girls I have?'

'No.'

79

'Four,' he said. 'It goes back to my childhood. Eleven brothers and sisters. Nobody ever slept alone.'

She had an image of a cajun cottage. The stairway rising from the porch to the *grenier*, the attic bedroom with its batten shutters against the hurricane winds. Looking over the swamps and the wild indigo. She had once, in college, driven over to the Teche country, to take pictures. Through the ghostlike cypress forests to the bayou which had been choked with hyacinths. Houses with mud chimneys had been built over the water on pilings. Jean Aucoin's house, possibly. And she had frightened herself with the sound of the tree frogs and the rush of a red-winged blackbird. Now she felt the fear creep over her again, like the brush of a feather.

'I told you. I don't care how many girls you have,' she said.

'Don't you want to know if I'm goin' to keep them, now I've met you?'

'No.'

'I don't know,' he said. 'That depends on us. How far this goes. What it turns out to be. How much time we can spend together.'

'None. If this is what you're going to do.'

'I can't help it,' he said. 'It's my nature. For instance last night when we were wheeling Mrs Greenblatt back to her room, and I saw your husband, the first thing I did was ask myself a question.'

'I don't want to talk about my husband.' She had a sudden vision of her two lives crossing like swords. Maybe she had meant for it, one day, to happen – the release that would come from circumstances out of control. It seemed fitting that the possibility had come about through the bombing. Through violence. The idea frightened and elated her.

'When I saw him, I thought – *Why me? Why anybody?*'

'I don't want to talk about it,' she said.

'Not your husband? Not the bombing either?'

'No.'

'Why not the bombing? It affects you, doesn't it?'

'I was a kid during World War Two,' she said. 'All I heard about were Nazis. Bombs and Nazis.'

'My papa shot the parish sheriff over a muskrat pelt,' he said. 'My papa wasn't a Jew and the sheriff wasn't a Nazi, but they hung my papa anyway. To me, you grew up *first-class*. That's the way it is. It's a chain. To a black man, a cajun like me is first-class. To me, a Jew is first-class. To you, first-class is playing Scarlett at Tara and looking for renegades like Rhett Butler.'

'How would you know?' She had an image of her grandmother's house. A corner double across the street from a barroom. She could still remember every single blaring verse of 'Lay That Pistol Down, Babe.' And the Salvation Army competing outside. Inside, the rooms followed each other like shotgun shells – the front room turned into a workshop for her immigrant grandfather, the tailor, the coatmaker. The three back rooms turned into the only kosher boardinghouse in New Orleans. The World War Two soldiers had come there to eat.

There had been a sergeant with a lot of curly black hair and a New Jersey accent. She was ten. He had promised to come back and marry her. There were times, long after that, when she'd stop whatever she was doing and look off into space and think: Bernie Friedman, whatever happened to you?

The Nazis had got him.

'It's late,' she said.

'*Fais dodo*,' he said. It had a double meaning. In the Louisiana bayou country, it meant 'go to sleep.' It also meant 'all-night party.'

'No.'

She rolled off the bed and went into the bathroom and closed the door. There were yellow stains in the sink and toothpaste speckles on the mirror. The sight of her face was intolerable. She washed it quickly and made it up. Then she came out and started to dress.

He was still lying where she had left him. 'Why?' he said.

'Why what?'

'Why did you come here today?'

She thought about other times, other lovers. Sometimes she came to get something; sometimes she came to give something; sometimes she came to wipe something out.

'Twenty years from now,' she said, 'when you're a successful doctor, and you've joined the country club, and you've married the mayor's daughter, you'll be changing into your white coat somewhere and you'll stop and think: Mollie Buchman, whatever happened to her?'

The Nazis got her.

'I'll be an old woman,' she said. 'But you'll remember me the way I am today.'

'That's bullshit.'

'You tell me.'

'You came because you like the fact that I steal *you* from that goddamned privileged world the way I steal everything else I need.'

She got into the coat with the fox hem, and pulled on the white knitted cap. 'I came here today because I hate myself.'

'You'll come back.'

'I don't think so.'

'You'll come back,' he said, 'because it's the only place in your life you can find what you're after.'

'What's that?'

'You don't know it yet, but you're after the truth,' he said.

'Don't count on it.'

At a quarter to four, through the study window, Reuben saw Attica's rusted Dodge pull up at the bottom of the driveway.

Attica stayed below.

Leila got out of the car. Gingerly. Then she started up the driveway, one foot ahead of the other, with care. Like she was carrying dynamite. Which she was. Wrapped in a dish towel.

At that moment, Simmons' cop came around a clump of magnolia trees, fifty yards from Leila. Reuben cursed himself. He had believed he was operating with reason and calm, but he had forgotten completely about the cop. Leila was moving at the pace of molasses. The cop stopped to take a good look, focused on the dish towel, then started to move in. Leila grinned like a madwoman, but she kept moving up the driveway.

Reuben streaked for the back door.

He opened it, then waved at Leila. 'I've been waiting all day for that *cake*,' he shouted.

He waved at the cop. The cop waved back.

Leila came the rest of the way, the dish towel package in two out-stretched arms, as far away from her body as she could get it.

She didn't look at him. She came in, past him, into the kitchen, and set the package down on the chopping block in the middle of the floor.

He closed the back door. Then he came across the brick floor and stood beside her. She looked up at him, twelve years of trust and eyes red from crying.

'Ain't nothin' gonna happen to Buster, is it?'

'No.' Reuben unwrapped the towel. The red sticks were nestled together and neatly tied.

'I ain't never been so scared in my life,' Leila said.

'I'm sorry about the policeman.'

'It ain't the policeman.'

'Did Buster steal the dynamite?'

'Nossir.'

82

'Who stole it, Leila? You can tell me.'

'I don't know. I had to talk and talk and I cried and I cried, and finally Buster went out. After a while he came back with it.' Her eyes went everywhere except to the dynamite.

'What was it stolen for?'

'I don't know, I don't know,' Leila said.

'It ain't a good thing for Buster to be mixed up in.'

'He ain't mixed up in it, I swear he ain't. I made him swear on Big-Mama's Bible. I cried and I cried and I said you got to trust Mr Buchman. Finally he said, "I got nothin' to do with it, but I'll go out and get it." Then when he came back, he said to me, "Mama, on one condition I'm gonna let you take that dynamite."'

'What condition?' Reuben said.

'He gave me a message for you,' Leila said. 'It ain't my message, I'm tellin' you that. And it ain't his. But he made me swear on Big-Mama's Bible that I'd tell it to you just like he told it to me.' She edged backwards towards the door.

'What's the message?'

'I didn't wanta give it to you, but he made me *swear*.'

'What is it?' Reuben said. 'You can tell me. You ain't never been afraid of me.'

'He said to tell you – ' She stopped and began to cry.

'What?'

'He said to tell you as far as them Klan bastards is concerned – *a Jew ain't nothin' but a nigger turned inside out!*'

He wrapped up the dynamite and put it in the Cadillac and drove to the police station.

He went past the cop on the desk and straight into Simmons' office and laid the dynamite down on the desk in the same spot he had put the bourbon the night before.

Then he unwrapped it.

Simmons eyed the dynamite. 'This ain't no ordinary thing that comes across my desk.'

'Check it with the Levitt report,' Reuben said. 'It's the same dynamite.'

'You been playin' detective?'

'Hell no,' Reuben said. 'It was at my house the whole damned time.'

'Ain't that interesting?'

'I picked it up myself from the job. I told one of Monk's boys to tell him it was me. But I guess he forgot.'

'Now what the hell would you be wantin' with dynamite?' Simmonds said. 'Especially with it bein' against the law and all.'

Reuben remembered the '47 law that prohibited the possession of dynamite by anyone whose occupation didn't warrant it. Minimum penalty, five years.

'I guess I forgot to tell you,' he said, 'I been plannin' on buildin' me a bomb shelter.' He met Simmons' eyes.

Simmons grinned. 'You're a real smart boy. That's why I always hired you any time I had need for a lawyer. I guess you're about as smart as they come.'

'I thank you for your kind words.'

'Don't mention it.'

'I been thinkin',' Reuben said. 'I been thinkin' about the possibility of the blacks doin' that bombin' and it don't make no sense to me at all.'

'You might be right,' Simmons said.

'I figured I'd just stop by and see if you'd tracked down that car.'

'Ain't that a coincidence. That's exactly what I been doin'.'

'A Rose County license tag, wasn't it?'

'You got a good memory.'

'A 1963 light blue Ford sedan, wasn't it?'

'Like I said, you got a good memory.'

'Who's it belong to?'

'Now why should I be tellin' you that?'

'Same reason I paid off the private detective your last wife put on you,' Reuben said. 'I believe I still have a copy of that file somewhere.'

'Don't put that blackmail shit on me,' Simmons said.

'Blackmail? I was talkin' about *gratitude*,' Reuben said. 'Three divorces and not a dime in alimony. How many men can say that?'

'Gerald Gunston the Third,' Simmons said.

'What do you know about him?'

'He's the man who owns the car.'

'What else?'

'He's from Rose County.'

'Black or white?'

'I ain't sure,' Simmons hedged.

'It was on the registration, wasn't it?'

'White,' Simmons said.

'Thanks,' Reuben said. It was too easy. Something about it was too easy.

'That was damned good bourbon,' Simmons said.

'We'll break out another bottle,' Reuben said. He wondered if

84

Simmons knew that there were Jews in the Confederate Army, and after that there were Jews wearing those vigilante white sheets. He wondered if Simmons saw it as ludicrous and insane and the violence of history catching him. He wondered if Simmons was one of them.

'I'd like that,' Simmons said.

'When I get back from Maryville.' Reuben watched Simmons remember that Maryville was in Rose County.

'Don't you go messin' in this,' Simmons said.

'I wouldn't think of it,' Reuben said. 'I'm goin' to a funeral.'

Ten

IT FELT LIKE NOVEMBER. The feeling of no known quantities. The sense of stalking, of being stalked. The knowledge that his senses were sharpened and wary. He could almost hear the sound of animals in the underbush. It was hunting season.

He dressed in a dark suit. Appropriate for the funeral.

Then he came over to the bed and stood over Mollie and looked down at her. With a clear head and a cold eye. She wasn't seventeen anymore. He could see that. He had known her at seventeen. What did he know about her today? Less than he knew about any of his clients.

Her lids fluttered. She opened her eyes. She looked pale and translucent, like the portrait. He heard Vernon Powell's voice. *When did she pass away?*

How many years ago?

'Good morning.' He realised he was staring at her.

She looked startled. 'I'll fix you some breakfast.' Her voice was husky with sleep. The sound of it was foreign. He wondered if he wanted to make love to her. He wondered if it would split his nerve ends.

'I don't have time,' he said. On Saturday night he had discovered he knew nothing about Justin. Last night he had discovered he knew nothing about Simmons. This morning he understood he knew nothing about Mollie.

'Coffee?' She was making offerings. He could see that. Meaningless offerings.

'No thanks,' he said. 'I'll pick you up at ten.'

She looked puzzled. 'What for?'

'Where the hell do you live?' he said. 'What the hell do you care about?'

'I don't understand.'

'Elena's funeral.'

She closed her eyes. He watched a slight shiver pass over her body. 'I don't like funerals.'

'It won't kill you,' he said.

The Williamsburg was closed on Mondays. He drove past.

The clock on the Cadillac dashboard said seven. He had three hours to get everything done.

He drove to the jail.

It wasn't much of a jail. A simple square of red brick, weathered by time and ivy, flying the state flag – the St Andrew's cross with thirteen stars. It occurred to him, now, for the first time, that the Mississippi state flag bore a Christian symbol.

He parked in front. There was nobody around. The jail held only men picked up for minor offenses or men who waited for trial. Convicted criminals were sent out to Parchman, the prison farm where Clyde Bowden's father had spent most of his life. Like father, like son. If not for Anny, he'd let Clyde rot.

He went inside. The interior had been built with the kind of space that happened in 1890. Big, but no waste. Because it had been built at the same time the new capitol was built, and the money had gone into that – a four-story replica of the national Capitol with a cathedral dome and an eight-foot gold eagle that looked out over the downtown district and lit up the city at night. Both structures, the jail and the new capitol, had been built after the Yankee left, and the new constitution had been drawn up with its grandfather clause and literacy test, designed to give the power and the vote back to the whites. And the blacks hadn't even put up a fight. Which was why, at seven in the morning, he was here to get a black man out of jail. If Clyde Bowden had been white, he would have left him here until summer.

He knew the cop on the desk. Every Christmas he and Justin distributed enough whiskey to the force to float a battleship – the whiskey was grease. Clyde had been charged with drunkenness. It took a fast thirty seconds to go through the formality of getting Clyde released into his custody. Then the cop gave him the keys.

He found Clyde sitting on his bunk in his cell, fooling around with the slide-guitar and singing the song that had got him arrested.

> 'Pick 'em up and lay 'em down . . .
> All the way from Selma town . . . '

It was the song Martin Luther King and his followers had sung from Selma to Montgomery on their march to the Alabama state capitol. King had once marched through Jackson. In the shopping centers in the white part of town, men had come out to wave Confederate flags and shout 'Nigger,' and had carried signs that read: THE ZOO WANTS YOU. Three weeks later Reuben had discovered that Mollie had gone to Lincoln Avenue to watch the march.

'What the hell happened?' Reuben knew what had happened. By now Clyde should have learned that nobody cared how much a nigger drank. It was what the whiskey brought out. Sometimes it brought out a knife in Clyde, and sometimes the radical blues. Clyde never learned.

Clyde stopped the guitar. He shrugged. 'It ain't nothin' different,' he said. 'Every Saturday night I get picked up on account of I'm black, and every Monday morning' you come and get me out on account of I'm black. I don't lose nothin' but my day in church.' He had a small sharp face the color of rye and he didn't have the size to back up his arrogance.

Reuben jangled the keys in the lock. Clyde stepped out, the guitar slung over his shoulder like a gun.

'Next time I'm gonna tell 'em to take that guitar,' Reuben said.

'Ain't gonna be no next time,' Clyde said. 'It didn't come out like a promise.

Out on the sidewalk, Reuben said, 'This is the last time I'm gonna do this. You tell your mama.'

He stopped at Sam Crawford's filling station and filled up with gas.

Sam was there like he always was, hopping around on one wooden leg and chipper as a bald canary. Sam didn't mention the bombing. For ten years, he and Sam had exchanged barbershop jokes and the weather. Now he found himself looking at Sam Crawford and wondering what the hell he really knew about Sam.

'Hey,' Reuben said, 'did you hear about the bombing?' He watched Sam's face.

'Jesus,' Sam said, 'I don't know what the world's comin' to.' He busied himself wiping the windshield. 'That's how come I'm goin' for Wallace. He'll keep peace in the streets alright. He don't fool around. This bus sure eats oil.'

Webster Asylum was ten miles outside of town. In the midst of a five-acre clearing surrounded by woods, a rambling one-story red-brick artifice was coated with moss and gnarled with barren wisteria vines. The asylum was filled with the senile who had been pensioned off by their children to live out their last years at the expense of the state in the company of the incurably mad. Elizabeth Higgins was supposed to be senile, not crazy.

The grounds were swarming with cats. He had never seen so many damn cats in his life. He came up the walk through the cats, and went under the portico and through the front door.

Immediately a guard blocked his way.

'I've got an appointment with Mrs Elizabeth Higgins.'

'No appointments today.' The guard, sporting a breastplate badge and saddled with a gleaming gun-filled holster, had a face like soft bread gone moldy. Three of his counterparts were taking a walk down the hall, moving past a lineup of closed doors, giving each one a sound tap with a nightstick.

'Buchman and Woods, Attorneys,' Reuben said. 'I'm Buchman. If I have to, I'll call the chief of police, the D.A., the governor. Whoever I have to call.'

'I got orders to clear the premises.'

'Where's the nearest phone?'

'She's in one-eighty-two,' the guard said. 'Down the hall and through the vestibule.'

Halfway down the hall, one guard stood outside an open door while inside, the other two were trying to wrench a cat away from a skinny old savage in a marabou housecoat. The guards had hold of the animal's head while she grasped at the hind legs, screaming at the top of her lungs like a railroad whistle, '*You motherfuckin' sonsabitches!*' The cat racked out between them, its eyes brimming with fright.

The vestibule was yellowed with weak sun streaming through a wall of dingy glass. A wheezing old man in high-laced boots and galluses was crocheting a string doily.

'Have you seen Abzug?' he said.

'No,' Reuben said.

Number 182 was on the other side of the vestibule. He rapped on it. The door opened a crack, and a moist eye smudged with mascara peered out.

88

'I ain't got none,' she said. 'Althea's gone. So's Tillie. That's all. Go away.' Her voice was a violin with a couple of broken strings.

'I'm a friend of Johnny's,' Reuben said. 'I want to talk to you about your son.'

She hurried him in, then slammed the door. He was enveloped by the scent of stale jasmine or decaying gardenias.

'I'm Reuben Buchman.' He took a good look at her. Thin hennaed hair frazzled with a curling iron. The mascaraed squint was buried in flesh, but above the eyes two thin black lines had been penciled, one slightly higher than the other, with a diligent vanity from some other era.

'I'm Lizzie.' The fat on her arms and neck had withered away into folds. Still, his image was third-from-the-left in a lineup of rose-trimmed garters.

Her presence on a witness stand would have about as much potential for Higgins' salvation as a thistledown wish.

She lowered herself into a wicker rocking chair. Beneath the Gauguin-printed wrapper, her breasts began to squirm and crawl in opposing directions.

He sat on the edge of the bed which was littered with movie magazines and empty Orange Crush bottles. At the foot of the bed was what looked like a green plastic sandbox. In it was cat litter, used badly and lately.

He was surrounded by clutter – a windup Victrola, a stack of quarter-inch records, plastic plants, china knickknacks, and a collection of plaster religious figurines decorated with fake pearls and glass gems. The room was no bigger than the cedar closet in Maryville where his grandmother had once stored everything in mothballs, the place he had hidden on rainy days among his dead grandfather's old boots and shotguns and stinking sheepskin jacket. The remembered smells mixed with the stale gardenia and cat litter. The one window was closed, the Venetian blind drawn tight.

'Johnny's in trouble,' he said. A sound like a shotgun blast went off outside, followed by a series of shrieks. Lizzie's left breast squirreled around again, and then a fur tail gushed from the neck of her wrapper. A lynxlike cap leapt to the floor.

'Tillie – ' Lizzie shouted. She was left with one bulging breast. She grabbed at it. Outside a second shotgun blast went off, followed immediately by another, a battery of them, like a firing squad.

Reuben went over to the window and flipped the blind. It looked like a battlefield. The grounds were littered with the dead bodies of cats. A dozen guards with shotguns were taking bead on the cats and firing. The animals were scattering in all directions, blood spurting from sudden bullet wounds. He recognised the guard who had stopped him.

He flipped the blind closed and turned around. A volley of shots sounded again.

'We feed the cats from the kitchen,' Lizzie said. 'They keep ruttin'. It costs the state too much money.' A black cat with white whiskers climbed out from Lizzie's wrapper. He remembered the woman in the marabou housecoat fighting for her cat. He remembered the old man with the crochet hook. Abzug was a cat. 'Althea –' Lizzie said. Now Lizzie was flat-chested. Althea curled up on her lap.

He could see how it was in a war. Death went on outside, but people remained wedded to their own preoccupations.

Insanity was relative. He had his own ax to grind. 'I need some information about Johnny.'

'Johnny's a good boy.' Lizzie stroked the black cat.

'Johnny's going on trial,' Reuben said. 'For assaulting a teenage boy. I have to defend him.' Why had he said *have to*?

'Johnny never hurt anybody,' Lizzie said. Outside, the gunfire went off again. Tillie had a silent spasm, but Althea didn't move a muscle.

'You're his mother,' Reuben said. 'You –'

'I ain't Johnny's mother,' she said. The shotguns went off again. 'Cora's my only natural child. It was Cora who found him. Johnny. Out in the woods. Cora was 'long about ten, I think. Johnny was a baby. We thought he was an Indian baby come from that reservation outside of Claymont. Except later he grew all that blond hair. Just like an angel. Then I knew he was marked to be a priest.'

'You mean he's adopted?'

'I guess so.' She got out of the rocking chair, opened a closet, and pulled out a big cardboard box. 'I kept all his things.' She picked up a cheap, worn-out baseball mitt. 'I kept everything. Just like he was born to me.'

'Did Johnny like girls?'

'What kind of question is that to ask a *mother*?' She dropped the mitt back into the box. 'Besides, I told you he was marked to be a priest.'

'Did he study for the priesthood?'

'He couldn't. He was always movin' around. I was a dancer, you know. We went all the way to Memphis and St Louee. Johnny and

Cora and me. A dime a dance. That was a lot of money back then.'
The gunfire went off again. She went over to the mirror and began
to powder rouge on her face. 'Then when we moved here, he was
seventeen. And that priest just looked at me and said, *We got to get
'em young.*' She sent him a smudged look in the mirror. 'He saved
them boys from drownin',' she said. 'He did a lot of good things,
Johnny did. Then he decided to be a dentist. I guess savin' teeth
ain't too far from savin' souls.'

'What about his black friends?' Reuben said.

'*Niggers?*' she said.

'Yes.'

'He didn't fool with niggers,' she said. Outside, a number of
shotguns blasted in unison. Tillie and Althea rubbed Lizzie's
legs.

'I'd like to send somebody after that box of stuff,' Reuben said.

'I don't know that I'd part with it.'

'You want to help Johnny, don't you?'

She went over to the Victrola and began to wind it. Then she
put on a record. It was a scratchy rendition of 'Ain't She Sweet?,'
loud and shrill. Outside the shotguns kept going.

'You can have it for a dance,' she said.

He didn't know anything about Justin, or Simmons, or Mollie,
or even Sam Crawford. But he knew all he needed to know about
Elizabeth Higgins.

He dug around in his pocket and found a dime.

Then he left.

It was nine fifteen when he got to his office.

When he came in, Olive was typing away.

'I sent flowers to Mrs Greenblatt at the hospital,' she said.

'That's fine.' He knew everything he needed to know about
Olive.

Luanne was back at her desk. She was wearing a blue micro-
skirt, a red shirt with white stars, and gunboat red patent oxfords.
She wiggled her fingers in the air at him and flashed an adoring
smile. He knew all he wanted to know about Luanne. He didn't
screw around in his own back yard.

He hung his overcoat on the brass tree. Justin's coat was already
there. At the top of the stairs, he went past Justin's office without
turning his head. Anything else he needed to know about Justin
would have to originate with Justin.

At his desk, he buzzed Olive.

'Cancel all my appointments,' he said. 'Or shift what you can to

Mr Woods and Mr Sandifer. I've got to go to my aunt's funeral in Maryville.'

'Oh – I'm so sorry,' Olive said.

'Thank you.'

'I wonder what the third thing will be?'

'What third thing?'

'Tragedy comes in threes.'

'That's very helpful information,' he said. 'Call my wife and tell her I'll pick her up at ten.'

'Yessir.'

'And get Bill Thatcher on the phone for me. You can probably get hold of him in his judge's chambers.'

'Yessir. Anything else?'

'Stop being a disaster hound.'

While he waited for the call, he went through the paper. An unmanned lunar module was orbiting the earth – prologue to setting two astronauts down on the moon. L.B.J. had made a speech in Dallas, promising no weakening of will in Vietnam. The President's National Advisory Commission on Civil Disorders had released a 1,400-page report on the summer riots of 1967 in Newark, Detroit, Chicago, and Watts. A fire in a mental hospital in England had killed twenty-two people. And there was a photograph of a frowning Simmons at the site of the bombing at 908 Maple. The caption read: WE'RE NOT GOING TO STAND FOR THIS IN MISSISSIPPI.

The red light flickered on the phone.

Reuben picked it up. 'How the hell are you?' He had known Bill Thatcher since law school. Bill had become the youngest judge in the state, a collector of Civil War memorabilia, and a dedicated southern historian. Bill's wife had died two years ago, no children – Bill's antidote to loneliness had become weekend quail hunts on his farm outside of Holmesdale. That was everything Reuben knew about Bill Thatcher – enough to come up with a way to get what he wanted without sticking his neck out.

'I'm fine. What's on your mind?'

'I need a favor. I've got a Yankee industrialist coming down in a couple of weeks – he's considering putting up a factory in Claymont. He wants to go quail hunting.' Reuben tried to imagine Isadore Rabin out there with a shotgun. A little urban Jewish man. Never. The biggest thing Izzy Rabin had ever hunted was a pastrami sandwich. But he had to make it an exchange of favors. He could not come out and simply ask for it.

'Why the hell not?' Thatcher said.

'What can I do for you?'

'Forget it. I'll hold it.'

'I like to pay as I go. Who've you got as public defender on the John Tyler Higgins case?'

'Are you kidding? There's nobody standing in line for it. We'll probably get stuck with an A.C.L.U. guy. Bastards –'

'How'd you like me to get that off your back?'

'That's a stiff price for a quail hunt,' Thatcher said, 'but you've got yourself a deal.'

'See you in court.' Reuben hung up. He grinned. He thought about Isadore Rabin shooting quail. Never. The grin vanished. He wondered if Isadore Rabin had gotten news of the bombing. Then he realised that Bill Thatcher hadn't mentioned the bombing.

He looked up and saw that Justin was standing in the doorway like a man who had something on his mind.

Justin came across the office and stood on the other side of the desk, and what he did was put out his hand.

Reuben looked at the hand. Then he looked at Justin's face. Then he put out his own hand. The handclasp was mute, with a lot of unsaid things in it, most of which Reuben needed.

'What the hell's that for?' Reuben growled.

'It's Monday morning,' Justin said. 'It's just the way I like to start the week.'

Then he was gone.

Eleven

IT WAS A two-hour drive to Maryville.

Outside of Holmesdale, the Cadillac passed tenant shacks perched on stilts, smoke streaming from chimneys askew on slanted tar-paper roofs, littered yards dotted with bright clothes flapping in the February wind. There was a cold, gray, colorless sky.

Thirty miles outside the city limits, Reuben watched the delta begin. The strip, a hundred and fifty miles long and fifty miles wide, had once been a riverbed. The Cadillac hugged the flat white road as he drove past the cotton fields – land newly ploughed up and ready to be planted in its cotton allotment; land lying fallow earning government money for idleness. One way or another the delta plantation owners pulled a quarter of a billion dollars out of the soil. But the soil meant more than money. Even to men like himself, who no longer lived on it or drew their livelihood from it, the soil meant identity. It was there with its assertion of continuity, like the Mississippi River or the Mississippi sun or the Mississippi sky. Like the three-dollar-a-day blacks who had been ousted by mechanised farming, Reuben lived in the city, worked in the city, and still, the soil belonged to him. The Yankee could never comprehend the southern truth. A man, black or white, didn't have to own the land to be of it.

In his grandfather's time, Maryville had been known as the golden buckle on the cotton belt. His grandfather's land remained the same. The same cycle of planting and hoeing and praying and picking. The ownership changed. The cycle remained. That made the land still his.

Beside him, Mollie was silent. He could see her from the corner of his eye. The bottom half of her face was buried in the Christmas mink. Her eyes were glazed and fixed on the road. He knew nothing about her. It remained a new thought. Then the corollary of this morning's discovery sprang to his mind. *She knew nothing about him.*

In the rear-view mirror he could see Frieda in the back seat, buried in caracul. For that instant, she, too, seemed a stranger.

He wondered if anybody ever knew anybody.

'What's going to happen?' Frieda said.

He looked at the dashboard clock. They were thirty minutes away from Maryville. 'I've got no crystal ball,' he said.

In the rear-view mirror she sent him a look he knew well. Her eyes lit with fear and aggression, then clouded over with pain. It was a look that provoked thoughts of Jesse.

He hadn't known Jesse. Jesse hadn't known him.

He remembered a Sunday. At the military school in Biloxi. Frieda had been ill with the flu. Jesse had driven down alone. *I want to go home, Papa.* His ass had been crisscrossed with black and blue marks. He had showed them to Jesse. Jesse hadn't blinked an eye. *Your mama thinks it's the right thing. You got to get a good education.* Reuben had shouted, *Goddamn you.*

Jesse had hit him.

'Slow down, please, Reuben,' Mollie said.

He looked at the accelerator. He was going ninety. When he looked out through the windshield again, he realised they were going through the three thousand acres the old man had once owned.

He pulled off onto the side of the road.

In the mirror, he saw Frieda's face. No need to explain it to her. It was the place he had stopped on the day of his father's funeral.

He got out and started to walk. He didn't look back.

There was the break in the fence that had been there then. He went through it, his back to the highway and the rich black alluvial land stretching out in front of him. The old man had once owned three thousand acres of the richest land in the state. The history of the Buchman family had been written here, in the furrowed dirt and the pines beyond. In the land was the reality of legacy, and the presence of the ghosts who had made it.

Each time he walked it, he went back. To see how it must have been when Joe Buchman laid eyes on this land for the first time. Each time he went back to that time in history, 1892, the Yankee gone, and the carpetbaggers defeated and the land swarming with blacks looking for a master. And he could see how it had been for Joe Buchman. Because, like the Jew, the South had survived captivity and bled under the heel of an oppressor. Like the Jew, the South had endured destruction of property, oppressive tax burdens, alien government, and unjust courts. Like the Jew, the South had been deprived of mastery of its own fate.

The Yankee had set out to destroy the southern world. He had succeeded at Appomattox but had failed in the crucial battle of mind and will. The desire to make over the South in the prevailing American image had failed. In 1892, when Joe Buchman arrived, the South was setting about to vindicate the will of a Calvinised Jehovah, which decreed that the South, like the Jew, would reclaim its primal tenets and rise again.

The Yankee and the czar were the same. The southerner and the immigrant Jew had both been victims. Both felt themselves chosen people, dedicated to reestablishing their dignity. In the affinity of the recently oppressed, the immigrant Jew and the trampled southerner joined hands in a common goal: reclamation of land, self-mastery, regional destiny. Joe Buchman had a goal; the South had a goal; the goals turned out to be one and the same.

And were passed on. The priorities of commitment remained the same.

He walked the land. In touch with his grandfather, with his father. Under his feet, now, was the section of land that had been earmarked for Jesse. Jesse had once walked it off with him, every step.

Jesse had told him how the land had been taken from him. How the old man hadn't expected to die, ever, and hadn't left a will.

And in the fight that followed his grandfather's death, Jesse, in anger, had announced to his brothers, *All I want is papa's cane!*

They had thrown in the tallis for good measure.

Jesse had carried the angry act of integrity to his grave. The tallis was ragged, moth-eaten; the cane was an old hand-whittled stick carved by an old black named Sampson, long dead. The tallis not used since Russia. The cane used in the last years of Joe Buchman's life.

That was his father's legacy. In goods. In property. But legacies were not measured in goods or property. The cane and the tallis remained. And the land remained. And he, Reuben, remained – born on the day of his grandfather's death, on the day that the '27 flood had swept everything off, born with the sense of one soul carrying on for another.

Now, as he walked, the images came up from the land. The depth of the legacy that went all the way back to 1892. Now today was to be dealt with. A light blue Ford that belonged to an unknown entity named Gerald Gunston III.

His grandfather's house had once been in the best part of town, but the blacks had moved in a long time ago. Reuben drove into the street, overrun with chickens and an occasional pig. The street hadn't been paved in forty years, but his grandmother Sarah had always refused to move as staunchly as she had held onto the old wood stove and the old-fashioned icebox. She had outlived the old man by twenty years. Reuben could remember how, in the last years of her life, Sarah had believed she was back in the Ukrainian *shtetl* as she sat in the rocker on the veranda and greeted the passing blacks with names from her childhood: *Shalom Moishe* and, *Gimpel*, and *Yitschok*. And the blacks would tip their caps and respond, having grown accustomed to it.

He pulled up to the house. It looked like it had always looked, maybe worse but not much. Willie had screened in the veranda thirty years ago; it hadn't taken long to rust and decay, and nobody had touched it since. The fig trees had closed in, and Reuben remembered that the porch was always in shadow, even at high noon in the summer, the porch and the house beyond as dark as a cave. He never laid eyes on the house without thinking: *It wasn't always like this;* although he had never seen it any other way. It was exactly as it had been when he was a kid, exactly as it had been the first time he had brought Mollie up from New Orleans, in the summer of '48.

He climbed out of the car. In his mind's eye, he could still see his grandmother, in the rocking chair on the screened veranda, and he had been bringing Mollie up the walk. He could still remember what Mollie had worn, a blue dress with puffed sleeves and a big straw hat. His grandmother was almost eighty and shrunken, but the bones had still been there, with a look to her that was slightly macabre, between the living and the dead a mere decimal of difference.

This is Mollie . . . he had said. Sarah had rocked back and forth. It hadn't been February, it had been the blazing heat of June, but the porch had been dark and damp.

Sarah's face had clouded over. *Rachel . . . ?* she had said. Reuben had no idea who Rachel had been; Sarah's faculties came and went. She beckoned to him. When he came close, she said, *Joe . . . you won't be happy with Rachel.* He realised she believed he was his grandfather. A strange look came over her face, a fluttering of eyelids, an unmistakable look of seduction.

I'm Reuben, he said, uncomfortable.

Reuben?

This is Mollie. He tried again. *We're going to get married.*

The rocker creaked. Sarah's eyes wouldn't leave his face. *I'll go to Moscow. I'll get a yellow card. Is that what you want?* She put a hand out and touched his cheek. *America,* she said. *You and Rachel and me. We'll go to America.*

Bubby – I'm Reuben.

She dropped her hand. She turned her head and looked at Mollie. *A shana madele,* she said. Then her eyes crept back to Reuben's face. *You're just like him,* she said. *Just like Joe. . . .*

He opened the car doors for Mollie and Frieda, then led them up the walk. There was no more pretense at a garden, only weeds and gravel, a few patches of grubby earth with a chicken pecking around. Then the door to the porch opened and there was Willie.

Willie looked exactly as Reuben remembered, his light hair still parted in the middle, though he was a bit thinner on top and all over too. The same elongated face with its tentative grin and colorless eyebrows, dressed in the county patrol uniform he had always liked to wear, even off duty. He looked shaken and frail – the stranger who had married into the Buchman family. Now Elena was dead, and Reuben could see Willie felt himself a stranger again, thrown back into being Methodist-Willie, the redneck farm boy who had run off and married Elena on the same day the old man's body had washed up. Afterwards, Elena and Willie had

7.

moved into the old man's house with Sarah, their wedding presents from the town never unpacked and gathering cobwebs in a closed room for all the days of their marriage until Sarah died.

He climbed up onto the veranda. Sarah's old rocker was there, creaking in the wind.

'The boys are all here,' Willie said.

From inside the house, Reuben could hear the sound of the boys – his father's brothers, all now in their sixties, but the description still fit and would until the day each was buried. Mollie and Frieda went through the front door. He stayed behind a moment with Willie.

'I want to see you later. Alone,' Reuben said.

Willie's face broke with gratitude. 'I knew it was gonna be alright.'

'I want to go over to City Hall. While the family's eating lunch.' The criminal records were kept in the sheriff's office located in City Hall.

'Anything you want.' Willie didn't ask why. His face flushed. 'You're a good man.' Reuben had no idea what he was talking about.

They went inside. The hall went the length of the house but no light came from the back door which had been bolted shut against the wind. To his left was the living room with its horsehair furniture, huge and out of scale, thrusting the black carved heads of eagles for arms and feet. Frieda stood by the piano with its array of old photographs. Mollie sat on the ottoman at the foot of his grandfather's chair. His uncles were waiting for him.

Itz, the oldest, stood by the fireplace, his long neck stuck out, looking like the failed eagle he was, guilt and defeat written over his face. It had been forty years since Itz lost his share of the land by gambling on the stock market; the crash had taken everything. After that Itz had become a Rose County bootlegger, a natural choice since he was the one who had always run the still for the old man. But Itz had never made enough to buy back the land; the state had been dry since 1908, there were plenty of bootleggers around. Then, two years ago, the state went wet, putting Itz out of business. The second defeat had reactivated the first; it was the face of a beaten man.

'You look fine, boy,' Itz said.

'He sure does,' Reb said. The middle one. Reb came around the overstuffed chair and clapped Reuben heartily on the shoulder. 'You sure look fine, boy.' Long and lean and still wearing the professional glasses, nicknamed Reb for *rabbi*, because he had once spent a year in his youth at an agricultural college, the only one of the Buchman boys to get any education. The education had paid off, once; Reb had been the one to suggest to the old man that they buy an old army plane and get rid of the boll weevil by dusting the cotton crop from the air. Old man Joe had agreed, and at the age of fifty-two, the old man who had been born in Russia had learned how to fly.

'Yessir,' Reb said, 'you look real successful.' Reb sent a look at Mollie, appraising the mink. 'Wish I could say the same, I sure do. But I done made my mistakes like the rest.'

Reuben understood Reb's mistakes. When the old man died, Reb had sold off his legacy, sold the land for the privilege of a business suit and a cotton broker's office. Then the government began paying the farmers for not planting cotton, and the traffic that passed through a cotton broker's office had dwindled away through the years. Reb's face had the look of a man who had gambled on the wrong card. Reuben felt a terrible satisfaction looking into it.

'What he means is,' Nate said, 'we ain't got no money for funeral expenses.' Nate was sunk into a horsehair chair, looking beefy and barrel-chested and unhappy to be there.

'I told you,' Willie said, 'I can call my brother in St Louis. I told you. My brother'll send me – '

'It's a family decision,' Nate said. 'We don't make no family decisions without Reuben.' He looked at Reuben. 'That's right, ain't it ?'

'That's right.' Reuben looked at Nate. Nate had held onto his share of the land by marrying an Atlanta aristocrat after she had lost a leg in a riding accident. She had brought class and she had brought money, along with a beautiful face, an artificial leg from Germany, and an iron will. At the moment, after thirty-five years of marriage, she was in the process of divorcing Nate and suing in court for the land. Reuben knew what the outcome would be. Like the other two, Nate had made a bad gamble and lost. Like somewhere up there, the old man knew what had happened and was paying them back.

'Nobody pays for a Buchman funeral except Buchmans,' Reuben said. They had taken the land, Jesse had taken only the old man's cane. The land was gone, the cane remained. They were big, Jesse had been the short one. They were here, alive; Jesse was dead. Yet Jesse seemed bigger than any of them, and more alive than they were. And beyond that, there was the presence of the old man, his grandfather, stronger than anything in this room. There was a question in that: How did that come to be?

'I knew you'd say that,' Reb said. 'I told 'em before you got here. I said Reuben ain't gonna let – '

'You're damned right,' Reuben said. 'Nobody but a Buchman pays for a Buchman's funeral, and it looks like I'm gonna do it because it looks like I'm the only Buchman around with a pot to piss in.'

'Have respect for the dead,' Frieda said.

'I hope to hell,' Reuben said, 'that the dead have some respect for me.'

He took Willie to lunch at the Downtown Cafe.

It was three blocks to downtown, laid around a square dominated by City Hall and the inevitable statue of the Confederate soldier. A few feeble attempts at modernisation like Aaron Pulitzer's drugstore only served to heighten the untouched state of the rest. Men on the street waved, greeted Willie, greeted him, men who planted and hunted possum and drank the same liquor and owed the same Memphis bank. Walking beside him, Willie was as nervous as a bucket of bass.

The Downtown Cafe was across the street from City Hall. Inside a jukebox was playing 'Moon River.' A counter on one side, a line of pink plastic booths on the other. The counter was filled, the third booth was empty; they took it.

'I got to tell you somethin',' Willie said. 'I can't hold it no longer.'

'I'm listenin'.' With Willie, he talked like Willie.

'They don't know it,' Willie said, 'but Elena left you the house.' His hands on the Formica table were shaking.

'Me?'

Willie nodded.

'Why?'

'You know why. It was the old man's house. She couldn't leave it to me. Elena was a Buchman. She had to leave the house to a Buchman. You're the old man's heir. That's how she saw it. She promised Sarah. Before Sarah died.' Willie's face cracked like an old china plate.

'I'll be damned,' Reuben said.

'Elena married me,' Willie said, 'but she never was anything beside a Buchman. Like all the rest of you. It didn't matter to me. I loved her. I loved your grandma too. It was like I was married to both of 'em. I took care of them and they took care of me. People thought I was crazy, but I never had much of a family before. I liked it. I don't wanna leave that house, Reuben. I know it's yours now, but I don't wanna have to leave it while I'm alive. 'Its all I got left.' Willie looked like a man waiting to be sentenced for a crime he hadn't committed but felt guilty of anyway.

'I have to think about it.' Reuben picked up the menu. The waitress came over. The menu was predictable: ham hocks and turnip greens, black-eyed peas and cornbread. Reuben ordered all of it. When the waitress left, he lit a cigarette.

'I tell you, Willie,' he said. 'I've got a little favor of my own to ask.'

Twelve

THE CITY HALL corridor was one of the caves of his childhood. Benches lined the walls. A couple of farmers waited for appointments wearing tough weather-beaten faces filled with stoic despair. Nothing had changed. Even the sign at the other end: $5 FINE FOR SPITTING ON THE FLOOR. In between, the portraits of local heroes marched solemnly across, prim bewhiskered faces with the stern expressions of men who posed for posterity.

The old man hung where he'd always hung, next to Theodore Bilbo. Each time Reuben came back there was always the moment when he looked at his grandfather and felt himself regress to the kid in the corduroy knickers. Frieda had made him wear knickers; everyone else had worn overalls. He used to come to the old man to talk about it. Then he had looked at Joe Buchman with the eyes of a kid. Later he had learned that in the early twenties, while Theodore Bilbo had been building the boat to Ship the Negroes Back to Africa, Joe Buchman had been initiating the first cooperative cotton gin in Rose County. Bilbo had been elected United States Senator, the old man had been elected mayor of Maryville. Reuben had learned there were many ways to immortality.

'I liked him,' Willie said. 'He was always runnin' me off, but I liked him anyway. He was somethin'. You know, the older you get, the more you look like the old Litvak.'

'Why'd they call him the Litvak ?' Reuben said. 'He came from the Ukraine. Litvaks come from Lithuania.'

Willie scratched his thinning hair. 'I don't know nothin' about them places. I ain't never been out of Rose County.'

'You better get to our business,' Reuben said.

'You're right,' Willie said. But he stood there, getting his courage together.

'We don't have a helluva lot of time.'

'You're right.'

'Goddamnit – '

Willie moved then. He scurried the length of the corridor and disappeared up a stairway. Reuben sat on a bench, lit a cigarette, and looked at the portrait of his grandfather. Behind the bushy white beard and the thick white brows was a face carved from contradiction and daring. How the hell did a man get the guts to come clean around the world to a place where he didn't even know the language ? Back then it must have been like it was now to think about going to the damned moon.

The story had come down in pieces. How Joe and Sarah had come from somewhere in the Ukraine. How they had started out with plenty of money, but Joe had given it all to a pregnant girl on the boat who had lost her husband. Without a nickel, they had landed in New York, ending up near the Bowery. Joe had taken a job as night watchman; his payment had been rags left on the floor which he would bundle up and sell until he'd been arrested for peddling without a license. Those were the facts of it. Then the old man had discovered the dream of Baron de Hirsch, the dream that matched his – the Jewish back-to-the-land movement. Joe and Sarah had left the land of dingy tenements and struck out for a commune in Louisiana with a hundred and fifty other Jews, unprepared for the ravages of heat and rain and mosquitoes and malaria and yellow fever. The colony's life had been short. Surrounded by deserted plantations and rattlesnakes and mosquitoes and floods, Jews who had fled from the czar could not cope with the land. But the old man had gotten a taste of it. He took the river up to Natchez and went in search of his own land, his own place. With nothing but guts and a dream in his head. And damned if he hadn't made it a fact. The old man had done it. Nobody – not Gerald Gunston III, not anybody – could destroy that.

It was twenty minutes and three cigarettes. Then Willie came back wearing a victory grin and carrying a manila envelope.

'You were right.'

'What'd you get?'

'He's got a record alright. I took the file to the City Clerk's office and xeroxed it. Nobody asked me one damned question.'

Reuben took the envelope. 'Let's go. We've got ten minutes to get to the funeral.'

'I did alright, didn't I?'

'You did fine.'

They came down the steps of City Hall. A farmer was asleep on the bench and three pigeons perched on the head of the Confederate soldier.

'I know the guy that arrested Gunston,' Willie said. 'I can take you out to talk to him after the funeral.'

'What's his name?'

'Doan Newberry. He's a night marshal. I know myself when I take somebody in, there's always stuff they leave out of the record. What a guy says, sometimes. They don't put that in a record.'

'You're a damned good detective.'

'I'm glad you like me,' Willie said.

They crossed the street and got into the car. Reuben locked the file in the glove compartment along with the forty-five. 'Whatever else happens, Willie, it's okay with me about the house.' He started the car. From the corner of his eye he watched Willie's face. Relief and guilt began a battle. Willie opened his mouth, then closed it again.

Reuben pulled out into the square. A small black sedan pulled out behind him. 'The old man, I think he would have liked that,' Reuben said. He headed east, towards the cemetery.

'I ain't a Buchman,' Willie said. That was the crime he felt guilty of; he confessed it.

'You are by me,' Reuben said.

A spiked wrought-iron fence marked off the cemetery, the wind blowing through with nothing to break it. Over the gate hung the fire bell that had once belonged to Maryville's first fire company. It was the only bell around that had escaped being melted and molded into cannon balls during the Civil War. It had been rung, for years, only for funerals. It could be heard throughout town. Nobody had rung it for Elena's funeral.

Willie headed for the gravesite where the handful of people had gathered. Reuben stood at the gate, looking at the bell, and remembering how when Jesse died, Jesse's friends had taken turns at it; the bell had rung for twenty-four hours straight. People had come from miles around, merchants and rednecks and landowners and tenant-farmers, fifty gentiles to every Jew, and twice as many blacks. Jesse hadn't been a saint but Jesse had been born to the delta and its people. There had been those who remembered Jesse as a wild young man riding the cotton fields with the Litvak and gambling all night in town. There had been those who remembered him later, in the general store: *By Gawd, I remember your paw when we used to hide the whiskey in the lettuce bin.* There had been those who had said to Reuben with honest pride: *We hear you done good, boy, over there in Holmesdale. Yessir, we hear about you.* It would have taken a dozen buses to cart the mourners away.

When he looked up, Monk was striding towards the gate, his overcoat collar pulled up around his ears, and grinning.

'Goddamn you,' Reuben said. He was touched.

'Hell,' Monk said. 'You came all the way down to New Orleans for my mama's funeral. Nobody else did that.'

They moved through the gate. Reuben had the impulse to ring the bell. But it was too late for that. He was grateful for Monk. At some other time in history, he and Monk might have slain dragons together. A hundred years ago, they might have hunted bear. What they were to each other now had to do with the times. Comrades through marriages and births and funerals.

'When the service is over, how about taking Mollie and my mother back to Holmesdale with you? I've got some loose ends to clear up here.'

'Sure,' Monk said.

'Thanks.'

'I owe you a favor,' Monk said.

'We're friends,' Reuben said. 'We don't owe each other.'

'Simmons called me about the dynamite,' Monk said. 'You got me clean off the hook. Where the hell did you get dynamite from?'

'I hatched it.' Reuben grinned.

'That was a damned good trick.'

'Maybe you'd better forget that dog and get yourself a night watchman.'

There was no crowd. Elena had lived as a recluse. Reuben could count the mourners on his fingers. There were those he had brought with him from Holmesdale. There was Aaron Pulitzer, the pharmacist, with his shock of white hair and tortoise shell glasses, a self-taught man who had been Jesse's best friend. Aaron Pulitzer's father had come from Kiev after the pogroms of 1905. Nobody else from town had showed up. Only the boys, his uncles, with two of their wives looking old and hard put together. Nate's estranged wife had stayed away. And there were none of the children, the cousins from his childhood, not one. Itz's son had been killed in Korea; his daughter had married a traveling salesman from Sioux Falls, Iowa. Reb had three daughters. The oldest, like her father, had gone to agricultural college, and was working in Washington for the government; the middle one had married an insurance man from Chattanooga, Tennessee; the youngest had gone off to work as a secretary in Memphis. Nate's marriage had produced one son who had been sent back, by his mother, to a military academy in Georgia, living on weekends with Nate's ex-in-laws.

That left Willie and himself. That was it – the pitiable remains of what had once been the wealth and power in the Mississippi delta.

And Rabbi Hellman. Come over from Greenborough. A small, bespectacled man in a yarmulke who had always been a transient part of their lives when God couldn't be avoided. It was Hellman who had buried Sarah, Hellman who had confirmed Reuben, Hellman who had married Reuben to Mollie, and Hellman who had presided at Jesse's funeral. Hellman had shared the honor with Lucius Honeycutt, the Maryville Baptist preacher, who had insisted on giving a sermon of his own.

The memory of Hellman's traditional words had dimmed. But Lucius Honeycutt was as vivid and real to him today as then – a tall, craggy man, master of rhetoric and charged gestures. He had spoken of sin and damnation and the wreckage of human lives; then of hope and salvation; of the dependence of men in faith. *Our roots are in the earth*, Lucius Honeycutt had said, *but the earth is not ours. It does not belong to us. We belong to it.* Then he had described the men who had come into the wilderness to tame it; he had pointed out the common denominator between men of different religious beliefs, addressing himself to the men who had come from the land and who would return to the land – men, like Jesse, who would never be forgotten.

Now it was Hellman who spoke. Hellman began with the power and the glory of the Buchman family, went on to a few regrets for their lack of religious piety, concluded they were all good human beings in the sight of God, Elena among the best. Then he began the Hebrew prayer. Frieda began to weep.

Reuben turned his back on it.

He went down the path until he reached Jesse's grave. The grave was in decent shape; Frieda sent a check every month to Aaron Pulitzer, who saw it was taken care of. He looked at Jesse's inscription:

Look not on his countenance, or on the height of his stature; for it is not as man seeth; for man looketh on the outward appearance, but the Lord looketh on the heart.

The inscription was from I Samuel:16. Reuben had picked it himself. He had selected it instinctively, had never questioned why. Now, as he stood there, the significance crept into his consciousness, unbidden, as if it had been patiently waiting there, biding its time. And now it came – the meaning of the inscription, the meaning of his relationship with Jesse.

Over Jesse, always, had been the shadow of the old man. There it was. He, Reuben, had imprisoned Jesse within the shadow of his grandfather. He, Reuben, had put Jesse into competition with old man Joe. For all of Jesse's life. And Jesse had lost.

Inside his chest, something cracked as he saw what he had no wish to see. In the words of the inscription, he had looked on his father's countenance, and on the height of his father's stature, and on his father's outward appearance – and he had made his secret judgments. And Jesse had understood the contempt that Reuben had felt for Jesse's failure as a man.

The long-buried source of his guilt washed over him. He stood at his father's grave, thinking about the man who had been his father – the man named for Jesse James who had once been known as a wild one; the man who had been tamed and civilised into something he was not, by forces he had never understood. The man who had worked sixteen hours a day so that Reuben could become what he was; the same man who had refused to take pride in Reuben's success because he could not collaborate in the secret, unspoken judgments that relegated him to the land of failure.

There was no way now to undo that. No way to go back. No way even to become friends. The idea of mortality was bearable, but the finality of death was not. He had judged Jesse with cruelty; he had forfeited Jesse; that could never be undone.

Someday, his sons would judge him.

I loved you. He closed his eyes. *I'm sorry.*

But he understood what had cracked in him, and he knew it had never been settled between them, and it would not be settled today. Because the cracking had been the irrevocable knowledge of loss – not the loss of Jesse in death, but the loss of Jesse in life.

I want him. I want my father. It was not Jesse he addressed. From somewhere, silent, the answer came. *Never.*

He moved on to the old man's grave.

Sarah had been buried next to his grandfather, the grave crawling with weeds. He made a mental note to have Willie clean it up and keep it that way.

He stood there, refusing to think anymore, sheltered by the belief that wherever his grandfather was, he wasn't beneath those weeds, and if there was anything to be said between them, it wouldn't be said there. Graveyards were for the living, not for the dead.

There was no inscription. Only the facts:

JOSEF BUCHMAN
BORN: NOVEMBER, 1867
DIED: MARCH 22, 1927

The day of the old man's death was the day of Reuben's birth. He had not been named for his grandfather. The Litvak had been carried off by the flood, his body not found for almost a week. In the hope that the old man had survived, Jesse had not named him for his grandfather. By Jewish tradition, to name a child for the living confused the heavenly bookkeeping system which maintained a place for each soul by name. Reuben was five days old when the Litvak's body was brought back by a convict who had been sent out in a skiff to rescue survivors. Sarah had paid fifty dollars for the body. Reuben had attended the funeral in his father's arms. The memory, though not recallable, had left its profound effect.

Reuben turned away.

That's when the old man tripped him. Nothing in the way except weeds and pebbles and wind. But his ankle gave way.

'You old sonofabitch – ' Reuben said. 'What the hell are you trying to do?'

He listened. Nothing came back but the wind.

Thirteen

WILLIE DROVE.

Reuben went through the contents of the manila envelope.

It was ten miles outside of Maryville, off the highway, and onto the gravel Chickasaw Road. Across the bridge that spanned Toby

Tubby Creek, named for the Indian chief who was buried at the mouth of the creek where it ran into the Pearl. After that the car bounced along through a patch of woods over a rutted dirt road.

The contents of the brown envelope jogged along in front of his eyes:

Gerald Gunston III
Age: 21
Born: Claymont, Mississippi; October 10, 1947
Occupation: None
Physical description: Six feet, one inch, 155 pounds; medium brown hair, hazel eyes; American eagle tattoo on left forearm.
Special characteristics: Is known always to carry on his person a Scofield Bible and Concordance.
Mother: Mrs Hattie Gunston; credit manager at Claymont Auto Parts.
Father: Gerald Gunston II; real estate salesman.
Siblings: Wilhelmina Gunston, age 17; Foster Gunston, age 14.
First incident: September, 1961. Cited for disturbing the peace during the first integration of Claymont High School. Tried in Juvenile Court. Reprimanded on condition of psychiatric help.
First Legal Offense: July, 1963. Arrested for possession of sawed-off shotgun. Eighteen months suspended sentence.
Second Legal Offense: December, 1967. Arrested for reckless driving, with companion, Frank Flowers. Possession of fully loaded .45-caliber machine gun, unauthorised deadly weapon. Released on bond. Tried one week later. Flowers set free by jury. Gunston did not appear. Later information reports that Gunston has left for the state of Alabama, and cannot be extradited for a misdemeanor.
Latest investigation reports that the submachine gun in question was stolen from a National Guard armory in Holmesdale. A fugitive warrant has been issued, but Gunston has not been found.
Known Associates:
Dean Leland Goss. Age 38; of Cranston, Miss.; owner and operator of Goss Electrical Co., doing business in Cranston and Holmesdale. Identified as a member of the White Knights of the Ku Klux Klan, and member and often spokesman for the Americans for the Preservation of the White Race.
Fred R. L. Watson. Age 26; self-employed sign painter and novelty salesman of Claymont, Miss. A member of the Americans for the Preservation of the White Race.

The name Fred R. L. Watson stopped him. Fred R. L. Watson was the Claymont redneck who had caused the trouble with Rabin at the Ko-Bee factory site. The same redneck Justin had promised the job of foreman.

He went back to his reading. *Known Associates* was a barrel of snakes:

Robert 'Army' Jones. Age 23. Truck driver from Holmesdale, Miss. Identified as a member of the White Knights of the Ku Klux Klan. Indicted in 1964 on state charges of illegal possession of 105 sticks of dynamite. Released on bond.

Elmos Rawlins. Age 35. Farmer in Harrisburg, Miss. Identified as a former state senator of the White Knights of the Ku Klux Klan. Federally indicted and convicted in 1964 on conspiracy charges against three civil rights workers. Released on bond pending appeal.

Floyd Rawlins. Age 32. Harrisburg, Miss. Employed as nightclub bouncer in Holmesdale, Miss. Indicted in 1964 on charges of assaulting a newsman. Found not guilty.

Frank Flowers. Age 54. Gulfport businessman. Identified as Grand Imperial Wizard of the White Knights of the Ku Klux Klan. Federally indicted and convicted in 1964 on conspiracy charges against three civil rights workers. Released on bond pending appeal.

His mind raced putting it together. Last December, Doan Newberry had stopped Gunston for reckless driving. Gunston's companion was Frank Flowers, grand imperial wizard of the Klan. They had a machine gun. Flowers showed up for the trial, was let off; Gunston disappeared. The bevy of cronies were all Kluckers, all indicted for crimes, and all walking around free as pigeons.

It was a barrel of *rattlers*.

Willie stopped the car at the end of the dirt road. In front of the car was a frame cabin that had once been two rooms but had been expanded with a porch running across the front and along the side. A chimney ran up each side of the cabin, and there was a dogtrot alongside enclosed with a fence. The cabin sat facing the road from the edge of a field that went on for about a mile and a half before the woods began. There was a small vegetable garden on the right and behind that, a lean-to shed. As Willie cut the motor, the quiet was shattered by a series of blood-curdling screams from the shed. The hound dog began to howl like a coyote. Then the door to the shack opened and a woman came out onto the porch wearing an apron and a man's sweater, wispy hair pulled back into a knot and a face that looked like wet sand. She recognised Willie and waved. The screams abruptly quit.

'Doan's hog-killin'!' she shouted.

Willie waved back. Reuben got out of the car. The woman went back into the house. The hound dog paced the dogtrot silently, waiting for his share of the carcass. The rest would go into cured hams and sausage and hogshead cheese and backbones and spare ribs and chitlins. Doan Newberry was late. Hog-killing time was usually in December; the pork eaten fresh in winter, and cured in the spring, and salted in the summer.

Willie led him around the lean-to. Two dead hogs were laid out, their throats slit from ear to ear, eyes bulging and blood soaking into the dirt. Doan Newberry wiped his hands on a butcher's coat, leaving a red-striped trail over the spatters that had already left their mark. He had a pale Scotch-Irish face, an angular nose, watery blue eyes, and a head of thin, corn-silk hair. There was one other singular feature. A piece at the top of his left ear was missing.

'Damnit Willie,' Doan said, 'you shouldn't bring no company without tellin' me first.'

'It ain't company,' Willie said. 'It's my nephew, Reuben Buchman.'

Newberry peered at him. Reuben saw the recognition flick up in the watery blue eyes.

'We went to school together,' Reuben said. 'Maryville Grammar School. Miss Callaway.'

'I'll be damned,' Newberry said. 'You're the Jew-boy who wore the knickers.'

'And you're the redneck who beat me up for 'em,' Reuben said. 'But I don't hold no grudges.'

Newberry's hand went to his left ear, as he remembered it was Reuben's ax that had severed the missing piece. Then he laughed, a sound like a whooping crane.

'I never woulda knowed you,' he said. 'Come on in. Come on inside.' He grinned. '*I don't hold no grudges. Hell!*'

He led them over to the house. When they reached the porch, he stopped and peered at Reuben again. 'Nossir,' he said. 'Never woulda knowed you.' He grinned. 'You *bastard*.'

Inside, the woman was stirring a pot on a black butane stove. There was the smell of dumplings and ham fat.

'Better haul them carcasses onto the side porch,' Newberry said to her. 'I don't want no foxes to have a good time with 'em.'

The woman nodded and went out.

Newberry opened a rusty icebox and brought out three beers, flipping the tops with his teeth and handing them around. Then he gestured at the hand-hewn board table. They sat down. There was a leftover pan of biscuits and a half-eaten apple pie.

'What can I do for you?' Newberry said. His eyes stayed on Reuben.

'He wants to know about Gerald Gunston,' Willie said.

'Goddamn, Willie, that's official business.'

'This is confidential,' Willie said.

'*Confidential?*'

'Confidential,' Willie said. They passed the big word back and forth. Newberry's eyes didn't leave Reuben.

'I don't know about that,' Newberry said. His hand went to his ear again. 'Hell. I don't know.'

'He's an attorney,' Willie said. He didn't say 'lawyer.'

'I don't know,' Newberry said. He pulled at the ear. 'Hell.'

Reuben slipped a fifty-dollar bill from a gold initialed money clip. Then he picked up the apple pie and set the bill under it. Fifty dollars was too much. Most of it was for the ear. 'Send me some sausage when you get it made,' Reuben said.

'I guess I could tell you a couple of things,' Doan said. 'Hell!'

'Like what?'

'Gunston's a mean bastard, I can tell you that.'

'What else?'

'Women like him,' Newberry said. 'Tall, skinny sonofabitch. A lot of curly hair and funny eyes. I don't see why they like him. He don't even like them much. Women. I mean, he ain't no lover. Still and all, the women follow him around like flies after a garbage truck.' He shook his head. 'Hell. I guess I ain't never gonna understand women.' He grinned at Reuben. Then he picked up the fifty-dollar bill and pocketed it.

'You picked him up the week before Christmas – ' Reuben prompted.

'Christmas Eve,' Newberry said. 'Picked him up with Frank Flowers. Sittin' there as big as you please. I hate them fellows. Too many law officers mixed up with 'em. Not me. I even put it on their record. Nobody else does that, nossir. It don't even belong on their record, whether they belong to the Klan or not. But I put it there. Sure do. Old Frank Flowers broke off and set himself up his own operation. Thinks he's somethin'. He ain't. Not by my lights.'

'What operation?' Reuben said.

'Hell. He ain't even part of the Louisiana Klan no more,' Newberry said. 'Broke off. Made a lotta people mad. Hell. I don't care which operation it is. I don't like none of 'em.'

'Where do you think Gunston is now?' Reuben said.

'Hell. Can't nobody find him,' Newberry said. 'The night I picked him up, he said he wasn't goin' to jail for no frame. Hell. I never framed nobody. I'm an honest lawman. Willie knows that.'

'What about Gunston?' Reuben said.

'Said he'd go underground,' Newberry said. 'Said he was a

minute-man. Whatever that is. Said nobody was gonna stop him from savin' the South. Hell. *He* can't save the damned South. Ain't nobody can. We can't fight the damned Yankee again. Too many of 'em down here. Stealin' our land. Stealin' everything. Gettin' the niggers to vote. Stealin' *everything*.'

'If you were gonna look for Gerald Gunston, where would you look ?' Reuben said.

'Hell,' Newberry said. He scratched his head. The blood on his hands and under his fingernails was beginning to coagulate. 'You got to know what he *likes* for that.'

'What does he like ?' Reuben said.

'He likes his Bible, that's all I know,' Newberry said. He laughed the crane laugh again. 'If it was me, you could look where there's a lot of fresh hog meat!'

Dusk came early. The winter shadows lay in the street when they got back to the house. The wind was whipping charcoal pieces of dirt in the air. On the porch, Sarah's old rocking chair flapped back and forth like a grounded bird.

Willie lit a fire in the living room. The light danced around over the overstuffed furniture and the eagles' heads like fireflies looking for a place to light but getting swallowed up instead.

Reuben wrote out a check for the funeral expenses. Willie's face turned red, and tears came to his eyes. 'You're the head of the family now, Reuben,' he said.

'No goddamned family left to be head of,' Reuben said.

'That ain't true,' Willie said. 'It changes. It falls apart and it comes together and it changes, but it goes on. I believe that. That's why Elena left you this house.' He turned away. 'I'll get us somethin' to eat,' he said.

Reuben let him go.

The ankle had begun to pain. He lowered himself into the big chair and put his feet up on the ottoman. The elevation reduced the pressure. He took a look at the ankle. It was swollen.

You old bastard. You leave me your goddamned house and then you sprain my ankle. What for ? I got no time for ghosts.

But he felt it happening to him, as he used to feel it when he was a kid. Sitting in this same damned chair. Back when he wore the knickers. He had always been able to imagine the house as it had been in 1905, when his grandfather had bought it from the Confederate colonel; and after that Reb and Jesse and Elena were born, all of them in the carved four-poster of the upstairs bedroom, under the patchwork quilt that had been made for Sarah by

112

the ladies of the Maryville First Baptist Church. And he, Reuben, as a kid, and now again, would become the old man, in front of the fire, just in from the fields, and in a few minutes Sampson would bring him his whiskey, and say: *How do the cotton look today?*

'All I could find was some baked beans.' Willie held two chipped plates like offerings, a brown coagulated mess at the center of each.

'I'm not hungry, Willie,' Reuben said. 'A drink'll do. One drink and then I've got to get on the road.'

'You're a good man.' Willie crossed the room and opened a cupboard and pulled down a bottle and two crystal glasses. Reuben watched the motions take twice the time they should have. Willie didn't want to be left alone.

Willie came back and sat on the ottoman next to Reuben's foot. 'How's the ankle?'

'Throbbing.'

'A drink'll help.'

'One drink.'

'I gotta tell you somethin',' Willie said. 'It's on my mind and I gotta tell you.' He poured two shots and handed one to Reuben.

'It doesn't matter.' Funerals brought out confessions. Reuben didn't want to hear Willie's confession. An affair with a waitress at the Downtown Cafe. He swallowed the bourbon. The warmth hit his ankle.

'I was lyin',' Willie said. 'What I said at the Cafe. About Elena and your grandpaw. I was lyin'.'

'It doesn't matter,' Reuben said.

'She was a tyrant,' Willie said. 'The old lady. Sarah. Your grandmaw.'

'It doesn't help to talk about the dead.'

'It helps me,' Willie said solemnly.

'Alright.'

'We run off and got married, Elena and me. You know about that. You know how the old man was always runnin' me off. *No backbone*, he used to say. You know about that?'

'I know.'

'So right before his body washed up, we run off. Five days after the flood. Then where could we go? I ask you? Elena cried all the time. So we came back here. Then after your grandpaw's funeral, the boys came, your uncles. I heard 'em when they came here and they said to Sarah: *What you gonna do? You can't live here alone.* And Sarah said to 'em: *Willie and Elena, they're gonna live with me.*

And Nate laughed. And he said: *How come?* I was listenin'. The old lady said: *No backbone.*'

'That's not true,' Reuben said. 'I saw it today. You've got a lot of backbone, Willie.'

'You're a good man,' Willie said. He stood up. 'Listen,' he said, 'I got somethin' for you.'

'You don't have to pay me back. I told you. Just keep the Litvak's grave up.'

'It ain't from me, it's from *him* – from the old man.' Willie reached up and tugged at the painting which had hung over the fireplace for fifty years. On the canvas, a cracked and faded cotton field bloomed – the first twenty acres Joe Buchman had ever owned, and on it the small cabin in which Itz and Nate had been born. In the last years of his life, the old man had commissioned a local artist to go out there and paint it. 'Damned thing's heavy,' Willie said.

'I don't want it,' Reuben said.

Willie turned, his face crooked. 'I won't miss it none.'

'It belongs here,' Reuben said. 'I couldn't think of it any other place.'

'If you say so.' Willie came back to the ottoman and poured two more drinks.

'I've got to go, Willie,' Reuben said gently.

'Please,' Willie said. 'Just one more.'

'Just one.'

'Those glasses were weddin' presents,' Willie said. 'The whole town sent us weddin' presents after they found out. We never even unpacked 'em till your grandpaw died. Sarah wanted everything like it was. Sarah wanted Elena like she was. Sarah did all the cookin', even. You remember that, don't you?'

'I remember.'

'Elena never spent no time away from her mama. I kept thinkin' to myself, *She'll grow up*. I kept sayin' to myself, *She married you, didn't she, Willie?* The most beautiful girl in the Mississippi delta and she married Methodist Willie Caldwell. But the old lady ruled everything. You remember that cow the old lady used to have? All that butter and cream for all those years. And then your grandmaw died and damned if that cow didn't keel over the very next day. They were cartin' Sarah off in the hearse at the same time the sanitation department came for the cow. Like that cow didn't dare live one more day after Sarah died.'

Willie stopped, choked up. Part whiskey, part memory. 'I ain't never got it all straight in my head.'

'It don't matter,' Reuben said.

'It matters.' Willie stood up again, ramrod straight, and marched over to the upright piano. He picked up one of the photographs that marched along the top, and brought it back. 'Maybe you'd like to have this?'

Reuben looked at the photograph. An old tintype. Familiar. The kid in the knickers had spent a lot of time looking at it. There was the old man, just sixty years old, standing beside Sarah, in tails and a top hat and a bushy white beard. Sarah, fifty-eight years old, was seated in a chair, her hands compliantly folded in the lap of a long white silk dress. The picture had been taken the day of the '27 flood. The day Reuben was born.

'I told you,' Reuben said. 'It isn't that I don't want it. But it belongs here. I want everything to stay here. Where it belongs.'

Willie looked at the picture. 'She wasn't no tyrant with the old man,' he said. 'Nossir. Anything the old man said, that was the law to her. You know where this picture was taken, don't you?'

'I never understood it,' Reuben said. 'After forty years, why did he want to marry her all over again?'

'Nobody else understood it either,' Willie said. 'Maybe he got crazy from the malaria. He got the malaria again – the third time he had it – when the river started up in January. By spring the river was stormin' against the levee. Maybe he knew it was gonna get him. Who knows? Anyway he made up his mind he was gonna have a weddin' for him and Sarah. Everybody thought he was crazy, but she went along with him. Sent Sampson around to invite the whole damned town, even me. He had food and music and a *chuppa* set up in the First Baptist Church. And then the old man, and your papa, and your uncles, rode in through the pourin' down rain on four big white horses. Like in the old country, he said. Everybody was up on the levee fightin' the river, but they all came down for the weddin' alright. He had a special table set up for the niggers with Sampson at the head of it. You and your mama was the only ones missed it, on account of you were bein' born,' Willie said.

'You got a good memory, Willie.'

'You're right about that,' Willie said. 'I remember all of it. You know how they got the rabbi to come down from Memphis?'

'No.'

'You wouldn't remember Bubba? He's the one did the cotton-dustin'. He's the one taught the old man how to fly that damned World War One plane. Like I said, the old man had the malaria, so he damned well couldn't fly. He sent Bubba and Reb up to Memphis to rent him that monkey suit and bring back the rabbi. It was stormin' and the river was comin' up and the rabbi hadn't ever been in a plane before. He said he wouldn't come. Rabbi Judah P. Feinman, I'll never forget. His papa had been a colonel in the Civil War. Said he wouldn't come. So they kidnapped him. Brought him back in the cotton-duster with a shotgun at his head, with Bubba doin' tricks in the storm all the way back. I ain't never seen nobody as mad and as scared as that rabbi – '

'I'll be damned.'

'That's right,' Willie said. 'That's the way it was.' He poured another drink.

Reuben picked up his glass and clicked it with Willie's. 'Here's to Rabbi Judah P. Feinman.' He swallowed the bourbon and thought about a kidnapped Memphis rabbi in a World War One plane, making *bruchas* with a shotgun pointed at his head.

'He made a big speech about it at the weddin',' Willie said. 'He said all Bubba and Reb had talked about on the plane was the boll weevil. He was hoppin' mad. He said he was gonna talk about insects, too. Grasshoppers, he said. He made a damned weddin' speech about grasshoppers. He stood up there and he said, *Every grasshopper gets a leap accordin' to his destiny*. Then he said your grandpaw had taken his leap from Russia to Maryville, but he had never taken *the leap to God*.' Willie grinned. 'The old man didn't like that much.'

'I wouldn't think so.'

'The rabbi said to your grandpaw, *You're a man who claimed everything, but you never changed nothin'. You never changed nothin' but your own small life*. Then the old man stood up, his face all red, and he hollered at the rabbi, *I ain't no goddamned grasshopper!*'

'What happened then?'

'That's exactly when the siren started screamin' and everybody started runnin' on account of the levee had broke through. That's the last time anybody ever saw the old man alive. That's the last words anybody ever heard him say. *I ain't no goddamned grasshopper*.' Willie shook his head. 'That's the way it was.' His eyes filled up with tears. 'The next week me and Elena ran off.'

'But you were here when they brought his body back, weren't you?'

'How come you askin' me about that?' Willie said.

'Sarah paid a convict fifty dollars for his body,' Reuben said. 'Isn't that the way it was?'

Willie stood up. 'That's the way it was.' He looked down at

Reuben. His face twisted. 'I gotta tell you somethin',' he said. 'I guess I gotta tell you somethin' I ain't never told nobody.'

'What's that?'

Willie buried his face in his hands.

'You don't have to tell me.'

Willie dropped his hands. 'I guess I can't,' he said. 'I want to, but I guess I can't.'

'Forget it,' Reuben said. 'I tell you what you do. How about you go upstairs to that big hall closet. How about you get me the old man's shotgun. That ain't part of the house. And it sure is somethin' I'd like to have.'

'Right away.' Willie fled through the door.

Reuben hobbled on the ankle over to the piano. He set the photograph back where it had always been. There were photographs of Jesse, and his uncles, and Elena, and one of himself at the age of three with long curls. He stood there looking at the pictures until he heard Willie come back. Then he turned around and saw that Willie was carrying the shotgun and a big metal box.

'I had forgot about this,' Willie said. 'The old man left a lotta papers. Sarah put 'em away in the closet with his things. It ain't part of the house either. I mean, it's part of him, like the shotgun, but not the house. I figured you might want 'em. He kept everything here. Right here in this box.'

Willie carried the box to the ottoman and set it down. Then he pried it open. Reuben hobbled over. He sat on the ottoman and went through the box. There were mortgages and notes and bank loans. There were contracts and land maps and detailed directions for making corn whiskey. Everything in it had belonged to the old man alright, none of it in order, and all of it anachronistic. There was one item of interest. A journal the old man had kept in his own handwriting. Written in Yiddish. To Reuben, it might as well have been Greek.

'You want it?' Willie's voice cracked.

'Sure I do,' Reuben said. 'Thanks. Maybe you could put it in the trunk of my car for me?'

'Maybe we could have another drink?'

'I'd like to, Willie, but I can't.'

'Sure,' Willie said. 'I can understand that.' He picked up the box. 'Sure. I'll take it out for you. You sure you can walk on that ankle?'

'Fine.'

'Forget what I said, will you?' Willie said. 'What I mean is – forget what it was I couldn't say?'

'It's forgotten.' Reuben hobbled to the door, carrying the old man's shotgun. Willie opened it for him. They went across the porch. Sarah's chair creaked. It was pitch black outside, and the wind was howling. When they reached the car, Reuben opened the trunk. Willie took a long time to get the box settled. Reuben laid the shotgun beside it.

'You'll come back and visit me, won't you?' Willie said.

Reuben slammed the trunk. 'Sure I will.'

He pulled off without looking back.

Fourteen

That's all there is, Reuben. The thing between a man and a woman, that's all there is. . . .

A half hour of road reeled out behind him, an hour and a half still ahead. The wind whistled around the car like a pack of coyotes. The road was lonely and isolated. He'd been up since six, his ankle was throbbing, he'd had too much to drink with Willie, no supper, and the ghosts of Maryville were clinging to his back.

He was beginning to feel the effects of all of it.

Behind him were his roots, his beginnings. Ahead of him was Holmesdale, and the threat of the bombing. Locked in the glove compartment, with the pistol, was the manila envelope and its list of barbarians.

And then there was Lea's voice. *That's all there is. . . .*

He lit a cigarette. There was moss in his throat.

God kept on making mistakes. But he didn't even have Him to blame – God, the angry Jehovah to whom he had been introduced by Rabbi Hellman in Greenborough, in the time of the corduroy knickers. Because God had become, for him, the old man, his grandfather. The face of God had become the face of the old Litvak, Joe Buchman, a long time ago. The mistakes had been made by the old man.

Lea was his own mistake.

But it wasn't a mistake. Lea had been a watershed. Everything before her had been one thing, and though his life looked the same afterwards, the course unchanged, it was not. It was only the surface that seemed untouched. Beneath, something in him had shifted irrevocably.

Why now? Why go over it again?

But there was no choice in it. The memory, when it came, came always with its own volition, its own will, its own life.

That's all there is, Reuben. . . .

The first thing to happen to him had been the sound of her voice, the strange timbre of it, as if dusk was at the core of her. It was her voice that came first.

The hottest night in August. 1962. After midnight, maybe one in the morning. He had gone back to sleep when the phone rang again, with Mollie sleeping beside him on her back, the child that was to be Phil stirring in her womb. Phil would come a month early, but nobody had known that then. If he had been able to read the future he might not have answered the phone when it rang again. But he answered it, in the dark, the hum of the air-conditioner going. And there had been the sound of Lea's voice. *I'm Lea Kraber.* . . .

He had known what her name would be. John Abrahmson had called earlier, waking him up for the first time that night. Nothing unusual about that – John had just left his wife then, Martha, not divorced yet, only separated, and was living with the quiet gentile secretary he later married in the house he had just built in the middle of downtown Holmesdale, a circular tower flanked by office buildings and stores on the last of the land that had been left by his father. And there was Martha, John's soon-to-be ex-wife, who was in the habit of driving by late at night and tearing up the newly planted azaleas or throwing kitchen knives at the windows. Reuben was the one John always called, never the police, because John simply wanted someone to tell it to: *You see how crazy she is, that bitch!* And Reuben listened because John Abrahmson paid him a retainer, and that's how he earned it. But it wasn't about Martha.

It was about a girl named Lea Kraber who had said she was working her way through the telephone book. Jewish names. She had started with John Abrahmson, and John had figured that he, Reuben, was next on the list.

' – crazy Yankee agitator,' John said. 'I told her. I said – listen girl, my grandpaw was here before the goddamned Civil War. My grandpaw once owned all of downtown Holmesdale. You ain't talkin' to no Jew, you're talkin' to a southern gentleman. Now you go peddle your papers somewhere else.'

'What does she want?'

'She's lookin' for a Jew to stick his neck out for her,' John said. 'Don't answer the phone. When it rings, you just don't even answer it.'

But when the phone rang later – he didn't know how much later, he had gone back to sleep – he answered it anyway.

'Yes.'

'I'm Lea Kraber. . . . ' In that voice. He had expected a harsh Yankee accent. There wasn't one. Maybe a finishing school in there somewhere, but he couldn't tell then. There was the depth of it, more like breathing than talking, a contrary act of nature that wiped out the memory of all other voices; but maybe that came later, he couldn't be sure.

'What kind of trouble is it?' he said.

'Vagrancy,' she said. 'That's what they call it.'

He knew what that meant. Another one about to be locked up in the fairgrounds. There had been more than a thousand all summer long. The jail not big enough to hold them, and still they kept coming. And nobody left to defend them. By then, Kornfield had given up and gone home. Kornfield had asked him to take over the defense. He had refused. The defense was turned over to public defenders whose loyalties were obviously on the side of the prosecution. Then Reuben had quit prosecuting. With the absence of Kornfield, the courtroom had lost its challenge – it had begun to feel like sending sheep to slaughter. Then Kornfield had begun to telephone, counting on a prodding residue of conscience. And he had continued to refuse to take on the defense.

'Why call me?' He expected to hear Kornfield's name.

'There're four of us,' she said. 'We get four phone calls. I'm doing the calling. One kike, one nigger, a wop, and a shanty. We figured I had the best shot.'

Then he understood. They were betting their dimes on the Jewish conscience.

'It's not my kind of case,' he said.

'I'm sorry.'

'How old are you?'

'Nineteen,' she said. He wondered what the face looked like.

'Don't you have parents to call?'

'There's nobody to call.'

'Look,' he said. 'You shouldn't have come down here. This isn't your place. You bring out the worst in it.'

'If it's your place,' she said, 'you should do something about it.'

120

'What would you suggest ?'

'You could start by helping me.'

'No,' he said. Then he hung up. He lit a cigarette and sat on the edge of the bed, smoking in the darkness and listening to the hum of the airconditioner. And looking at the phone.

She didn't call back.

Two days later, he put Mollie in the hospital. It was a hundred degrees in the shade, the humidity unbearable. Phil wasn't due for two months, but the pains began anyway. Mollie was confined to bed at Sinai and given shots and tranquilisers. The longer they could delay it, the better for the baby.

There were difficulties. Joe had just finished up with the mumps and immediately Leila came down with them. A fluke. Later he believed in fate. Leila was put to bed for a month. Joe was only six. He packed a suitcase and took Joe to stay at Monk and Sheila's. He might have seen he was getting ready for something, but he didn't think about it.

When he thought about it again, he told himself he had the need for a mitzvah. A good deed to bring good luck to the new baby. Still, he put it off another two days, the girl's voice haunting him. He took a dozen red roses to the hospital. He went to see Joe at Monk's house and he ate dinner there with Monk and Sheila and Joe and Monk's three sons. When he left, he found himself driving to the fairgrounds.

He stood outside a long time, looking through the hastily constructed barbed wire at the makeshift quonset huts. The inmates at the fairgrounds were being fed on a diet of cornmeal mush, and at night the heaters inside were turned on to bring up the summer heat to a hundred and twenty. So when their thirty days were up, they'd get the hell out of the state. And tell their friends. He had prosecuted hundreds of them. But now it had become personal. Whoever she was. Lea Kraber.

When they brought her out, she was glossy with sweat, and shaking. Thick coal-black hair down to her waist. She looked like some wild creature who had been penned up but not broken. Her eyes, the color of amber, were glowing with fever and rage. She was tall. That surprised him. Dressed in faded tight jeans and an undershirt that had been dyed a purplish-blue, the body lithe, and the chills moving her like a dancer. And big, expressive hands that wouldn't be still, like they were caressing some invisible person; when he saw the hands he should have known, but he didn't let himself know.

She came out with the three of them. There was the nigger, as big and black as any chain-gang member; and there was the wop, small and wiry with a lot of curly black hair; and there was the shanty, in a bedraggled red beard and sandals. But she was the leader of them, he could see that. They fell back and waited for her to deal with it.

'What about my friends?' she said.

'Screw your friends.' For a minute he thought she wouldn't go with him. For that minute, he was relieved, and he saw she could feel it. She knew she couldn't push it. She went back to her friends, and said something to them. He couldn't hear what it was. It took a minute or two. Then she came back.

'Okay,' she said.

He put her in the car. He had been driving a 1962 green airconditioned Oldsmobile. The night was hellish hot, but he turned off the air. He could see she was ill. He hadn't thought about it before – where he would take her.

'Where do you want to go?' he said.

'Anyplace.' She was no supplicant.

'You'll get picked up again.'

She shrugged. 'I'll think of something.'

He stopped for a light. He thought about where he could take her. He couldn't think of any place.

'Do you have any money?'

'How much will you give me? Ten? Twenty? What should I do with it?' She was looking at him with an intensity that disturbed him. The red light seemed to go on forever. Then it changed. The solution came to him.

'I have some friends in New Orleans,' he said. 'Zack Rosen and B. V. Grossman. They'll take care of you.' He thought about Zack. Zack provided people with what they needed. On his nineteenth birthday, Zack had provided him with a whore. Happy Birthday. He thought about the Creole cottage on Toulouse Street that Zack shared with B. V. The slave quarters in back were rented out to Playboy bunnies and stewardesses. Zack provided what they needed too. Abortions, loans, or one-way tickets back to where they came from. Zack would give her a place to stay and find her a doctor, and wouldn't ask questions.

'Why?' she said.

'Why what?'

'Why would you go to all that trouble?'

'I don't know.' He didn't know. He felt she knew. He had always believed there were women who were born with something that gave them an immediate knowledge of some kind of truth a man couldn't see. An interior vision.

'I'll drive you down there.' He believed it was an impulse. He understood that need was the mother of impulse, but he had no idea what need propelled him.

'Why?' she said again. In that voice.

'I don't know,' he repeated. He looked at his watch. It was nine thirty. New Orleans was a three-hour drive. He would get there after midnight and be back before dawn.

'You're a strange man.'

He headed out to the highway, keeping his eyes on the road. She didn't say anything more. Nothing. She seemed to have no curiosity. She seemed to have no need to know where she was going, or what she might find. Fifteen minutes went by. She said nothing. As if she had completely relinquished herself.

Finally, he turned to look at her. She was gone. Slumped over into the seat. The big, expressive hands hanging down, and the coal-black hair tumbling over them.

He was halfway home from Maryville. The wind whipped the car. He didn't want to go back there. But the memory had hold of him, carrying him along, like the road. And the memory would carry him now, all the way through it. Through the beauty and the pain of it, and the inevitability that had not, then, occurred to him.

He turned the car around. He took her home. To the house he and Mollie and Joe had lived in, back then, the house on Oak Road, a gray frame house with a gabled roof and a tulip garden, and the front door that was painted moss green.

In the darkness he carried her into the house.

He had never been any good with women. He had always thought of women as strange inaccessible creatures. In his childhood there had been the corduroy knickers which separated him from the children who came in by bus, wearing overalls or flour-sack dresses, and shoeless. With a knowledge he didn't have. They had seen animals breed in the open; had watched a cow give birth; slept, at night, in the same room with brothers and sisters and parents. No mysteries to them. Sex as natural a part of their lives as the knowledge that a red sunset brought rain or low-flying swallows brought wind. He had been reared by Frieda to be neat and respectful; told what was nice and what wasn't; had gone over to Greenborough every Saturday – driven by the black boy in the truck from the store – to study for his confirmation with Rabbi Hellman, knowing that he was different from the others, but told that being a Jew had nothing to do with it, the difference. He had come to the conclusion that the difference was sex.

He had been lonely then. More lonely later. There was the military school, nothing but boys. The homosexual professor who had terrified him. The inevitable whore in Biloxi where he had lined up, his senior year, with the others; when he'd got inside he had paid for her promise not to tell the others he hadn't *done* anything, and he could tell from the look on her face that it wasn't a special or unusual request.

After that, there was the whore on his nineteenth birthday. The present from Zack Rosen. At Tulane. And, after that, there was Mollie. As neat and respectable and conflicted as he.

That was his history with women.

Nothing like Lea. Ever. Nothing.

There was the residue of some primitive, atavistic memory perhaps; she stirred it. But the memory had been unfinished, incomplete; he had always felt there was a truth, and there were those who knew it and those, like Lea, who embodied it. She didn't live mystery. She lived the moment, called that truth. In the time he knew her, she never told him a lie.

She stirred as he carried her in. She opened her eyes and looked around. She was being carried, but he knew he wasn't in charge of it.

He carried her into the bedroom and laid her down on the bed, but not before he had pulled back the spread with the neatness of a cat burglar. She didn't miss that, she didn't miss anything.

'I'll fix you some soup.' He had never taken care of anyone before.

'I'd rather have a hot bath.' She was shaking, the tremors running over her body. 'Will you help me?'

Mollie was private. Lea had none of that. None of the need for the circle of inviolate space that was the self-protection of women. Her need was the opposite; she had the need to involve him in the sensations she experienced. The accompanying demand was that he leave himself behind, enter a foreign landscape; she would show him how to explore it – he, Reuben, this man who lived in a dull reality built of clay.

He felt it that way.

He filled the tub with hot water. He undressed her. He helped her wash her hair. He felt himself becoming someone else; in his own house, his own skin. The Reuben Buchman he had known began to disappear in the flow between them. It originated with her. He followed. The long female body slightly distorted by the bath water, simply there, without asking in it or denial in it. Simply there, if he wanted it. As sensual as he might want to it be, as compliant; no questions, no answers, no bargains to be made in advance; nothing beyond the unspoken fact that the power of the thing between them was obvious. The need could be given its name later.

He wrapped her in his terry-cloth bathrobe. With his hairbrush, she brushed out her hair, the color of a crow's wing, her face flushed from the fever and steam of the bath.

He left her there. In the kitchen, he heated a can of bouillon. He believed that when he got back she would be gone. He believed she was a product of his inner dementia. He had not known he was capable of inventing such a creature. But when he came back, she was propped up against the pillows, and grateful for the bouillon.

He sat on the edge of the bed while she sipped the bouillon from Mollie's china cup.

'Why did you come down here?'

'I came with Cody.' Her eyes studied him, bright, like gold glittering in a pan of water.

'Who's Cody?'

'The *nigger*,' she said. 'I'm his bagel baby.'

He wanted to hit her. She didn't miss that either. But she kept talking. She told her story as if she were talking about someone else, some other girl she had once known who was spirited and driven by the need for experience to keep her from despair.

Her father imported textiles. Manhattan. A brownstone in the East Sixties. Her mother was Ethical Culture. Whatever that was; he had never heard of it. She had a younger sister in school in Boston learning to be a speech therapist. At fifteen, she had run away from home. She had cracked up, emotionally, was brought home, given an abortion. And five hours a week with an analyst. She was only fifteen, but she had already given herself up to the ethic of eroticism. Whatever that was; he had never heard of that, either. She was only fifteen, but she already understood that eroticism precipitated self-knowledge; her self-knowledge told her she was brighter than the analyst was. It had taken her only three months to defeat him. She was put into a finishing school. A wretched place.

'I didn't want to be canonized,' she said. Her cheeks were too bright, her nose too short, her mouth too full, her eyes glazed with some kind of tortured victory. He didn't understand a lot of what she said, but he understood that she negated everything he had ever believed about women.

He was still wearing his business suit, the only thing left of him still recognisable to himself. Later, he could remember the sight of his clothes draped over the wing chair, the navy blue jacket neatly hung on the back, the shirt, the knitted tie, the trousers folded in half; the last of himself left there, on the antique chair that had come from some pre-Civil War plantation. Knowing that the last man to be with her had been a black man. Later, he could remember that thought as his last earthbound impulse.

After that, he began to live two lives. He watched Lea come back to health with the subtle arrogant feeling of having created her. The opposite was true. She was creating him. Some moments he saw her as the Yankee girl, the enemy – moments when he compared himself to the Goths, with the lust for Rome, the conquering of the Roman woman. The opposite was true. She was the conqueror. Alone, he had fits of brooding despair, followed by intense excitement and the anxiety that he might lose her.

He showed his face at the office, made imaginary outside appointments, and left as soon as possible. Clients were an invasion. He passed them on to Justin or got rid of them as soon as possible. Justin saw nothing amiss, didn't question him. The obvious perceptions were always the difficult ones between people familiar to each other, he counted on that.

Once, each evening, he made the trip to Monk's and saw Joe; and once, each evening, he made the trip to the hospital. But the sight of Mollie became less and less real. There were the ordinary things to be said and done, the things that had once made up his life, but they became vagaries, extraneous burdens, to be gotten out of the way so his life could begin.

He knew it was madness. The madness made him canny and efficient.

He waited for Lea to mention her friends. She didn't. She seemed to have left them behind. He asked for their names. He telephoned and had them set free: Cody and Dixon and Palmisano. It took only a phone call. He was still, legally, an appointee for the prosecution. He used the title. He had her friends set free on the condition that they would leave the state in twenty-four hours. Then he knew they were gone. After that, he believed it would become simple for him.

He and Lea went nowhere. During the time he was gone he left her there, in the house on Oak Road, the drapes pulled. He came back to her there, all discoveries made there. He discovered two things. The first was the nature of love – the strength of inarticulate gestures, touch, scent, the depths of light and darkness, nothing he could get hold of – it got hold of him, consumed him. The second thing he discovered was that he could not remember who he had been, and he could not define who he had become, and there was no such thing as time, or the passing of time, or the coming of some future time.

The day after he had her friends released, he returned home to find her gone. There was no way to tell if she would return or not – she had no clothes to take or leave behind. Only herself. Lea. The possibility of loss brought with it the feeling of annihilation of soul. There was a sudden urgency to think of her as undesirable. He stood in the bedroom, looking down at the bed, focusing on the thought of her other lovers. Seeing himself queued up for her in a succession of panderers, holding out a tin cup for the disbursement of love; as if she gave out coins, copper pennies, dimes, but he could not calculate the sum of it, only hear the clink as they fell into a bottomless well. He tried believing that he had been made a victim of a grueling sexual extortion. Even that didn't enrage him; somehow, instead, he felt ennobled. And felt, finally, that the repudiation of Lea would be the dispossession of his deepest being.

He left the house and began to walk. Somehow, he knew how long it would take. It was two hours. When he returned, he found her naked in bed, reading, wearing eyeglasses.

'Where did you get the eyeglasses?'

'Cody.'

'You saw him?'

'That's all over,' she said. 'I told him. It's you. I want to stay with you.'

'What did he say?'

'He said, *Good luck, baby*.'

He came over to the bed and sat on the edge of it. 'I love you.' It was the first time he had said it.

'You can't love me.'

'Why not?'

'I'm a nihilist,' she said. 'I'm the flesh I am, that's all. And sometimes I think I'm out to destroy that.'

'I don't understand.'

'I flirt with death,' she said. 'To demolish the barriers. I flirt with death as a positive act. That's the only belief I have.'

'What about us?'

'There's no *us*. There's a screwed-up Yankee girl on a course of self-destruction. And there's a half-dead southern man who can't see what his life is, or who he is. That's us.'

'Why are you doing this?'

'It's inevitable,' she said. 'Why not do it now?'

'I'm not ready.'

'You don't *claim* anything,' she said. 'You're not going to claim me.' She shook her head. 'Your soul isn't torn, it's *rusted*. You think you're a Jew. You think you're a southerner. You think you're a man. You haven't claimed any of it.'

'What about you?' he said. 'You claim death?'

'I claim nothing,' she said. 'That's a claim. Nothing. Don't disturb it. I don't want it disturbed. You can't go all the way. Don't disturb it.'

'I love you.'

She shook her head. 'No.' He set about to claim her.

All through September he found himself remembering the months before as the months of his childhood.

He made love to her. Afterwards, he would lie there and remember the month of May, and the sight of the field hands chopping the weeds in the cotton fields.

He made love to her. Afterwards, he would lie there and remember June and July in his childhood, when the squares appeared on the cotton plants and after that the bloom came, looking like hollyhock, in three days turning from cream to pink to bright red.

He made love to her. And saw August. Full white bolls of cotton stretching out into the sea of white that had once been his childhood. Southern. He knew he had set about to claim that much. And in claiming it, he wanted her to see it. Needed her to see it. As it had been for him.

The September dusk was hot and sticky. She wore the jeans and the undershirt. September 28, 1962. In a paper sack, she carried a French bread, some cheese, a bottle of wine he had picked up from a local bootlegger. It was the first time they had been out of the house together. It was a month. They had been together one month.

He took the highway to Maryville. Thirty miles before Maryville, he turned off onto a gravel road. Down that road were the cotton fields of what had once been the Cosgrove plantation. The Cosgroves were gone, the land worked now by tenants. He remembered the February day that his father had taken him out there to hunt without a shotgun. The old man Joe had taught Jesse, and then Jesse taught him. After that, Jesse showed him the clearing, what was left of the old Cosgrove place.

It was fourteen miles off the main highway. He pulled off and parked. The field hands were gone, the fields empty. He and Lea walked out into a streaked sunset, the hot colors turning the cotton bolls into patches of fire, then mauve, then deep violet; then finally the bolls gleamed phosphorescent white in the coming of night.

It had been years. He had a brief glimpse of what he was doing. Living his time over, with Lea.

By the light of a flashlight, he found the path through the woods, the same path he had taken with Jesse. He held her by the hand and led her through the speckled night shadows thrown by tall thin pines, the frogs hopping away from their footsteps and from somewhere the cicadas starting up in concert. He felt the two of them connected by something primeval, now made fitting and right, in the woods, of the woods, the uncivilised thing between them brought to its natural uncivilised place.

When he stopped at the pine, he couldn't be sure if it was the same tree; if he was looking at it now, or if he was looking at it with the eyes of the boy he had been. He aimed the beam of the flashlight at it, the light traveling up the length of the trunk until he found what he was looking for. It was there. The burrowed cave, close to the top.

'Hold the flashlight on me,' he said.

He could hear her breathing. The cicadas grew louder. It had been more than twenty years, but he didn't think about that. He found a stick and began to climb. First it was more difficult than he had expected; then suddenly it grew easier as he became filled with the power in it, and filled with the sound of his own breathing, which was the sound of hers down below, too, and with the light following him from below.

Then he reached the cavern, near the top. He stopped. Listening. He couldn't tell if there was anything in there or not. He gripped the trunk with his legs. Holding on with his left hand, he swung out and poked the stick inside. The sense of the nest of warm, furry bodies came through the stick to his hand. They were in there. He could feel the shapes.

He settled on one. Turning it around with the stick until he had it right where he wanted it. Then he brought the animal along, poking it with the stick, until he felt it in the right position, and in a minute the tail came out first – four inches of it, in front of him, waving in the beam of the flashlight.

He caught hold of the tail. With one swift motion, he slung the squirrel out in an arc, into the air, then brought it back, and slammed its head against the side of the tree trunk. Blood spattered.

The squirrel fell limp. He let it go. He heard the sound of it as it hit the ground below.

Look boy, this is how you do it.

He poked around with the stick again. He separated another one. They were huddled together. He brought the tail out, caught it, then made the arc, and came back with the same fierce battering blow. The thump. Once. The squirrel was dead. He let it go.

Now he could hear the rest of them chattering inside, frightened, as the stick slid in again. He could tell how many were left now. Three. *Look boy, this is how you do it.* The old man had taught it to Jesse, and Jesse had taught it to him. The tail waving out. Another arc. Another shattering deathblow. The blood flew. The squirrel fell to the ground.

He looked down into the beam of the flashlight, like looking down into the eye of the sun. Lea. Partner in love. Partner in violence. *I flirt with death. To demolish the barriers.* He was obsessed. Caught up in the compulsion of mastery and godlike power.

He kept on until the last two were dead. Down there on the ground.

Then he climbed down towards the eye of the sun and stood looking down at the five dead squirrels – he, master of the senseless death. Not even the need to cook and eat them. Master of death, and so master of life. Master of Lea. Next to him was the sound of breathing, and her eyes glittering, and he saw there was blood on his hands as he reached for her. And he realised that he had claimed something. There was this in the South. There was gentility and grace and violence. And this in him.

He brought her down onto the ground, the leaves, the pine straw, dirt and brambles. And he met her own need for violence and death – the repudiation inherent in the recognition. One with the sounds of the animals around them, as compulsive as the killing of the squirrels. Everything in it come together, life and love and death and violence, out onto the other side, where life was possible.

Afterwards, the night carried them.

The return completed itself. To the clearing, where the house appeared in the darkness in front of them, as if it had come to them, not they to it. Not much of it was left: rotted wooden pillars holding up the shell that had long ago been gutted by fire, and through the years carried off, piece by piece, for firewood. But he could still see what it might have been, and she could too. Back before Grant's soldiers had gutted it on the way to Vicksburg –

that was one legend he told her. There was another legend, the one that said that Confederate Colonel Cosgrove's wife, Eugenie, had been unfaithful. That Cosgrove had come home to find her with a Union officer, and had shot her and shot himself. That his last dying act had been to set a match to the drapes, and the ghost of Eugenie had come back to put out the fire. The ghost of Eugenie still roamed through the land and through the house.

He threw the beam of the flashlight up onto the porch. Lea went ahead, climbing onto what was left of the gallery, picking her way by the light. Then, suddenly, she stopped and turned. She grasped one of the rotted pillars with both hands and laid her cheek against it.

'I'm Eugenie. There's a war going on out there. I can hear it.'

In the beam of the flashlight, she might have been the ghost of Eugenie Cosgrove. It was all in her, every truth, every illusion, she could have been any of it.

'Who will save me from death?' she said.

He came up onto the gallery. 'There's no war,' he said. 'It's 1962.' But he wasn't sure.

He went inside. A gaping hole filled with the straw of birds' nests was all that was left of the chimney. She came in behind him, and sat down, and began to lay out the stuff from the paper sack.

He sat down beside her. He opened the bottle of wine. The blood had dried on his hands. On her cheek were dirt smudges. A long thin scratch traveled the length of her forearm.

'I love you,' she said. She turned off the flashlight. Patches of moonlight filtered down through the burnt-out roof and lit her face. There was the sound of a rat scurrying off in the darkness somewhere.

'It's not real,' he said. But he couldn't be sure. He had killed five squirrels. She might be Eugenie Cosgrove.

'I have sixty-five thousand dollars,' she said.

He felt the biting anguish of sanity come over him. The narcotic chill of reality. 'No.'

'My grandfather left the money to me,' she said. 'We could take it. We could go as far as we wanted to go. As long as it lasts. The hell with all the tomorrows, there aren't going to be any.'

'You're a nihilist.'

'It's all dying out there,' she said. 'People are dying from a war that doesn't even have a name. You're one of them. You've built some gray insulation. But you broke through it. You'll never find me again. I'll never find you again. We'll search all our lives and we'll never find us again.'

'I know that.'

'That's all there is, Reuben. That's what I've been trying to tell you. The thing between a man and a woman, *that's all there is.*'

The day after that was September twenty-ninth. 1962. At eleven twenty-three p.m., Phil was born.

Reuben telephoned Zack Rosen.

He put Lea on the midnight plane to New Orleans. *I'll be down there. As soon as I can. . . .*

The next morning he bought red roses and a diamond bracelet for Mollie.

It was noon the next day when the telephone call came from Zack. In the slave-quarters apartment behind the house on Toulouse Street, Zack Rosen had found Lea. Dead.

Twenty-four hours later he arranged to have himself appointed to defend freedom riders.

Fifteen

A SIGN on the highway said: Holmesdale 53.

He was leaving Rose County.

Lea was gone. It happened like that, in memory as it had in life. She appeared to take him over, then she was gone.

He had not gone to her funeral.

Zack had telephoned her parents in New York. The story he told was close enough to the truth. Lea had appeared. He had given her a place to stay. She had gone to the corner drugstore, bought a child's jump rope, and hanged herself from the wooden rail of the hayloft bedroom.

Her parents came for her body.

He was left with the void. He called her a visionary, a volcanic force, a wraith, a delusion, forcing her into whatever shape would condemn him the least. Whatever shape would make him less culpable. He was besieged by anguish, and confusion, and fury at her.

In the courtroom, he defended her counterparts.

The road veered to the left. There was nothing but darkness on either side. The winter landscape was desolate. He kept his eyes on the ribbon of light thrown by the headlights onto the road ahead.

Maryville was behind him. Lea was gone. There was Holmesdale ahead. And the manila envelope in the glove compartment. It was a start. In a battle, information constituted arms. The use of the arms would require a plan. He was too tired to go beyond that. He did his best work while he slept. Tomorrow he'd wake, and a plan of action would take shape. He trusted his processes. Justin did the computerised thinking. He allowed solutions to surface.

Then he saw it.

He thought it was weariness, an illusion of fatigue, exaggerated by the pain of the ankle. But it wasn't. It was a car, parked about a quarter of a mile up on the highway. Looking like some animal that had lumbered out and gone to sleep there.

He thought about Frank Flowers, and he thought about Gerald Gunston, and he thought about Doan Newberry standing beside two bleeding hogs with their throats slit.

The car was there alright, parked across the road. A ravine on one side and a rise on the other. No way around it. Whoever it was had picked his spot.

He kept going.

He eased up on the accelerator and leaned over to the glove compartment, keeping his left hand on the wheel. But the glove compartment was locked, with the gun inside. He had locked the damned envelope in. And the keys were on the ignition.

He tore at the key ring. It broke. Keys scattered. Still moving, he felt around on the floorboard until he found the key. He got the glove compartment open.

The car was directly ahead.

He hit the brakes. The Cadillac met a gravel patch at the edge of the road and skidded, the rocks spraying out like bullets.

When he stopped, he had the gun in his hand.

He rolled down the window. The glare of his headlights lit up the other car. A small black sedan. It looked empty.

A moment went by. He could hear the clock on the dashboard whirring around. He could hear the thumping of his own heart.

He shouted, *'Get the hell out of there with your hands up!'*

Nobody answered. Another moment went by. He felt himself go clammy. He shouted again: 'What the hell do you want?'

Nothing. Darkness and silence and the wind. And the small black car, lying there.

He gripped the gun in his right hand. Slowly, with his left hand, he pushed the car door open. In a stooped position, he slid out, his body protected by the door, his head down. He cocked the muzzle of the gun over the window and slowly lifted his head.

Nothing.

Then he felt the steel rod of a pistol press against the small of his back.

'You can stand up now, Mr Buchman,' a voice said. Cold and clipped. Reuben rose slowly. 'Drop the gun,' the voice said.

He weighed the odds. He dropped the pistol. It fell at his feet. A hand swooped down and picked it up. The voice said, 'You see how easy it would be for any one of them?'

'Who the hell are you?'

'You can turn around now, Mr Buchman,' the voice said.

Reuben turned.

Relief diluted the fear.

The man was tall and broad-shouldered, wearing a hat and a black overcoat whipping around in the wind. Under the hat brim was an expressionless lantern-jawed face. An all-American face that had begun to age badly. But formidable. Not a face to screw around with.

The face belonged to Tom Barksdale.

Barksdale held out Reuben's gun. 'Put it away.'

Reuben climbed back into the car. The glove compartment was still hanging open. He shoved in the pistol and slammed it. Barksdale came around the headlights and climbed into the passenger seat.

'What the hell is this –' Reuben's heart was still pounding. He could still feel the steel of the pistol pressed into his back. It was a feeling a man didn't forget quickly.

'Sorry I had to do that.'

'You scare the shit out of a man.' Reuben lit a cigarette. His hand shook.

'It was a lesson,' Barksdale said. 'If you're going to play cops and robbers, you'd better understand what's involved.'

Reuben stared at Barksdale. It began to come through. He understood he had been followed. Every step. 'What right do you have –' He stopped. It occurred to him that an F.B.I. badge gave a man the right to do anything he damn well pleased. The thought chilled him.

'It's not a game,' Barksdale said. 'We want you to know that.'

Reuben studied Barksdale's face. Beneath the insignia and the manner had to be a man. He tried to remember what he knew about Barksdale. From Chattanooga – he had heard that somewhere. Probably educated at Fordham. Law. Most of the F.B.I.

men were lawyers. Married, he knew that. He tried to recall Barksdale's wife; he had an image of a big-boned, utilitarian woman. A couple of children. An Episcopalian – Justin had told him that.

'You didn't run me down in the middle of the night just to teach me a lesson.' Reuben had felt the thrust of the gun.

'Of course you're right.' Barksdale's manner appeared straightforward. Direct. A slight hint of a southern accent buried somewhere. Turned out in some Washington basement, a native son sent back to maintain law and order in Dixie. Something nagged. A muted hostility beneath the façade.

'What's this melodrama about?'

'I didn't think it advisable that we be seen together in town.'

'For my protection or yours?'

'Both.'

'I'll buy that much.' Reuben wasn't sure that he did.

'I have a message for you.'

'I've got nothing to do but listen.'

'Directly from the Bureau. To your people. There's concern in Washington. We want you to know that. Washington is aware of the effect of the bombing on the Jewish community.'

'What the hell are they doing about it?' Reuben watched the anger flick up in Barksdale's eyes.

'We're working on it,' Barksdale said. Cold as ice. 'I can't be any more specific than that at this moment. You know we work under the regulations of the Department of Justice. We can't lay out what we're doing. Not to the press. Not to anybody, until it's time for indictments. Hysteria serves nobody. You're a southerner. I don't have to tell you how touchy the issues are.'

It came back – in '64 when the three civil rights workers had been killed and Robert Kennedy had put pressure on Hoover, Hoover had come down to meet with the governor, and after that Barksdale had been sent in. As a Klucker specialist. But it had taken Barksdale and his force months to find the bodies, and years to get indictments, and now, four years later, Frank Flowers, grand imperial wizard, was still running around loose on bond, companion to Gerald Gunston III.

Reuben leaned over across Barksdale and opened the glove compartment. He ignored the pistol. He pulled out the brown envelope. 'You can stick a gun in my back,' he said, 'but they're running around loose.'

Barksdale shook his head. 'You've put yourself in a great deal of personal danger in order to acquire one paragraph on a handful of men. We have complete files on all these men. And more. Much more. We know who they are, and what they're doing, every minute.'

'Then why the hell don't you arrest them?'

'We're not interested in arrests. We're interested in convictions.' Barksdale took the envelope from Reuben and put it back in the glove compartment. 'You know a local charge always supersedes a federal charge. You know, in most of these crimes, a local charge is involved. The criminals are tried first in local courts. Mississippi courts. You know the history of civil rights cases tried in Mississippi courts. You were once involved in such matters yourself.'

Reuben wondered if Barksdale was referring to Lea. Was Barksdale saying they had a complete dossier on him? Why? Why was Barksdale going to all this trouble? There was more to it than a lesson. Or a message.

'I'm always involved,' Reuben said. 'I'm not a man who likes to sit on his ass.'

'We're not against an aroused citizenry,' Barksdale said. 'In fact, it can be helpful.'

'How?' Reuben had the distinct feeling he was being manipulated. Skillfully. By a bright, shrewd man.

'In Phoenix, for instance, we had a Mafia situation,' Barksdale said. 'Aroused citizens raised funds. We can't tell you to do that. But it was very helpful to us.'

'Funds?'

'That's right. It's not common knowledge, but I assume you know most of our information comes from informers. Most of our witnesses are informers.' A faint smile broke the lantern jaw. 'That's why our files are bigger than yours.' The smile vanished. 'Of course, in the courtroom, the defense lawyer always asks our witnesses: *Were you paid by the F.B.I. for this information?* The answer, naturally, is: *Yes.* You can see what that does to perfectly valid testimony.'

'I can see that.' Reuben knew Mississippi judges. He knew Mississippi juries. He'd be up against that kind of misguided provincialism in the Higgins case. Barksdale was making perfect sense. Still, he felt something wrong in it.

'I'd like you to think about the value of informant funds coming from a source other than the F.B.I.,' Barksdale said. 'I'd like you to think about the possibility of that kind of cooperation from your people.'

Your people, Barksdale said. Did he simply mean the people you're associated with? Or was it anti-Semitic? How many Jews were there in the F.B.I.? Reuben realised he didn't know. The F.B.I. was like the marines; the F.B.I. was the rescuing cavalry in a western film. That's how the public thought about them. Call in the F.B.I. The men in the neat blue suits with the country behind them. The courageous, incorruptible sons of Uncle Sam. He had never questioned it before himself. Why the hell was he questioning it now? He believed in the power of the F.B.I., and he wanted the bombers, but his instincts kept insisting there was something wrong with all of it.

'I'll think about it,' Reuben said. 'But I think you'd better understand something.'

'What's that?'

'I'm a lawyer,' Reuben said. 'I'm representing a client. Technically, the client is Rabbi Greenblatt. In reality, the client is myself, my family, my community, my roots. I intend to fight like hell for all of it.'

'I'm offering you a way to fight with us,' Barksdale said. 'If your people decide to do this, I wouldn't expect you to simply turn the funds over to me. You'd be in on the undercover operation. Every step of it.'

'How?'

'I can't go into that without a commitment on your end.'

It was reasonable. Too reasonable. Five minutes ago it had begun as melodrama. Now it had become an alliance. As if Barksdale were two men – one hard, one soft. Then he remembered the F.B.I. usually worked in pairs. One hard, one soft. Barksdale had managed both.

'I'll think about it.'

'For your own protection, I'd suggest you keep this meeting between ourselves.' Barksdale pulled out a card and handed it to Reuben. 'My private number.' There was a pause that lasted a fraction of a second. Then he said, 'Sorry I had to delay you. Goodnight, Mr Buchman.'

Then he was out of the car and gone.

Reuben watched the black sedan turn itself into the road. Then it pulled off. The taillights twinkled into the distance and vanished.

He lit another cigarette. His hand still shook.

He thought about the fact that there was a kid in every man. The kid that was awed by the power of God and the F.B.I. That's what they worked on. The kid in the corduroy knickers.

But he wasn't a kid anymore. And Barksdale had been right about one thing. *It's not a game. We want you to know that.*

He became aware, suddenly, of the darkness around him. He opened the glove compartment and laid the pistol on the seat beside him.

Then he pulled out into the road.

It was fifty-three miles to Holmesdale.

And his ankle was hurting like hell.

Inside the city limits, he stopped downtown in front of a drugstore across the street from the old capitol building. He limped inside and closed himself in a phone booth and dialed Justin's number. Through the plate-glass window, he could see the lights on the double pavilion of the old capitol, which had been left as a museum and monument. It had been built by slave labor twenty years before the Civil War. Andrew Jackson had been there, and Henry Clay, and Jefferson Davis, and the Irish comedian who had written 'The Bonnie Blue Flag,' the battle song of the Confederacy. And Judah P. Benjamin, the highest ranking Jew in the South. The old capitol belonged to him as much as it did to anybody.

Irene, the black maid, answered the phone.

'He ain't here,' she said. 'Him and Miss Caroline, they gone to a church meetin'.'

He came out of the phone booth, limped past the shelves of mouthwash and deodorant, and bought an Ace bandage. Then he sat on a stool behind the pharmacy counter and taped up the ankle with a dexterity left from his football days at Tulane. He was halfway done when he caught sight of a woman through the glass fence. Thirty feet away, she stood there hesitating, looking around as if she were temporarily lost; small and dark-haired with a sensitive face and fragile gestures, and for a moment he thought it was Mollie. She sensed his eyes. She looked at him and smiled tentatively. Then she crossed to the counter and said something to the clerk. He kept his eyes on her, knowing she felt them. She looked back, smiled again. He had a fleeting fantasy of picking up the woman. The clerk handed over a carton of cigarettes. He watched her hands. It seemed important to see if she was wearing a wedding ring. She was. She was on her way out when the insight surfaced: He had the feeling he had been watching Mollie, without her knowledge, looking for some nameless clue to some nameless puzzle.

He dismissed it.

Barksdale had engendered more than one kind of paranoia tonight.

The parking lot at St John's Episcopal Church was filled. Through stained glass windows, tinted aureoles of light broke the windy darkness. Christ bleeding on the cross; St Francis in a sea of pigeons; Peter by the sea.

He parked and got out. The tape had relieved the worst of the pressure on the ankle. He started to walk, looking for Ritzy, the black midget caretaker who lived in the rectory, took care of the grounds, and collected tips for opening and closing car doors. He found him sitting on the hood of a white Lincoln, his stubby knees propped under his chin, puffing a cigarette and star gazing up at the church spire. When he saw Reuben, he jumped, the cigarette flying off into the darkness like a tiny red comet. Then he hopped down from the hood, and held himself erect, hardly taller than Reuben's belt buckle, turning up a flat shiny ageless face, his hair as white as cotton under the visored cap. They had him dressed in a red brass-buttoned coat. On Easter Sunday, Father Farnswell allowed him to occupy the last seat in the last pew, in order to celebrate the resurrection of the tall blond son of the God who had made Ritzy three feet tall and black.

'How are you, Ritzy?'

'Fair to middlin',' Ritzy said.

'What's going on inside?'

'Regular church meetin'. You lookin' for Mr Woods?'

Reuben peeled off a five-dollar bill. 'You think you could get him out here without disturbing anybody?'

Ritzy snapped up the bill and took off. Reuben watched him disappear through the side door of the church. In a minute he came back, hurrying across the parking lot in a short-strided, bow-legged gait. 'I got to him alright,' Ritzy said. 'But Miss Caroline, she say you wait your turn on God.'

'You got a place I can wait?'

'I could let you in the rectory.'

'That's fine,' Reuben said. 'When Mr Woods comes out, you tell him I'm waiting. How much longer you think God's gonna take?'

Father Farnswell's study was as sparsely furnished as a monk's cell. Two straight-back chairs, a hat rack, a framed rendition of 'The Last Supper,' and an orderly serviceable desk. There was one note of life. In the corner, by the window, was a neat, covered bird cage. Except for that, it was a virtuous room, cold and damp, as austere and ascetic as an aging virgin. His nostrils twitched. The room had been sprayed lately with a disinfectant that smelled vaguely of ether.

Reuben fixed his eyes on the bird cage. He imagined a parrot. A bright-colored bird with a sunflower beak, trained by a seaman. The bird shrieked filthy phrases at weepy matrons with tea cups.

He got up and crossed to the bird cage. He lifted the cover enough to look in. A pale canary slept on its perch like a glob of clotted cream.

He went back to the sofa and sat down. The air in the room was dead. He had a sense of dried bones and pressed flowers. He thought about Harris. He thought about men who were dedicated to the notion of God, and the rooms they lived in. He thought about men who earned their living by being guardians of the souls of others, Harris Greenblatt and Benjamin Farnswell. The power of prayer usurped the power of living, and created a dry, pompous vanity until life became a series of pronouncements, warnings, and laxatives. Dust. What kind of service was the abnegation of life ? He thought about Barksdale. Barksdale might have made it as a man of God. Anesthetised nerve ends and cold authority. But a passionless man didn't equal a saint. Bloddless rage was the kind that killed. He thought about himself. Fifteen years in the court-room had worn away his innocence, but not his passions. He could conceive of death, but never old age; never wistful sex, or impotence, or helplessness, or cheerless piety. He had never believed that, in the end, God would arrive with the impersonal touch of a night-duty nurse. God would come as a judge. One question : What the hell did you do with the life I gave you ?

He crossed to the desk and picked up the telephone and dialed his house. Leila answered.

'Miss Mollie ain't here.'

'Where is she ?'

'I don't know. She didn't say.'

'Are the boys alright ?'

'They asleep.'

'Thanks.' He hung up. He thought about the woman in the drugstore. He tried to imagine her in bed with a man. It wouldn't come to him. Instead he saw her seated at a dressing table applying cosmetics, drawing eyes, a mouth, in that detached concentration women had when they worked on their public masks. The notion of betrayal evaded him. It felt like a legal problem. The concept that emerged was destruction of property.

He crossed to the sofa and sat down. He heard the muted sound of organ music swell across the parking lot outside.

Ten minutes later he was sitting in Justin's study, looking out through the window to the courtyard that was filled with big-leafed plants and a fountain that sprouted from the mouth of a concrete dolphin.

Justin's desk was an English hunt table. Justin sat behind it, his back to the flashing fountain. On the other three walls, bookshelves were filled with law and southern history, and photographs of Caroline, two daughters, and Justin's father during his term as lieutenant governor in the late thirties.

Justin put on a pair of black spectacles and read through the contents of the manila envelope.

'You'll have to handle Watson,' Reuben said. Fred R. L. Watson, leading protester against the Rabin factory, listed as a friend of Gunston's and an associate of known Klan members.

'After Barksdale.' Justin took off the glasses and replaced the Xerox pages. His face had paled out. The freckles stood out like specks of dust. 'Give it to me from the beginning again.'

Reuben swallowed some Scotch. He looked at Justin over the rim of the glass. He thought about the fact that strangers knew each other instantly, but intimacy spawned a clouded vision. He thought about the fact that every need came packaged with its accompanying fear. The need for friendship came with the conception of treachery.

He went over it again. He watched Justin's face. He started with Sunday, getting the dynamite from Buster and taking it to Simmons' office where he picked up the lead on Gunston. He went through Maryville and his use of Willie. He recited the meeting with Barksdale verbatim. The hard part. The soft part. He included his own impressions and doubts. It was a chaste, concise version with no trimming.

Then he waited while Justin picked up his pipe, struck a kitchen match and pulled life into the bowl. When Justin looked up, his mouth was a thin, white line.

'What are you going to do?' Justin's voice was oddly quiet.

'I don't know. It doesn't smell right.'

'Why don't you consider simply cooperating?'

'Fifteen years,' Reuben said. 'When my instincts tell me something's wrong, I listen. You were one of them. You know how they work.'

'You want me to tell you how they work?'

'I want you to tell me what's wrong with it.'

'You provide the instincts, I provide the information.' Justin rose and crossed to the window. The fountain changed colors, from pink to green. 'One of these days I'm not going to have the information. Then what will you do?'

'I'll put you on a pension.'

Justin turned. 'Barksdale thinks you've trapped him. That's what's wrong with it.'

'Trapped him?'

'With the dynamite.'

'How?'

'It doesn't smell right to you that an F.B.I. man should put you through a hostile drama, then ask for help or money. And you're right. Barksdale doesn't know about your instincts. All he knows is you've put him in a box, and you've got an ex-F.B.I. man for a partner.'

'You think I've implicated you?'

'I assume Barksdale thinks you knew what to do because of me,' Justin said.

'What the hell did I do?'

Justin came back to the desk and sat down. He knocked out the pipe into a silver ash tray. Sparks of flame glowed in the brown moss. He studied the tobacco. 'I'm going to lay it out for you. Not because I want to, but because I've got no choice.' He looked up. His eyes looked like celluloid. 'But whatever I tell you, I'll deny if you ever call me on it. Do you understand that?'

'Yes.' Reuben could feel Justin's tension. Justin was a man who despised weakness, most of all in himself. Reuben could feel him wrestling with something.

'What I say may not make sense in the beginning,' Justin said. 'But in the end it will.' Behind his back, the dolphin sprouted a full rainbow. Reuben searched for a gesture of reassurance. He couldn't fine one. A handshake. A clap on the shoulder. Behind any of it would be fifteen years. What the years meant to both of them.

'Start with the Bureau,' Justin said. 'Start with Hoover. Point One. Start with what Hoover requires from his field offices. I've been there. I know. He requires *absolute loyalty to Hoover*. Beyond that, he requires a near-perfect conviction record.' He hesitated. 'Have you got that?'

Reuben nodded. 'Hoover doesn't like men who think for themselves, and he doesn't like arrests that don't result in convictions.'

'Right.' Justin got up and turned his back and looked out the window at the fountain which was turning from blue to green.

'Point Two,' he said. 'Hoover's the man who chases criminals and spies. Hoover's the man who infiltrated the Communist Party and the peace movement. But he's never broken the Klan. Hoover doesn't give one damn about civil rights and he doesn't care if the Klan operates or not. He's got a deal with the southern coalition in Congress to stay out of their business, which he did until Kennedy forced him down here in sixty-four. The F.B.I. office has been here four years. In four years there've been hundreds of incidents, all of them perpetrated on blacks, and not one criminal brought to trial. Which brings us to Point Three.' He turned around. 'Which is Barksdale.'

'The so-called Klucker specialist,' Reuben said.

Justin shook his head. 'He's a good agent,' Justin said. 'And he's also a decent man. But his hands are tied. All Hoover wants is as little trouble coming out of here as possible. He's got Hoover to satisfy. So if he gets mixed up in a case, he's got to be damned sure he's got enough evidence to give Hoover a conviction. That's not a simple thing to do in a Mississippi courtroom. So he stays on the safe side by remaining, in most cases, in the realm of "preliminary investigation." You pushed him off the fence when you walked into Simmons' office with the dynamite.'

'How?'

'The Civil Rights Act of 1960 allows the F.B.I. to enter a bombing case on the "rebuttable assumption" that the explosives were carried across state lines with the "knowledge or intent that such will be used to destroy or damage property." What was Simmons doing? Simmons was busy trying to pin the dynamite on a local source.'

'If Simmons could claim it was Monk's dynamite, then Barksdale was out of the case?'

'That's right.'

'Then either Simmons was helping Barksdale or Simmons wanted Barksdale out of his business?'

'Then you come up with the dynamite. Which Barksdale construes as pressure. Knowledgeable pressure. You put him right back in the case.'

'And Simmons doesn't like being topped, so he sends me off on a goose chase?'

'That's right,' Justin said. 'But you're dealing with Barksdale now. You're dealing with the Bureau. Hoover's the only man in this country who's held office for fifty years. Nobody plays at that kind of power.' For the third time he went back to the desk and sat down. Then he leaned across it. 'You want the Bureau on our neck? You want out files investigated? You want to be followed the way you were today? How about a tap on your phone? Or your old love affairs dug up? Is everything under your roof that pure?'

An image of Mollie flashed. Mollie undressing. A curve of neck. Breasts. Thighs. It melted into the image of the woman in the drugstore, then turned into Lea. 'I don't know,' Reuben said.

'That's how Hoover stays in office. He's got dossiers that go back to 1924.'

Reuben thought about a man who had spent fifty years poring over the sins of others. Hoover might have had the makings of a rabbi or a minister. 'Screw Hoover.'

Justin's face drained. Reuben watched the color recede. Together he and Justin had professional skeletons. Every partnership did. He wondered what Justin's personal skeletons were. Nobody lived by a moral blueprint. He could feel the tension coming out of Justin like a fever. Suddenly he realised what it was.

He rose and crossed to the desk. 'I want you to know something,' Reuben said.

'What?'

'I want you to know I'm not going to do anything to damage your political career. I know how you feel about it. It's your legacy. It's what you got from your father. I want you to know I understand that.'

Justin looked startled. 'I appreciate that.'

'You and me, we love this place,' Reuben said. 'Mollie can't understand that. Neither can Monk, or my mother – it's not their place. They don't feel the way we do. You stuck your neck out tonight for me because you know I'm fighting for my roots. I want you to know I feel the same way about yours.'

'You don't have to – '

'I want to see you up there in the governor's mansion. It's as good for me as it is for you.' Reuben grinned. 'I'll come for brunch. You can pour molasses all over my scrambled eggs.'

Justin fumbled with his pipe. 'That's a date.'

Reuben felt suddenly strange. 'Between the two of us, there's nothing we can't beat,' he said. But the steam had gone out of it. He waited. Justin opened the desk drawer and pulled out a can of tobacco. Finally he looked up.

'We're a good team,' Justin said soberly.

Reuben lowered himself back into the chair. The ankle had begun to throb again. Methodically Justin began to pack the pipe. Outside, the concrete dolphin was spitting another rainbow.

Justin struck a kitchen match. It blazed. The aroma of sulphur and pipe tobacco filled the study.

'How do we deal with Barksdale?' Reuben said.

Sixteen

MOLLIE took the highway back to Morningside Drive.

She went past the Williamsburg. There had been times in the past when she had stopped, with complicated elaborate stories of where she had been. The Williamsburg was closed.

Tonight, for the first time, she had said it. To Jean Aucoin. Aloud. *I don't love him.* Reuben. *I don't love him.*

At the end of Morningside, she came round the corner. The big colonial house was lit up at the top of the hill, looking as if it belonged to somebody else. Some mythical perfect woman of grandeur and serenity who had no need for erotic contacts meant to keep her from domestic death. She realised each new one surprised her, each new one more deeply alien than the one before. She wondered if she had settled for erosion instead of death.

Attica's jalopy was parked at the bottom of the hill. The driveway was empty, Reuben's car not back yet. When she came in through the kitchen, Attica and Leila were sitting at the table over chunks of corn bread and glasses of buttermilk. She realised she hadn't eaten since lunch in Maryville, but the sight provoked nausea and the irrational impulse to flee.

Reuben had telephoned. Once.

There was one other message. Zoe, her sister, had called from New Orleans. Important. Call back.

The children were asleep. Phil had an earache. Leila had tied a bag of camphor around his neck.

The rabbi hadn't come in yet.

'Thank you, Leila.' Her voice sounded hollow. Attica tipped a worn plaid cap. 'Good night, Attica.'

They left, those who took care of her. They were paid for it. What else did she know about them? Nothing. Why didn't she ask? She didn't want to know. The house, behind them, had an empty sound. *I don't love him.* She didn't want to know.

She dialed Zoe's number in New Orleans. Zoe's line was busy.

She climbed the stairs. When she reached the bedroom, she could hear Attica's car pulling off. She went into the bathroom and turned the water on in the tub full force, filling the tub to the brim. Then she lay there a long time in the steaming bath. She scrubbed away the sex, the smell of Jean Aucoin. The beginning of a decision was taking place in her. She knew it would come to her.

She got into the blue fleece robe and sat on the edge of the bed and dialed Zoe's number again. Zoe had married a doctor. She had married a lawyer. In the end they had both done what they were supposed to do. Maybe that was the sentence for having been born guilty of some terrible crime, born female; nobody had ever come out and said what the crime was, but it had been made perfectly clear what the price was. Their lives.

Zoe's line was still busy.

She went over to the window and looked out. Remembering the snow that had been there on Saturday. It never snowed in New Orleans. The need for snow had been her own invention; the need that had precipitated the idea of Switzerland; the failed flight of a crippled bird with the obsession to carry her babies with her.

For the first time it occurred to her that she might leave them behind.

Always, before, the thought of leaving had come with the image of snow: snow as a virginal blanket, a hibernation, a white death, a bright rebirth; deep snow, mountains of snow, blue-white and undefiled – she had dreamed of snow, the same dream, since the day Phil was born. But it had never before occurred to her that she might go alone.

Why not ? They weren't babies anymore.

In the birthing of babies, she had found her only release. In pregnancy. Didn't she owe them something for that ? The only times in her life she could remember peace, the peace made up of the absence of self-contempt, her body undeniably doing its job as a woman, impervious to all hallowed authority anywhere. It had been seven years before she became pregnant with Joe; her failure; seven years of battling with the body that continued to repudiate its own nature. She had dealt with those years in her own way. She had worked to put Reuben through law school; her penance, her absolution, her pact with virtue, for the guilt that had not emerged in full regalia until tonight.

Tonight she had said it. *I don't love him.*

And on its heels had come the knowledge that she had never loved him, was not capable of loving a man, any man, for whatever reason, whatever trick of fate.

She could see how it had happened. She had needed protection and safety, had been willing to pay for these things, had chosen Reuben deliberately, his value calculated in some secret inner computer. He was a certain kind of man who would accept tokens and symbols because he had no real knowledge of women, and so she had appeared to him to be a wise and mysterious and fragile girl. She had known she would marry him from the first moment she had set eyes on him. She hadn't known why, only that it was right, the perfect evasion of the thing she had been evading all her life. Now she could see how it had been. Sixteen, when she had met Reuben – a time for conceiving escape out of need and weakness, the things that had appeared to him as choice. Fraudulent.

It had caught up with her at Phil's birth.

Between Joe and Phil had been two miscarriages. A hundred trips to the gynecologist's office, her body laid out in a refrigerated room on a Formica table like a piece of meat. The sex organs hidden inside, dependent upon the certification of strangers. Another confrontation with special vulnerability, physical, the helpless nature of the female bound to the facts of biology. And the fear that her body would no longer do the thing that might save her.

Then, finally, she had been pregnant with Phil. And had known the peace, again, for that time. But the day after Phil was born, she could remember opening her eyes in the hospital room, and Reuben had been standing there, holding the roses and the jeweler's box with the diamond bracelet inside, and she had looked into his face and felt it for the first time – the blistering hatred. She had looked at his face and hated him.

It had not gone away. It had persisted. It had settled down upon her, an irrational bone-melting rage. The doctors had called it post-partum depression; it was not; it was the corrosion of hatred, eating at her. It had come from nowhere and then it focused itself on the sight of him, the slope of his shoulders, the color of his eyes, this stranger; this stranger who had mounted her, back to the earth, and violated her; this stranger, Reuben, whom she hated.

A year later, at the end of her second affair, the first insight came to her. It wasn't Reuben she hated; it was herself. And the hatred for Reuben, which she had believed was an inversion of love, had vanished. And left, in its place, nothing.

Nothing.

Nothing was what came out of the inability to love and the oppression of guilt.

She left the window.

She went down the hall to Phil's room. The room smelled of camphor. On a table, a pair of hamsters were circling in their cage. She went over to the big acorn-carved bed and bent over Phil and untied the camphor bag Leila had hung around his neck. Then she kissed him. He didn't stir. She wondered if she could leave him; how it would feel, without him; how he would feel, without her.

Then she went into Joe's room. The sound of his breathing told her he wasn't asleep. She came across the braided rug and sat down on the other twin bed, looking at him by the light of the winter moon coming in through the window.

'How's your life?' she said.

His eyes came open. 'Fine,' he said. 'I guess.'

'What's the matter?'

'Everybody treats me like a kid.'

'You're not a kid,' she said.

'I know what's going on around here. I know why the rabbi's here.'

'What do you know?'

'I know the bombing stinks.'

'I agree,' she said.

'I want to know what's going on.'

'I don't know any more about it than you do.' She realised that was true.

'Sure.' He didn't believe her; grown-ups were supposed to know. How would she feel, without Joe? How would he feel, without her?

'Nobody's going to let anybody hurt you.' She hoped that was true. 'You know that, don't you?'

'I guess so,' he said.

She leaned over and kissed his cheek. Then she tucked in the covers. 'You're a very special guy,' she said. 'You'll get your own crack at life. When you grow up and you're running the world, maybe there won't be so many mean things happening.'

'I hope not,' he said.

She went back into the bedroom and began to pack.

One suitcase. Sweaters. Warm things. She didn't know where she would go. Wherever it was, there would be snow.

She laid the suitcase on the bed and began to fill it. From a life of nineteen years she would take one suitcase. That seemed fair enough. To Reuben. The difficulty came in deciding what to put in it, what not to put in it. That decision had to be made first. The when and the where would come later.

When she had it packed, she set it in the back of her closet. She couldn't remember what she had packed. She had a vision of herself in some strange hotel room, snow outside the window, unpacking the suitcase with a kind of surprise; as if one of herself had packed it, but there would be another woman who would unpack it – with a tender pity and only a vague remembrance of the life left behind.

Later she would deal with the pain.

For now, it seemed settled.

She went downstairs into Reuben's study and picked out a volume from the encyclopedia. She looked up Vermont. The average snow-fall was ninety inches annually. More than two-thirds of the state was covered with forests. There were white-tailed deer. There was a place called Lake Champlain, a valley between the Green and Adirondack mountains.

There was a picture of children ice skating on the village green of a town called Norwich, in the Connecticut River valley near a place called White Junction. She liked the sound of it. White Junction.

She closed the book and put it back in the shelf.

It seemed settled.

She remembered how Reuben had reacted to Jesse's death. He had gone through valiance and guilt and denial and faith in God and anger. The grief had come later. He had laughed too much, or broken down and cried; he drank a great deal and made love to her with a ferocious despair – small acts of murder and orgasm meant to wipe out her existence and his. Then it was over. He got through it. He reacted badly to loss, but he knew how to get through it. She no longer blamed him. For anything. She had come with her own denials, bred to her, fed to her; nurtured with hothouse precision, she had bloomed into one of those perfect flowers without fragrance or texture. She had chosen a man who could not call her on it. Then she had gone looking for anyone who could.

She went into the kitchen to wait for Reuben.

She opened a can of chicory coffee she imported monthly by the case from New Orleans. *Béte noir*, it was called by the Louisiana Creoles. *Béte noir* – nightmare, black beast, dark forces. Her own.

She was dripping hot water by the tablespoonful through the grounds in the white enamel pot when she heard the back door open. But it wasn't Reuben who came into the kitchen, it was

Harris. The first time she had found herself alone with him since Saturday afternoon before the bombing. It seemed a long time ago. And there was no place to run.

'How is Frances?' she said. It didn't matter. She, Mollie, would be gone.

Harris shook his head. He looked tired and drained. His moustache looked like it had been chalked onto his face by a child. 'She keeps crying for Cherry. Maybe I'll get her another poodle. What do you think?'

'I don't know.' In Vermont it wouldn't matter. White Junction. There was integrity in the idea of living out her own truth; alone; no betrayal in it, ever again.

'I could use some coffee.' Harris sat down at the table. She poured two cups and sat down opposite him. She knew what was coming. It didn't matter.

'Tell me, Mollie, why did you quit teaching Sunday school?'

'I don't know.' She stirred in sugar and cream.

'That's no answer.'

She sipped the coffee. 'Faith comes from other places,' she said. It was somebody else's phrase. Her head was filled with phrases like that. Quotations she had read a long time ago. She could never remember the source. The child is father of the man. It is better to be the tail of a lion than the head of a jackass.

'What kind of arrogance is that?' His left eyebrow shot up.

'Maybe Judaism is the arrogance.' She had read that too. Somewhere. She felt a sudden clarity of thought.

'You don't know anything about Judaism.'

'It's up for grabs,' she said. 'Nobody knows what it is anymore.'

'The concept of one God,' Harris said. 'The concept of man's responsibility to that God.' The eyebrow came down. He leaned across the table. 'The basic concept doesn't change.'

'One God,' Mollie said. 'The Jews came along and said to everybody, your gods are no good, only mine, only my God who has chosen the Jews. If the Israelites had the only God, why didn't they win all their wars, why did they suffer, why didn't their only God make it easier for them?'

'They displeased Him.'

'Obviously they had to be guilty of something,' Mollie said. 'Why else would their one and only powerful God deal out defeat and persecution? So to hang on to their arrogance of one God, they invented guilt.'

'You'd better do some thinking, Mollie,' Harris said.

'I don't want any more,' she said. 'I don't want any more *guilt*.'

'What's bothering you, Mollie?'

'Nothing.'

'I'd like to help you.' He reached across the table. She saw he was staring at her.

'Don't touch me,' she said.

'Mollie – '

She could feel the clarity become fear. Like Joe's fear of the bombing. The nightmares of children. As if she had defied her father and now she must disappear. She wanted Harris to say to her what she had said to Joe: *Nobody's going to let anybody hurt you.*

'Leave me alone,' she said.

Then she fled.

When the phone began to ring, she didn't know how long she had been lying across the bed in the darkness, the pillow soaked with tears. But she knew she had fought and lost. In a land of chill, damp temperatures and swaying palm trees, telephone poles and a tangle of trolley-car tracks, she had been riding somewhere. She had been able to hear the night clanging of the trolley that had carried her into a hopscotch drawing, three blocks two arms a block a pair of mother arms: *Don't kiss my hand, it's not nice to kiss people's hands.*

The phone rang again.

She thought: You have either been very crazy and you are shifting into some kind of sanity, or you are cracking up.

The phone rang.

She crawled across the bed and picked it up.

Zoe's voice came through the wire with its familiar ring of cracked crystal. The voice was like Zoe, beautiful and fragile and slightly off key.

'Mollie – ?'

'Hellow, baby.' *Baby*. Zoe wasn't a baby anymore. The capsule of adolescent defiance had long been spent. Its aftermath was an incoherence meant to fracture reality into brilliant pieces in order to make it bearable.

'I don't want to bother you, Mollie.'

'It's alright,' Mollie said. In the past few years, Zoe's self-deprecating fragility verged on hysteria or collapse.

'Farrell picked up Maw-maw,' Zoe said.

It took Mollie a moment. Farrell was New Orleans' D.A., Maw-maw was Zoe's mother-in-law. 'What do you mean he picked her up?'

'It's all over the front page of the evening papers. "D.A. Cracks Down on Abortion." Her name and everything. Mrs Myrtle Stein.' It came out in one breath.

'What happened?'

'I can't believe it. My husband's a gynecologist and his mother hits the papers as an *abortionist*. I mean, that's really Freudian. You know? And all these years I thought she was a midwife. Sol says Farrell's trying to build an image so he's going around picking up the small fry. I was thinking about going down to talk to him. I met him at Zack's on Mardi Gras, you know the Mardi Gras party Zack always gives, and he was really looking at me. But Farrell's six-foot-four. I mean, that's a little too *much*, don't you think?'

'How is Sol taking it?' Mollie said.

'You know how poor they were? How can he do that? I mean, she's the one who put him through med school. I can't believe it. He's pretending she's *not his mother*. There's a lot of Steins in New Orleans, you know? He's telling everybody he never heard of her. I mean, he owes her *something*, doesn't he?'

'I don't know.'

'He says when he was little, he never went to the same school twice, they were always running from the creditors. I can't believe it. He says they were so poor he used to go out and look for coal along the railroad tracks, and one day a freight killed his dog. I mean, he could cry for that dog. What about his *mother*? He says he was always discriminated against by the best Jewish families because all their daughters had gone to Maw-maw for abortions. It all just came pouring out of him. I don't know what to do.'

'Does she have a lawyer?' Mollie said.

'I called Paw-paw,' Zoe said. 'You know what he does now? He bought that bar out by the waterfront. The longest bar in New Orleans. He makes book. I can't believe it. He said: "We got to find the man in Baton Rouge to pay off. I'll get up the lettuce. We can't leave her in the joint." I don't even know what he talking about. He said he knew Sol wouldn't want to stick his neck out. Sol's got respectable, he said. I told him I'd call my brother-in-law in Mississippi. I didn't know what else to say. But I can't talk to Reuben. You know that. Reuben scares me. I thought, maybe – you know? I mean, I don't want to *bother* you.'

'I'll talk to Reuben.'

'She's not a bad woman,' Zoe said. 'I mean, I always liked her. You know? I know she doesn't have an education and you know how she *looks*, half-Spanish and half-French and all of that, but

152

everybody doesn't have to be kosher, do they? I mean, even Daddy ate ham in restaurants.'

'How are they taking it?' Mollie said.

'They keep calling every five minutes to reassure me that it's not Sol's fault,' Zoe said. 'They keep saying Sol's a *good man.* They're terrified I'm going to leave Sol and I'll never find anybody else to take care of me. Mama keeps telling me it's really not important Sol doesn't sleep with me anymore. There are *other* things. I can't believe it. *What* other things?'

'Security,' Mollie said. 'Second-generation American. We were programmed to get in.'

'You're so smart, Mollie. You always were. I don't know why you're so good to me. I mean, I just can't stand the idea of Mawmaw in jail. You know? She is Jason's grandmother.'

Mollie thought about Jason, Zoe's only child. Also fragile. And fractured. And sensitive. *What do you see with?* Mollie had once asked him. *My shoes.* Jason had said. *I put on my shoes and they take me for a walk and I see things.*

'Don't worry anymore' Mollie said. 'I'll talk to Reuben and I'll call you tomorrow.'

'What time?' Zoe said.

'I don't know.'

'I met a man from Neiman-Marcus.' Zoe said. 'I'm having lunch with him. He thinks I'm *incredible.* I think he's got problems. I mean I'm not incredible. I can't understand it. I always attract weak men. What do you think?'

'I'll call after lunch' Mollie said.

'I wish you needed something' Zoe said. 'I wish you needed something I could do for you. I love you Mollie.'

The image that came to her mind was the victory garden. During the war. They had grown radishes and lettuce and string beans and corn in the vacant lot in back. Zoe had been eight. She had been ten. Her father had been thirty-eight, too old and too many dependents to be drafted, but he had enlisted anyway. She and Zoe had sat on the back steps popping string beans into a small enamel pan.

'I love you, too,' Mollie said. 'Now don't worry anymore.'

She hung up.

She sat on the edge of the bed and lit a cigarette and teetered between the urge to laugh and the desire to cry.

The two of them had sat on the back steps snapping beans and Zoe had asked solemnly: *Do you think the Nazis will come here?*

Of course not, silly!

What are you going to do, Mollie?

I'm going to join the Girl Scouts and wear a uniform too.

Tomorrow, she would ask Reuben to go down to New Orleans and get Myrtle Stein out of jail.

She went into the bathroom and pawed through the drawer. The vial of tranquilisers was empty. But there were still a couple of sleeping pills. She swallowed both of them.

She remembered falling into bed. The last thing she remembered was lying there and sensing Reuben's presence as he came in and crossed over to the bed and stood there, looking down at her, for a very long time. Then, from the bottom of a deep, dark well, she heard him say:

My God, Mollie – I'm so lonely. . . .

Seventeen

IN HIS SLEEP the pain had felt like the throbbing tension of sex. But when he woke he found it was the ankle. And Mollie was gone, the bed empty beside him.

He imagined her outline on the sheet. He imagined her turning over, smiling, giving out the scent of lemon and spring earth. He imagined the two of them nuzzling and twining like soft, warm animals. He imagined the spontaneous thrust of entering her, like plunging into blindness in search of brilliant oblivion.

It wasn't like that.

It had not been like that since the new and fumbling innocent years of beginnings.

He dressed. The ankle was swollen. He couldn't get his shoe on. He limped down the hall wearing one shoe and one bedroom slipper. The boys were still asleep.

She was standing at the stove wearing canvas jeans and a V-necked fisherman's sweater, pouring boiling water from a copper teakettle through the white enamel pot. The kitchen was filled with the smell of the chicory coffee and the damp earth of newly watered windowsill plants. She had set the table for two with yellow pottery.

He came up behind her and slid his arms around her waist. Her hair smelled fresh, like a clean breath of wind through his nostrils. She turned around. Her face was milk white. Her features looked as if they had been plastered onto a mask. Then it slipped, like a Modigliani painting, and fireflies and shadows went darting across her eyes. He had the sense of a vital, tenuous moment as slim and evasive as a needle's eye. Her eyes filled with tears. She began to weep, silently, against his chest. He held her. He stroked her hair.

'What is it?' he said.

A small, almost inaudible noise came from her, like a bleat. Then she pulled back. She shook her head. He handed her a hand-kerchief. She blew her nose like an obedient child.

'What happened to your foot?'

'I sprained my ankle.'

'You should have it X-rayed.'

'I'm going to.'

She gave him back the handkerchief without meeting his eyes. 'Do you want an ice pack?'

'No, thank you.'

'I made coffee. Would you like breakfast?'

'Juice and coffee.' He sat down at the table, old and scarred, purchased nineteen years ago in a junk shop near Ole Miss for seven dollars. A memento of crazy joy and thunderstorms. He had memories of cracks of lightning and tears as thick as rain. He wondered how they had come to live in the surcease, which was loneliness.

She set a glass of orange juice in front of him. 'I haven't seen you,' she said.

'We were at the funeral all day yesterday.' He was suddenly aware that he hadn't spoken to her yesterday. The thought increased his feeling of loneliness.

She brought the coffeepot to the table. Then she sat opposite him, her back to the window, the winter light catching reddish glints in her hair. He had a vision of her naked, sunning herself in some private hell. He felt it as a premonition. He dropped two saccharine tablets into his empty cup.

'Any news about the bombing?' she said.

'No.' One's own lies were tolerable. Protective.

She poured the coffee. The black liquid hit the saccharine tablets and sizzled. He could feel a restling going on in her.

'I drove out to the rabbi's house this morning,' she said. 'The sun was just coming up. It was terrible.' A shudder went through her.

'You shouldn't have done that.'

'I'm trying to face – whatever there is,' she said. An odd look came over her face. He felt suddenly claustrophobic. He knew something was coming that he didn't want to deal with.

'I've got a lot on my mind, Mollie,' he said. 'I've got the Higgins case to get together, and the Rabin factory, and the bombing – ' He shook his head. 'It's a lot to handle.'

'I packed a suitcase last night,' she said. 'I have to leave.'

'Switzerland again?'

'No. I'm not going to try to take the children. I'm going alone. I can't live with my own lies anymore. We don't have a marriage.'

'Nineteen years is a marriage,' he said.

'Listen to me – ' she said. He could see the strain and determination pinching at her eyelids and the corners of her mouth. 'It's not your fault,' she said. 'It's my own flaw. There's something wrong with me.'

'Do you want to see a psychiatrist?'

'I'm having an affair.' She looked at him directly, unblinking. He felt the blow as outrageous, followed by a numbness that disguised pain into a high-pitched ringing whistle. He picked up the spoon and stirred at his coffee. In the void of silence, time crawled.

The first coherent thing that came to his mind was Barksdale, and Justin's voice last night: *Is everything under your own roof so damned pure?* He remembered the phone call he had made from Father Farnwell's study. The painting 'The Last Supper' stuck in his brain. *Miss Mollie ain't here,* Leila had said. He felt a part of him struggling with a primitive fury, the desire to kill her. But another part insisted on reason; there had been his own affair with Lea; there had been the nights of letting off steam down in New Orleans at Zack Rosen's; there was the objective reality of physical betrayal to be seen in a perspective of sophistication. The third part of him was seared by pain, the conception of loss, the need for her.

He looked up finally. 'Who is he?'

'It doesn't matter. I don't love him. And it isn't the first affair.'

The second blow followed the first, with precision and the absence of cruelty. He felt honesty in her, and pain, and he recognised the integrity of risk. He understood that he had always counted on her weakness. Seventy-two hours ago, his life had been solid and intact. Now he had a sense of the beginnings of a landslide, the pieces of his life beginning to fall away.

'Who is he? What's his name?'

'It's not important what his name is. He just happened to be there.'

'What's important?'

'I don't want to hurt you more – that's important. I'm sorry. I know my timing's lousy. I don't want to make it harder for you.'

'This new affair – how long?'

'Since Saturday,' she said. He realised she had begun the affair on the day of the bombing.

'How many others?'

'It doesn't matter. They were all the same man. All for the same reason.'

'What reason?'

'I don't know,' she said. 'All I know is I can't keep living like this anymore. I went out there this morning. I looked at it. It frightened me. But there was something else. I stood there looking at that bombed-out crater and it seemed as if it hadn't just happened. I felt it had been there all along. And maybe we had planted grass over it. Maybe we were pretending to have a picnic on the grass. And that was our marriage. That was the way we live. Both of us knowing it was there underneath, all the time, so it was a relief to look at it. And I knew, then, I couldn't live it any longer.'

Through his own numbness, he felt her pain. 'Is there anything I can do?'

'I don't know. I don't know if we have anything left. It's not your fault.'

He stared for a long time into the black pool of untouched coffee. Finally he said, 'I need some time. I need some time to think about it.'

'Why don't you hate me?'

'I don't hate you.'

'How *do* you feel?'

'I don't know.'

He got up. He left the kitchen. He limped across the entrance hall and pulled his overcoat from the closet. He got into it and buttoned each button slowly, carefully. When he came back, she was still sitting there.

'I'll see you,' he said.

She sent him a painful smile. 'Have a good day.'

He started across the kitchen towards the back door.

'Reuben – '

He stopped. He turned around. He waited. She didn't move.

'I hate to bother you – '

157

'That's alright.'

'It's Zoe,' she said. 'Zoe called last night. Sol's mother's in jail. Farrell's gone on a cleanup campaign. He picked her up for doing abortions.'

'Zoe wants me to help Sol's mother?'

'I know you can't – '

'Call Zoe. Tell her I'll take care of it.'

'Thank you.'

'Have a good day,' he said.

Book Two

Eighteen

HE HAD BEEN nine years old when he watched a chicken snake devour a live chicken. Fascinated and repelled, he had been rooted by fear to a spot of dirt in the chicken house where he had been sent by his grandmother to gather eggs. The pullet's head disappeared first. Then the body. Last to vanish had been the two waving clawed feet. He had been able to see the shape of the chicken in its belly as the snake moved off through a knothole. The whole thing had taken three minutes.

Mollie's act of murder had taken less time than that.

The Cadillac hurled him at ninety miles an hour towards the Louisiana state line. It was three in the afternoon, and the sun was out, but he felt cold rage whistling through him like night wind on the desert. The protective armor of numb despair was gone. Rising, in its place, was a full-blown attack of madness.

He reached out and touched the old man's cane. It lay on the seat beside him. The act was an attempt at deliberate sanity, self-rescue. He ran his fingers over the crudely carved stick, feeling it as a talisman, proof of his belief that the life of a man begins before birth and ends long after death. The notion of immortality had become vital. He had seen it happen to others. Continuity became vital when a man lost control of his immediate life. Others turned to lawyers, like himself, who handed out reason; or to doctors who dispensed pills; or to priests who doled out arbitrary concepts of God. For himself, there had always been the old man.

He had left the house this morning and stopped at the Williamsburg.

He had hobbled in. He had asked Frieda to go home and get the cane. She had said, 'What cane?' He had heard himself shouting,

159

'The only thing Papa ever got from the old man and I've been paying for it since the day I was born!'

He had felt something let go in him and he knew it was raw because Frieda was suddenly crying. He found himself hanging onto her and holding her and they had both been shocked by that.

The car raced towards New Orleans.

Hatred and self-pity vied for his soul. He cursed Mollie.

Yesterday he had been a man whose legacy was threatened. This morning, his marriage had shattered. By extension, tomorrow, what else would be at stake?

He thought about Barksdale. He cursed Barksdale. He cursed himself for taking it on. Why the hell had he assumed responsibility for the whole damned Jewish population of Holmesdale? His identity had never been rooted in Judaism. He hurtled towards New Orleans knowing that neither God nor Myrtle Stein had anything to do with it. For the first time in his life he was fleeing. He had been in charge of everything. At the moment he was no longer in charge of his own pain.

In the rear-view mirror he looked back. There was no one behind him. He had an image of Barksdale tracking Mollie. Taking notes. Dates, times, names, places – pain categorised in a small pocket-sized F.B.I. notebook.

There were dizzy streaks of light on his eyelids. He wanted to kill her. He felt nausea and the urge to murder and the fear of death.

She was the mother of his children.

All deep emotions, in the end, were ludicrous. He wanted to kill her. Instead he was on his way to get drunk, to get laid, to lose his sensibilities.

This morning, from the Williamsburg, he had put in a call to Zack. The phone rang for a long time. Zack, out in the Quarter every night with B. V. Grossman and an assortment of girls, never got up before noon.

'It's Reuben.'

'Screw you, it's the middle of the night.'

'Screw you, it's important.' He pictured Zack in the French Quarter bedroom with the mirrored ceiling, sitting on the edge of the round velvet bed scratching a bearlike chest, then laying his hand on the satin-skinned ass of some version of a *Playboy* centerfold. Zack's life had once included a six-week marriage to a schoolteacher, but that had been a long time ago.

'What is it, you sonofabitch?'

Reuben laid out the saga of Myrtle Stein. Zack, like everybody else, had seen the headlines.

'I want to make a deal with Farrell.'

'What kind?' Zack said.

'What kind of man is he?'

'Ambitious.'

'Find out what he'll go for. Money, broads, an exchange of favors? Tell him my partner's got the governor in his pocket.'

'I'll talk to him.'

'Don't go back to the broad.'

'Tell Mollie to hang onto her chastity belt,' Zack said.

The car rushed forward, companion to glacial rage.

She had gone against everything.

They had both lived their lives in the South, wed to the white-womanhood-purity myth, the foundation of southern existence.

Mollie had abandoned her pedestal.

For whom? For how many? Why? How had their marriage become one of those deadly relationships based on an exchange of lies?

And why hadn't he seen it? felt it? How had he gotten locked into a blind vision? He had seen her as Zack saw her. Chaste. He had seen her as feminine without being female. He had seen her as intelligent without being brainy. He had seen her as there when he needed her and wrapped in cotton when he didn't. She had her children and her cameras and her role as his wife.

That was over.

Bitch.

He had loved her. He had believed in that. There had been the girl on the sea wall who had told him he could do anything he wanted to do. He had believed in her first, then in himself afterwards.

The rage turned hot, then cold again. In the desert of his mind, he heard the sound of coyote laughter and he saw her as carrion for vultures.

He saw himself growing old, without Mollie.

The interdependency of people grew intricate and complicated over a number of years. But was that love? What the hell was love? Not a manly preoccupation, thinking about love. Love belonged in movies and women's magazines. Society rewarded those citizens who loved the least. He hadn't invented the rules of the marketplace. He sold his time and his talent in order to pay for the

11   161

right to give it away to men like Higgins. But there was always a charge. Society extracted its price. Most of any man's energy didn't go into *love*. It went into maintaining a tenuous footing in the shifting earth of the outside world.

Last night he had asked Justin, 'How much money?'

Justin had said, 'How the hell should I know what an informer costs on today's market?

'Make a guess.'

'Forty, fifty thousand. Maybe more, maybe less.'

Reuben considered the sum. 'For that kind of money, they're going to want a guarantee. How the devil can Barksdale guarantee a conviction?'

'He can't.'

'They're not going to go for a subsidy.'

'There's a simple solution,' Justin said.

'What?'

'You tell Barksdale you'll pay for convictions – or bodies.'

Last night the idea had shocked him. Today, the idea of bodies had begun to make sense.

Mollie had struck a match in a kerosene-drenched field.

This morning, while he waited for Frieda, he had seen the two newspaper items. Side by side. The announcement that the F.B.I. was making a 'preliminary investigation' of the Greenblatt bombing was printed alongside a piece that named Reuben Buchman as defense attorney in the John Tyler Higgins case.

He had looked at the items, and he had imagined the voice on the telephone. He had imagined the face that went with the voice, reading the items side by side. And he heard it again. *Count your days, you dirty Jew.*

Distortion had taken him over. The need was for murder. Anybody's murder. The murder of Mollie was justifiable and impossible. He would settle for Gerald Gunston III. Or his own temporary death. The night ahead in New Orleans which would bring a blotting out of his senses.

He hung onto the cane.

He crossed the state line. He hit the ribbon of road that Huey Long had built in the thirties. Long was a man who had believed in immortality. He had left few monuments behind – the university and the sea wall, a couple of hospitals, a spillway, and the New Orleans airport. B. V. Grossman's father had been one of Long's lieutenants, later federally indicted for income tax evasion along with Isaac Katzman, who owned the Regent Hotel and who had become famous for changing his clothes every hour on the hour down to the color of the carnation in his buttonhole. B. V.'s father had begun as a dry goods merchant and had ended up as president of the levee board. Four years later, the railroad terminal had been named for him, and he had set about to put his name on every possible part of the terminal including the plumbing fixtures.

Years later, when the name was changed, it had cost the state a hundred grand to wipe out the name of Grossman.

B. V. had inherited enough money from his father never to have to worry about money again. Reuben saw himself in the dining room of the Creole cottage on Toulouse Street, sitting with Zack and B. V. over Black Bertha's jambalaya. *How about five grand apiece for a couple of corpses?*

Whose corpses?

Gerald Gunston's. And Mollie's.

I don't hate you, he had said. He had said, *Call Zoe.* He had been saying she was still his wife. It was still his home. He was still in charge.

Another lie.

The road rushed under him. He was consumed by bitter, vindictive pride.

He had gotten through the day.

How? He had driven to Sinai. How? He had limped down the corridor to Emergency, where an X-ray told him what he already knew: the ankle was sprained, not broken. He had sat in a chair with the cane beside him while an intern had taped it up.

'Where do I know you from?'

'I assisted Dr Schraft on the Greenblatt operation.'

'You're not from around here?'

'Louisiana,' he said. 'Louisiana cajun.'

For no reason at all, he had wanted to hit him.

He had gone upstairs to see Frances instead. Her left arm was in a cast up to her shoulder. It was an airless gray room with a bolted window that looked down on the parking lot and a radiator underneath going full blast. Frances' face was a match for the ivory of the wilted gladiolas next to her bed.

'How are you?'

She turned a pair of vague, empty eyes on him. 'Fine, just fine,' she said, with blank toneless cheer. He was conscious of women, and lies. He saw that her lies were gratuitous, meaningless. 'It's a

163

good vacation,' she said. One lie following the other because she didn't believe it was possible to live with the truth of things, and for those who were helpless, it wasn't. But she gave him something, the thing he had come to get. A reaffirmation of his own power and the right to use it.

He had still been in control of himself.

In the lobby, he got change, then locked himself in the phone booth and went through a dozen dimes. Barksdale, whatever he was doing, hadn't gotten around to tapping the pay phone at Sinai.

He set up a meeting. Tomorrow night.

He selected fewer than a dozen men who, together, were worth ten million dollars. A year ago, most of them had raised the money for the construction of the new temple. Tomorrow night, he'd inform them they'd have to raise the money to protect it.

He had completed the last phone call when the one thing Barksdale hadn't mentioned became suddenly obvious. Justin hadn't laid it out either. Why not? Fewer than twelve men sharing a common concern and worth ten million dollars might make more than a ripple on the Potomac. He went over a mental list. There were Jews on the Supreme Court and Jews of both parties in Congress and Jews who wielded other kinds of power in Washington. None of them immune to a complaint by an organised body like, for instance, the Anti-Defamation League. *I have a message for you,* Barksdale had said. *Directly from the Bureau. To your people. There's concern in Washington. We want you to know that.* The dynamite had been the accidental catalyst. The real issue was the fact that Hoover didn't want an organised southern Jewish complaint stirring the waters of Washington. He began to understand what his real handle was.

Screw them. The Jews.

He cursed Harris.

The second year he had been at the military academy in Gulfport, a hurricane had struck the Gulf Coast. He could remember the odd, deceptive quality of the quiet that had preceded it. And then the rumbling echo of muted sound as it had moved across the water. Then it had struck, for only minutes, and gone on, leaving wreckage and debris behind.

The bombing had been like that.

This morning, Mollie had been like that.

It had become one event in his mind. He had looked at her face as she told him about driving over to Maple Street. There were few things in his life he had ever seen with such clarity. He had listened. He had answered her. Underneath had been the bellowing roar of pain and loss and fury and betrayal.

The road rushed through the Louisiana swamp. The sun sliced in behind hackberry and cottonwood. A flock of blue geese, down for the winter, streaked up from the Spanish moss shoreline.

Who were they? How many? At what point in their life had the affairs begun?

Late afternoon sunlight set fire to the cypress ghost forests as the car sped past. Somewhere he had learned that the cypress had been killed by the inroads of salt water. The Louisiana swamps didn't drain into the Mississippi. They served as catch basins for overflow waters, and as hunting grounds for muskrat and alligator, and as fishing beds for croakers and sheepshead and illegal shrimp. Somewhere he had learned all of that.

From Mollie.

When he met her, she had been studying photography at Newcomb, the women's campus adjacent to Tulane. Her project for the year had been the cajuns. It was Mollie who taught him that the cajuns were descendants of the royalist families who had been driven from Nova Scotia after the French Revolution and given grants of Louisiana land by Great Britain. She had driven out to the swamps with her camera and found beauty in the peculiar isolation, in the poverty and ignorance of white men who were little better off than the blacks who worked in the sugarcane fields.

From Mollie he had learned all of that. And something else. *You can do anything if you really want to.*

Screw her.

The road careened through the swamps, in and out of the night shadows thrown by the Spanish moss. Gnats plastered the windshield with instant death.

He forced his mind away from Mollie. He thought about Zack and B. V. He thought about screwing and gambling and the sybaritic existence.

B. V. Grossman had once been married to a red-headed mambo instructor who had run off with a black drummer.

It was a funny story. It didn't make him smile.

He couldn't let go of Mollie.

It wasn't anybody he knew. Was it? Why had he assumed she had slept only with strangers? *They were all the same man,* she had said. *All for the same reason.* What reason? *I don't know.*

It was Monk.

How could it be Monk? Why not? They were both from New

Orleans. She didn't even like Monk. That's what she *said*. What she said meant nothing. Mollie. Bitch and liar.

He went back over the sound of Monk's voice on the phone this morning.

'What's it about?' Monk said.

'You'll find out at the meeting like everybody else.'

'Hey – this is your buddy you're talking to.'

'I'll see you tomorrow night.'

'Wait a minute. I want to tell you. I put Buster on as night watchman. You think that's okay?'

'Hell no.'

'He's your nigger, isn't he?'

'That's right. And I'm telling you. Get somebody else.'

'It's none of my business,' Monk said, 'but you sound like hell.'

It wasn't Monk.

Forget it.

Forget Mollie. Forget the insanity of trying to figure out *who* and *when* and *where* and *why*?

Keep your eyes on the road and one hand on the old man's cane. In less than an hour, you'll be in New Orleans. In less than an hour you can wipe out all of it.

It was Justin.

He thought about Justin. Justin and Mollie. Women liked Justin. They liked his carefull gallantry. They liked the goddamned pipe. Justin was a challenge. His cold, passionless exterior inspired female fantasies of cracking through to some long-buried, heretofore hidden depth.

His wife and his partner, that was classic. Why not?

Because Justin wouldn't sleep with a Jew.

How did he get to that? He felt it was true. Why? Because Justin hadn't touched on the possibility of Jewish pressure in Washington? Because Justin had done a lot of talking about Hoover and none about Jews? Because Barksdale had called them *your people* and Justin hadn't called them by any name at all?

The night of the bombing he had gone directly to Justin. What instinct had kept him from telling Justin about Mollie this morning? Pride? Vanity? Self-protection?

He had told himself it was because Justin had his hands full. Because the Vernon Powell hearing had been set for this afternoon and if the judge ruled for Powell, which was likely, a court order would be issued to get the African Republic militants off the land, which might be tantamount to a sheriff's license for a bloodbath.

And there had been a call from Rabin, who had read about the

Greenblatt bombing and was having second and third thoughts about putting a factory where there might be trouble.

And there had been another moment of cold anger because Justin had read the announcement about the Higgins case.

And he had wanted to shout: *I'm as good as anybody. I'm a Jew and a southerner, and I run my life according to my own conscience.* And then, for the first time, it had struck him that maybe he was neither. Neither Jew nor southerner. Maybe he had lived his life somewhere in the abyss between. There was a word for it. Alienation.

There were gentiles who believed that Jewish women, like the Chinese, were made sideways. Or that Jewish women were as passionate as blacks.

Maybe Justin was one of those.

Justin hated Kornfield. Kornfield was a Jew.

When Justin had built his Federalist house, he hadn't even asked Monk to bid on the contract.

None of Justin's personal friends were Jews.

But Justin had made the call to the governor for Myrtle Stein. And the governor had called Baton Rouge, and Baton Rouge had set it up through Zack who had contacted Farrell, and there would be a governor's pardon waiting for Myrtle Stein when he got there.

Justin had done that, hadn't he?

In the same way he had sat it out with Justin in the hospital in Harrisburg when Justin's mother had been operated on, last year, for cancer. Minna, small and gray as a mouse in the hospital bed, and both of them, like brothers, lying to her, and he had filled the room with flowers.

It wasn't Justin.

Forget it.

Forget Mollie. Bitch and liar.

Forget Justin and the law practice. Forget Barksdale and Harris and the Jews. Screw all of it.

The road hurled itself out of the swampland.

Ahead of him, the white concrete strip, shimmering blue and purple in the sundown, stretched out flat and clear all the way to New Orleans.

Nineteen

HE REACHED the Quarter at dusk. Ten square blocks dedicated to jazz and sex and drugs and rites of passage. The area between Canal Street and Ursuline Avenue was second in his psyche only to Maryville. He believed every man had two versions of home – the place of his birth and the place of his loss of innocence. The first was sacred; the second had remained an ongoing force in his underlife.

He drove through the narrow cobblestone streets, the shops closed and the nightclubs not open yet, a few scattered pedestrians, but the cars bumper to bumper along the curb. During the day, the filth and the litter turned the Quarter into a seedy old bum selling pencils to tourists; at night, it became a garish old whore with a knife in her garter. But twilight was kind as candlelight to a bad face lift. The time that was neither day nor night settled onto the place that was no longer old or new; the one brief hour when Jackson Square and the St Louis Cathedral and the wrought-iron balconies of the Pontalba Apartments claimed their dinity and identity by temporarily ceasing to look like glossy postcard photographs.

He went three times around before he found a parking spot, on Toulouse, in front of a school that had been recently replastered and painted magenta, one of the colors acceptable to the Quarter Commission which dictated all renovation.

He was a block and a half from Zack's. He got out of the car, carrying the cane, and began to walk. The air was damp. It always had been. Rain was always just going to start or just over, and in between everything mildewed and rotted. In New Orleans, he was always conscious of air, the moisture moving along with him like an invisible presence.

The presence was Mollie.

How many times had he walked these streets with Mollie?

He reached for a cigarette. The pack was empty. He crumpled it and threw it into the gutter.

Get the hell away from me, bitch. Then he realised he had said it

aloud. Behind him, someone giggled. He turned. An undersized
kid beat it around the corner. From a candy store window, two
dozen stuffed black cotton Aunt Jemimas grinned at him.

He went inside. A man buried in glandular fat sat just inside the
doorway reading a newspaper. Reuben asked for a pack of cigarettes. The man sighed, then got up ponderously and went behind
the counter. Reuben reached for his money clip.

The money clip was gone.

The kid who had giggled behind him? Bastard. Was it? He
went through his day. He hadn't even gone out for lunch. The
Higgins tapes had come in the mail and he had spent two hours
listening to Kornfield seesaw between being a hawk with a hammer and a Hebrew schoolteacher who wanted to be Christ.
Luanne had brought him a sandwich. He hadn't reached for the
money clip all day. *Little bastard.* Mollie had given him the clip.
His initials in gold. Christmas, 1965. Nearly two hundred dollars
in it. His day for loss. Not loss. Theft. All kinds of theft.

He dug in his pocket and found enough change to pay for the
cigarettes.

He tipped the fat man with his last quarter. Some perverse need
to strip himself and walk the rest of the way without a dime in his
pocket. The act was meaningless. Zack would cash a check for
him. He nursed the fantasy of divesting himself of everything and
joining the ranks of the degenerate Quarter bums. He understood
the urge. Fury turned inward.

Zack's Creole cottage sat directly on the street, its gabled roof
outlined against a moss-colored sky. He stopped in front. The
clapboard sported a new coat of gray paint. Long storm shutters
were bolted shut from the inside to ensure quiet and privacy. Once
inside, the outside world would cease to exist.

He entered what appeared to be an alley. Three feet off the
street he was stopped by a wrought-iron gate adorned with a
design of pineapples, the New Orleans symbol of hospitality;
Mollie had taught him that. Damn Mollie. He pushed a button.
The buzzer grated. The gate swung open, then shut behind him.
He went down a flag-stoned walk and came out into the lush inner
courtyard that was the beginning of the seduction. Here one shed
reality. Here a man who owned one lame black servant and a case
of brandy could sit out a lifetime. The house on Toulouse Street
had always engendered the notion that everything was possible
and nothing was worth doing.

On the other side of the court were the six apartments that had
once been slave quarters, connected, by an additional wing, to the

main house. He looked up through the gallery. Behind the second door on the left, Lea had hung herself with the jump rope. He couldn't make himself feel anything. As if Mollie had used up his quota of pain.

He tapped on the glass panes of the French doors with the old man's cane. When they opened, Zack barreled out, looking like a red Russian bear in a white turtleneck and holding onto a glass of vodka. They embraced like Italians. Zack's drink sloshed over. Reuben's cane clattered to the brick court.

'You Mississippi riverboat sonofabitch – '

'You Quarter-rat bastard – '

Zack picked up the cane and handed it back. 'You don't dance as good as you used to.'

'You're not my type.' Reuben followed Zack into the house.

'How can you hurt my feelings like that ?' Zack said.

From the kitchen, Black Bertha shouted, 'For God's sake, close the door.'

'Bertha would like this dance.' Zack grinned. Then he closed the French doors and headed for the bar, broader than he was six months ago and his hair getting newly thin on top, and Reuben felt a twinge at the evidence that said they were all getting older. It was more than twenty years since the day Zack walked into the fraternity house on Audubon Street, a World War Two veteran, and veteran of a number of other things, all of which he had passed on to Reuben. Like a big brother, more worldly, more lived ; an age difference of five years was a lot back then.

'Double Scotch.' Reuben pulled himself up onto a gilded bar stool and propped the cane against the bar. He watched Zack pick up two cubes with a pair of silver tongs and drop them into a diamond-cut glass. The room was reflected in mirror. Mollie disappeared into polished floors and thick rugs and cypress panel-ing and fanlight windows and crystal chandeliers and the warmth of a coal fire going in a marble fireplace.

'What's with the cane ?' Zack sloshed Scotch to the rim of the glass.

'Sprained my ankle.'

'I'll be damned.' Zack handed the Scotch across the bar. Reuben felt a moment of awkward silence. Zack's face looked pressed against an invisible pane of glass.

'Where's B. V. ?' Reuben said.

'He's got his own place now.'

'How come ?'

'He got tired of all the people running in and out.' Zack shrugged. 'I like people.' Zack couldn't be alone. 'He still comes for dinner.'

Reuben took a good slug of Scotch. 'Here's to getting laid.' It burned going down.

Zack refilled his vodka. 'Betty gets off around midnight.'

'How is she?'

'Good as the last time I hope.' Zack made an obscene gesture. In the mirror, Black Bertha's figure appeared like a massive apparition. She pointed a wooden spoon at his back, like casting a spell. Reuben remembered that, during her off hours, Bertha still made Devil Oil and East Life Powder and Get Together Drops for the underground market near Congo Square.

'She's still wanderin'.' Bertha had been obsessed for the past couple of years – every house in the Quarter had its ghosts, most of them tortured slaves who groaned and wailed and rattled chains; Bertha insisted Zack's house now had Lea.

'Leave him alone,' Zack said.

Bertha mumbled something in a corrupted French, *gombo*, then vanished. Reuben swallowed most of the Scotch.

'I can't shut her up,' Zack said.

'Forget it.'

'Seventy years old and she still *schtupps*. Her boyfriend's younger than you. What do you think of that?'

'That's fine.'

'What's the matter? If you don't want Betty, I can get you somebody different.'

'Betty's fine.' Reuben held out his glass.

'Two, three times, that's it for me. Maybe you want somebody else?' Zack poured Scotch into it.

'Betty's fine.'

'It's all set with Farrell. He didn't like it worth a damn, but he signed.'

'Thanks.' Reuben drained half the glass.

'All we have to do is go down and open the cell door.'

'Thanks.'

'What the hell is it – that crazy bombing?'

'That's part of it.'

'They're nuts in that state. I keep telling you. You ought to get out of there.'

'Maybe you're right.'

'I've got all the contacts you need down here. Three years, you'd be the richest shyster in town.'

'You want a roommate?'

'You're splitting with Mollie?'

'She's been screwing around.'

'I'll be damned. Who'd she lay?'

'I don't know.'

'What kind of *schmuck* detective did you hire?'

'No detective. She told me. This morning.'

'She's in love with somebody else?'

'No.'

'She's probably lying. How long since you laid her?'

'What the hell do you know about marriage?'

'It's Russian roulette. Played it once, didn't like it.'

Reuben finished off the Scotch. 'Fix me another drink.'

'Before you sock yourself out, why don't we go get Myrtle Stein?'

'Screw her.'

'She can be had,' Zack said.

Zoe was waiting on a bench in the anteroom, looking small and fragile and frightened.

She rushed across the tiled floor, her heels tapping and echoing, and threw her arms around Reuben and wept all over the front of his jacket. Zack came to his aid. Zack pulled her away like chewing gum from a shoe sole.

'C'mon little sister,' he said gently.

Mascara streamed down her cheeks. 'You're fabulous,' she said. 'I really thank you. How can I ever thank you?'

'Try a week from Friday,' Zack said. 'My place or yours?' He gave her his handkerchief.

She rubbed at her cheeks, her eyes lowered. 'Underneath all that, you're a good man,' she said.

'Don't bet on it.'

'Where the hell is Sol?' Reuben growled.

Zoe turned bright red. 'He's at the hospital. He had an emergency, you know? I mean, it just happened. You never know when a baby's going to come. I mean, who can plan that?'

'You're a liar,' Reuben said.

'Let's get it over with,' Zack said.

Reuben had seen Myrtle Stein only once in his life, twelve years ago, at Zoe's wedding, a small kosher orthodox affair filled with Zoe's hysteria and Sol's frozen respectability, and somehow he had gotten Myrtle Stein confused with a little old lady in a babushka who kept kissing the groom.

It was another robbery.

She came floating out in a clinging black dress and platform shoes and a rhinestone necklace, blowing wet scarlet kisses at the inmates.

Zack said, '*Mother* –' Then he took Myrtle Stein by the arm and escorted her across the tiled anteroom and out into the street. Zoe fluttered beside Reuben, saying, 'You're fabulous, Reuben, I mean, you're really incredible –'

'Leave me alone,' he said.

'I'm sorry –' She sounded like Mollie. He lit a cigarette to have something to do with his hands.

On the sidewalk, Myrtle Stein stopped and took three deep breaths which inflated her massive breasts.

'How much lettuce?' she said.

'Paw-paw sent some money to Baton Rouge,' Zoe said, 'but that's not –'

'How much? Who got paid off?'

'I don't know.'

'It's taken care of,' Zack said.

'Who the hell are you?'

'Maw-maw,' Zoe said, 'you remember Zack. Zack was at the wedding. Don't you remember the nice present he –'

'Which wedding?'

'*My* wedding.'

'For Christ's sake, Zoe, Harry's been married four times, how should I know what wedding you're talking about?'

'The one with the gefilte fish,' Zack said.

'Who the hell is Harry?' Reuben said.

'Sol's brother.' Zack tapped his forehead. 'He's a racetrack tout. One of my best buddies.' He rolled his eyes.

'What is he – crazy?' Reuben said. 'And where the hell is he?'

'Listen, you Mississippi bastard,' Myrtle said, 'just because you sprung me don't mean you can talk dirt on –' She lapsed into a string of curses, part French, part Yiddish.

'*Cochon-schmuck*,' Zack said.

'Let's get the hell out of here,' Reuben said.

Zoe caught his arm. 'Thank you, Reuben. You're fabulous. It's really *incredible*. I mean, Mollie's so lucky. She tells me all the time how lucky she –'

'You listen to me,' Reuben said. 'You and your goddamned sister have given me more trouble today than a man needs in a lifetime. Now, you just put that broad in your car, and you get her the hell out of my sight. And the next time anybody in your goddamned family gets in trouble, you just holler for Jesus Christ.

Because that ain't me. Do you understand that? *I ain't Jesus Christ!*'

'Anybody can see that,' Myrtle said.

The drive back to Zack's was silent. On St Charles Avenue, under a streetlight, three Ursuline convent girls in navy-blue pleated skirts and white sweaters and pea jackets waited for a trolley. The last trolley line in the city. The trolley Mollie had taken to Newcomb every day, twenty years ago. A few blocks beyond, they passed the new Jewish community center, the only modern edifice for blocks, looking like a big white brick oven.

Back at Zack's, B. V. hadn't arrived yet. Zack fixed Reuben another double Scotch. 'There's plenty of fish in the ocean,' Zack said.

'Screw all of them,' Reuben said. Nausea threatened.

'That's the spirit,' Zack said, like a coach.

Reuben carried the Scotch to the bathroom, papered in a big black-and-white print – bare-breasted Greek maidens with brazen expressions. He washed his face at a marble sink, gold fixtures shaped like female legs. There were three traditional framed prints on the wall. He turned them around. On the backs were paintings of copulation, humorless, pornographic. A carved wooden box sat on the back of the toilet. He opened it. Inside, two ivory figures were making it. Zack had said: *Two, three times, that's it for me.* Zack had made his accommodations to the recognition that a woman who knew how to please also knew how to hurt. Zack had worked his life out around trivial pleasure and trivial cruelty, the role of a great-uncle playing sexual Santa. Comfort and safety. Why not join Zack? It was open to him. Why, then, did he have the sense of moving through a series of rooms, and doors closing?

He came out of the bathroom. He could hear voices at the bar. B. V. had come in. He climbed the stairs to Zack's bedroom. He went across the white fur carpet and lay down on the round scarlet velvet bed and stared at his reflection in the mirrored ceiling. There was a knob on the headboard. He turned it. Colored lights played over the room. He tried to imagine a bare-breasted Greek maiden beside him.

She's probably lying, Zack had said. *How long since you laid her?*

Regularly. Mute, remote, ritualistic, lonely. Maybe Mollie had been as lonely. The passion of early discovery had never become depth. Sexual mediocrity. Lea had been his blinding burst of light. Who the hell had turned on the light in the cave for Mollie?

174

She had violated their life. It would never be the same. *I can't live with my own lies anymore,* she had said. Some portion of his being had been relieved.

He sat up. He reached for the princess phone. He pressed the buttons. It began to ring. After a moment, Mollie answered.

'Hello,' she said. He listened. 'Hello – ?' He felt himself go clammy. His heart began to pound. 'Who is it?' she said. Rage flooded him.

He hung up.

He lit a cigarette. His hand was shaking.

Dinner began at eight.

Zack sat at the head of the long narrow table, B. V. at the foot, snorting like a water buffalo, small-eyed and thick-skinned and mammoth, puffing on a cigar with the sullen self-centered expression that went with inherited money and a small intelligence.

He laid the cigar on a silver ash tray and tucked a napkin under his chin. A pinky ring gleamed. The canary diamond had been a gift from Huey Long to B. V.'s father. Then he picked up the cigar again. He smoked through dinner. B. V. liked his pleasures simultaneously.

'Be glad she didn't run off with a damned African,' B. V. said. He laughed. 'Sugar ran off with a damned African.'

Reuben focused on the table. Set with silver and china and crystal. Flowers. Everything glittering under candlelight on starched linen. And the aroma of Black Bertha's Creole cuisine floating in from the kitchen.

'What the hell,' Zack said. 'A friend of mine, he came home one day, found an empty house. His wife took everything, even the toilet seats. You know what he did? Called me up. Laughing like a damned hyena. Turns out he's been trying to get rid of her for years – '

'Screw it.' Reuben knew what it was. The camaraderie of the cuckolded. Somewhere an ex-mambo instructor with flaming red hair was running around with B. V.'s balls. Maybe Zack's were missing too. Why the hell had he come here? What the hell was he doing here? The kitchen door swung open, and Black Bertha entered, carrying three platters of raw oysters, half shells laid out on beds of cracked ice, lemon wedges, silver containers of ketchup and horseradish.

'Ain't nothin' worked,' Bertha said. Single-minded. She set a platter in front of Reuben. 'I done tacked up a horseshoe on the door. Nothin'. That girl, Lea, she's got a stubborn spirit. I done

175

burned sawdust and sprinkled ashes and turned my pockets inside out, and it don't help nothin' – she jus' keeps on roamin' and cryin' – '

'Screw it,' Reuben said. That seemed to be the extent of his vocabulary. He felt like a captive. He looked at his watch. It was two hours until Betty. The oysters stared at him.

'How come I don't hear her ?' Zack said.

'You pass by a cemetery not holdin' a child by the hand, you'll hear her,' Bertha said. 'You'll wish you didn't.' She set a platter in front of Zack.

'You keep going up there and lighting them candles, you're going to burn the damned place down,' B. V. said.

'It ain't your place no more,' Bertha said, 'on account of you're scared of that girl's ghost and don't be sayin' you're not.' She set the last platter in front of B. V., then shook a long bony finger at Reuben. 'That girl ain't never gonna rest 'til somebody makes them a trip up to New York and leaves them a bottle of white chicken feathers on her grave. Ain't nothin' else gonna get rid of the *gris-gris*.'

'You go,' Reuben said. 'I'll buy you a plane ticket.' He swallowed an oyster. Without ketchup. He couldn't taste it.

'Not me,' Bertha said. 'I ain't goin' up north.'

'She ain't never left Congo Square.' B. V. grunted, then attacked the oysters. Bertha went back through the swinging door. Reuben looked at his watch again. Time had stopped. He felt suddenly disoriented and slightly dizzy.

'Eat your oysters,' Zack said. 'They're good for your cock.'

B. V. belched. His oysters had vanished. He picked up the cigar and began to puff on it.

Reuben mixed horseradish and ketchup, dipped in an oyster and let it slide down his throat.

'They're all alike,' B. V. repeated, 'every damned one of them. I don't miss Sugar none.' He grunted.

Reuben forked a dozen and a half oysters like a man on a belt line, washing them down with wine. The candlelight blurred.

'They're good for you,' Zack said.

'Good for your cock.' B. V. laughed.

'A woman's nothin' but a little piece of mink,' Zack said. 'You can't let it make you crazy.'

Black Bertha came back with pompano, sauced with sherried cream and small Gulf shrimp; and more talk about Lea. Ghosts. 'She don't come past the chinaberry tree in the court,' Bertha said. She poured more wine. Reuben swallowed the wine.

'Cut it out – ' Zack said to Bertha.

Bertha claimed her authority. Her grandmother, Congo Annie, had been a legendary figure, six and a half feet tall, two hundred pounds, and wearing a necklace made out of every ear, eye, and nose she had gouged off in a fight. Congo Annie had operated a floating brothel. When she died, her body was put on her barge by her twelve coal-black sons, and all of them had floated down the river, never to be seen again.

Reuben could see her clearly. Congo Annie.

'That was Sugar.' B. V.'s voice came from far away.

Bertha served artichokes stuffed with Parmesan and garlic sausage. 'Twelve o'clock, she starts roamin'. Every night.' She poured more wine. Reuben drained his glass.

'How the hell do you lay a ghost?' Zack said. *Lea.* Reuben could see her clearly. Then she turned into Mollie.

'You eat a lot of oysters.' B. V. laughed.

Bertha served jambalaya. Oysters and shrimp and ham and sausage, hot as hellfire, on a bed of white rice. 'You'll hear her,' she said. 'You'll hear her tonight, alright.' Lea.

'I had a friend,' Zack said. 'One day he came home, found his wife in bed with a Chinaman. You know what it was? Turns out she was a damned Communist.'

'They're all alike,' B. V. said. 'Every damned one of them.' He lit another cigar. Reuben watched the candles drip onto the table-cloth. He knew he was drunk. And empty. He never got drunk. Only when he was empty. Voices had begun to echo. *Mollie.*

You've got to get over it, Zack said.

A broad's a broad, B. V. said.

You can't let it make you crazy, Zack said.

Screw her, B. V. said.

Calas tout chaud, Black Bertha said, bearing a platter of hot fried rice cakes, sprinkled with powdered sugar.

And hot, thick coffee. With chicory. He didn't drink it.

And imported brandy. Two. He drank three. Then B. V. held out a cigar.

Reuben stood up. The room circled him.

B. V. laughed.

Zack said, *I had a friend* – The rest blurred together.

The floor came up to meet him.

He woke clear and cold as a block of ice. To a mound of accessible flesh. The dismal craftsmanship and detachment of a professional hand on his groin.

He was in the hayloft bedroom of one of the slave-quarters apartments. There was a light on somewhere downstairs. Somebody had carried him up, undressed him. Probably Black Bertha and Zack. The old man's cane was propped against the bed.

A pair of breasts wobbled in front of his eyes in the semidarkness. The hand grew more enthusiastic. He pulled away.

'Cut that out.' He sat up. He reached out and switched on the lamp. Beside a blue telephone on the night table, his wristwatch said three o'clock.

'What's the matter?'

He looked at her. Betty. Tousled blond curls, big green eyes, creamy skin. Coldly he calculated the sum of her. Not a bad broad. No husband. Two kids to support. She worked eight hours a night in a bunny costume, and she didn't sleep with just anybody; partly from fear of the clap, and partly from a half-assed integrity that came out of a flat mind and a decent prosaic heart. She liked him. He had never beaten her. He had never tied her to the faucets of a bathtub and walked barefoot on her aching back.

He didn't answer her. The calculator shifted to Mollie.

He picked up the cane and got out of bed and crossed to the cedar rail fence and looked down into the two-story living room. The bird's-eye view brought a feeling of omnipotence. He would do what he had to do.

He felt the need for action. Something startling and immediate and final. Something to separate him from Zack and B. V. His need was to claim his manhood.

It came to him. What he had to do about Mollie.

The thought was followed by an image of Justin. A man needed two beings. A man needed a woman to love him, and a man to witness his life. He knew what Justin would say: Don't make waves; no more upheavals; you can't handle a separation, motherless children, Barksdale, the bombing. Keep everything afloat until things calm down. Dissemble. Serve your own best interests.

He couldn't make his decisions from Justin's perspective.

He was capable of strategy and lies and self-protection, but he was ruled by his feelings, his need to push life to the limits, his need to follow his own conscience. His truth, at this moment, was his hatred for Mollie. He knew he would act on it. He gripped the cane. Justin was not his witness. The old man was his witness.

'I'm sorry,' Betty said, from behind him. She sounded like Mollie.

He turned around. She was leaning against the pillows, waiting, holding open the door to that world where any woman became all women. He had an image of Zack saying to her: *Reuben's wife ran off with his balls*.

'Get the hell out,' he said. 'I don't need you.'

He watched her face. She knew he was talking to someone else. She was accustomed to being someone else. Lea. Mollie. Elena. He suddenly remembered the summer he was twelve he had fallen in love with Elena. He had wished Willie dead. Every time somebody hitched up a horse outside of Jesse's store, he rode off on it. Every morning he got up early enough to scrub off his sheets with a washcloth.

Betty didn't move.

He came back to the bed and picked up the phone and dialed. He turned his back. The line began to ring. Then Mollie's voice came through, fuzzy with sleep.

'Hello . . . '

'I want you gone when I get back,' he said.

'Reuben – ?'

'When Leila comes in the morning, you pack and get out.'

He listened to a deep silence. Finally, she said, 'Alright.'

'The children are mine. You agreed to that.'

'Yes.'

'There's three thousand in our personal account. Take all of it.'

'Thank you . . . '

'You did this,' he said.

'You have a right to hate me.'

'Who was it?'

Another silent moment passed.

'I don't give a damn,' he said.

'I'm sorry . . . '

'*What the hell did you want?*' he said.

'I don't know.'

'Let me know where you are.'

' . . . Alright.'

'I'll see you in hell,' he said.

He hung up.

When he turned around, Betty was laid out like the Duchess of Alba in a blond wig. With the distorted vision of absolute accuracy, he saw her components – animal vitality and indolence and fear; feathery eyelashes fluttering over ignorance and pain. He felt her pain. The blood began to course through his body. His groin ached, swollen with fury.

'Don't hurt me . . . ' she said.

Time extended itself.

She became Mollie. Lea. Frieda. Eula Williams. She became Justin. Zack. Barksdale. Jesse. Man, woman, child, tree, earth, sky, all of it, everything. A dozen murders took place in which his violence spent itself.

When it was over, the word that wrote itself across his brain was *Gehenna*. The summer he had fallen in love with Elena he had learned the word from Rabbi Hellman in Greenborough. *Gehenna* was the suffering on earth which felt like an encounter with living hell.

He said, 'I love you.'

Twenty

IT WAS no longer Mollie.

The thought brought no pain. He felt only a perfect knowledge of where he was, and who he was, and what it was he had to do.

Cold and damp, the morning air invaded his pores with a sense of his own power. He thought about Phil and Joe. The boys would have to be told, as gently and firmly as possible. He'd make sure their lives didn't change. It had always been Leila who cooked their breakfast, bandaged their knees, cured their colds. It had always been Attica who taught them to chop wood, to plant tomatoes, to know the difference between a twig and a moccasin down by the river. After a short burst of hysterics, Frieda would pitch in.

He set his watch by the clock in the belfry of the St Louis Cathedral. It was seven fifteen. The church was locked up. Inside, under the altar, saints were buried. The thought initiated a surge of victory. He was alive; in charge, again, of his own life.

In Jackson Square, a bearded kid wearing a back pack was washing himself in the fountain. The kid waved. Reuben didn't wave back. He felt no kinship, this morning, with the rootless.

He gripped the old man's cane, tapping the brick sidewalk at a brisk determined pace. He went past deserted bars, a couple of passed-out rummies, closed art galleries, a black woman scrubbing steps with a wire brush. Mollie had severed the bond between the two of them, but she had not severed him from himself. His commitments remained, stronger than ever. He felt himself as a hardened warrior, girding for battle, with the forces on the other side still uncounted.

He stepped off the curb and headed for the pale yellow column-ed walkway of the French Market. Produce trucks vied for the street like contenders in a bullpen. Through the river mist on the dock, he could see the stevedores unloading giant purple bunches of plaintains. The sight seemed simple, naïve, from some other era. Lea had said, *There's a war going on out there. I can hear it.* Back then, it had been moving in. Tonight, in Holmesdale, the men would assemble. He would lead them into a battle plan. Armed, then, he'd confront Barksdale.

Inside the Café du Monde, he sat on a stool at the mirrored marble counter and ordered a mug of chicory coffee and three square puffed doughnuts. As he went through the traditional Quarter breakfast, his mind leaped ahead, touching all bases. The voice on the telephone reechoed: *Count your days, you dirty Jew.* The evil crackling voice was his enemy. The enemy would be flushed out of hiding. *Tell Barksdale you'll pay for convictions – or bodies.* Justin had known, before he had, what kind of war it would be. *Is everything under your roof that pure?* It was reason-able to assume that Justin had known about Mollie too. There were those who were tuned in to the subterranean tunnels of life. Some, like Lea, died from the knowledge. Some, like Justin, protected themselves from the consequences. He felt himself as a different breed. Unlike Lea, he would survive. Unlike Justin, he would fight.

He finished his coffee.

Then he headed for the fish market, looking for Cora Higgins Stimpson.

She was almost as tall as Higgins, her hair dark blond and streaked with pewter, wearing a hard-bitten face and a neat starched apron that spelled out a straight-backed pride.

'You want shrimp or catfish?' She was a sentinel behind the mounds of bewhiskered catfish with glazed eyes. Laid out on a bed of ice were big gray shrimp and oysters and luminous red snapper.

'Cora Higgins – ?'

'Who wants to know?' she said. He remembered that doughy sex kittens like Elizabeth Higgins always produced huge, utili-tarian daughters. He remembered something Justin had once said about women: Handle a small woman like she's made out of steel, and a big woman like she's made out of glass.

'I'm Johnny's attorney,' he said. Gently.

She searched his face, going over it with a primitive Geiger counter. 'What's your name?'

'Buchman. Reuben Buchman.' He gave her a card. She studied it.

'I heard he was in trouble.' She fingered a small gold cross, then dropped the card in her apron pocket. 'I don't believe none of it,' she said.

'I'd like to buy you a cup of coffee.'

She picked up a snapper and carried it over to a chopping block and began to scale it. Then she severed its head with a cleaver. Her motions were quick and deft, without anger. He knew she was doing what other women did with knitting needles – thinking her way through it. When she came back, she said, 'Why? Why do you want to help Johnny?'

'He was framed.'

'That ain't what I mean.' Suspicion colored her face. 'I mean, what do you care about Johnny?'

At another time, he might have said, *I follow my own conscience* – the phrase he had wanted to hurl at Justin; or *I believe in justice*, as he had to Eula Williams. The impulse had once sprung from a need to take a moral position. Now, he had been assaulted from without by the bombing, and assaulted from within by Mollie; now, this moment, he understood that his commitment to John Tyler Higgins was an assertion of self.

He watched her face. Her eyes turned transparent and watery. She stood like a bulwark. All through Mississippi, there were thousands like her. The paramount thing in her life was most likely her superiority to the black man. She smelled like fish.

'He's your brother. I thought you might want to help him. Maybe I was wrong.'

She stared at him in willful silence.

He gave her thirty seconds. It was the thirty seconds he had learned in the courtroom – the time he allowed in awareness of the capacity of any human being to come up with some unpredictable grand-scale gesture. Everything contained its opposite. In a redneck woman, there was sometimes a queen. The odds were the same as the possibility of finding a cuckoo in a sparrow's nest.

The half minute went by.

'I guess I was wrong.' He turned around. He started off.

'Wait a minute.'

He stopped. From the corner of his eye, he saw her pulling off the apron. She came around the counter, her big face twisted in obscure conflict. He couldn't read it. She stopped in front of him, clutching at the gold cross with a big, work-reddened hand, a thin wedding band on it. His information said she had married a truck driver, Harry Stimpson, seven years ago. Then he read it. He saw the small girl made out of glass who was terrified of God and Harry Stimpson.

'He's not my brother,' she said.

'I know,' Reuben said. 'You were ten years old when you found him in the woods.'

'I was fifteen,' she said. 'I'm his mother.'

Twenty minutes later, he set out for his car, carrying the package of wrapped catfish.

Cora had said, *I'll testify if it'll help him.* He had been startled by her courage and touched by her naïveté. He pictured himself telling a Mississippi jury that Michelangelo had been a bastard. Michelangelo had also been a homosexual. *Forget it*, he had said. She had kept a scrap book, secretly; she would send it to him. She had offered him money. He had taken the half-dozen catfish instead.

He went over it as he walked. The senile taxi dancer, Elizabeth Higgins, locked up at Webster, had wanted Higgins to be a priest, Cora had said, *I never told him I was his mother.* It happened often. A good lawyer learned more about his client than the client knew himself. Maybe Higgins had the psyche of a priest – or maybe Higgins knew who he was, and how he came about. *His father was a man who paid a dime to dance with Mama in Memphis.* Maybe the key to Higgins was as simple as a temper tantrum. In defiance of a society that would obviously reject him, Higgins had aligned himself with every available underdog. Higgins had become a civil rights dentist, had hired a female black assistant whom he also screwed, had stuck his neck out for a teen-age runaway boy, had invited retribution and punishment. The role of rejected-priest/bastard-son had been laid out a long time ago. The summary had its own kind of absurd logic. As much sense to it as Higgins being defended by a Jew whose grandfather had been chased by the czar of Russia. As much crazy sense as being able to figure out everything about a man he had never spoken to, and not knowing anything about a woman he had lived with for nineteen years.

That was over.

He looked at his watch. Leila had arrived at his house an hour ago. Mollie was gone.

He turned the corner at Jackson Square. The street which had been deserted earlier was beginning to take on life. A couple of early-bird sidewalk artists were setting up easels and chalk boxes, one of them coaxing a reluctant tourist into a twenty-five-dollar souvenir portrait to be hung over a mantel in Davenport, Iowa. He went past a display of leopards painted on velvet, tacked to the spiked wrought-iron fence. He might have been twenty. Everything on the street was as it had been then. He wasn't twenty. He was forty. He lived in a different season. In Holmesdale, it waited for him.

He stopped to light a cigarette. When he looked up, he saw an old man coming walking towards him reading a Hebrew newspaper, an old giant wearing a yarmulke and a face that gave credence to the theory that the American Indian had been one of the lost tribes of Israel. *It's none of my business*, Monk had said, *but you sound like hell*. He had said, *I've got to go to New Orleans and get Sol's mother out of jail*. Monk had said, *Listen, if you run into my papa wandering around, see how he's doing*. He watched the old man turn through the gate and head for a bench infested with fluttering pigeons. He hesitated. Time prodded. How long would it take? Monk had lost a day at Elena's funeral. Alright. Get it over with.

He went through the gate and across the grass. The old man was engrossed in the newspaper.

'Mr Levitt – '

Monk's papa looked up, puzzled. Then he said. '*Reuben* – ' A smile cracked the old leather face into a crisscross of wrinkles. '*Shalom*, Reuben.' He got to his feet and grasped Reuben's hand with both of his own. 'With a cane. I didn't know you.'

'How are you?'

'A little poetry, a few friends, a little health – what more *nachas* for a seventy-year-old man?' He made an open-palmed gesture. 'Tell me, how goes your family?'

'Fine.'

'And Milton? Still mad on me? He sent you? Talk some sense into a crazy old man?'

'Milton's fine,' Reuben said. 'I'm here on business. I was just leaving – '

'Come. I'll walk with you to your car.' Old man Levitt rolled up the newspaper and tucked it under his arm. They began to walk. 'Such a tragedy, that bombing. A rabbi's house. Like Germany, it feels. *Meshuganas*. Such a place. Years ago I told Milton. It was written. *And the Lord said unto Abram: Know thy seed shall be a stranger in a land that is not theirs*. Go to Israel, I told him. Now look at Israel. From Jews, they, too, have become soldiers. What do you think?'

'I don't know.' They came out of the square into the street. The catfish was beginning to stink.

'I'm an old man. Too serious. I see Zack in the street last week. He tells me a joke. *To a Jew "To be or not to be," is an answer.* Always, Zack makes me laugh.'

They passed the candy store. The porcine proprietor was setting a six-foot plastic Aunt Jemima out on the sidewalk.

'My car's up ahead.' Reuben saw a ticket was stuck to the windshield. They reached the car. He pulled the ticket off and stuck it in his pocket. Then he put out his hand. 'I'll tell Monk you're fine.'

'This is my house,' the old man said, 'right here.' He gestured at a wrought-iron gate. 'In the back. Across the court.' His face clouded. 'I might have to move. My friends come, they play music at night. My landlady's an old woman. She screams. In Vietnam, they should be? You're a lawyer. Tell me. Can she make me without my friends? Can she make me without music?'

'Mail me a copy of your lease,' Reuben said. 'I'll look at it.' He opened the car door and slid in. He laid the catfish and the cane on the seat beside him.

'I'll get it. Right now – I'll get it.'

'I can't wait. I don't have time.' Reuben shut the door.

'One minute it'll take me – ' the old man shouted. He hurried through the gate. Then he vanished.

Reuben opened the door and got out. He lit another cigarette. Up ahead, on the wall of a grocery, he spotted a phone booth. He pulled the cane out of the car and headed for it. When the operator came on, he made a credit-card call to his office.

Olive answered.

'Is Mr Woods in?'

'He's on long distance with Mr Rabin.'

'Tell him I said to set up a meeting for me with Barksdale. To-morrow morning. He'll know how to go about it.'

'You've got an adoption case in court in the morning.'

'What time?'

'Eleven.'

'Then tell him to make it before eleven. Way before eleven.'

'The appointments I canceled yesterday afternoon – I made them for this afternoon. Shall I let them stand?'

'I'll be back by noon. Tell Mr Woods I want to see him. Tell him to clear his lunch.'

'He's got lunch with the governor.'

'Screw the governor.' He hung up. He pushed the door open

with the cane, then closed it again. He took the coin out of the slot, put it back in, then gave the operator his home number.

Leila answered. He asked for Mollie.

'She done left here a few minutes ago with a suitcase,' Leila said. 'She went off in a taxi.'

'What did she say?'

'She didn't say *nothin*'.'

'Thank you,' he said.

When he got back to the car, Monk's papa was coming through the porte cochère, carrying a big brass samovar.

'My friends, they're good people,' he said, 'but sometimes they *gonif* a little, it's not a good thing. This belonged to my papa. You'll just put it in your trunk? I don't want something to happen to it. You'll just give it to Monk for me? Me papa, in Russia, he used to put a leather boot on top. You'll tell Monk? Alright?'

'Alright.' Reuben opened the trunk. Inside was the box of his grandfather's effects he had taken from Willie in Maryville. The Yiddish journal on top. And the old man's shotgun.

'What's the shotgun?'

'It was my grandfather's.'

'From Monk's grandfather a samovar, from yours a shotgun?'

'Where's the lease?'

The old man shook his head. 'I forget. Milton has it. Milton paid up the rent. Six months. I forget because charity it feels like.'

Reuben took the samovar out of his arms, and laid it in the trunk beside the box of papers. Then he picked up the journal. This is in Yiddish,' he said. 'I'd like to get it translated. What do you think? Is fifty dollars a fair price for someone?'

Monk's papa took it. He flipped through. 'It's your grand-father's?'

'Yes.'

'Better for you to have this than a shotgun.'

'I wouldn't want to leave it with just anybody.'

'Fifty dollars is too much. Thirty. Plenty. A Yiddish scholar it shouldn't take him too long.'

'Maybe you could find time?'

'For what I should take your money? For a simple thing like this?'

Reuben scratched out a check and tucked it in the old man's pocket. 'Take your girlfriend out to dinner.'

The old man flushed copper. 'A widow,' he said. 'Only fifty-eight. Don't tell Milton. You give me your word?'

'I won't tell him.' Reuben climbed in the car. The old man stuck his head in the window. His eyes glittered.

'It's a mitzvah. I know. It'll be written down for you in *Gon Aden*.'

'Forget it,' Reuben said. *Gon Aden* was paradise. He drove off. Headed in the opposite direction.

Twenty-one

THE TAXI ROLLED.

The back of the driver's neck was smooth and freckled as a robin's egg; two Camel cigarettes stuck behind his left ear; the meter clucked along like a mechanical hen. The addition of such meaningless details did not keep her from waves of anguish.

What's the matter, Mama? Phil said, at breakfast.

It's the bombing, Joe said. *She's worried about the bombing. Isn't that right?*

You're not to worry about that, she said.

When's the rabbi gonna get out of here? Every time he sees me, he pinches my cheek. I'm not a kid anymore.

That's true.

How come you got up this morning to fix us breakfast? Phil said. *It's not your car pool day.*

I just felt like it. . . .

The taxi halted.

'Here you are, lady.'

She sat still a moment, looking at the glass doors of the air terminal. The sight blurred. The driver opened the door for her. She got out with a feeling of swimming in a sea of unshed tears.

He set her suitcase on the sidewalk. 'You want me to carry it in? Fifty cents extra.'

'No. Thank you.' She fumbled in her purse. She handed over a couple of bills.

The taxi drove off. She stood there another moment, blinking in the winter sun. Then she picked up the suitcase and went through the glass doors.

187

Who is it?

Mollie . . .

An hour ago, Jean had opened the door, still in his hospital coat, just in from the hospital, the night shift, nine to nine.

Mollie – ?

I came to say good-bye. My plane leaves at eleven.

The big terminal clock said ten twenty.

She crossed to the ticket counter. She gave her name. Her voice sounded hollow. Into the hollow came a terrible insight. One does something irreconcilable. Driven by guilt, one then does something one can face less.

Last night, she had walked through each room. Touching each piece of furniture. Trying to make contact with anything that had once been. She had sat beside Phil's bed in the darkness, listening to the hamsters run in the cage. She had wept over Joe, asleep, on the verge of moving into manhood. The days had gone slowly. The years had gone fast. Nobody went back. Life was a one-way street.

The ticket slid across the counter, her luggage check stapled to it. She picked it up. How had she not known it would feel like walking off the edge of the world?

Where are you going? Jean said.

Vermont. An alternative to the irrationality of Switzerland. Conceived as penance. Loneliness. Redemption of self. The fantasy that whatever came afterwards would be just.

What happened? Jean said.

I told him. Reuben.

About us?

About me. He doesn't know about you.

Why?

I don't know. What had she expected to come from it? A solution, like alchemy, from the magic of truth? Her life had been buried in lies. One truth had not set her free. The truth she had chosen had simply revealed to her what she was – the sum of ignorant, self-destructive outcries, radiating from some doomed center.

For God's sake – you know I didn't mean to break up your marriage.

She bought a magazine she could not read. She went into the coffee shop and ordered a cup of coffee she could not drink. She opened her purse and swallowed one of the tranquilisers Jean had given her. Inside was the money clip. Initials in gold. R. B.

I taped up your husband's ankle. Yesterday morning. Here. Take it back. You may need it.

Two hundred and sixty-three dollars in it.

Jean – Why do you do it?

You're going to Vermont. That's your way. I'm going back to the bayou. I want to build a clinic. That's my way.

You'll get caught –

How should I raise it? Beat a few million garfish to death with a canoe paddle so my mama can make wind chimes out of the scales? Get some society women to organise a charity ball to raise money for cajuns? You'll find out what it's like out there. There's no such thing as morality. There's economics, that's all. And whatever decent human exchange you can find along the way.

Good-bye, Jean.

I didn't just take you to bed. I want you to know that.

What was it?

It'll come to you, he said.

She came out of the coffee shop. The corridor that led to her gate stretched out before her. A wave of dizziness swept her. She made an attempt to tabulate her inner resources. All that came up was *loss*. Where had she lived? In a vacuum. Her need for prisons had driven her to create a prison of self. What had she asked of Reuben? Protection. The cotton batting had kept her infantilised. She had no means with which to deal with the world. The confession to Reuben had been possibly the first act of courage of her life.

She turned into the ladies' room.

She sat at a white tiled counter and stared at her face in the mirror.

She tackled the panic. She was a photographer. She could work. She wouldn't starve. Neither would she live alone if she chose not to. In nineteen years of marriage, there had been six affairs. Why wouldn't there be somebody else? But Zoe had once quipped: *Finding a man is like finding a job; it's easier to find one when you already have one.*

She fought tears, and the desire to faint. The real crux of her pain. How could she live without Joe? Without Phil? How could she have succumbed to a bout of madness that had cost her the only two small beings she had ever really loved? How could she leave them?

The choice had been made.

Behind her, a pay phone beckoned. She rose, moved slowly to it, put in a dime, then dialed. It rang a long time.

'Leila?'

'Yes, ma'am.'

What was there to say? 'You be sure Attica gets Joe to his drum lesson this afternoon.'

'Yes, ma'am,' Leila said. 'I sure am glad you called. I didn't know where to get hold of you. They done called from Phil's school.'

'What's wrong with Phil?'

'He ain't sick or hurt or nothin' like that, I done asked 'em. It's just that the teacher wants to see you and Mr Buchman this afternoon.'

'You'd better leave word at Mr Buchman's office.'

'I done that,' Leila said. 'What's the matter, honey? You didn't look so good this morning' and you don't sound no better now.'

'It's alright . . . I just have to go away for a while.'

'You havin' a nervous breakdown, Miss Mollie?'

'Something like that. You take care of the boys – ?'

'Lord Jesus, I'm gonna put in my prayers you're soon gonna be your darlin' self again.'

'I love you, Leila,' she said. She hung up.

She stood there, weeping, until someone came in.

When she came out into the corridor, a loud nasal voice through the loudspeaker was announcing her flight.

The Cadillac stank from catfish.

He came into the city limits. The catfish needed to go on ice.

He'd have Leila cook it for supper. Before tonight's meeting, he'd come home and eat with the boys. Fried catfish and hush-puppies. To remind Joe and Phil of the times he and Attica had taken them fishing. Reinforce the good times, before he told them.

The clock on the dashboard said eleven.

There was plenty of time. He'd drop off the catfish, break the news to Leila. After that, he'd tell Justin at lunch. On his way home, this evening, he'd stop at the Williamsburg and tell Frieda. No histrionics. One step at a time. Calm and simple.

It was over.

He pulled up in the driveway next to the station wagon. He saw she hadn't taken the camera equipment. He hadn't given her time for that. He had done what he had to do. Like discovering one had to lose an arm. Better to amputate than chew it off one piece at a time.

He got out of the car. Through the trees he could make out Attica's shadow in the greenhouse.

Let Leila tell Attica.

He let himself in through the back door and came into the kitchen. The kitchen was empty. The old man's cane rang on the brick floor. He laid the catfish on a refrigerator shelf and poured himself a glass of milk. It occurred to him that he would be the one, now, to leave a note for the milkman. How much milk did the boys drink every day? Leila would know. Where the hell was Leila?

He shouted Leila's name through the intercom.

When he turned around, Mollie was standing in the doorway.

It took him a moment to recognise her. She was wearing a short plaid skirt and a black sweater; a lot of chains hung around her neck, and there were deep circles under her eyes. She no longer looked like a girl.

He felt nothing. The empty-air twitches of a missing limb.

'What the hell are you doing here?'

'They called from school. Phil's in some kind of trouble. They asked to see both of us. I thought – '

'Get in the car,' he said.

He drove in silence.

Schoolteachers in his day had been spinsters with big hands, coal-miner faces, cardigan sweaters, and brogans.

Times had changed.

Jacqueline Carruthers was young and pretty, an unblemished face the shape and texture of a honeydew melon, a bright tooth-paste smile radiating health and authority.

'I'm glad both of you could come.'

'What's the trouble?' Reuben said.

'Please, sit down.'

The classroom was empty, except for Phil, seated at the back of the room, hands clasped in front of him like a tiny prisoner waiting to be sentenced.

Miss Carruthers pulled two chairs alongside a scarred teacher's desk. She sat down. Reuben waited. She ran a hand through a mass of dark curls. Thin penciled half-moon arcs rose high on her forehead. A scarlet mouth pouted. Sharp pointed breasts thrust over the desk. *Phil had tried to rape her in the cloakroom.*

'What's the trouble?' Reuben repeated.

'I don't know how to tell you this – '

'Straight.' Reuben felt a burst of anxiety. Beside him, Mollie leaned forward. He felt a primary bond reassert itself. The bond of parents.

'We're all enlightened people,' Miss Carruthers said. 'I'm sure you understand that a confusion of identity in a young child can be quite serious.'

'Are you talking about Phil ?' Mollie said.

Miss Carruthers picked up a pencil and began to tap it against the desk. 'Phil insists he's *black*,' she said.

Relief flooded Reuben. He felt the tension leave Mollie. He smiled. 'I see.'

'It's not funny.' Miss Carruthers laid the pencil down with great care.

'All children try out different roles,' Mollie said.

'Roles are bad for classroom discipline,' Miss Carruthers said. 'And I must tell you, I feel Phil is a very disturbed child.' She leaned across the desk. 'An identity conflict could deter his intellectual progress and have grave effects on his emotional development.'

'Why don't we talk to him ?' Mollie turned around. She beckoned to Phil. He sent a questioning look at Miss Carruthers. She nodded. Phil got up and shuffled up the aisle, his head down.

'Do you want to tell your parents what you told the class ?' Miss Carruthers said.

'No,' Phil said.

'You can tell me,' Mollie said gently. 'I won't be mad. I promise. Have I ever broken a promise to you ?'

'No.'

'Then, trust me.'

'I used to be a frog,' Phil said. 'You remember ?'

'I remember,' Mollie said. 'When you were little, I used to turn you into a frog, and you used to hop down the driveway and get the mail from the box.'

'I'm not a frog anymore,' Phil said.

'What are you now ?'

'I'm black.'

Mollie put her arm around Phil. 'Who turned you black ?'

'Attica. I asked him. He said okay. Till I was twelve. When I'm twelve I have to turn white again and he has to call me "mister." That's what he said.' Phil looked at Reuben. 'Why does that make Miss Carruthers so mad ?'

'Hold out your hands, Phil,' Miss Carruthers said. Phil obeyed. 'Now. What color are they?'

'Black,' Phil said. Reuben watched his face set defiantly.

'Now, Phil, you can see perfectly well what color – '

'Black,' Phil said.

'It's alright,' Reuben said. 'Don't you worry about it, son. Why don't you run out now and play with the other kids.'

Phil grinned. He scurried off, his legs going like a windmill.

Reuben rose. 'I appreciate your concern, Miss Carruthers, but I find it a harmless fantasy.'

Miss Carruthers looked up at him. 'Of course.' Her acquiescence was formal, polite. She flashed the toothpaste smile again. Nothing happened to her eyes. The young melon face turned a deep crimson. 'I understand,' she said. She rose. 'Every family handles these things in their own way.'

He drove home in silence.

He pulled up in the driveway and left the motor running. Mollie made no move to get out. He lit a cigarette. Then he shook one from the pack for her. He lit it for her.

'Thank you.'

'You didn't pack your camera equipment.'

'If I had, it would be on its way to Vermont right now.'

'Why didn't you go?'

'I couldn't – '

'We're both too smart to believe that children can hold a marriage together.'

'You're the lawyer,' she said. 'What do people do?'

'They make arrangements.'

'Time out?' She made an attempt to smile. It didn't come off.

'Your timing was lousy.'

'Im sorry.'

'I've got a lot on my mind. We could make a temporary arrangement. Send the rabbi to Jake Gorman's. You move into the guest room. Nothing between us.' He pitched his cigarette out the car window. 'Think about it.'

'For how long?'

'Until things settle down. No lies in it. No love, no hate, no anger.' He sent her a cold smile. 'Maybe we'll get to like it.'

'Alright.'

'One more thing – '

She shook her head. 'That's over.'

'I don't give a damn what you do,' he said. 'But you ought to know the F.B.I.'s probably following you around.'

She looked startled. Frightened. The old impulse to reassure her swept him. It vanished. 'They're looking for leverage. It's complicated. I forced them into the bombing case.' He watched her absorb what she could of it.

'Can they hurt you?'

'I'm a titan,' he said.

He leaned across her and opened the door. She sat still a moment. Then she put out her cigarette and slid out. She turned back, holding the door open.

'You were fine – with Phil,' she said.

'Forget it,' he said bitterly. 'A Jew's nothing but a nigger turned inside out.'

Twenty-two

HINDS STREET was dark as the river bottom, a short stretch of commercial warehouses, not lit nor intended for nighttime use. His was the only car on the street as Reuben pulled up in front of Abrahmson's Cotton Storage, and waited while the freight train roared past along the I.C. tracks in back. On the other side of the tracks, the Oyster Bar began. Beyond that, the cotton fields began, the highway to Maryville. The dashboard clock said twenty till eight; the street was lonely and isolated; no Monk.

He cut the lights. Carrying his briefcase and wielding the cane, he unlocked the door, then walked around inside, turning on hanging bulbs, and pulling cotton bales around in a circle to form seats. Most of the men had been here before. Once a month, John imported a pro from the Gulf Coast to run a big game. Big stakes. Tonight's meeting would be a different kind of game; another kind of stakes. Fifty grand. The 1968 price for being Jews in Holmesdale.

A hand-lettered sign read: NO SMOKING. He lit a cigarette to dispel the silence, then sat on a cotton bale waiting for Monk. Monk had left word with Olive. *Meet me at 7.30. Important.* Where the hell was he?

He went through the cigarette, remembering the last time, the last meeting; these same men, a different kind of problem. An embarrassment. To be settled, back then two years ago, in the name of charity. And he, Reuben, had been the messenger. The fatalism on Arnie Feinstein's face had remained with him long afterwards. In the quiet, now, it came back to him. . . .

The man called Arnie Feinstein had been tall and angular and hawk-nosed, obviously Jewish-looking, big hands stuck in the pockets of washed-out overalls, a face and body made up of bones like some museum dinosaur, eyes sunk deep, a stubble of graying beard. Reuben had gone to see Feinstein in a ratty one-room place, not far from this warehouse – a bare mattress on the floor, a straggly wife, two straggly children, all of them waiting for the verdict. Arnie Feinstein had said he could work with his hands. Good with his hands, he had said. He had set out from Chicago, south, where he had heard it was better – heard it from the blacks he had worked with – though he was now dispossessed, stranded in Holmesdale; but he would work his way through, he had always worked his way through. All he needed was a job.

A job for Arnie Feinstein had been the issue at the last meeting.

A meeting like this one. The same men. All the representatives of Jewish money and status in Holmesdale. There had been Jake Gorman's scrapyard, a natural solution, but Jake had said he couldn't work a Jew that way, couldn't work a Jew like a nigger. There had been Victor Karp, groomed like a Latin gigolo from the proceeds of seven Mississippi and Arkansas oil wells, but Victor had said he needed young men, tough men, not worn out *kochers* like Arnie Feinstein. There had been Dave Colman's luggage factory, but Dave had said that Yankee Jews – he had once been one – were accustomed to unions, and he didn't want any Yankee Jews organising any union in his luggage factory. And they had gone through the possibilities, until the problem had become clear. John Abrahmson had been the one, finally, to put it into words: There had never been a poor Jew in Holmesdale. Not as long as anyone could remember. What did one do with a poor Jew in Holmesdale?

They had bought Arnie Feinstein and his family four tickets back to Chicago.

He dropped the cigarette and ground it out with his heel. Around him, the silence grew shrill. He felt suddenly uneasy. His watch said a quarter to eight. Where was Monk?

He went to the door and looked out. The street, cold and empty, moved off into shadow. *If you're going to play cops and robbers, you'd better understand what's involved*, Barksdale had said. *It's not a game. We want you to know that.*

They walked in shadow. Whoever they were. All he had was a license plate, a name, Gerald Gunston III. A list of Klan names. Frank Flowers and Goss and Army Jones; the Rawlins brothers. Unknown entities. *We have complete files*, Barksdale had said. *We know who they are and what they're doing, every minute*. But there was a price tag attached. *Aroused citizens . . . funds . . . We're not interested in arrests. We're interested in convictions*.

Why the hell should it cost fifty grand to work within the law?

The doors to courtroom of self came open. The voice of the internal prosecutor began.

Your witness.

– Answer the question.

It seemed reasonable when Justin laid it out. *Hoover doesn't give one damn about civil rights and he doesn't care if the Klan operates or not*. Barksdale's first priority is to Hoover. Hoover requires convictions, and convictions require informers, and if the informers' testimony is to hold up in court, the money to pay them has to come from some source other than the F.B.I.

– Hearsay.

Sustained. Strike it from the record.

– Leave Justin out of it. What about you? What about alternatives? What about the Anti-Defamation League? What about Jewish pressure on congressmen? Direct complaints to Washington? The South's another country, but it's still part of the United States. Why the hell are you taking charge?

He lit another cigarette. He considered the question. Who was he to take charge? Why had he done it? All his life he had done it. Leaped in. Taken hold. Always of the thing no prudent man would touch. Like Higgins. Like Lea. It was Lea who had said there was always the man among men who was more than a lump of clay; the man in whom, for no discernible reason, a fire had been lit; and so he became to those around him a source of warmth, source of protection, source of light, source of sparks from which other fires were lit. It was Lea who had claimed he was one of those men, aware of the mysteries of life, the uniqueness of earth, the possibilities of men. *Bullshit*, he had said. Bullshit.

– Why, then?

Because I'm crazy.

He pitched the cigarette into the darkness. The sound of a car answered him.

He looked for Monk's truck. It wasn't Monk's truck.

In a moment, a long black Lincoln came into sight and purred to a halt at the curb. Not Monk. The figure who emerged was half

Monk's height and twice Monk's width, fanatically groomed, suited, button-down shirt and crocodile moccasins, sleek as an overfed water rat. Dave Colman, Yankee turned southerner, came mincing carefully across the sidewalk, his expression telegraphing a message usually relegated to private midnight insomniac moments: *If there's going to be any trouble, count me out.*

Dave was the cork.

Behind him, a series of cars pulled up, spilling out a river of men.

No Monk.

Jake Gorman and Mickey and Leo arrived – Jake looking like an encrusted old fisherman who had pulled out two rarefied sons, gifts from the sea – the three of them a family of defendants. Written on their faces was the discovery that their lives were not inviolate, unassailable; the knowledge that they, all three, had been partially blind to this society with which the original pact had been made, not knowing what the pact was, knowing only that it had been shattered.

Behind them came Max Nathan, smelling of verbena and shaving lotion and the musk of Gina's perfume. Max's tentative smile came out like fish sucking air, fearful of suffocation, emitting a plea: *Help me.*

No Monk.

Jack Schraft appeared, a skeleton dressed in a suit, pale as cardboard and watery-eyed, but determined and rational and coldly appraising: *I came for the facts.*

Then Victor Karp emerged from his chauffeured limousine, a carnation in his buttonhole, a sober, ritual, white-moustached face – a man who had lived for sixty years as an elitist, subsidising culture with Arkansas oil wells, deliberately removed from the rest of the Jewish community, yet who came when he was summoned, proof of his democracy. 'How are you, Reuben,' he said. The message was: *I hope this won't take long; I have other, more important, more social, considerations.*

Harris arrived, with a military bearing, swallowing hard like a stiff-necked goose, his anger repressed under piety and virtue; the need to serve God in direct proportion to his need for a watchdog over his violence. His message was a double one: *I am able to suffer anything.* And: *Are we going to get those bastards, or aren't we?*

Lewis Eisenberg, president of Gold Variety Chain Stores, came next, dressed like a floorwalker and wringing his hands mechanically, his face twisted by anguish and denial and confusion and monstrous fear: *How did anybody let this happen?*

Behind Lewis came John Abrahmson, playing the clown, his cherub face ruddy, looking like an aging acrobat juggling money and family and eccentricity and fear, huffing and looking wild, sending out the unmistakable message: *Let me out of here.*

The men filed by. From the doorway. Reuben watched them assemble themselves on the cotton bales. There were men's places in the world. There were locker rooms and hunting camps and army barracks and football fields; poker games; the altar. There were sacrosanct places preserved for men only – and this, tonight, was another one of those, a secret gathering bound by a common purpose. Men came together for the purposes of winning, fighting, killing, self-preservation; seldom to build. Another freight rumbled by. The warehouse shook. In a moment, the walls settled down. He hung onto his grandfather's cane, feeling like Moses, and knowing that he wasn't – knowing that he was simply better equipped to deal with threat than anybody else around. His business was crisis. Crisis was one moment piled on the next moment and what came out of it. His task, tonight, was to garner these disparate men into a unit based on the tenuous bond of a religion which no longer constituted faith. The greater bonds were survival, self-interest, anger, and fear. The simplest unification was to tap the dark side. He didn't want to do that. It seemed important to do this another way; search for, and find, some other way.

His watch said eight. The street was empty. No Monk.

He closed but didn't bolt the door.

Then he stood there a moment, concerned about Monk. But the problem of Monk was superseded by the crucial nature of the moment and the dilemma which, suddenly, began to come clear.

In a moment he would move through the warehouse and step into the circle of light. He could hear the men talking, arguing, morose, angry. He would tap the cane on the concrete. They would quiet. He would wait. Each would look towards him. As children. Frightened. Furious. Cowed. Rebellious. And he would look at their faces, knowing each of them, their lives, their sins, their fears; knowing the size of each of them; knowing they trusted him simply because they had no choice.

The choice was his.

He could lie to these men; lie to them and frighten them and manipulate them and handle them – and come out with the money. He could complete his alliance with Barksdale and Justin. Because Barksdale had tapped into his fear, and his arrogance, and his own belief that he was not like the rest of them. And Justin had tapped into his southern heritage: his love of the land; his bond to his grandfather; his loyalty to all things native and southern.

But he was also a Jew.

Like politics, conspiracies were built on the premise that no one in one's own camp was trustworthy. If a man lived long enough, everybody betrayed everybody. Even Mollie. Yet, if survival lay in a loyalty to all camps, how did one hang onto one's soul?

The crux of the moment became clear. He could lie. He could play on their fears and insecurities and sell the Barksdale position as truth. Or he could take the risk of trust. He could tell what he knew, what he felt − all the facts, his own misgivings, the alternatives; let each man weigh the information as it stood. Because his alliance, whether he liked it or not, was with them, these men, for better or worse, whatever they were, however frail or fearful or less than perfect.

They were all Jews.

Southern and not-southern; weak and graceless; ignorant and overfed and argumentative − this was his camp.

God help him.

Buster watched the taillights of Levitt's truck pull away through the darkness; standing there, at the edge of the building site, until the little red sparks were gone. Imagining Eula, out there somewhere, the bright red car streaking through the night on some highway; or maybe parked now, Eula in some worn-out motel room, lying in bed and thinking about him; but gone.

He turned around and started to walk, circling around the newly poured foundation, an acre of land; everything pitch-black except for the bulb Levitt had left burning in the shack where the tools and the lumber and the dynamite were stored, and the stained glass windows that had come all the way from Israel. The shack was padlocked, but Clyde could get a lock open and shut again, make it look like nobody had ever been near it. Then Clyde would take the dynamite to Brendon Hollyhoke, waiting, on Spring Street, in the big paintless rotting house, because Vernon Powell had been to court this afternoon, and the judge had handed down a court order, and the sheriff was going to march at sunup − but there wouldn't be nothing to shoot at but a bare piece of land. Hollyhoke had made the decision that if it was going to turn out to be a war, the old house on the edge of the Oyster Bar was a better fort than a barren piece of land.

Why did it feel like it wouldn't make a damn? Martin Luther King was marching in Memphis with the garbage collectors, and Brendon Hollyhoke was holed up on Spring Street; violence or nonviolence, Jesus or the vote – it all felt like the wind, the dynamite nothing more than a talisman against the raffling off of his soul. The act of taking it simply meant that he would not become Attica. But Reuben Buchman had taken the dynamite back on Sunday; nothing to do but to send it back by Leila. And now Monk Levitt had set him out here with a gun – the gun, like the dynamite, making him more powerless; no black man wanted a job where he held a gun in his hand, meant to protect the white man's property. He imagined a thief appearing. A white man. The possibility of death in the weight of the pistol was his own death. If a white man came out of the night, it was him with the pistol, night watchman, black, and maybe killing a white man, any kind of white man – he would be signing his own life away with that bullet. Because if it happened, it wouldn't matter that it was a white man who had put the pistol in his hand, and it wouldn't matter that the white man he shot was a scavenger; it would matter only that he was a nigger with a gun who had pumped a bullet into a white man. And if they didn't hang him, there'd be no work for him ever again, he'd be hunted, haunted, chased down, framed. He'd be a dead man.

So what if Clyde came in a little while, another half-case of dynamite – so what ? A handful of black men on Spring Street, what was that ? The end of it might be a couple of dead black men, and maybe a couple of dead white men, but he, Buster, would still be looking down the same road, and that road didn't change, might never change, not for him. He belonged to a generation of martyrs. On the bodies of the dead, maybe their children might walk to freedom; maybe. Hollyhoke, with his African Republic, was asking for death. Martin Luther King, with his marches, was asking for death. Clyde, tonight, with his lock-picking tools, would be asking for death. And him, too; Buster Jackson; asking for death. Because the white man had a dog as tall as a mountain and as wide as a city, and the dog had grown fat on the meat of history, and had grow fierce on the flesh of black men; and the dog guarded the kingdom of the South. He had seen it in his dreams – the wings of a bat, and the hide of an elephant, the claws of a wildcat, the laugh of a coyote, the teeth of a lion. Driving black men into the slavery of the North, or pawing them to death in the earth of the South.

What you gonna do when I'm gone ? Eula had said. *Every Sunday you gonna go out and look at that forty acres that somebody said your grandpaw used to own ? And think about gettin' it back when you ain't never gonna get it back ? All you got here is what used to be. And what used to be was nothin' but worse than what you got now.*

But he hadn't listened, hadn't heard her, because being run by a woman was a nigger thing; like Vaseline was a nigger thing, and the automobile was a white thing, and the telephone was a white thing, and stealing was a nigger thing, and killing was a white thing, and singing was a nigger thing. But now he heard her, and now it seemed to him that no matter how much he hated it, he couldn't change it; nothing to be in this place but two things, a nigger, or a white man, one or the other, and he could be neither. It was nothing more than a hunt, the white men with the bat-winged dog set loose, and the game was the black man's soul.

He stood still in the darkness, the bulb in the shack shining far away and glimmering like a small moon, and the night sounds around him, cicadas and frogs, and the sound of a car moving somewhere out there, then passing on; not Clyde. And in that moment, his decision was made. Tomorrow morning, he would pack up and go north. He would take the pistol. And when he got there, wherever it was, he would step down from his truck and go in somewhere, wherever it might be, and he would say, loud and clear, *I'm Buster Jackson.* And the first man who said, *It ain't gonna be no different up here for a nigger like you* – he'd level the pistol and blow his brains out.

And maybe he could find Eula.

'Let the F.B.I. pay its own goddamned informers,' Leo said.

'What are you – a Communist?' Lewis Eisenberg said. 'I'm a *good American.* I built nine stores the American way. Nothing about America's ever let me down, and I'm standing up for the F.B.I. Whatever they say do, I'm ready to do.'

'I agree with Leo,' Jake said.

'You ain't been nowhere but the junkyard and the hospital for twenty years,' John Abrahmson said. 'How the hell would you know how to do anything except *agree with Leo?*'

'You lay off Papa – ' Mickey said. He peeled off his glasses and glared at John.

'*You* want to go to Washington?' John said. 'You gonna take time off your business? Go sit in congressmen's offices? You want *Yankees* fighting our battles for us?'

'I don't want any trouble,' Dave Colman said. 'I want to do it the way that's not going to make any trouble.'

Reuben orbited the circle tapping the old man's cane on the concrete. Nobody paid any attention. Out of truth had come chaos.

'Anti-Semitism's trouble,' Jack Schraft said. 'Any way you look at it, anti-Semitism's trouble.'

John waved a pudgy fist. 'Don't be callin' no names. My family's been here since before the Civil War and we ain't never run into what you're talkin' about.'

'I ran into it Saturday night,' Harris said. 'Maybe you don't remember what happened Saturday night?'

'It's not going to happen again,' Max Nathan said. 'In the same place twice, lightning doesn't –'

'Shut up!' Reuben shouted. The room hushed.

'I resent that,' Victor Karp said. 'I won't be spoken to in that tone.'

'We're not going to have this.' Reuben had taken on the role of authority, and before it was over he would be loved and hated, hailed and reviled. Before it was over he would throttle every damn one of them. He damned the thing called conscience, or arrogance, or whatever it was had got him into this; and he damned the old man, who had left it to him. 'One man at a time,' he said. 'One man at a time gets to talk. Then we make a motion. Then we vote. That's the way it's going to be. Anybody who doesn't like it can leave right now.'

Victor Karp stood up. 'Good night,' he said. He moved across the circle of light.

'Just a moment,' Reuben said. Victor Karp stopped. He turned. 'Yes?'

'I want something clear,' Reuben said.

'Yes?' Victor Karp stood unruffled. Not much touched him, ever. Seven oil wells constituted a great deal of insulation. Behind Victor, Reuben saw the warehouse door open. With relief, he recognised Monk's silhouette as it entered. The sight was an affirmation. Monk had arrived. Whatever happened, he could count on Monk to back him up.

'I don't give a damn if you stay or not, Mr Karp,' Reuben said. 'I don't give a damn if you vote or not. You were, however, invited here tonight because you happen to be a well-heeled member of the Jewish community. So what I do give a damn about is how much money you plan to contribute to our decision tonight. Trips to Washington take money. F.B.I. informers take money. Any plan we might evolve will require money. How much, Mr Karp?'

Victor Karp didn't blink. 'Ten thousand dollars,' he said.

'Thank you.' Reuben said. Behind him, the men began to murmur. He tapped the cane. The men fell quiet. Ten thousand dollars bought a lot of quiet. Victor Karp turned and made a military exit. His figure became a shadow. Monk's shadow moved in and turned into Monk, and crossed directly to Reuben, his face strained and angry.

'Look at this – ' he said. 'Goddamnit, look at it.' He waved a newspaper. Reuben took it. THE CAUCASIAN COMMUNIQUE leaped out in banner headlines. 'I found it on the seat of my truck tonight,' Monk said. '*Look* at it.'

There were photographs of prominent Jews. Bernard Baruch and Henry Morgenthau and David Dubinsky; Felix Frankfurter; others. A big headline read: THE COMING RED DICTATORSHIP. The subhead read: ASIATIC MARXIST JEWS CONTROL ENTIRE WORLD AS LAST WORLD WAR COMMENCES. THOUSANDS OF PLOTTERS PLACED IN KEY POSITIONS BY INVISIBLE GOVERNMENT. An editorial note read: *The information printed here is not available from any of the regular channels of information which are controlled by our enemy.* The enemy was 'the Jew,' including a 'Jew Plan' which outlined a plot to take over the world by means of revolution, integration, mongrelisation, war, usury, depression, the U.N., and other assorted phenomena.

It was no better, no worse, possibly slightly more ignorant than all classic hate-literature everywhere. As he read, the silence Victor Karp had left behind deepened. Then Harris rose, took the newspaper out of his hands, sat down again, and began to read. Reuben saw the blood drain from Harris' face. Harris handed it on to Leo. Jake and Mickey read over Leo's shoulder. The printed accusations were familiar even to those who had never read a hate-sheet before; those same accusations stretched back thousands of years – the Jew as alien. Reuben had always believed the Jew was no more alien in Mississippi than the Frenchman who drove out the Indians, or the Spaniard who came afterwards, or the Anglo-Saxon pioneer with his Bible and his ax and his whiskey. The alien here, like the alien everywhere, were the ignorant and the violent.

Monk broke the quiet. 'Sonofabitch. I found that thing on the seat of my truck. Then I went home to change and got a goddamned telephone call. *A dirty Jew*, he called me. A lot of other crap. *Pass it on*, he said. *Tell your Jew-lawyer friend who's defendin' Higgins –* '

'Tell me what?' Reuben felt his pulse accelerate.

'Who the hell is Higgins?' John Abrahmson said.

'I think that's the dentist who hired the black technician,' Leo said. 'Wasn't he picked up on a homosexuality charge?' He frowned at Reuben.

'That's right,' Reuben said.

203

'Trouble,' Dave Colman said. 'Nothing but trouble.'

'Did you take on that goddamned niggerlover?' John demanded. 'What the hell did you do that for? No wonder they're after us.'

A hush fell. Reuben felt each man snatch at the unlikely explanation. The need for a scapegoat rippled through the room. Leo passed John the newspaper.

'I don't want to see that crap.' John handed it on to Jack Schraft.

Beside him, Reuben could feel Monk's rage coming out like waves from a radiator.

'Why the hell didn't you tell me you got a phone call the night of the bombing?' Monk said. 'Why the hell are you foolin' around with Higgins? Goddamnit – you know that's askin' for it.' Monk was a gun, the trigger cocked, ready to go off. Reuben could remember what the voice on the telephone had kicked off in himself – the depth and power of his own capacity for violence.

'Shove it,' Reuben said quietly. 'I take the cases I want to take. Nobody tells me what cases to take.'

'Maybe you should drop it,' Jake suggested.

'Goddamned right,' John said.

'It's not worth it,' Leo said.

Mickey murmured his acquiescence. Lewis Eisenberg's head bobbed like a cork. Max Nathan stared at the concrete floor.

Reuben grasped the cane. 'I've handled cases for every one of you – a lot of goddamned cases that weren't worth the enemies I made or the time I spent. Nobody tells me what's worth it and what's not. I follow my own goddamned conscience – which included calling this meeting tonight to plan action. But you don't want action. All you want is somebody – or something – to blame. Screw it. Take your meeting and shove it –' He turned and began to walk. Then he felt a hand grab his shoulder.

'For Christ's sake, you can't walk out on us,' Monk said.

Reuben stopped, turned. 'Why the hell not?'

Monk swung an arm over the assembled men. 'Look at 'em,' he said. 'They're waitin' for somebody to tell 'em what to do. I need you to back me up. Because I'm tellin' you what we got to do. I say we hire a goddamned torpedo to find the bomber and blow his head off!'

'What the hell are you talking about?'

'They're Nazis. I say we get 'em. I say we hire somebody to get 'em!' Monk was speaking to the men. Reuben watched their faces. Higgins was forgotten. Almost as a unit they recoiled. A number of still, cold seconds marched by.

Finally, Jack Schraft said, 'I'm a doctor. I don't kill. I heal.'

'It was a goddamned doctor who shot Huey Long,' Monk said.

'We're Jews,' Harris said, 'not killers.'

A strange quality of quiet blanketed the room, as if the lessons of history – fear, humiliation, self-doubt, self-hatred, despair – had asserted their weight. What Reuben felt coming from them was not integrity but an acceptance of impotence.

He released his fury by rattling the cane against the concrete floor. 'The choice is not to be *killers* or *victims !*' he said.

The silence broke. He heard a rumble of assertiveness run through the men. He had them back. A shabby army. What the hell was he going to do with them ?

'I'm going out to smoke a cigarette,' he said.

On the sidewalk, he said, 'Listen to me – '

'Screw 'em,' Monk said. 'In Germany they would have marched into ovens.'

'Look – Saturday night I felt the same way you do. A newspaper's not personal. A telephone call is. I know how you feel. But there's more to it than that.' Quickly he filled Monk in on the dynamite, the Maryville information, the meeting with Barksdale on the road. 'I'm trying to find a way to deal with it,' he said.

'What if you can't ?'

'You go along with me.' Reuben said. 'If it turns out I can't – we'll do it your way.'

'You and me. We'll do it ourselves ?'

'I don't know.'

'Why the hell not ?'

Reuben looked at Monk. He remembered going through the cemetery gate in Maryville thinking that he and Monk in some other time might have fought dragons together. The time might come.

'Alright,' he said finally.

Monk put out his hand. Reuben took it. The handclasp felt cold and strange. On the tracks behind the warehouse, another freight rumbled past. The sound of a train whistle filled the air, then died.

'I saw your papa in New Orleans. He's fine. He sent you a samovar.'

'Stubborn old bastard,' Monk said. 'Sheila told him a hundred times she didn't want that samovar.'

Reuben tapped the cane. The men fell quiet.

'Alright,' he said. 'Are we going to raise the money or not ?'

'I don't know,' Jake said. 'It's not the money. We've all got the money. God knows we were trained to make money. . . . ' He sighed an old man's sigh. 'I've just been thinking about it. I remember when I was a boy in the Ukraine – the czarist police used to come around and ask my papa, and the neighbors, for money. They'd promise protection. If we didn't give the money, there'd be a pogrom. If we did give the money, they kept it, then accused the Jews of bribery, and a pogrom was mounted on the charge of corruption. . . . I don't know. . . . ' He sighed again.

'Papa – this isn't the Ukraine,' Mickey said gently.

'I don't know what you're talkin' about,' John Abrahmson said. 'My grandpaw built the first temple here, and all of downtown. My papa built the Sinai Hospital and the Holmesdale Hotel. Ain't nobody around here ever gonna tell *me* what to do.'

'I want to do whatever is going to cause the least trouble,' Dave Colman said.

'Listen, Reuben,' Leo said, let's have it straight. If we raise the money – you trust this Barksdale or not ?'

'No. I don't trust him because I don't even know him. But I don't intend to hand the money over. I don't intend for us to be silent partners. I intend to have a say through every step of this thing. Now let's vote on it. All those in favor – '

A silence ensued. Nobody moved. Nobody spoke. Nobody raised a hand.

Finally Jack Schraft said, 'I don't think it's our decision, Reuben. You're the one who'll bear the brunt.' He looked around at the men. 'I think we have to hand it back to Reuben.'

'I agree with that,' Max Nathan said.

'So do I,' Lewis Eisenberg said.

'Anybody oppose it ?' Jake said.

Another silence fell.

Reuben raked at his hair. Forty-one in March. On the day of the old man's death. Except for Mickey, he was the youngest man in the room.

He looked at Monk. *You and me,* Monk had said. *We'll do it ourselves.* Except for Monk, they had all become children.

His eyes swept the circle, resting a moment on each face. Each face relinquished its choice to him.

'Alright,' he said. 'You raise the money. I'll go and see Barksdale. Tonight.'

Twenty-three

THE TELEPHONE was at the rear of the warehouse.

He stopped in front of it, pulled out Barksdale's card, and read the private number by the flame of his cigarette lighter. Then he thought about Monk, waiting for him outside; his oldest friend, Monk, and the offer of justifiable violence – the direct frontier solution sanctioned by southern tradition. An eye for an eye, burning for burning.

He wasn't ready to accept that. Not yet.

He had been born a Jew, and he had been born a southerner, but he had *chosen* the law. He believed that the battle of good and evil could be fought in a courtroom. *I believe in justice,* he had said to Eula Williams. *I get my kicks in the courtroom.* He believed in the courtroom when he was in it. He believed in his own power as a lawyer. He was one of the few men in the South who could turn a lynch mob into a jury. *I believe in myself,* he should have said. The real question had never been tested: How much did he believe in southern justice ?

He clicked the lighter again and dialed Barksdale's number. Barksdale was the available law-and-order alternative, committed to a questionable authority which had nothing to do with the welfare of the South. Beyond that, even given a dedicated Barksdale, the same question remained. Arrested terrorists would be tried first in a local court. How many Klan members would end up on the jury ?

The line rang three times. Then Barksdale picked up. 'Yes ?'

'This is Buchman. I want to see you tonight.' He felt the release of motion. From motion came action. From action came solution or error. Error was preferable to passivity. His decision had been made as he dialed. The Barksdale proposition had to be fully explored.

'We have an appointment at nine in the morning. Your partner made it.' Barksdale's voice was brisk as an autumn wind, twice as cold, with the promise of winter.

'I'm switching it. Tonight. You pick the place.' Reuben waited.

A draft of chill air rushed by, like Barksdale's spirit. Finally Barksdale said:

'The Greyhound Bus station. The Coffee Shop. Fifteen minutes.' There was an abrupt click. Reuben was left with the dial tone. He hung up. He looked at his watch by the flame of the lighter. It was ten forty-five.

He went through the warehouse. He could hear the men at the business of money raising. It sounded like an auction. Each one of them bidding for the prize of immunity. The burden of decision, and consequences, had been left to him.

On the sidewalk, Monk waited.

'Did you get him?'

'I'm going to meet him now.' The air had turned damp. The moon was hidden by clouds and there was the smell of rain. At midnight, it would become the first day of March. March always rained. In April, the tulips came up.

'Do you want me to go with you?'

'Uh uh.' He unsnapped his key ring and extracted a key. 'The Williamsburg's closed. Let yourself in and wait for me there. Make us a couple of pastrami sandwiches.'

Monk took the key. 'Rye?'

'Mustard and pickles. No mayonnaise.'

He lowered the car windows. As he drove, the damp air swept past him. The streets were dark, the moonlight obscured by powdery clouds.

He kept the speedometer at thirty. The warehouse was close to the bus station. He didn't know where Barksdale was coming from. Fifteen minutes. So Barksdale lived fifteen minutes or less from the bus station. What else did he know about Barksdale? Nothing. Barksdale had files on him; he had nothing. He wondered if Barksdale knew who Mollie had slept with. . . .

The last thing he wanted to think about tonight was Mollie.

He went back to Barksdale. Barksdale had files; he had instincts and speculation. What kind of man was Barksdale? What were his vices? Maybe he gambled. What was behind the super-American image? What kind of scars did he bear? Nobody got through life untouched. Assurance was style, not always content. Doubt bred doubt – any good lawyer knew that. Assurance was halfway to any kind of victory. What kind of victory did Barksdale want? Barksdale had said they both wanted the same thing. Barksdale wasn't the enemy. The real enemy was out there. Barksdale constituted a possible alliance. Within the law. Barksdale had a Bureau behind him and all he had was a handful of Jews. Then he remembered the Bible was filled with odds like that. David had leveled Goliath with one smooth stone.

He turned into Main Street.

The sidewalks were wet, newly washed, gleaming under the passing streetlights. Brightly lit windows were arranged like stage sets, frozen actors waiting for cues. Mannequins, like Barksdale, presenting unblemished fronts. Barksdale was a man bound by government codes and Bureau stipulations. How bound ? Justin had laid out the Bureau position. Was Barksdale a man who would act only according to red tape and orders ? Or was Barksdale a man who would go beyond Bureau restrictions ? Tonight, he had raised the money. He understood that he, Reuben, went with the money. The next step meant a total involvement, wherever it might lead. With a man he knew nothing about. The choice was a crucial one. What kind of core did Barksdale have ? Was there any integrity he could count on ? Or did he simply need Barksdale to be what he wanted him to be because the alternative was Monk, and Monk's way ?

On the road Monday night, Barksdale had taken his personal measure. Tonight it was his turn.

The bus station was across the street from the railroad station. The same parking lot served both. He pulled in. There were a couple of service trucks and less than a dozen cars. Nobody rode trains or buses anymore. Blacks going north; civil rights workers going south; the poor and the social-minded.

He went through the terminal and into the Coffee Shop. Barksdale hadn't arrived. The place was nearly empty. An old rummy had passed out in a back booth, and a redneck family with string-tied suitcases and two sad-eyed children filled a table. That was it. His watch said he was two minutes early.

He took a stool at the gray tiled counter. The counterman took his time shuffling over. Reuben ordered coffee. In front of him was a plate of soggy doughnuts. A fly was trapped under the plastic dome. He watched the fly buzz around in the sticky sugar and hurl itself against the invisible walls of its prison. It occurred to him that most men lived in invisible prisons, hurling themselves against forces they could neither see nor name. For him, set the forces had made themselves visible. He lifted the dome and the fly free. One simple act. The difference between flies and men.

The counterman came back with the coffee. He looked at his watch again. It was on the nose. He turned around. Barksdale was coming towards him, tall and angular, a long-strided gait. Under-

14   209

stated. A bloodhound. The quarry was human. Whether the man was or not remained to be discovered.

Barksdale took the stool beside him. Under the overcoat, Reuben caught a glimpse of a sweater. Beige cashmere. Off-duty clothing. The counterman brought over another cup of coffee. Barksdale stirred in three spoonfuls of sugar. Then he saw that Barksdale was ticking off the details as accurately as he was. Taking his time. Silence was a tool. Most men were uncomfortable with silence; silence bred paranoia; silence gave a man time to read his own doubts and fears into the simplest gesture. He allowed himself to imagine his own worst fear: Barksdale would turn and say, *What kind of man are you? You can't even handle your own wife.*

Without turning, Barksdale said, 'What is it?'

Something in the tone made Reuben's tactical decision. Barksdale was a lawyer. He couldn't play lawyer with Barksdale. Barksdale was trained. He couldn't trap Barksdale into revealing any information he wasn't prepared to reveal. Reuben had one strength. His instincts – the inner seismograph that was tuned to measure the discrepancy between what a man said and what a man was.

'We had a meeting tonight,' Reuben said.

Barksdale turned. It was a swift, quiet face, without mercy. A message came through. He had been aware of the meeting. 'What was the outcome?'

'We can put twenty-five thousand dollars at your disposal,' Reuben said. He recorded the slight lift of Barksdale's left eyebrow, a slight hint of a frown.

'I'm not sure that's adequate,' Barksdale said. Justin had said forty or fifty. Where had Justin gotten that figure? From Barksdale? Or was Barksdale aware of the outcome of the meeting? Had his question been moot?

'We raised fifty,' Reuben said. 'I'm a gambler. I'm betting half. If your way doesn't pay off, I've still got alternatives.' He watched Barksdale go over the alternatives. There was Washington. There was also the possibility of sending out word himself. It was a poverty culture. For twenty-five grand some starving redneck would turn in the names of the bombers and his grandmother besides. Barksdale could see all of that. But it didn't show. Nothing showed on his face, an F.B.I. face, gentile, reserved and secretive. Then another message came through. He had caught Barksdale off base. Barksdale had been expecting a hysterical Jew, looking for guarantees and reassurances.

'I'm sorry,' Barksdale said. 'I can't accept a half commitment.' It came through as half-truth.

'You came halfway, I came halfway,' Reuben said.

'We have an appointment tomorrow morning,' Barksdale said. 'On the basis of a full commitment, I'll be glad to share all the files which hold information relevant to this case.'

'Why don't we start with who did the bombing?' Reuben said.

'I don't know who it is,' Barksdale said. Reuben felt the lie. Barksdale would hold back until he chose not to hold back. Barksdale would turn over those files he chose to turn over. If he involved himself fully, there was no way to get around a dependency on Barksdale's integrity, or lack of it.

'How would it work?'

'I make contact,' Barksdale said. 'You attend all preliminary meetings if you wish. I don't touch the money. All payment of funds will go directly from your hands into the hands of the informants. You take your own risks. The F.B.I., under this set of circumstances, can't be responsible for your life or safety. Obviously, however, we'll do everything possible to guard your welfare.' It came out straight. Not a lie in it anywhere. Whatever else Barksdale was, he was at home with a battle plan.

'How much risk is involved?'

'There might be a little, there might be a lot. You realise we're dealing with a lunatic fringe.'

'Between the two of us, how would it work?'

'I'm trained for it,' Barksdale said. 'I call the shots.'

'No,' Reuben said. He didn't follow it up. He let it lie there. A long moment went by. He felt Barksdale wrestling with it. Then he felt some conclusion settle. He couldn't read the outcome.

Carefully, Barksdale said, 'What do you propose?'

'I figure it this way,' Reuben said, easy and quiet. 'If I did it alone, with fifty thousand dollars, I'd take the risks – I'd call the shots. I bought your offer only because I want to stay within the law. But I can't give up all my prerogatives. The most I'll do is share them.'

Barksdale hesitated. Then the conclusion came up. 'You'll be informed of every step to be taken. That's as far as I can go.'

Reuben studied Barksdale's face, openly, like a man taking inventory. 'In your business, alliances are made on the basis of a common enemy,' Reuben said. 'In my life, I make collaborations based on trust. It's a quirk in my personality. I don't trust authority figures – I only trust men.' He met Barksdale's eyes in a direct gaze.

Barksdale broke the tension. He turned away, picked up his coffee. Reuben watched Barksdale's chiseled profile as he brought the cup to his lips. Then Barksdale set the cup down and turned. 'We suffer from our own image,' he said. The briskness had gone out of his voice. The exchange wasn't in the manual. 'I've been in the F.B.I. for twenty years. Right out of law school . . .' He paused again. 'I'm married,' he said. 'My wife is eight months pregnant. I have a twelve-year-old son and an eight-year-old daughter. I asked for this assignment. Because I'm a southerner.' He laid some change on the counter. He rose. 'Good night,' he said. He turned and walked off.

Reuben watched his back move across the Coffee Shop. Tall and angular and long-strided. Through the plate-glass window, Reuben watched Barksdale cross the terminal. Then he disappeared.

Reuben sat still. He waited for the verdict. There was Barksdale's tone in the last exchange; the tone had seemed honest. There was also the content; Barksdale had told him nothing he could have discovered by a quick check. *My wife is eight months pregnant.* The one personal piece of information in the small speech which might have been a ploy – or might have been the most that Barksdale could manage, conditioned by twenty years of training.

The verdict came back: a hung jury. At best, it was going to be an uneasy alliance.

Reuben picked up the cane. He wondered what the old man would have done. He didn't know. But he knew himself. Whether it was Mollie, or Justin, or Barksdale, he knew he couldn't live half and half. But the choice was not that simple. The choice had become Monk's way or Barksdale's way. Monk waited for him. Monk offered twenty years of trust and the promise of swift violence – an exercise in southern manhood. Barksdale offered an uncomfortable collaboration and a fifty-fifty chance of law and justice – a commitment to the beliefs of his chosen profession. Then he saw what it came down to – a weighing of personal priorities. He was a Jew, a southerner, a lawyer. Three codes. One would have to take precedence.

Which one ?

He didn't know.

On the wall, a pale blue Schlitz neon blinked on and off, the only light in the Williamsburg. They sat at a table near the bay window.

'I don't get it,' Monk said. 'You took his temperature, you're

212

not satisfied with the reading – but you're going to go along with him anyway?'

'That's the size of it,' Reuben said. He looked out through the tiny panes. The parking lot, the street, the shopping center on the other side made up a deserted moonscape. He and Monk might have been the only two creatures alive. 'Why the hell don't we forget it for tonight. I've had it.'

'Screw it,' Monk said. He opened two more beers. A half-dozen beer cans and the remnants of two pastrami sandwiches littered the table. The Schlitz clock said three minutes until midnight. 'What happened in New Orleans? All you told me about was my papa –'

'What do you want to know?' Reuben said. 'Zack doesn't change, B. V.'s a pig, Myrtle Stein was a bitch. I got drunk, I got laid. I interviewed a witness for the Higgins case and I saw your papa. That was it.'

'Was she any good?'

'Who?'

'The lay.'

'I was so damned drunk, I don't remember.'

'Listen –' Monk said, 'how's the thing with you and Mollie?'

'I don't know what you're talking about.' Reuben bristled.

'You know what I mean.'

'What kind of question is that? How's the thing with you and Sheila?' A shaft of pure hatred thrust through his abdomen. They were friends. He and Monk. Twenty years. They had shared everything – even the possibility of going out together to kill a man. Yet the thought of Monk knowing about Mollie was an intolerable one.

'That's what I'm talking about,' Monk said. 'What the hell do you *do* about it?' He swallowed more beer, tipping his head back and guzzling. Reuben wanted to hit him.

'Do about what?' Reuben felt every muscle tense.

'Listen – you were best man at my wedding. I was best man at yours. What the hell did we know? You marry a Jewish girl – that's all we knew. Virgins. *Screw virgins*,' he said. He took the beer can in both hands and twisted it. Then he popped open another one. 'I'm not saying Sheila doesn't screw, but, hell – if I didn't get out of this town every couple of months, I'd go nuts.' He leaned forward. 'Didn't you ever wonder how it'd be to be married to a *broad*? Every night you ball your brains out.'

Reuben grinned. The muscles let go. He swallowed some beer. 'I never thought about it,' he said.

'Sure you did,' Monk said. 'Hell, I've known Mollie since she was in kindergarten. She was always a professional virgin. I keep trying to tell Sheila – for Christ's sake, it's 1968. There's a sex revolution going on. You should hear what they're doing out in California. I said – listen – we'll have a nude swimming party as soon as it warms up. What do you think? She screamed so loud, she woke up all the kids.'

Reuben finished off the beer. Fatigue washed through him. 'Maybe we'd better get home,' he said.

'In a minute,' Monk said. 'I've got to ask you something.'

'What is it?' Reuben said. His head had begun to pound from beer and exhaustion. The blue neon blinked on and off in his eyes, throwing Monk's face in and out of darkness.

'We've been friends a long time,' Monk said. 'If anything was bothering you, I'd be the first one you'd tell, right? And if anything was bothering me, I'd come to you first. That's right, isn't it?'

'That's right,' Reuben said.

'I want to ask you something. Did you ever lay a black broad?'

'No,' Reuben said. An image of Eula Williams flickered on and off with the neon.

'I've been thinking about it,' Monk said. 'Every guy I know has gotten some black stuff. I figured out it's on account of we're Jews – a gentile broad's bad enough. But there's this girl that used to come around to see Buster. Not even light-skinned – black as the ace of spades, but she sure has got something. I told Buster, "Get her the hell out of here, I don't like women on the job." She hasn't been back in a couple of days. But I found out who she is, where she lives. I've been thinking about it. Buster's not there tonight – I'll bet that girl's pretty lonely. I thought maybe you'd go with me. Tonight. We'll go see what it's all about.'

'You've had too much to drink,' Reuben said. 'Come on. We're not going to the Oyster Bar. We're going home.' He gathered up the beer cans. He didn't want Frieda raising hell in the morning. He carried them over to the garbage can in back of the meat case and dumped them. He was on his way back to the table when his head cleared suddenly. Monk had said, *Buster's not there tonight.*

He came across the brick floor. The cane echoed. He stopped at the table. 'Where's Buster?'

Monk looked up. The blue light flickered on and off across his face. 'You know where he is. I put him on as night watchman.'

'I told you to take him off,' Reuben said angrily.

'I'll take him off tomorrow,' Monk said. 'What the hell's the matter with you?'

'Let's go,' Reuben said.

Monk got up. 'You're the one who pulled out on me. What the hell right do you have to be sore?'

Reuben headed for the door. Monk came behind him. The bell tinkled. They went through.

'Give me the key,' Reuben said. Monk thrust the key at him. He locked up. When he turned around, Monk was climbing into the truck.

He climbed in the other side. 'Drive to the temple site.'

'What the hell for?'

'I'll tell you later,' Reuben said. He wouldn't. He had given his word to Buster. Buster was one of his own. *His nigger*. As a white man, he might screw Buster's wife, or cheat Buster out of a year's profit on ten acres of cotton – a black man expected to get taken in the areas of sex and business. But a white man took care of his own when they were sick, saw that they never literally starved, and never broke a protective promise. Buster would count on that unwritten code which still bound the races. He could pull up with Monk, send Buster home, and Buster would know he had kept his word.

The truck tires squealed as Monk backed out, turned around, and headed for the road. He turned right, then left on Forest Drive without pausing for the stop sign. A mile down the road was the temple site. The truck rattled. Monk pressed down on the accelerator angrily.

Then, through the windshield, the darkness shattered with the sound of an explosion. Over the rooftops of the houses and through the trees, a bright burst of orange light filled the moonless sky. An earth rumble passed beneath them. The truck trembled as it rolled forward. Then an eerie silence settled, and the terrible light gaped like an open wound in the hide of the night.

'Jesus – ' Monk said. 'It's the temple.'

'Keep going,' Reuben said.

A pair of blinding headlights suddenly came into view and sped towards them. The car whizzed past, a blue of blue. Reuben spun. The back of the truck was piled high with lumber, the view through the back windshield obscured. He cursed violently.

'You think that was them?'

'I don't know. *Keep going.*'

It came into view. Flames, out of control, streaked skyward, shooting off sparks and eerie dancing fire balls. Monk hit the brake. The truck careered to a stop.

'*Duck!*' he shouted.

Another explosion shattered the night as the dynamite in the shack went off. Reuben hit the floorboard, hands clasped over his head. The sound shrieked in his ears. Debris hit the roof of the truck. The windshield cracked and rained down like hail.

Then it turned quiet.

He started to rise.

'*Stay down!*' Monk shouted, crouched, on the other side of the floorboard. '*That damn shack's full of dynamite!*'

He ducked.

Another explosion thundered, followed immediately by another. A moment went by. A third blast of dynamite went off. The truck rocked. The sky turned to daylight. The earth split with the sound of an avalanche.

Then the silence came back.

He waited.

Finally Monk said, 'I think that's it.'

He slid back onto the seat. He saw both hands were bleeding from splinters of glass. He was shaking. He looked at Monk. Monk's hands, like his, were speckled with blood. Lit by the flames, Monk's face was ashen.

'Are you alright?' Reuben said.

Monk nodded. He opened the truck door. Reuben's door wouldn't come open. He slid out behind Monk. The bonfire spread out in front of them, a sheet of solid flame, crackling, eating up the sky.

'Bastards –' Monk said hoarsely. 'Four months of goddamned work. A *temple*.' Something glittered on Monk's rough jaw. Tears of fury. Reuben closed his eyes. The sound of the flames seared his brain.

'Buster –' he said. 'Where's Buster?'

Monk grabbed his arm. 'Nobody can get in there.'

From a long distance away, the wail of sirens filled the air.

'What if he's in there?'

'If he's in there, he's dead,' Monk said.

Twenty-four

MARCH RAINED.

A flash of lightning streaked across the sky, some thunder rolled like God's echo to the explosion; then the rain began to come down, spearing the flames and making instant mud of the earth. It was after midnight, the first day of March.

The sheriff's car with its whirling red light came first. Four fire trucks came next, sirens screaming, loaded with men in black slickers. Then the crowd began to arrive, a sea of umbrellas.

Reuben followed Simmons, lumbering through the debris, skirting the flames; wet ashes and pieces of concrete foundation and big chunks of colored glass – the windows from Israel; at the edge of the chasm, Simmons threw the savage beam of flashlight. Then he said: 'He's a dead nigger.'

The ghost-white ambulance came. To pick up Buster.

Reuben watched them sling Buster's dark, limp, blood-soaked body onto the stretcher. The face still recognisable, eyes open, filled with terror and shock; the entire left side of his torso blown away, raw meat and intestines exposed; and one leg hanging by a thread.

The stretcher moved through the rain.

Reuben followed it. Past the spectators perched on car fenders like parade watchers, or vultures, quiet and curious like Wednesday-night revivalists waiting their turn to testify for Jesus.

It was Buster. Dead.

The blessing of shock would not come. The disbelief that follows immediately after tragedy would not come. The rain poured down, and the flames still raced under the hoses, and the demolished site spread out into the darkness, and the ambulance doors opened, like the gates of hell. And it was not like the television images that flickered in his bedroom at night; the sight of Buster's blood was not the ketchup of a screen shootout, or newsreels of riots and war. They, the violent ones, were not out there – halfway around the world or across the country, products of the press – but here, in this spot, here, in his own life.

But it was not like the last time. He hung onto the old man's cane, but he made no plea for his roots. The alien here, like the alien everwhere, were the senseless murderers.

And he would kill them.

He watched them slide the stretcher into the ambulance.

He would have to tell Leila. He would have to be the one.

It was Buster. Dead.

They had gone against everything; had gone against the way it had always been, the immutable law of the South that said a man had his wife, and his children, and his *niggers* – not a hundred or more like it used to be, only a handful, but these an integral part of his life, his integrity dependent on the bond that still told him who he was – still, no matter what the world might say. And the un-written law said: Nobody touched a man's wife, or a man's child-ren, or a man's niggers.

The law had been broken.

The ambulance doors slammed, and somebody shouted, 'Let's get outa here!'

He stood still. He watched the ambulance pull slowly away through the rain. And the knowledge came to him that anything could be destroyed, at any moment.

They had done this. They had assaulted his destiny. They. Out there. The small blue car rushing past; the voice on the telephone. There were men who committed murder. There was also reckon-ing. He was a Jew and a southerner and a lawyer – and a man. Life was not a courtroom. The need for vengeance came slow and cold, like the cold raw rain coming down.

He would kill them. Before the tulips came up.

He went looking for Monk. He found him in the cab of the truck, the rain pounding down on the roof. Monk slid out. Reu-ben climbed in. Monk climbed back behind the wheel. Reuben lit a cigarette. His overcoat was soaked.

'Take me back to my car,' he said.

Monk switched the ignition on and turned the truck around. The headlights swept the scene, then veered down the road. Monk drove slowly, barely able to see through the shattered windshield, Reuben didn't look back.

Monk pulled into the parking lot in front of the Williamsburg, got out, let Reuben slide out.

'We'll do it your way,' Reuben said.

'When?'

'As soon as I can find out who it is.'

Monk climbed back into the truck. Reuben watched the truck pull off through the rain.

He went back into the Williamsburg.

He went through the store, to the back, into Frieda's office. He pulled off his overcoat. Underneath, his suit was damp, but not soaked through. A number of wraps and sweaters and coats hung on wall hooks. He found Syd Kaminsky's raincoat and got into it.

He stopped at the walk-in cooler and picked up a ham and a turkey. Behind the counter, he shoved each of them into a plastic bag.

Then he came back out into the rain, locked the door, climbed back in his car, and drove to the Oyster Bar.

Leila's street had turned to mud.

The house was dark.

Carrying the ham and the turkey, he climbed the stairs to the porch. Then he stood there a moment as a bolt of lightning cracked the sky. The thunder rolled. He waited. The rain beat down on the roof of the porch. Finally, he rapped on the door. No one answered. He knocked again, louder. He couldn't make himself call Leila's name. He knocked again. A light went on inside. After a moment, the door opened. Through the screen, framed against the light, Leila stood with an old coat thrown over her nightgown. He couldn't see her face. She said, 'Oh my God – Mr Buchman –'

'Can I come in ?'

She pushed open the screen. He came through. He saw Attica was standing beside the kerosene stove, a flannel shirt pulled hastily over longjohns. He went past Attica and set the ham and the turkey on the oilcloth-covered table. When he turned around, Leila was standing beside Attica, holding onto him. She was Buster's mother. Somewhere, in her, she already knew. What she held onto was denial. The rain was coming down with the sound of drums.

'It's Buster.' His voice broke.

Neither one of them spoke.

'They bombed the temple,' he said. Leila shuddered. He felt her sharp intake of breath. 'Buster's dead.'

'No,' Attica said. 'He ain't dead.'

'I'm sorry.'

Leila screamed.

The scream filled the room, then became a moan, like the rushing of the Pearl River; and mixing with the sound of the rain, 'Oh, Jesus . . . Jesus . . . Jesus, *Jesus !*'

Attica let her go. She fell into a chair and buried her face in her hands and began to sob. Her body rolled inward, away from the

219

moment, sounds coming out of her, pain and fury and terror.

Reuben moved over to her. Attica went to the sink and stooped down and pulled a bottle from behind a curtained shelf. He poured some colorless liquid into a glass, swallowed half, then carried the rest back to Leila. As he handed it to her, his eyes met Reuben's; dead and cold, like marbles swimming in a glass. Then his lids closed over them. Leila took the glass. She swallowed, choking.

'Hush . . . ' Attica said. 'Hush now . . . '

She looked up at Reuben. 'He's dead?'

Reuben nodded. Her eyes rolled back in her head, then fastened on him again. She began to rock her body, back and forth, hands clasping her arms, as if she were rocking a child. Her eyes fixed on him. And he knew she was remembering the dynamite he had come here to get, on Sunday; the dynamite she had talked Buster into returning. As if, somehow, that dynamite – not the dynamite tonight – had been the cause of it; as if, somehow, they together had led him to tonight.

'We'll get the men who did it,' Reuben said.

She quit rocking. 'I know.'

He realised what she was saying. She was saying a white church had been bombed tonight, not a black one. She was saying she knew white men avenged their property – the death of a black man was secondary. She was saying white men got justice. She had never heard of Barksdale or Hoover or southern coalitions. A Jew, to Leila, was a white man, simply a white man; white men got justice.

He stood there looking down at her, wanting to put his arms around her, wanting to say, *I loved Buster* – but owing her no lies, owing her that much tonight. He had bought Buster's shoes, had paid for Buster's appendectomy, had gotten Buster the job with Monk. On Sunday, he had taken the dynamite. Each act had been an act of castration – and she had helped him. She had castrated her son in the name of survival. In the name of what had he done it? Only tonight, for the first time, had he seen Buster's guts, tissue and muscle and organs, exposed, blown apart, his first recognition that the dead man had been a living man. Alive and black, it had been Buster who had sent the truth to him. *A Jew ain't nothin' but a nigger turned inside out.*

'I'm sorry,' he said.

He felt Attica move away. Then, abruptly, the sound of the rain filled the room. He turned. Attica had opened the door and was standing beside it. Outside, the rain slashed down from the porch roof in a solid sheet.

'We'll be back to work after the funeral,' Attica said. 'Tonight – you leave us be.'

He took the highway back to Morningside.

At the corner of Forest Drive, he stopped at the stop sign and looked to his left. The sky was dark. The fire was out.

He kept going, past the dark houses lined up, the rain beating down on the windshield. The clock on the dashboard said a quarter to one. Five hours until dawn.

He came around the corner and pulled up into his driveway.

Then he saw the small black car waiting at the top, motor running, impatient puffs of smoke coming out of the exhaust.

He halted the Cadillac directly behind it.

In the beam of his headlights, the back door of the car opened and a man got out, carrying a big black umbrella. The man came towards him. He rolled down the window. Then he recognised the face, the familiar, square, stubborn face.

'Let's go,' Justin said.

Twenty-five

FLOYD ALBERT RAWLINS could tell the weather. He had told Elmos on Sunday, when the sun set behind a bank of clouds, it would rain before Thursday, and now the rain was beating down like hailstones on the roof of the Hunt Club, where he worked as a bouncer, the only damned job he'd been able to find. Nobody had asked him a lot of questions and it had worked out alright.

He sat hunched at the end of the bar, listening to the sound of the rain and looking in the mirror that ran behind the rows of glasses, the pale blue light coming down on it. He looked past his own image to the three men at the corner table – Justin Woods and his Jew partner and the third one, the F.B.I. man, which meant they would get something settled tonight. They had come in a few minutes ago, just after one o'clock, two of them carrying big black umbrellas, and the Jew with the cane – looking like any three members on an off night, looking for a drink before two o'clock.

But he knew they weren't just men come out of the rain – they had come looking for him.

Still, there was nothing to do but sit and wait. It might take them the whole hour to get to it; sitting there, the three of them, talking, looking no different from the other men who came up here looking for whiskey and deals – never knowing what it was to hunt for something alive and dangerous, like him and Elmos, when they were kids. Elmos had once got a rattlesnake big as a stovepipe.

There were all kinds of rattlesnakes in this world. Justin Woods' papa had been one of them.

Floyd bent his head and massaged his neck. It had started to hurt again; six hours on the job without the brace. He had ended up bad in the fight with that television news cameraman, the Yankee who had caught him coming out of the courthouse with Elmos after the trial, right after Elmos and Frank Flowers and the rest of them got convicted of conspiracy; and Elmos had said, *What the hell' conspiracy, they're dead, ain't they ?* – the three civil rights workers, two a Jew, and one a nigger. And the fight had ended him up in the hospital with the neck injury, and Frank Flowers hadn't put up one dime for the hospital bill, or the time afterwards when he couldn't work.

He was lucky to get this job.

The neck bothered him, but nobody could tell. He looked back at the mirror, his own image, looking pretty damn good in spite of the paunch, and the cleft in his chin like his papa.

Papa would kill him if he knew what he and Elmos were up to.

The men were still talking, he could see that. The one talking was the Jew. Buchman. The one with the cane. He could see the Jew was the one who said what to do and what not to do. Two things Papa had always said to watch out for – lawyers and strangers.

But Papa wasn't always right about everything. He had been the one to say it would rain. Three frosts in February, rain in March. And the niggers always said if it rained the first day of March, then it would rain the whole month through. The niggers hoping for that so they couldn't work the fields; that was the way a nigger was, not thinking about tomorrow – not thinking about nothing but fatback and liniment whiskey and making more pickaninnies who would grow up with no more luck or sense than they had. Not that it mattered anymore. Papa hadn't had tenants in thirty years.

But back when he did, he knew how to handle them alright. It never was the niggers, Papa had said. It was the cotton that made the trouble. Floyd could see that. Before you even planted it, you mortgaged it – you had to have money for seed and supplies and the blacksmith and feeding the niggers. After that you prayed that the floods didn't wash the seed away, and the hailstones didn't beat it into the ground; and if the boll weevil didn't eat it up, and if it didn't rain on St Swithin's Day, then there might be something to take to the gin. By that time the money was gone, spent, and if the price was down, the sale of the crop didn't even pay off the mortgage. So Papa moved into the next year paying off for the last. That was the way it had been. Still Papa wouldn't plant anything but cotton.

Now the rain was coming down on cotton not even planted. Fourteen acres was all they had left. Fourteen acres didn't mean nothing – except to Papa; it meant he still owned land. They had cut down all the timber for the sawmill; and then they had brought in the bulldozers and dug it all out until the land wasn't even there to look at anymore. The land became part of the reservoir which held up the rain that came pouring down from the hill country – his papa's land gone for the flood control to protect the land that belonged to the politicians. And all around the reservoir now were fancy weekend cabins and boats, belonging to doctors and lawyers.

In the mirror, he could see the three-piece orchestra playing a number. There was one couple on the floor. The girl was blond, too much glue on her hair and no meat on her bones. She was wearing a silver dress and ballet shoes. She danced past the table where the three men were sitting but none of them looked at her.

They were too busy talking about Floyd Rawlins.

He looked at his watch. Only ten minutes had gone by. It might take them a while, no need in worrying it like a bone. He had other things on his mind. Like the rain meant he'd better get some lumber tomorrow, and see about patching the roof – he'd get Elmos to help him. But Elmos was hardly good for nothing these days, jumping at the hoot of an owl, waiting for his bail time to be up. Then they'd come and get him, lock him up, just like they were going to lock up Frank Flowers, finally. It had all happened four years ago. That same damned leak came back every year, no matter what they did. Mama used to say it was jaybirds building nests in the eaves. But Elmos had killed all the jaybirds with a shotgun, and the leak still came back. Like Papa carried the Irish potato in his pocket, but the rheumatism came back anyway. He could remember the smell of the catnip tea Mama used to drink for her headaches, and her hands had looked like they were carved out of wood. Elmos had been ten, he had been eight, when she died.

He could remember the day like yesterday.

They had been out in the woods with the dog that didn't have a name, because there had been too many animals to bother with names – chickens and ducks and dogs and cats and even a pet raccoon. But Elmos had finally sold the coon's hide for two dollars. He could remember being out in the woods with Elmos, vines and pinoaks and Elmos roaring through the thicket, fast and skinny as a knife, and Elmos could hit things with a shotgun Floyd couldn't even see. And the dog had gone digging around in a dirt mound and come up with a Chickasaw's bone. And Elmos was swinging two squirrels by the tail. And when they got back, Mama was dead.

But they had still had the land then – four hundred acres. Even through the depression, Papa had held on to the land, cotton fields and woods and the creek running through, filled with bass and brim, and the smell of rain and honeysuckle. And the three of them, after Mama died, had done fine with it. He could remember that was the summer they had hollowed out gourds to make nests for the stone martens who ate the mosquitoes, painting them silver and hanging them on poles and Papa had said it looked just like the city.

Then the government men had come around, and Papa had run them off with a shotgun. But after that, it was old man Woods, Justin's papa, their neighbor, coming around with the contract, crooked as a dog's hind legs, and saying he had signed up himself. Papa believed it. And the contract turned out not to be worth its paper – eighteen dollars an acre and the promise to lease it back for seventy-five cents an acre, but there was no way to lease back the bottom of the reservoir. The land was gone. And Woods got to be lieutenant governor.

He looked at Justin Woods in the mirror. He was the one doing the talking now, wearing the same cold dead face and the birds' eyes he had when he was a kid. Nobody had been able to tell what Justin Woods was thinking, even back then, not even when Justin was getting beat up – the blood coming out of his nose, and him not fighting and not running and not falling down either, like nothing could hurt him.

For a minute it looked like the Jew was going to get up and leave, but then the F.B.I. man said something, and the Jew sat back down, and the nigger waiter ran over to take an order for another round of drinks. Floyd knew what they were arguing about. The

Jew wanted to know what he was going to get for his money. On Monday Floyd had gone to see Justin. Reminding Justin about Harrisburg, how they had all been kids in Harrisburg; how Minna, Justin's mama, who played the church organ on Sundays then, was still giving piano lessons in the musty parlor, to Elmos' kid – Elmos saw her sometimes, sure did; Minna liked to talk to Elmos. He and Elmos knew a lot of things. Like who done the bombing on Saturday night. Might take a little money. That was back on Monday. Tonight was tonight. Another bombing. The price would go up. He watched the Jew's face. The Jew was listening to Justin. Justin could talk a redbird out of his red pajamas.

They'd get the money. Him and Elmos. All they had to do was keep Papa from finding out what they were doing. Papa would kill both of them. Still, he figured it was time to live his own life. Those two men last month had known right away he had class; one of them with an Italian name – he had written it down. They had talked to him about coming down to New Orleans, a place called Gretna. He had thought about it a lot since then. Sometimes he thought about getting on the *Southerner*, maybe drinking his way down in the club car, with the train tracks swaying underneath him. Sometimes he thought about flying on Delta, with the stewardess in those short skirts and valentine hats. And sometimes he thought about buying a brand new red Maverick and driving down on the highway that went through the swamps and clean across Lake Pontchartrain on the longest bridge in the world.

But he had to get Elmos some money first, so Elmos could go down to Mexico. He couldn't stand the idea of Elmos cooped up in a jail cell. Elmos hadn't done nothing but stood up for his birthright – them Yankee kids, two Jews and a nigger, had no damn right to be down here making trouble. Elmos had warned them. And, afterwards, he had gone all over the state trying to raise money for Elmos; but Elmos wasn't a hero anymore, and all he had got for his trouble was making Frank Flowers mad. Flowers gave him two hundred dollars to shut his mouth and go home. That's all the money Flowers had ever put out, so he and Elmos didn't owe Flowers nothing. They had their own hides to take care of. That's all he was doing.

In the mirror, he could see it was the F.B.I. man doing the talking now, the other two listening. Then the Jew said something and the F.B.I. man shook his head. The Jew stood up again. Then the F.B.I. man began to talk again. The Jew nodded, then sat down again, and picked up the cane and began to fool with it. Floyd could tell it was getting settled. He'd have some money soon, him and Elmos. Elmos could go on to Mexico, and he could start thinking about what he was going to do. For one thing, he'd get himself a girl, a girl as pretty as Army Jones' girl; she was prettier than either one of the Miss Americas from Mississippi. Maybe a schoolteacher, like Army Jones' girl. A pretty schoolteacher who wouldn't just lay anybody. And tomorrow he'd go and get himself a new suit. It wasn't the same as going down to New Orleans, Gretna; but it would mean he was getting ready for it. He'd pay a little down and put it on layaway, a brown suit with brass buttons and a yellow tie to go with it. He wouldn't tell Elmos, or Papa, or anybody. It was his life. Then he thought about the rain still coming down on the roof, and he thought maybe what he'd buy was a raincoat. It rained all the time in New Orleans.

He looked back at the table in the mirror. There were only two men, now, sitting there. Justin Woods wasn't sitting down anymore. Justin Woods was headed across the dance floor, coming straight his way.

He sat still. He waited. He kept his eyes on Justin in the mirror. Then Justin came up right behind him, and nodded. He nodded back. Justin kept going, down the length of the bar, and through the men's room door marked *Colonels*.

Floyd waited another moment. He let the moment go by, listening to the rain coming down. Thinking about how he was going to buy a suit and a raincoat too.

Then he got up and moved down the bar and went through the door marked *Colonels*.

Justin was washing his hands at the sink. Against a skylight, the rain came beating down like a stampede of horses. Four years ago, Elmos had tried to get Justin to defend him, but Justin had said no. That was four years ago. Elmos hadn't known then what they knew now. Now they had Justin.

He came up beside Justin and turned on the water in the adjoining sink. He felt like a television doctor, scrubbing up before an operation.

'Friday night,' Justin said. He shut off the water. He pulled off a paper towel and dried his hands. 'Midnight. At the fishing camp.' Between them, unspoken, was the thing they both knew about Justin's mother. Justin pitched the towel into the trash basket and walked towards the door.

'We'll be there,' Floyd said.

In the mirror, he watched Justin go through the door. Then he looked at his own reflection, smiling. It was all going to happen.

226

Maybe tomorrow he'd get a suit and a tie and a raincoat, and a brand new suitcase.

He'd go down to New Orleans in style.

Twenty-six

IT WAS AFTER two when he let himself in the back door.

In the kitchen, the stove light was on. There was a pot of fresh coffee. In the semidarkness, at the table, Mollie was wrapped in the blue fleece robe.

'The phone's been ringing all night. . . . ' Her voice trembled. She gestured at a legal pad on the counter. He picked it up. Barksdale had called. Justin. Harris. Jake Gorman. John Abrahmson. She had written down the times. Tonight, Barksdale had said he called Justin when Reuben couldn't be found. The time of the message backed it up.

He laid the pad down. 'Buster's dead.'

She nodded silently. Her eyes brimmed. She lit a cigarette. Next to her coffee cup an ash tray overflowed.

He filled a cup and carried it to the table and sat across from her. Twenty years ago, in a barracks apartment, studying for law exams, they had shared coffee after midnight. Tonight she no longer looked young, or pretty, or familiar.

'I can't tell the children,' she said. 'You'll have to do that.'

'I'll stay for breakfast.' He dropped in a couple of saccharine tablets and swallowed the coffee.

She dug a place in the ash tray and ground out her cigarette. The ticking of the kitchen clock filled the room.

'I'm frightened,' she said.

He set his cup down. He looked at her. In her eyes, the bombing went off again. He saw Monk's face, the flames flickering over it. Buster – dead. He heard Leila's painful scream.

'I'm sorry.' He felt cold and weary.

'Reuben – ' she said. He could feel her anxiety, like a vapor.

'I've got all I can handle.'

He knew who it was now. He had forced Barksdale to level. *Army Jones* listed on the Gunston report as a 'known associate.'

Robert 'Army' Jones. Friend of Gunston's. Heir to Gunston's car. Truck driver in Holmesdale. Identified as a member of the White Knights of the Ku Klux Klan. Indicted in 1964 on state charges of illegal possession of 105 sticks of dynamite. Released on bond. Army Jones. Walking around free. Because it couldn't be proven – in court. The F.B.I. evidence was 'circumstantial,' Barksdale had said at the Hunt Club. Because he had threatened to walk out. And finally Barksdale had come up with the name. *Army Jones.*

I don't know who it is, Barksdale had lied at the Greyhound Coffee Shop. Another lie. How many lies were in it? How did Justin end up playing mediator at the Hunt Club? With Floyd Rawlins, at the end of the bar, watching them in the mirror. Barksdale said Rawlins had contacted him on Monday. The Rawlins brothers, Floyd and Elmos, were ready to sell the kind of information that would hold up in court. He had felt another lie in it somewhere. Then Justin had made contact. Friday night, midnight. An isolated fishing camp on the Pearl River.

'You know who it is, don't you?' she said.

'Yes.' *Army Jones.*

'What are you going to do?'

'I don't know.' The decision was there to be made all over again.

'Please,' she said. 'Please, Reuben – talk to me.'

'About the bombing?' Tomorrow, at nine, he'd pick up the files from Barksdale. He'd find out everything he could find out about Army Jones.

'No.'

'What do you want to talk about?'

She shook her head. 'Nothing.'

He stood up. He picked up the cane.

'How's your ankle?'

'Alright.' He headed for the door.

'Reuben – ' Her voice broke.

He stopped.

She said, 'Where do you want me to sleep tonight?'

He didn't turn around. 'I'll sleep in the guest room,' he said. He went through the door.

'Mama's fixing breakfast,' Phil said. 'Leila's not here today. Maybe Leila caught my earache.'

'Earaches aren't catching,' Joe said.

'Are they, Dad?' Phil said.

'No,' Reuben said. Mollie slipped a plate of bacon and scrambled eggs in front of him. He didn't look at her face. The hand wasn't steady.

'Then what's the matter with Leila?' Phil said.

'Buster was in an accident,' Reuben said. 'Buster – died.' The rain beat against the windows.

Phil started to cry. Mollie moved around the table and stooped and held him. 'Don't cry. . . . '

'I don't want Buster to be dead.'

From outside, a car horn sounded. 'There's your car pool,' Mollie said. 'C'mon, let's get your raincoat on.' She got Phil into his raincoat and walked him to the door.

Joe said, 'What kind of accident?'

Reuben forked a piece of bacon. He looked at Joe. Joe was twelve. A clear, curious gaze. Almost a man. Still a boy. The bridge to manhood stretching out in front of him. Reuben could remember how it was to be twelve. Fear and confusion and daring – it all showed on Joe's face. Then something else came back to him. At twelve, there were two intolerable things. The first was a lie. The second was the suspicion that your father was not the man you had once believed him to be.

'I'm going to level with you,' Reuben said. 'Man to man.' He heard the back door slam. Joe straightened in his chair, reaching for manliness through imitation. Looking at Joe was sometimes like looking into a mirror of his own youth. 'You know the rabbi's house was bombed?'

'I'm not a kid anymore. I know what's going on,' Joe said. Reuben felt Mollie come back into the kitchen.

'You know we're Jews. . . . '

'Sure. I'm going to be confirmed in June. I know about the Maccabees. Grandma won't eat ham. I know all that.' Joe frowned. 'Is something the matter with being Jews?'

'You know Uncle Monk's building the new temple over on Forest Drive?'

'Sure.'

'That was bombed last night too,' Reuben said.

'Is it a war?'

'In a way,' Reuben said. 'Uncle Monk put Buster on as night watchman. Buster got killed. I guess that makes it a war.'

'Are they going to bomb us next?'

'They're never going to bomb anybody again,' Reuben said.

'What are you going to do to them?'

'There're different ways a man can go,' Reuben said. 'You know I'm a lawyer. There's the law. There's the courtroom. . . . ' He

229

looked directly at Joe. 'But I'm also a man,' he said. 'When the other side has no respect for the law, sometimes you have to go back to an older law. Sometimes you have to see about justice yourself.'

'Which way are you going to go?' Joe said.

'I don't know.' Reuben picked up his fork. 'Now eat your breakfast. You can't go to school on an empty stomach.'

The rain kept coming down.

Hart, Mississippi
February 11, 1968

Source advised that from approximately 9.30 p.m. to almost 12.00 midnight, Frank Flowers, Robert 'Army' Jones, Elmos Rawlins, and Dean Leland Goss, gathered at rural highway 84, west of Harrisburg, Mississippi, on the night of February 10, 1968.

Source stated that the purpose of this meeting was for Frank Flowers to give additional instructions concerning dynamiting to Robert 'Army' Jones, and that Dean Leland Goss was there to listen in order to help give these instructions at a later date to Jones' 'assistant.' Source stated that Goss told Jones that Gunston had 'gone underground,' but would return if needed. Jones stated he could 'do the job' alone.

Source stated that Frank Flowers feels that he and Elmos Rawlins will very shortly be incarcerated in jail, and that he is having Dean Leland Goss, who will be the next Imperial Wizard, begin to take over responsibilities. Since Flowers broke contact with both Alabama and Louisiana klans in 1967, they are 'on their own' and known as Unit III.

Source advised that Frank Flowers again gave instructions concerning the use of a clock and a timing device and instructed Jones to practice with a clock, battery, flashlight bulbs, and wires, in order to become familiar with a timing device. He also instructed that Goss use his knowledge as an electrician to supervise and perfect said timing device.

Source stated that Jones told Goss that he intended to go to the outskirts of Holmesdale, call a Negro cab driver he knew, and when the cab driver came to that vicinity to pick up 'a customer,' he would then shoot him and hang him from a bridge as 'a warning' to the African Republic. Source advised that Frank Flowers and Goss and Rawlins disagreed with Jones, and agreed that all efforts should be directed at the present time towards Jews, and no more efforts directed against Negroes. The point was to 'get even' with the federal government for the injustice done to Flowers and Rawlins in the 'conspiracy' trial for the '64 murder of three 'outside agitators.'

Source stated that Rawlins asked Flowers if the explosives buried on his father's land should be dug up. Rawlins told Flowers he believed he was 'being followed by the F.B.I.' and the explosives might be 'safer someplace else.' He listed explosives at 900 pounds of dynamite; several canisters of explosives, the kind used in shooting oil wells; sixteen ounces nitroglycerin in a castor-oil bottle; two rolls of primacord; two hand grenades stolen from the National Guard armory; three packs of malleable plastic explosives; and an unknown number of satchel paks, the type used in demolition by the military.

Source advised that Flowers agreed that explosives should be moved, and meeting broke as Jones, Goss, and Rawlins left to relocate explosives.

Reuben looked at his watch. It was after twelve. The meeting with Barksdale and the adoption case had taken the morning. He buzzed Luanne and sent her out for a sandwich. His next appointment was at two. It would take all of the two hours to go through Barksdale's files.

There was a photograph of Buster's body, taken at the morgue. Front and back.

There was a photograph of Gerald Gunston. *Women like him*, Doan Newberry had said. Tall and young and wild-eyed.

There was a photograph of Army Jones. Reuben studied it. Tough and muscular in a short-sleeved shirt, a tattoo on his upper arm reading 'Jackie,' shirt open at the neck, a hairy chest, a simian sexuality, a package of cheroots in his shirt pocket, one lock of dark hair hanging insolently over his forehead.

There were other photographs, names he didn't recognise. Bennie Walton, in big black eyeglasses, a triangular jaw, a broken nose. Joe Gherkin, reed slim and wrinkled-faced. E. L. Martin – as all-American looking as Barksdale.

BIO. – FRED R. L. WATSON. Kleagle; field organizer. Gets $3.00 for each new Klan applicant. Also sells Klan flags, standard bearers, and leases robes on consignment. Also sells subscriptions to the *Caucasian Communique*.

BIO. – DEAN LELAND GOSS. Spokesman for the Citizens for the Supremacy of the White Race. Active in campaign of George Wallace. Appeared on state-wide television during which he compared the CSWR with the signers of the Declaration of Independence. Arrested in 1957, in Birmingham, Alabama, and charged on two counts of assault with intent to murder. The arrest followed a violent dispute at a Klan meeting over Klan leadership and accounting for Klan funds. Two men were shot. Goss freed on $20,000 bond. State charges dropped. Arrested in Houston, in August 1961, and interrogated by city and county officers about his presence near recently desegregated schools, and then released. Further questioned in September 1961, in Claymont, Mississippi when riots began over school integration. Goss acknowledges his ability to incite crowds, has referred to himself as a 'fiery' speaker, and addressed a crowd of 900 in Holmesdale, Mississippi, January 1968, accusing the courts of trying to 'mongrelise' the races.

There was a photograph of M. K. Taylor in uniform. The cop who had arrested Higgins. The cop he had punched last Saturday night, right after the rabbi's house had been bombed.

Attached to the photograph was one paragraph:

Source reports that around December 21, 1967, Virgil Carter made it known to fellow Klan members that his cousin, a member of the Holmesdale Police Department, told him, 'For God's sake tell them not to do anything while I am anywhere around, because I don't want to get hurt or get in a fight with my friends.'

A cold sweat broke.

He picked up the phone and put in a call to Kornfield in New York. Kornfield's secretary said he was on another line.

'I'll hold,' Reuben said.

He went on to the next item in the file:

September 26, 1967
Holmesdale, Miss.

Source advised that *The Dixie Review* is the official publication for the Citizens for Supremacy of the White Race, which is a front for the White Knights of the Ku Klux Klan. (See attached copy of *The Dixie Review*.) Source reports meeting in Holmesdale offices of *The Dixie Review*. Present were Frank Flowers, Joe Gherkin, Dean Leland Goss, Gerald Gunston III, 'Army' Jones, and Dr E. L. Martin, chiropodist. Discussion of bombing of the synagogue in Holmesdale ensued. Flowers made the statement that such a bombing would impede integration activities in Holmesdale as the 'Jews would be too busy with their own affairs to meddle.' Mrs Leo Gorman was named as president of the League of Women Voters and an 'agitator.' Gherkin stated they should not attempt to bomb the temple as this would be a federal offense. Source estimates that there appear to be forty or fifty active members of the Klan in Holmesdale County. Plans were made for the swearing in of a new member (unnamed) at the kleagle school on Kelton Road. Source states that Flowers announced he had gone to New Orleans and made a copy of the film *Birth of a Nation*. Gerald Gunston and Dr Martin were elected to show the film around Mississippi.

'Your party is on the line,' the operator said.

Kornfield came on. 'Reuben – ?'

'Thatcher set the trial date this morning,' Reuben said. 'Higgins goes on trial Monday afternoon. Closed court, Mississippi morality – spectators are allowed at a murder trial, but trials with sexual implications are closed courtroom. When do I get Higgins?' Reuben fingered the file. The next item was a copy of *The Dixie Review*. The lead article was entitled 'The Jewish Peril.'

'Higgins doesn't want to come back at all,' Kornfield said. 'Can

232

you guarantee his protection? They bombed your temple last night, didn't they? Killed a black man – ' Kornfield hesitated. 'How are you on the Bible? Maybe you remember the message Mordecai sent to Esther? *Think not that thou shall escape in the king's house, more than all the Jews. . . .'*

'Shove the sermons,' Reuben said. 'By next week, the bastard who did the bombing'll be dead or behind bars.' He pulled out the photograph of Army Jones and propped it in front of him.

'Whose word do I have on that?' Kornfield said. 'Simmons' word? M. K. Taylor's word? Or maybe you want me to count on Hoover?'

'Count on me.' Reuben looked at the photograph. He had Barksdale's word. Barksdale's files. Was Army Jones the man? He realised, suddenly, that either way he went, he was going on Barksdale's word. 'When do I get Higgins?' he said.

'Monday,' Kornfield said.

'Alright. I'll make do with it.'

'One more thing,' Kornfield said. 'I understand your partner represents a black man named Vernon Powell. Yesterday, the court awarded Powell an Injunction to Quit. Has the sheriff gone out there yet?'

'This morning,' Reuben said.

'What happened?'

'Not a damned thing. Hollyhoke's moved his crew to a house on Palmer Avenue. Near the Oyster Bar.'

'Will you take a message to Hollyhoke?'

'Hell no.'

'I hear the F.B.I.'s moved into the case.'

'I don't know anything about that.'

'They've been known to set up ambushes.'

'Screw Hollyhoke,' Reuben said. 'If he's crazy enough to play African chief in Mississippi, he's asking for anything he gets.'

'By those standards, so was Higgins,' Kornfield said.

'I've got all I can handle,' Reuben said. 'That's it. That's final. Take your Bible somewhere else.'

'Good luck in court.' Kornfield hung up.

Reuben worked his way through a ham on rye and rest of the contents of the file. The conversation with Kornfield rankled. *Think not that thou shall escape in the king's house, more than all the Jews. . . .*

Screw Kornfield, he thought. Let Kornfield stick to his territory north of the Mason-Dixon line.

This was his earth, the South – he knew what he had to do.

Geral Gunston   Age: 16   IQ: 115   September 12, 1961
Psychiatric Report   Dr Edmund Whitfield
    Patient, Gerald Gunston III, arrested, and sent by Juvenile Court to
Webster for two-day psychiatric examination.

    Reuben began to read.

    In August of 1961, patient reports having felt increasing anxiety over
possibility of school integration. Patient reports telephoning Holmesdale, the state capital, and informing officials of the possibility of
'trouble.' Patient called in for questioning by F.B.I. and released. On
September 5, patient participated in school riots instigated by Dean
Leland Goss, in which several students were injured. Afterwards,
patient was kept out of school at request of principal. During this time,
patient reports he read the Bible 'day and night,' and became friendly
with Goss. Patient reports chagrin at inability to join Klan because of
his age. Patient reports regular church attendance in Cranston, Miss.,
until he was met by church members at door of church and asked to
find himself another church.
    Patient reports family ambience as 'quarrelsome.' He is the first of
three siblings, sister, age 13; brother, age 6. Father listed as real estate
salesman – labeled by patient as 'alcoholic.' Patient reports violent fights
between mother and father, particularly over father's excessive drinking. Patient reports a desire to 'be good,' and has held a job at local
grocery store, and a paper route.
    Patient has come to feel that authorities of all kinds, particularly
police authorities, the F.B.I., and judicial authorities, are persecuting
him.
    Evidence of marked feelings of hostility; indications of a paranoid
condition.

    He quit reading abruptly. Kornfield still rankled. Screw it, he
thought.
    He went back to his reading. Gunston's psyche:

    In the paranoid condition, suspicion is heightened; subject feels his
life is interfered with, troubled by, alien, dangerous, or unfriendly in-
fluences. Accompanied by an expression of grandiosity, the need to be
exceedingly powerful in order to compensate for the uneasy sense of self.
Gunston obsessed with a study of weapons. Also extensively sunk in the
Bible, immersed in reading authoritative texts over and over, deriving
from this some strong feelings of ego support. He was raised in an
emotionally disturbed environment (constant quarreling between
parents, and finally, divorce) and finds tremendous difficulty in aligning
himself with figures who can be helpfully supportive. Exhibits an
inability to establish adequate feelings of love, security, identification,
with figures close to him. Exhibits the need to choose some very broad,

sweeping, pervasive item which has the symbolic implication that he is a worthy person to engage in combating such a potent organisation (i.e., 'Communism' or 'the Jewish Plot'). He feels he is on a sacred mission to rid country of aliens and Communistic influence. Finds justification in the Bible. His judgments, ideas, expressions, behavior are grossly, markedly disturbed. Treatment highly recommended.

He buzzed Luanne.

'Get Dr Whitfield on the phone for me. He's at Webster Asylum.'

He shut the file. It was a visit to a subterranean world of ignorance and obsession. Only forty or fifty Kluckers in Holmesdale County. Probably less than a couple of hundered in the entire state. Enough explosives to blow the state up. Why hadn't Barksdale got them?

The F.B.I. was busy setting up an ambush for Brendon Hollyhoke. Why not for Frank Flowers?

Hoover doesn't give one damn about civil rights and he doesn't care if the Klan operates or not, Justin had said. That was now obvious. He saw that Army Jones was token. What about the rest of them? Kill Army Jones – then wait for the violence to flare up again?

He dug in the file and pulled out the picture of Buster. At the morgue. His side blown away. Kornfield had quoted the Bible to him. There was an earlier quote. *An eye for an eye, a burning for a burning.* . . . Killing Army Jones would constitute vengeance for Buster, and a clear solid warning.

But there was still the question of the law. He had spent twenty years serving the law. Higgins didn't want to come back because Higgins didn't trust the law. He had insisted that Higgins come back. Was he willing to put another man's life in the hands of the law – when he wouldn't put his own there?

Luanne buzzed. He picked up. He looked at Mollie's portrait. Her face looked back at him, like a death mask. *How long since she passed away?*

'Dr Whitfield won't be in until late this afternoon,' Luanne said.

'Leave a message for him. Tell him I want to see him on the Higgins case. If I'm not here when he calls back, set up an appointment.' He remembered the cats at Webster. 'At my office,' he said.

'What do I do about Mr Rabin?'

'What about Mr Rabin?' Isadore Rabin had telephoned this morning, after getting news of the bombing. Justin had pacified him again – seduced him into agreeing to come down, one more time, next week, for a final evaluation of the Ko-Bee factory.

'He keeps calling back. Every ten minutes. I keep telling him

Mr Woods is out to lunch. Do you want to talk to him?'

'No,' Reuben said. Justin was better at smoothing fur than he was. 'Tell him everything's under control. Tell him the governor's delighted with him. Tell him Mr Woods'll get back to him as soon as he comes in from lunch.'

'What about Mr Levitt?' Luanne said. 'He's on the other line. Do you want to talk to him?'

'Put him on hold.'

'What about –' Luanne began; he cut the line.

He lit a cigarette. He slipped Buster's photograph back into the file. He thought about Buster's funeral, tomorrow afternoon. He thought about Army Jones, walking around free. He thought about the meeting at the fishing camp with the Rawlins brothers, set for tomorrow night. He thought about the Bible, and he thought about the law. Justice by gavel, and justice by gun.

He picked up the phone.

'Have you got anything for me?' Monk said.

'I'm working on it.'

'Who did it?'

'I don't know yet.'

'We'd better meet and talk about what we're going to do.'

'Saturday morning,' Reuben said.

'That's day after tomorrow –'

'I need forty-eight hours,' Reuben said. 'Then we'll do what we have to do.'

'Did you get any more phone calls?'

'Why the hell would they call us? We were there.'

'We'll bury 'em,' Monk said.

He hung up. Then he got up and crossed to the French doors and pulled the drapes open. It was still coming down, dark and steady. Outside, on the rooftop patio, the rain had broken the necks of all the azaleas.

Twenty-seven

THE RAIN QUIT at two on Friday. The sun didn't come out. Dull gray light filtered down through an afternoon darkness of low dirty clouds.

Reuben took the boys out of school for the funeral. Leila had raised his sons. Her son, now, was dead. He felt a sense of quiescent guilt and unpaid debt.

They reached the church just before three – a small clapboard church in the Oyster Bar, grim and stoic and crippled and enduring, needing paint, like everything else in the Oyster Bar; needing the hand of God. A small sgin outside read: CHURCH OF PROVIDENCE, 'SERVANTS OF GOD,' PRESIDING: MARTIN GALLAGHER. THE FUNERAL OF BUSTER JACKSON.

Reuben led the way inside. Heads turned, murmured, nodded, deferred. They took seats in the last pew – Mollie, then Joe and Phil, then himself. Stretched out in front of him, the sixteen unvarnished pews were filled. There were more women than men – black women dressed in rustling black dresses, hats and veils, white minstrel gloves; black men wearing shiny mismatched hand-me-down suits, charred shirt collars, sober faces eaten away by subservience. He and Mollie and the boys were the only whites in the church – intruders and royalty, benevolent complicated visitors to the simple black foreign land of oppression and Gospel faith.

On the altar one small spotlight shone radiant through the gloom, lighting a silver cross which had been bedded in plastic lilies. In front of it was Buster's casket, white velvet, open, tented with gauze; the rain had brought out the flies.

Leila and Attica and the three little girls sat in the first pew. He recognised Clyde Bowden's back, a few others – servants and charity cases; women who had served him, men he had helped. *I've got friends in the black community*, he had once told Kornfield. Kornfield had laughed. *You would have made a good feudal lord*. Reuben had said, *You'll never understand it. You have to be born here.*

Anny Bowden climbed up onto the altar. With awkward dig-

237

nity, she sat down at the organ and sounded a chord. The church hushed. Anny began to play; the same hands that made him muscadine jelly. The strains of 'What a Friend We Have in Jesus' filled the church. Around him, voices joined the organ, rich in faith and tragedy. Reuben felt a vibration move through the pews, then felt it touch him. Unable to name it, he recalled the varying explanations for the black man's belief in a white Jesus. Some said it was a carryover from the secret societies of Africa; some maintained that the white plantation owner had sold a passive faith to his blacks in order to insure a slavery mentality; some believed that the same white man who had outlawed the teaching of reading and writing to blacks had nevertheless generously shared his own God. Now, at this moment, he felt none of the theories as truth. What he felt, instead, was a simple, unique, direct connection between the voices rising around him and God, whatever god; he felt the knowledge that there were other gods around, beyond the ones he knew, beyond what he acknowledged; and he felt a sudden yearning for whatever kind of faith it was that existed beyond the kind of religion that was offered by a sanctimonious Harris, beyond the remote answers available in a pasteurised, homogenised, organised, institutionalised faith. The cane was propped across his knees. He fingered it, knowing he had clung to his grandfather; his own god had been his grandfather.

There was dirt engrained along the bottom of the cane, Mississippi earth. In the story of the cane was a basic truth of the Mississippi earth. The old man had been a rural Solomon. The cane had come to be whittled because Sampson's son had stolen a ham from Joe Buchman's smokehouse. The old man had called Sampson in and offered him the chance to make his own reparation. A week later, Sampson had brought the cane to Joe Buchman, hand-whittled, seven nights of labor. The old man, having no need of a cane then, said, *You want I should break my leg, Sampson?* Sampson shook his head. *Nossir. I want you to live to be an old man and use it.*

No Yankee could understand a story like that. Kornfield had never understood that he, Reuben, lived with the knowledge that something had gone wrong, already done, before him; that his pride came from the knowledge that he had inherited a legacy corrupted – but indestructible. And no man, Yankee or Klucker, would deprive him of his inheritance.

The music ceased.

There was a moment of full silence; a deep quiet that held a belief in the continuing revolution of days; hope and grief united.

It came through as an indictment.

He felt a sudden awareness of guilt, without the knowledge of guilt; in the silence he felt an unspoken question: *Who is responsible?* And he knew, suddenly, that if Buster had been kidnapped, castrated, and hanged, it would have been clearer than the chain of guilt that laid itself out. Because Buster had died from Reuben's own benevolence, from Monk's lust, from Hoover's negligence, from the Klan's brutality. So it was not a question of guilt, it was a question of action. In every man was a taste for violence, greed, erotic obsessions, and savagery – which was why guilt, by law, lay always with the hand that held the gun. And the hand that committed the violence had belonged to Army Jones, first lieutenant in an army of hooligans. And Buster had been his, *his nigger;* and one way or another, he would avenge Buster's death – in the name of whatever god was present, today, in this church. . . .

The singing quit. Attica watched Martin Gallagher mount the pulpit, a tall bearded honey-colored black man in rimless glasses, come to sermonise Buster when he didn't even know Buster. Buster had quit church a long time ago, and Buster never went to the Holmesdale College for Negroes where Gallagher taught picture taking, but it was Gallagher standing up there now and saying, 'If Buster Jackson is absent from his house on earth, then he is in the House of the Lord, brothers.'

– and the congregation saying, '*Amen.*'

– and Gallagher saying, 'So we are here today to sing the gospel of joy. Hand clapping and shouts make the Lord a little closer. *We've been shoutin' since slavery.*'

– and Leila, next to him, with the rest of them, shouting, '*Amen !*'

– and Gallagher saying, 'The gospel is an anthem of victorious salvation, of triumphal entry into heaven. The gospel is an assurance that a life of slavery – to man, to work, to pain, to suffering – does end in eternal song!'

– and everyone saying, '*Amen.*'

– and Gallagher saying, 'Let us all sing: "Move On Up a Little Higher." '

– and Anny beginning to play again on the organ.

But Attica couldn't bring himself to sing, thinking about Buster, dead, and maybe free, but maybe not; thinking about how it had all started, how it had all happened. Because if they had still been on the land, maybe none of it would have happened. But the land was gone, had been gone, since '35; because of his papa's brother, Samuel, they had lost the land; and then they allowed him to rent it back, until it was taken again; and now Buster was dead; taken.

Because his Uncle Samuel had been the one with the deed to the land, forty-five acres it had been, claimed by somebody after the Civil War, and hung onto, no matter what. But Samuel had owned that pair of prize mules, handsome as any pair of mules a man could lay eyes on; and the way it turned out, it was pride in them mules that brought on the downfall.

Because Samuel plain refused to sell those mules. Not to no-body. No matter how hard Samuel was pestered, no matter how hard his white neighbor farmer pestered him plenty; once a week at least, and sometimes more, the white neighbor crossing over the fence and coming up to the house, always at dinnertime, Samuel's black wife cooking dinner, and the white man saying, *C'mon now, what you want for them mules?* And Samuel shaking his head and saying, *I won't take nothin' for them mules, ain't nothin' I'm gonna take for them mules.*

And it got to be like a game. The white neighbor farmer always asking the same question, and Samuel always coming up with the same answer, and the black wife shaking her head and saying to Samuel, *Even a blind horse knows when the trough is empty.*

But the white neighbor farmer wasn't as smart as a blind horse, or a mule either, and so he didn't learn that; didn't intend to learn that, the way it turned out. Going into town one day, with four friends, white, five in all, and getting down the bottle, and the whiskey bringing on the thoughts of that prize pair of mules. The thought getting stronger and stronger and fixing in the white man's head until that's all he could think on was that prize pair of mules.

That's when he and his friends left town together, carrying the whiskey, and the shotguns over their shoulders, and heading back to Samuel's land and Samuel's shack, it still early, and Samuel still out in the fields. Finding only Samuel's black wife in the shack, the pot going on the wood stove for the evening's dinner and them, the five of them, white, coming into the shack with the whiskey and the shotguns, and him saying, *I come for that prize pair of mules.*

And the black wife saying, *Samuel ain't here, he's still in the fields.* And him, the white man, saying, *I can wait, I done waited this long, I can wait.* And drinking away from the corn whiskey, passing it from one to another, and around again, until another one of them, white, said, *What we gonna do while we're waitin', huh?* That's when the second idea took hold, as strong as the idea of that prize pair of mules; Samuel's black wife right there, and all of them seeing the idea at once, because hadn't it been lying there, that idea, for more than a hundred years?

And when they were through taking turns with her, she was dead.

The pot still boiling away on the stove for dinner. And they laid her out on the bed and covered her up with a sheet, and then they sat there, drinking the whiskey, and waiting for Samuel to come in from the fields looking for his black wife and looking for dinner. Waiting for Samuel, to get that prize pair of mules.

When he came in, Samuel, and saw them sitting there with the waiting on their faces, Samuel said, *Where's my wife?* And one of them got up and went over to the bed and pulled back the sheet, saying nothing, but letting Samuel look for himself. Long enough for Samuel to see what it was, but no longer than that, before he laid the sheet back; then the white neighbor farmer said, *I come for that prize pair of mules.* And Samuel saying, *Please – let me bury my wife first.* And the white man saying, *Get a shovel, then.* And Samuel opening a cupboard and grabbing for the Winchester rifle, hidden there, and turning around with the Winchester rifle and letting go with it.

And when he was through, there were three of them lying drunk and wounded, and two of them lying dead.

Then Samuel laid down the Winchester, and took the shovel, and went into the fields and dug a grave and buried his wife.

Then he went to Chicago. Rode the freight.

And they came and got Attica's papa. And hung him.

And he, and his mama, went and cut him down. And gave him a funeral.

Like this one.

The preacher saying, *In death, there is life eternal. Your family loved you, but God loved you best.*

And everybody singing, 'Move On Up a Little Higher.'

His papa gone. The land gone.

And now Buster gone too.

Mollie watched Martin Gallagher on the pulpit, listened to his voice. Remembering the day of the bombing, Saturday; she had gone to Holmesdale College on Saturday morning, the snow on the ground. And Martin Gallagher had said, *You can't study here. We don't want you here.* He had said, *You won't find it here, baby. Maybe you'll find it somewhere. Maybe with your camera.*

From the pulpit, he said, 'A funeral is a celebration of life. Buster Jackson is on a great and joyful journey to Jesus.'

Around her, the black voices said, '*Amen.*'

He took photographs of funerals. Martin Gallagher. New Orleans jazz funerals. She saw herself through his camera eye. A woman of instability and charm, carrying the baggage of a marriage in bankruptcy, decay, and bitterness, in search of a way to lose herself; another self-defeating act of volition; another furtive and incomplete revolt. She was able to do that – see herself accurately through the eyes of a man, whatever man – he gave back a reflection of herself. She saw what she was, what she had been, saw the need to hand herself over; and Martin Gallagher had said, *You won't find it here, baby.*

From the pulpit, he said, 'A white man killed Buster Jackson.'

Mollie felt a chill run through her.

She looked at Reuben. His face was hard and tight. She knew he felt her eyes, but he didn't turn. There was the pact. She had agreed to the pact; and she had been unable to run. She saw the pact for what it was. Hopelessness and marking time.

The congregation said, '*Amen.*'

Gallagher said, 'You and me, brothers, we don't *hate* the white man. We *know* him. We've been in his house, in his life, all our lives. But *he doesn't know us.* To him, we're foreign creatures who disappear, after dark, into some netherworld he's never seen or entered. And so he *fears us.*'

Mollie's eyes found Leila.

In the front row, Leila was weeping.

Leila's son was dead, in the white velvet casket.

Mollie felt her own tears come. For Leila. For Buster. For the knowledge articulated by Martin Gallagher. She didn't know Leila. But knew, now, for the first time, that Leila had been born into ownership, and knew it, and had learned to lend herself. She saw that the real Leila lived somewhere else, here, in this church, and in some hidden corner. And Leila's love for Mollie had always been the simple, unspoken message: *I would rather you owned me than somebody else owned me.*

And behind the insight came a question: Had she taken that as her own condition? And what would she do if she owned herself?

'*Amen.*'

Martin Gallagher said, 'The white man will destroy himself –

with his own fear, and his own brutality. Those who deny identity to others lose their own sense of life.'

The *amen* rose and echoed.

Mollie's eyes went back to Reuben.

I would rather you owned me than somebody else owned me. Her marriage to Reuben had not been the free act of a free person doing a willful thing. She had offered the original pact – handed herself over. He had required it, accepted it. And each time, afterwards, that she had set out to take her life into her own hands, she had done so in a manner guaranteed to end her where she began.

With the punishment built in.

What would she do if she owned herself?

Leila was shackled by history. By what was she shackled?

Those who deny identity to others lose their own sense of life.

What would she do about that?

She was thirty-six years old. She had lived in the South all her life. She had defied the conventions, but she had accepted the conditions.

For the first time, she caught a brief glimpse of the criminality of her native land.

Martin Gallagher said, 'In the Bible, moral guilt is inherited. It is not the black man's burden. *It is the white man's burden!*'

'*Amen.*'

'Let us pray to Jesus Christ.'

243

Book Three

Twenty-eight

AT A QUARTER after eleven Friday night, Reuben reached the highway. He pointed the Cadillac north towards the rendezvous point, the Byrd Conoco station thirty miles up. The pistol, loaded, was in the glove compartment. He was to park behind the station, switch his headlights on and off twice, then Barksdale would appear. He was to get into Barksdale's car. Barksdale would drive the rest of the way to the fishing camp.

He considered the possibility that it might not happen like that.

He considered the possibility of a trap, an ambush, a double cross, the possibility of killing, the possibility of dying. He dwelt on none of it. He knew what the risks were. He had decided to take them.

His headlights pressed sluggishly through the cold slow drizzle which had started up again, the color of smoke. He went back to this afternoon's funeral – the sight of Buster's body in the white velvet casket as he filed past, after the service, holding Phil by the hand. It was at that moment, this afternoon, when the knowledge had struck him: he was linked to history by those he loved who were dead – the old man, and his father, and Lea, and Buster. He, Reuben, alive, was committed to each of them.

From the dead, as well as the living, came strength and purpose. He had promised Buster: *I'll get that bastard.*

The Conoco station was closed, dark, isolated, an island unto itself – nothing around for miles. He pulled in behind it, left the motor running, took the pistol out of the glove compartment, and blinked his headlights twice. Then he waited. Behind him, in the fogged-over darkness, the land stretched out into woods. From somewhere, a fox yelled. He heard the cry of a mourning dove. Then a strange hush fell. Few of the wilderness creatures were moving.

Sixty seconds went by on the dashboard clock. He thought about Army Jones, the photograph from the F.B.I. file indelibly engraved in his head. The insolent face. The pack of cheroots in a shirt pocket. An upper arm tattoo that read 'Jackie.' He had promised Buster: *I'll get that bastard.*

Barksdale's car pulled up beside him.

He dropped the pistol into his overcoat pocket. He got out carrying the cane, locked the Cadillac, and climbed in beside Barksdale. Barksdale pulled off without a word. Seven minutes up the highway, Barksdale turned off into a gravel road. For the first time, he spoke.

'How do you feel?'

'Ready,' Reuben said.

'I don't expect any unusual trouble.'

The gravel turned into dirt. The car chugged through mud and potholes. Then a clearing appeared. In the headlights Reuben could make out the outline of a canebrake and, beyond it, a shack.

Barksdale cut the lights and the motor. A drumming sound filled up the silence. The water of the Pearl, dense and black, was moving the way it had back when it was used to transport logs; five hundred miles of it, moving down to Louisiana. Jesse had once taken him fishing in Honey Island Swamp, in the delta, where the Pearl became a maze of channels, and the bass had been so thick they jumped up on the hook. He knew he was reaching back for a hand to hold.

He held onto the old man's cane.

'Let's go,' Barksdale said.

He got out of the car. Around him, pines stretched tall and black through the fog. The woods were wet and gray, filled with solitude and isolation. He walked beside Barksdale. Tiny frogs jumped out of the shuffling quiet of their footsteps. From its camp on a rotted log, a bullfrog croaked. He could make out the shape of the conical muskrat houses on the shallow shore where the dark waters curled around tree roots. A jackrabbit scurried past.

A dim light came from the small window of the shack. Barksdale stopped. Reuben stopped beside him. Through the window, they could see two men sitting, waiting. They moved on. The shack wasn't any more than shelter, homemade, three feet off the ground on pilings, some weathered boards, a tar-paper roof, and some

246

rickety steps leading up. The river rushed past. Barksdale went first, Reuben behind him. Barksdale rapped three times.

The door came open a crack. 'Who's out there?' The voice was harsh and guttural.

'Barksdale.'

The door creaked open. Reuben followed Barksdale inside. Floyd Rawlins, burly and hulking, closed the door behind them.

The room was small, cluttered with shotguns, sleeping rolls, fishing equipment. On a kerosene cook stove, a cold mess congealed in a pot. There was a cot in the corner. Under a pile of blankets a little girl slept. At a table, by the light of a kerosene lamp, Elmos Rawlins was skinning a possum with a long-bladed knife. Reuben recognised the face from the file photographs – the same ones used by the newspapers, in '64, when Elmos Rawlins was tried with Frank Flowers and five others for conspiracy after the murder of the three civil rights workers.

'Set yourself down,' Elmos said, a shrill voice. A small clipped head merged imperceptibly into a long, narrow body. His face was small-eyed and pallid, ignorant and shrewd; anger so long impacted that Reuben knew he no longer felt it as anger, but felt it as part of his nature, God-given, fundamental. The sight of him inspired a queasy shudder – the urge to run, the urge to kill.

The choice was a couple of straight chairs, a camp stool, an old cane rocker. Floyd took the camp stool, folded himself down into it like ladled lard. Barksdale took a chair at the table; Reuben did the same. The bloody carcass of the possum was laid out under the eerie light of the kerosene lamp. In the corner, on the cot, the sleeping child stirred. Reuben felt it as obscenity, piled up one upon the other. He fought a short burst of profound fury at the indignity of paying for witnesses, making deals with bastards.

Elmos laid the bloody knife on the table. A moment of mutual appraisal lay heavy, primitive. From outside, the sound of the Pearl River drummed against the shore. Reuben remembered that Willie had taught him how to read the trails in the mud bank of the Pearl: how to recognise the tracks of a she coon and her family looking for crayfish; how to recognise the tracks of a muskrat digging in the bank; how to recognise the signs of a marauding wolf, robbing the traps. Tonight, these two men were like that: wolves, marauders, predators. He recognised the signs. The possum lay there, like a ritual sacrifice.

The waiting went on. Reuben looked at Barksdale. It was clear Barksdale had no intention of taking the lead. Elmos waited. Floyd waited. Wolves, by instinct, waited.

Cautiously, Reuben said, 'What have you got?'

Elmos grinned abruptly. 'What do we get?'

'Gardenias.' Reuben felt the cat walk begin around a parapet of greed, mistrust, suppressed rage.

'I'll take mine in cash,' Floyd said. Reuben made his appraisal. Floyd was the leader. Elmos skinned possums, killed civil rights workers, committed the violence – but Floyd supplied the cues.

'Come on, boys . . .' Barksdale used the tone of a benign father. 'You know why Mr Buchman's here. So why don't we all settle down. Everybody's going to get what they need.'

'*Need?*' It burst from Elmos. 'Wouldn't be no need if you bastards didn't come down here from Washington. What do you know about how it is down here? I got me a little girl – ' He swept his arm towards the cot in the corner. 'You want me to sit in jail with Flowers? You want my girl to be an orphan? Her mama got killed in a auto wreck. Good thing, too. I woulda never took her back. It ain't easy. They could kill us. My own papa would kill me if he found out I was – ' He stopped, out of breath.

'That ain't none of their business.' Floyd sent Elmos a killing look. Barksdale had tapped a sewer pipe and the rotten water had come gushing out. But there was more to it than that. Reuben saw what Barksdale had done – set himself up as big daddy, arbitrator between the moneyed Jew and the good old boys.

'What about the money?' Floyd said to Reuben.

Screw Barksdale, Reuben thought. He'd drag him into it. He fought the impulse to hurl himself across the table and throttle the two of them, wring their necks like chickens.

'We've got the money,' Reuben said. He'd play it until he got what he was after; as much information as he could get. How he used it, afterwards, was a decision still to be made. 'You know we Jews have got the money,' he said. 'Now, what have you got, and what do you want? Lay it on the line.'

He watched Floyd and Elmos exchange a look. Elmos picked up the bloody knife and began to toy with the mutilated possum.

'Okay,' Floyd said. 'I'll tell you what my brother wants. That's his little girl over there, like he said. He don't want to go to jail. Me, I want some cash. I can take care of myself after that. Him, he wants some cash, some deal made for the appeals court trial, and a one-way ticket to Mexico. That's the deal.'

'I've got the cash,' Reuben said. 'You want to talk immunity, Mexico – that's this man here.'

He handed it back. He watched Barksdale.

'Why don't you three settle the money thing first?' Barksdale said. 'We'll talk about the other things later. Now, what are you boys planning on giving Mr Buchman for his money?'

'What do you mean what we're gonna give him?' Floyd said. 'We done the givin' already. Ain't got nothin' for it yet.'

Barksdale came in quickly. 'Now Mr Buchman here, his rabbi's house was bombed, his temple was bombed – he's the injured party. It's up to Mr Buchman to decide what he wants for his money.'

Reuben absorbed the exchange. What had Floyd already given? A name? Army Jones? What else? Why the hell was Barksdale laying the burden of the meeting on him? Reuben understood the value of tactics, but it wasn't tactics – it was deliberate evasion.

In the corner, the child stirred. Elmos got up and went over to the cot and tucked the blankets around the child. Then he came back to the table. Floyd sent him a look.

'Okay,' Elmos said. 'What do you want for your money?'

'I want the same thing Mr Barksdale wants.' Reuben watched Barksdale. Barksdale stirred slightly, nothing that revealed anything. There were times when Reuben could read the twists and turns of a human mind, could read a face, a gesture, a nuance, an inflection. He knew his own anger was in the way tonight.

'What do you want?' Elmos said to Barksdale.

Barksdale hesitated. It was resistance. A brief moment of silence. Then he said, 'We both want you to go into court.' Swift and reluctant.

Floyd bristled. The smell of sour fury came from him. 'Up yours! We go to court, we're as good as dead.'

'Damned right.' Elmos scowled at Reuben. 'You want us killed? You want a fuckin' lot for your money, don't you?'

Reuben felt something snap. 'I don't want a goddamned thing,' he snarled. The possum-skinning knife gleamed in the light of the kerosene lamp. He saw himself plunging it into Elmos Rawlins. He stood up. 'I'm getting the hell out of here.'

A silence fell. He heard himself. His own echo. The practiced third ear of the courtroom played it accurately back. The reality of his situation washed over him. He had come here, in Barksdale's car, to this isolated spot. Here he was, with two enemies, a quasi-ally, a bad ankle, a cane, and a gun. And what he had just done was given Barksdale his role back.

'Look boys,' Barksdale said, 'no need in harsh language.' He sent Floyd a quiet, assured look. 'You've got what Mr Buchman

249

wants. Mr Buchman's got what you want. Mr Buchman's lived down here as long as you boys have. He knows the decision to go into court is a tough one for men in your position to make.'

'They get federal protection, don't they?' Reuben lowered himself back into the chair, the assessment made. His task, now, was to control his anger; to call on the lawyer in him; get what information he could; see what kind of bargain he could drive.

'Federal protection's there for them,' Barksdale said.

'I don't want no federal protection,' Floyd said. 'I ain't gonna take no witness stand.'

'I'll take depositions,' Reuben said. 'We keep you under federal protection and available. We won't bring you into court unless it's absolutely necessary.'

'We ain't goin' into court,' Floyd said. 'Not one way and not another way.'

'Then what the hell are you prepared to give?'

The room went quiet. The drumming of the Pearl River came through from outside. Then, from a distance away, a rattling sound could be heard. Reuben tensed. He watched Floyd send a look at Elmos. Reuben knew it was another car approaching. He slid his hand into the overcoat pocket and felt the cold steel of the gun.

'We want forty thousand dollars,' Floyd said. Cold. 'What we're gonna give you is the time and the place of the next bombin'.'

The next bombing. Reuben heard it. He heard himself explode. A stream of invective poured from him. Savage.

'Goddamnit to hell – ' Floyd shouted, 'what the hell are you *doin'* here? I saw Justin on Monday. I laid it out. *Army Jones.* I said, *Your Jew partner wants more, let him come get it.* We're goin' on good faith. *What the hell are you doin' here if you don't wanna pay?*'

Reuben stared at Floyd. Again he heard it. *I saw Justin on Monday. Army Jones. Your Jew partner wants more, let him come and get it.*

Floyd looked at Elmos and jerked his head at the door. Elmos got up and went to the door and opened it. The rattling sound was closer, moving in. Reuben saw Barksdale stiffen. *I saw Justin on Monday.* The blatant lie. Floyd hadn't contacted Barksdale; Floyd had contacted Justin. Since Monday Justin had withheld the information from him. Justin had contacted Barksdale instead.

Elmos shut the door. 'It's Papa – ' His shrill voice croaked.

'I'll handle it.' Floyd got up from the stool and took the chair

Elmos had vacated. He peered at Reuben, evil, angry, and frightened. 'Goddamnit,' he said, 'yes or no?'

The rattling sound was loud now, almost upon them. Reuben
looked at Barksdale. Nothing to be read in Barksdale's face. Why
hadn't he remembered Justin's code – caution before loyalty.
What was a fifteen-year partnership stacked up against the power
of the F.B.I.? On Monday night, Barksdale had stopped him on
the road from Maryville. *I saw Justin on Monday.* On Monday
night, Justin had spelled out a dozen reasons for cooperating with
Barksdale. Why? Why did Justin want him involved? What was
Justin protecting? Why did Barksdale want him involved? To get
the Jews off his neck? If there was one lie in it, how many other
lies were there?

'He's here – ' Elmos said. The rattling quit directly outside.
Elmos left the door and crossed to the cot where the child slept
and sat on the edge.

'Yes or no?' Floyd said. 'Goddamnit, I want a fuckin' answer.
Yes or no?'

Outside, a truck door slammed. Then a pair of heavy boots
tramped up the rickety stairs. Reuben looked at Barksdale. Barksdale's eyes were fixed on the door.

'*Yes or no?*' Floyd slammed a fist on the table. The possum
carcass ricocheted across. The door came open. The voice came
first.

'*What the hell are you doin' with that kid out this time of night?*'
The voice crackled.

Reuben heard it.

The man came next. The man that went with the voice was a
weather-beaten lanky skeleton, baked into red clay by the kiln of
the Mississippi heat. Skin like elephant hide, parched, laid over
a narrow face, pale eyes, a cleft chin. Reuben saw a baked,
blistered man, whose life radius had been a hundred miles; whose
fear was of falling off the rim of the earth; who would be pleased
by the sight of a nigger strung to a pine, shocked by an erotic
movie.

Rawlins slammed the door. 'Who the hell are you?' He addressed Barksdale. The voice crackled and stirred an echo.
Reuben knew the voice.

'They come to ask us questions, Papa,' Floyd said. 'We told
'em. We don't know nothin'.'

From the cot, Elmos nodded vigorously. 'Nothin', Papa.'

*What we're gonna give you is the time and the place of the next
bombin'.* The F.B.I. had reported that ninety pounds of explosives

had been moved from where it was buried on old man Rawlins'
land.

The old man tramped over to the cot and picked up the child.
'Ain't no heat here, nothin'. You want her to freeze to death?'
The voice crackled.

The voice on the telephone.

The old man sat down in the rocker and began to rock the child.
'Get the hell off my property,' he said.

Barksdale rose.

Reuben stood up and crossed to the rocker. He looked directly
into the old man's face. The child was blond, flushed with sleep.

'How old is she?' Reuben imagined himself beating the old
man to death with his grandfather's cane.

'Seven. Plays the piano like she was grown,' Elmos said.

'I've got children myself,' he said. Icy.

'We know,' Floyd said. 'Two boys.'

A chill passed through Reuben. He felt Barksdale come up
behind him.

'Good night, gentlemen.' Barksdale took Reuben's arm. Reuben looked down at the old man.

'You make one more telephone call, bastard, and it's your last
one,' he said quietly.

The old man quit rocking. Hr showed a mouthful of teeth,
black with tobacco stains. 'Get the hell off my property.' he said.

Reuben turned. He and Barksdale walked towards the door.
He could see Floyd, at the table, over the dead possum holding
the knife. Elmos stood in a corner, neat a shotgun, probably
loaded, ready for hunting.

The idea of killing was easier to come to terms with than the
idea of dying.

He went through the door and down the steps. Barksdale came
behind him. The door slammed. The old man's truck was
parked directly in front, muddy and decrepit. A stream of moonlight cut through the mist and hit the black water, like ink,
strumming against the tangled shore. Reuben dug the cane into
the leaves and wet pine straw as they moved towards the car.
Barksdale climbed in and started the motor. Reuben climbed in
beside him.

'Look,' Barksdale said.

Reuben looked back. Through the window, he saw old man
Rawlins move across the room. The old man slammed Elmos
across the mouth. Elmos shouted something, then leapt at the
old man. Floyd moved in to separate them.

'The old man might turn them around.' Barksdale pulled the car out onto the dirt road and headed for the highway. 'We've got to move fast.'

Reuben lit a cigarette. 'I'll let you know.'

Twenty-nine

THE SATURDAY post-rain twilight was streaked with gold and lavender. Reuben ignored it.

A couple of hawks circled overhead. He paid no attention.

He kept his eyes on the twinkling red lights at the rear of the truck ahead. Monk was driving it fine. Careful. Monk had cleaned out the junk and the lumber. The back was empty. The truck bounced along, rattling, just under the speed limit. A slat-backed job, a dented cab, a brand-new windshield. It looked ordinary. And innocent.

Foot light on the gas, he let a few cars pull ahead on the highway. Like it was ordinary. Like there weren't two loaded guns locked in the trunk. Wrapped in blankets. Under the two suitcases. His suitcase and Monk's. Enough clothes to last a couple of days. Whatever it took. He couldn't say to Monk how long it would take. Neither one of them had ever killed a man before.

He looked at the clock on the dashboard. Half-past six. The plane for Memphis was scheduled to leave at 7:10. Their timing was fine. It was working out. All the details. Except for the final one.

It was sixteen minutes on the highway that fanned out from downtown. Reuben glanced in the rear-view mirror. Ordinary Saturday traffic. He caught a glimpse of a face under MacArthur sun-glasses, pale and angry – his own. He yanked off his tie and laid it on the seat beside him. He lit a cigarette. Neither act pleased him.

The traffic thinned out. He kept his eyes on Monk's taillights. The exit appeared. HOLMESDALE MUNICIPAL AIRPORT.

Monk's truck veered to the right and down the exit. Reuben followed.

The airport had been expanded a year ago. A new blacktop road cut through a long stretch of virgin woods. New buds on

253

dogwood and redbud splashed dots of color through the pines. A jaybird was screaming, and owls had already started up. *What we're gonna give you is the time and the place of the next bombin'.* There wouldn't be any next bombing.

The airport road was deserted. Only the two of them crawling along. Monk's truck in front, his own car in back. The final sun splashed the rain-washed woods with crimson. The road took seven minutes by the dashboard clock. At the end of it, the parking lot spread out in the March dusk. There were a few scattered cars, not many, bright spots of color. The number would do. Enough people to notice when you wanted to be noticed.

Monk went through the gate and parked. Reuben pulled in a discreet distance behind and parked fifty yards away. He watched Monk climb out, lock up, look around, dressed in his work clothes, jeans, cowboy boots. Monk nodded, then headed for the gate. Reuben jammed the tie in his pocket, got out, then went around to the back and opened the trunk. The samovar and the box of his grandfather's things were still there. He pulled out both suitcases. Carry-on size. The guns lay nestled in blankets, old navy blankets from the Korean War. Monk had provided the blankets. He had provided the guns. His grandfather's shotgun, cleaned and oiled; his own hunting rifle. Fifty-fifty, he and Monk had agreed. They would take the risk fifty-fifty.

He set the suitcases down on the asphalt and relocked the trunk. He thought about Army Jones' photograph; Buster's photograph. He thought about Army Jones, walking around, eating, drinking, sleeping, fucking. He thought about what Army Jones might be doing when the bullet struck him.

He picked up the suitcases and went across the parking lot. At the gate, Monk took his suitcase and fell into step. On the pavement in front of them, their two shadows wriggled under the fluorescent street lights that were just coming on.

'Did Justin buy it?' Monk said.

'Yes.'

'What about Mollie?'

'For Christ's sake – '

'We don't want any women screwin' this up. What'd you tell her?'

'Same thing you told Sheila. We're flying up to Memphis to bid on a shopping center. We're going to stick around politicking until the bids are opened.' Reuben stopped. The terminal was close enough to count the bodies inside. He set the bag down. He took count. Enough people around.

'Okay,' Monk said. 'I charge the tickets so there'll be a record. We make a lot of noise so everybody notices us. We take the plane into Memphis and catch the next plane back, using phony names and paying cash for the tickets. We leave my truck in the parking lot like a neon sign and take your car. Is that all of it?'

'That's all of it.'

'Let's go.' Monk picked up his suitcase. 'With luck, that sonofabitch'll be dead by morning.'

The plane engine droned.

Mollie leaned back, eyes half closed, caught in the limbo of twilight sky beyond the window. Gone from one place, not yet at another.

She couldn't go forward. She had decided to go back. She wondered if it was running. It didn't feel like running. She wondered what it was. *It's not what you think,* she had said to Reuben. Then, what was it? He no longer cared enough to ask her. They were even now. She didn't love him; he didn't love her. There was an old Negro spiritual – 'Lay your burden down. . . .'

'Where are you going?' Reuben had been packing. Late afternoon. She had come into the bedroom and found him packing.

'Memphis.' There had been something wrong with his mouth.

'How long?' she said. It was a small bag. It couldn't be long. He pulled a pair of trousers from the closet and laid them in the bag. He didn't look at her.

'I don't know.'

She watched him cross to the crimson antique chest and take out two shirts. He brought them back to the bed and laid them in the bag. Behind him, the drapes were open. The misting rain had quit. Sunlight came through the French eyelet curtains.

'Are we going to keep this up?'

'What?' He went back to the chest and gathered some sox.

'This.'

He turned around. 'It's better than lying. Isn't it?'

'What's in Memphis?'

'Monk's going to bid on a shopping center.' He shoved the sox in the bag. His face was alien. Something in it she had never seen before, something cruel and reckless. She turned her eyes away. She didn't want to look at it; she didn't want him to catch her looking at it – whatever it was. She focused on the black wallpaper, a white daisy, its yellow center.

'Maybe I'll get Frieda to move in for the weekend. Maybe I'll

255

go down to New Orleans.' She hadn't known she was going to say that. It had begun like that, a nonvolitional voice, a non-volitional urge. She was grateful for something to carry her.

From the corner of her eye, she saw him look up. 'What's in New Orleans?'

'It's not what you think.'

'I've got other things to think about.'

The second decision came on top of the first one. She went into the dressing room and dug into the bottom of a velvet-lined jewelry box. Her fingers closed around the gold money clip, the money still in it. In the mirror, she caught a glimpse of her face. There were no more mysteries in it. The confused mating of hope and destruction was close to the surface. She saw something else. A cry for help. Then she felt it crystallise – a need for assertion, a small piece of action, an attempt to disrupt fear with a small piece of truth. She came back into the bedroom, the money clip closed in her palm, and stood at the foot of the bed, waiting, wondering if she could go through with it.

He clicked the bag shut. 'For Christ's sake, don't stand there staring at me.' She could feel a cold anger radiating from him like the vapor from dry ice. She saw it was the wrong moment; then knew it was always, somehow, the wrong moment; but something compelled her. She wondered if she wanted his anger turned on her. She wondered if the need for truth was inextricably woven with the desire to die.

She stretched out her hand, palm open. A shaft of sunlight caught on the money clip. For a moment, it blinded her. 'What the hell is that?' she heard him say. Then she watched him recognise the clip. 'Where'd that come from?'

'I got it from him.'

'*Who?* What the hell are you talking about?'

'He taped up your ankle. Tuesday morning.' She watched him go back four days. A lifetime.

'That *cajun doctor?*'

She nodded. 'Yes.'

He picked up the money clip. 'What is he? A goddamned thief?'

'No.'

Reuben flung the clip across the room. It hit the wall and fell to the yellow carpet. '*Why the hell are you telling me now?*'

He picked up the bag and left.

* * *

The plane engine droned.

The sky outside the window had turned black. It had been thirty-five minutes into Memphis, a fifteen-minute wait, now they were on their way back. Reuben sat beside Monk, not looking at Monk, looking out the window into the darkness. In twenty minutes, the plane would come down. The hunt would begin. Like trailing a buck. *It's about time you got initiated, boy.* He heard Willie's voice. It was Willie who had taken him out to shoot his first buck. The first Christmas winter he had come back to Maryville from the military school. A cold, sharp winter. He had been helping Willie saw wood into stove lengths for his grandmother's stove. And Willie had stopped, held a wet finger straight up to see where the wind was coming from, and said, *It's about time you got initiated, boy.*

This morning, at eight, he had met with Monk at the Williamsburg. When he left, the drizzle had quit. The air, like the commitment to kill, had turned sharp and cold.

He had dropped off the old man's shotgun to be cleaned and oiled. He had talked about hunting. He had made arrangements to pick it up at four. Then he drove straight to the office and went directly to his own desk. He found a fire going, the drapes open; outside, on the patio, Olive had propped up the azaleas. His desk was piled high with neglected work. Deliberately, he immersed himself in the task of catching up. Underneath, one of the undercurrents, was a wondering how long it would take Justin to come in.

He interviewed a client who was to be indicted on charges of school-fund fraud. Then he waded through the paperwork on an industrial accident case. After that, Dr Whitfield from Webster Asylum came in. Whitfield turned out to be a man in his late forties who looked the way a psychiatrist was supposed to look, including the gray at the temples and the small pointed beard. Whitfield was quiet-spoken and intelligent. They discussed Higgins, what might be done, agreed on a fee. They compromised on a plan of action. Half of what Reuben wanted, and twice what Whitfield thought could be done. Whitfield left. Reuben started on the transcript Olive had typed from Kornfield's tapes. He had been halfway though, making notes in the margin, when he looked up and found Justin standing in front of his desk. Looking controlled and decent, nothing furtive or guilt-ridden, no gesture that spelled out deceit. Which meant nothing. Every good lawyer was an actor. Maybe Justin had talked to Barksdale this morning, and maybe he hadn't. Either way, Reuben had already made the decision not to be the one to raise it. He held out a file.

'Look this over. See what you think.'

Justin took it. 'What is it?'

'A guy who's been defrauding the Mississippi public school system. Charging all the cafeterias for first-class meat and boot-legging in inferior stuff. Pocketing the difference. Over a period of five years, it comes to a couple hundred grand and a lot of kids with ptomaine. He wants us to defend him.'

'I'll take a look at it.' Justin tucked the file under his arm. Reuben scanned Justin's face. Nothing came back. Justin had always been better at waiting than he was.

'What's with Rabin and Ko-Bee?'

'Rabin's coming back. The governor's arranging a black-tie affair. Show him how civilised we really are. Olive's making up our invitation list. Give her whatever names you like. A little old southern hospitality.' Justin grinned. 'Rabin's a *Yankee*.'

'And a Jew.' Reuben watched Justin's smile vanish. Why the hell was he never able to leave anything alone even when he had decided to? Cunning always failed him. Justin's strength was cunning. His was combat. 'How's the little old African Republic?'

'They're still holed up in that house near the Oyster Bar. It's Simmons' baby now.'

'And Barksdale's.' Kornfield had said, *I hear the F.B.I.'s moved into the case. They've been known to set up ambushes.* Army Jones was walking around free. But let a nigger stir up the woodpile, and the F.B.I. was on his neck.

'I don't know anything about that.' Justin didn't react. 'How'd it go last night?'

Reuben took the time to light a cigarette. 'Fine.'

'What happened?'

'You knew them in Harrisburg. You know what they are.'

'Hoodlums.'

'Why the hell didn't you tell me Floyd Rawlins contacted you, not Barksdale?'

'You've been a time bomb since Saturday night. I know what the Rawlins brothers are capable of. I didn't want you running off without federal protection.'

'What the hell gives you the right to make those decisions for me?'

'Fifteen years,' Justin said. 'Floyd Rawlins contacted me on Monday. I passed the information on to Barksdale. For your protection and mine. I don't want your life insurance, I want a partner.'

'What about Monday night? What about all that crap you

fed me on Monday night? About the F.B.I. About Hoover – '

'I leveled with you.'

Reuben got up and crossed to the window and looked down into the street. It was Saturday. Glory Christmas was foraging in the garbage cans. Behind him, he felt Justin's presence, waiting. Justin's plea was 'Guilty. With extenuating circumstances.' Twenty years in the courtroom had taught him that a man will always plead guilty to the lesser crime. He knew there was something else, but he couldn't get hold of it. He turned around.

'They won't testify in court. For forty grand, they'll come up with the time and place of the next bombing.'

'What are you going to do?'

'What would you do?'

'I don't know.'

'What's at stake for you? Does Barksdale have something on you? Does Hoover have something on you? You said it yourself – nobody's house is that damned pure.'

'I'm not being blackmailed by Barksdale.'

'What is it then? What made you do it? What made you lie to me? At the Hunt Club?'

Justin hesitated. Slight. 'I won't be cross-examined. We've got fifteen years of good faith. You've done things to protect me. I've done things to protect you. I'm not your enemy. Neither is Barksdale. Your enemy's the Klan. And, at the moment, it's your own paranoia.'

'I'll tell you what,' Reuben said. 'I'm going to let you decide whether or not I should go along with Barksdale and Floyd Rawlins. I've got to go to Memphis with Monk on a shopping-center deal. I'll be back Monday afternoon, for the Higgins case. When I get back, you let me know what you think I should do.'

'I can't take that responsibility,' Justin said.

'We're partners, aren't we?' Reuben came across the room. He put out his hand. Justin hesitated again. Then he took Reuben's handshake. 'It's Saturday,' Reuben said. 'It's just the way I like to end the week.'

The plane came down into the New Orleans airport.

In the terminal, she stopped in the flower shop and purchased two dozen jonquils, wrapped in fern and waxed green paper. She became a woman, crossing the terminal, wearing a purple dress, a gold silk kerchief, carrying a bunch of spring flowers.

There were taxis lined up outside. The color of the jonquils. She climbed in, set her bag at her feet, held on to the flowers.

'Where to ?' He didn't look back.

She spoke an address; an old remembered address. She was surprised at the sound of a remarkably unstrained voice – as if she had gone back there already, to the girl who had once been an impertinent amateur, childish and spellbound, filled with a clumsy, overwhelming sense of life.

The authority behind the wheel pulled off, acting on the calm assumption that she knew what she was doing, where she was going; the cab became another vehicle on the Saturday night highway into the city. She rolled down the window, felt the damp air on her face – warmer than Holmesdale, still drizzling here, the streets as slick as black satin under the passing street lamps.

The house in the Garden District filled its small plot of ground; white with painted shutters, a flight of steps, a balcony; subdued by evergreens, and a ragged look of dissolution. In some level of her consciousness, she understood the house had been forsaken; she discounted it as fear. *What's in New Orleans ?* Reuben had said. *It's not what you think.* She had given him the money clip as proof of the absence of treachery.

'Will you wait ?'

'It's extra.'

'That's alright.' She left her bag. She got out of the cab, carrying the jonquils, her coat thrown over her shoulders. She shivered, then marshaled her courage. Prodded by some swift and unseen force, she climbed the stairs. There were ten of them; she remembered that too. There had once been flowerpots on each side of the front door; they were gone. In her mind's eye, she saw the pink azalea trees, carefully pruned, in full bloom. Her heart began to pound wildly.

She pressed the doorbell. The chimes pealed through the house. In the ensuing silence, she heard footsteps approach. An outside light came on, bright as a spotlight. Then a stranger opened the door – a balding man in shirt sleeves, reading spectacles pushed up on his forehead.

'Yes ?'

'I'm looking for Mr Donovan . . . Burke Donovan.'

'He hasn't lived here in five years.'

'Do you know where I can find him ?'

'No. I'm sorry.'

'Thank you.'

He closed the door. She came back down the steps and climbed into the cab. 'Would you drive around the corner, please ?'

'Why not ?' He circled the block.

'Here,' she said. 'Stop here.'

The cab pulled to the curb in front of a small house that was directly behind the big house around the corner. It had once been the carriage house. The entire block had gone black. New Orleans was laid out like that – in the middle of an all-white neighborhood, several all-black blocks would appear; what had once been carriage houses, servants' quarters, sold to the blacks as housing, making way for other blacks to move in. The black-white relationship in New Orleans was a special one, partly because of the juxtaposition of living quarters, partly because most of the blacks were Catholics, and partly because the French-Spanish Creole intermingling broadened the definition of who was black and who was white. In the East, the gentile was WASP, Anglo-Saxon, remote. In New Orleans, the gentile was Spanish, Italian, French – Mediterranean, less alien; the possibilities of assimilation attracted both the mulatto and the Jew. And those blacks for whom assimilation was not possible propagated their own Creole caste system, as rigid and as chauvinistic as anything ever conceived by the white man.

She emerged from the cab and went up a short walk. Then she recognised the azalea trees on either side of the door, tiny buds on them, ready to bloom. She rapped. In a moment, the door came open. A small, wizened, light-skinned Negro peered at her by the half light that came through the doorway.

'Raymond ?' She had the urge to hug him. This afternoon Reuben, on his way out, had stopped in the kitchen. From the doorway, she had watched him stop, watched Leila turn around – her face thick from weeping, swollen pouches under her eyes, an air of muffled grief. She had watched a look pass between them, silent, a self-contained meaning in it, something shared. Through the window, she had seen Attica, some inner sentinel moving him in a drugged ragtime step through the rose garden. Then Reuben had left. And she had crossed the kitchen and wrapped her arms around Leila, holding her, both of them crying; in it, a mutual appeal and no release.

'Miss Mollie ?' Raymond said. 'Is that you ?'

'It's me.' A sharp pain pierced her. She drew a strange strength from it. It struck her that women organised their lives around pain – the pain of menstruation, of childbirth, of subjugation, the pain that was loss, the pain that was yearning.

'You ain't changed a bit,' Raymond said. 'Not one bit.'

'How are you ?'

'My girl's a nun. I guess you didn't know that. She's with the order of the Holy Family.' He beamed, oblivious to the fact that the Catholics practiced their own segregation; Mollie knew the Holy Family was the only order of nuns open to blacks.

'That's fine.'

'My boy, he had a hard time,' Raymond said. 'Got put in jail a while. He's out now. Down there on Dryades Street – belongs to Thugs United; they beat up all them dope peddlers comin' around black neighborhoods. I worry about him. Don't see him much. You raise 'em, and then they go. How long's it been? More'n fifteen years, I guess?'

'He's not living in the big house – ?'

'Sold it. Five years ago. Gave me this one. Free and clear.'

'Where is he?'

A troubled look scurried across Raymond's face. 'He ain't seein' much of people.'

'I want to see him.'

'I'll get to him,' Raymond said. 'I'll get to him, then I'll let you know. You give me a number I can get you. I'll let you know.' He frowned. 'You ain't in trouble, are you?'

She scratched out a phone number on the back of a check and gave it to him. He folded it, shoved it into his pocket. 'Thank you.' She leaned over and kissed his cheek lightly.

'It's good seein' you,' he said.

She went back to the taxi and gave the driver another address. In a few minutes he pulled up in front of a big Spanish house in a dead-end circular street off Fountainbleau. She paid him. Her heels rang up the clay tile steps and across the porch. She rang the bell beside a massive arched door. The chimes pealed. The taxi pulled off. Zoe opened the door.

'Mollie – !'

'I brought you some flowers.'

The plane came down and taxied along the Holmesdale airstrip. It didn't pull up to the terminal. Shuttle flights to Memphis and New Orleans unloaded directly on the field.

Reuben and Monk sat still as the passengers filed by. They fell into the tail end of the parade. When they reached the bottom of the steps, the passengers headed for the terminal gate. Reuben turned, Monk behind him, and cut across the field to the parking lot. In a moment, the Cadillac was streaking down the airport road.

He took the highway back downtown. The clock on the

Cadillac dash said 9:05 when Reuben pulled into the service lot behind John Abrahmson's warehouse.

Reuben climbed out. A party of crickets began to screech. Overhead, the sky was dark except for a thin slice of moon, and the flickering red star of an airplane moving off through the night. He could hear the rumbling sound of a freight train coming closer from off in the distance.

He walked the length of the car. Monk was waiting. The freight began to career past not thirty yards away. Reuben opened the trunk. He unwrapped the hunting rifle and handed it to Monk. Then he unwrapped his grandfather's shotgun. The samovar gleamed.

'When it's over, take the samovar.'

'Screw it.' Monk pulled a flask from his pocket and swallowed.

Reuben closed the trunk. The last car of the freight rattled past. The whistle sounded, filled the air, then died.

'What do you want to do?' Monk said. 'Drive or shoot?'

Thirty

WILLIE had taught him patience.

He had been thirteen. *You figure on a long, careful hunt,* Willie had said. City hunters came for sport. Local hunters went after meat. Willie had been a meat hunter. *It ain't kosher, your grandmaw won't cook it,* Willie had said. *I got some friends who'll cook it for us. You ever ate venison? It's about time.*

It didn't take long to find him. Army Jones. He didn't have the sense of a buck. A buck was aware of the hunt. *You hunt straight into the wind,* Willie had said. *So the deer don't pick up your scent* The dog trailed behind them through the woods so the hound didn't trample the tracks, and Willie kneeled, studying the imprint of blunted hooves in the wet leaves and soft ground. *There's this about a buck. He sticks to where there's trees. Cover. He don't like the open, none.*

Army Jones didn't have the sense of a buck. On the other side of the massive arched glass window, the Penny Arcade was brilliantly lit. As sharp and clear as a figure on a stage, Army Jones was pitching balls down a ten-foot alley, a scoreboard lighting up his prowess directly above a shelf stacked with prizes – dolls and ash trays and vases and cheap figurines. There were two men with him – one Reuben didn't recognise; the other, without his cop's uniform, was M. K. Taylor. He watched M. K. Taylor move across the arcade to the fortune-telling machine – press a lever, wait for the waxen Madame X to shuffle mechanically through a deck of cards and send a card through the slot. From across the street where Monk had parked, Reuben watched M. K. Taylor read his card. Whatever it said, Taylor wasn't too happy with it. He let it drop to the floor. Army Jones' scoreboard suddenly lit up like a Christmas tree.

'Look at that sonofabitch – ' Monk said. 'Hopping around like a crazy man.'

It was Willie who had shown him how to hold a rifle ready for action. Thumb on the hammer. Ready to pull it back and shoot instantly. *When you sight the buck, don't jump it. Wait. Bide your time. Take your aim.* There was an old deer hunters' saying: *One shot – one deer; two shots – maybe one deer; three shots – no deer.*

One shot. He would do it in one shot. It struck him how easy it was to stalk a man. How easy it could be to kill a man: Army Jones, right now, clasping a figurine to his chest; a man filled with boisterous joy, unaware he was in a running war; unaware of the two men parked across the street, the rifle even with the window ledge, leveled and ready to shoot. Reuben remembered the sight of the buck's huge and graceful gray body topped by its rack of horns. He remembered how the buck fell. Heavy. Toppling over onto the earth.

The old man's cane was propped on the seat beside him. His ankle was better. This morning he realised he no longer needed the cane. He carried it anyway. It was evidence. The old man had survived a Ukrainian pogrom. Reuben had looked up the word, once, in the dictionary, and found it defined as an organised massacre, a slaughter, a butchery. The old man had somehow survived, by daring and strength and determination and luck. And the old man had made his covenant with the South, with its flaws as well as its virtues, and Reuben had made his covenant with the old man. And the silent vow made to Buster, dead, in the white velvet coffin, was part of it. Army Jones would die. His finger on the trigger of his old hunting rifle, Army Jones in the gunsight. It was going to be easy. Easier than he might have ever believed – with cold purpose, to stalk and kill a man as if were a beast.

'They're coming out,' Monk said.

264

There was Army Jones in the middle, young and insolent – the anonymous one on the left, M. K. Taylor on his right, all three of them coming towards the exit. In a moment they would hit the sidewalk.

'Not now,' Reuben said.

'Why the hell not ?'

'One of them's a cop. I don't want a gunfight with a cop.'

'What do we do ?'

'We follow them. We wait until we get him alone.' *One shot. One deer.* One killing shot. A wounded beast ran until it felt safe from pursuit, then it lay down to suffer, alone, until death. A wounded man got away. He would kill him. With one shot.

He watched Army Jones climb into a '67 tan Chevrolet. M. K. Taylor got behind the wheel. The third man got in. The car pulled off. Monk switched on the motor, but not the lights.

'Keep them in sight,' Reuben said.

Monk pulled out, keeping a steady distance behind. At the corner, the tan Chevvy turned left, into Andrew Jackson Avenue. Monk switched on the headlights and followed, falling into the line of steady Saturday night traffic moving towards Main. The Chevvy's taillights headed north, past old mansions and high-rise apartments – the artery, like Holmesdale itself, was wed to the values of the past while having a full-time affair with progress; the same men who recalled *it used to be better* lived by the slogan: *It's going to be super*.

'Where the hell do you think they're going ?'

Reuben held the rifle across his knees. 'We'll find out.'

Ahead of them, the Chevvy stopped for a light at the intersection of Andrew Jackson and Main. Main Street was lit, the marquees of the two movie theaters blazing. There was a line in front of *Bonnie and Clyde*, waiting for the last show. The Chevvy crossed Main and kept going. Monk followed. The traffic thinned out. At the highway exit, the Chevvy turned off. Monk turned after it.

'Lay back,' Reuben said. The Chevvy picked up speed. Monk let the distance widen, then held it. It was the road Reuben had taken last night. Thirty miles up was the Conoco station. Seven miles beyond that was the gravel road that led to the Rawlins' fishing camp. Reuben looked back. Through the rear windshield, a short distance behind, a pair of headlights gleamed. If the Chevvy was headed for the fishing camp, there was the possibility that the car behind was another set of Kluckers headed, also, for the fishing camp. Or it might be one of Barksdale's men, following

Jones, or following him. Or it might be a nobody, a man on the road, but that wasn't a possibility to count on.

Monk felt his tension. 'What is it?'

'There's a car behind us.' If Monk slowed, let the car pass, they'd get a look at it. But whoever it was would get a look at them too. 'Keep it steady.' Reuben's fingers tightened on the rifle. There was nothing to do except keep the sandwich going, the distance even – see what happened.

Nothing happened. Monk kept looking back in the rear-view mirror. The car behind maintained an even pace. The miles began to add up. The Chevvy's taillights twinkled in the darkness ahead. Monk kept his hands steady on the wheel, his foot steady on the accelerator. Then, up ahead, on the left, the Byrd Conoco station appeared. The Chevvy went past. Monk followed. The station was closed, dark, a night apparition, as the Cadillac went by. The car behind remained steady. Seven miles beyond the Conoco station, the Chevvy turned off into the gravel road.

'What do we do? Follow him?'

'Keep going,' Reuben said. Monk drove past the gravel cutoff. Reuben looked back. The car behind turned in – the headlights veered, then vanished. 'Sonofabitch!'

'What do we do now?'

'Find a place to turn around. We can't get him tonight. There're too many of them.'

'You think they're having a meeting?'

'That's what it looks like.'

'Why the hell didn't we make a bomb?' Monk said. 'We could get the whole goddamned nest of 'em.'

'We'll get him tomorrow.'

'Bastards.' Monk pulled off into the gravel, then made a U-turn back onto the highway. 'You think they're planning another one?'

'I don't know.' *We're gonna give you . . . the time and place of the next bombing*, Floyd had said. He hadn't said what he planned on doing was setting it up. Reuben did battle with another wave of cold rage. 'When Jones' body turns up, they'll give it another think.'

'Why the hell didn't we get a machine gun?' Monk swallowed some whiskey, then handed the flask to Reuben. Reuben took a deep draught. The Cadillac sped past the gravel road. There were two cars of them, maybe more. While the F.B.I. sat by and nothing. It would turn up a week from now in a file. *Source reports a meeting. . . .*

'We'll spend the night at the Ramada.'

'It's full of jingoes.'

'Damned right. The only whites spending the night there are Yankees – we're not likely to run into anybody we know. Use the same names. I'm Lawrence Smith, you're Jack Busby.'

'Why the hell don't we go to his house and wait for him?'

'I told you. You want a gunfight with a cop?' M. K. Taylor. His instincts had been right all along. Now his instincts told him to lay low until tomorrow.

'Shit. How the hell are you going to know where he's at to-morrow?'

'He'll be in church,' Reuben said.

Mollie slept until ten, a deep pitiless sleep at the center of the earth. She woke to the sense of searching.

Downstairs, she found Zoe wandering around the cave-dark kitchen in a clinging snakeskin dressing gown, dark hair tumbling uncombed around a small wan face.

'The maid didn't show. Coffee'll be ready in a minute.' Zoe had two numbers, hysteria and depression; this morning, depression had taken over.

Mollie sat at a red covered table and fought the claustrophobia of Zoe's recently done kitchen – charcoal gray paneling, black slate floor, stairway balustrades at the windows like bars. It kicked off the memory of the first apartment she and Reuben had had at the barracks at Ole Miss – she had painted the walls black. Then she thought about Leila, the real slavery. Her own and Zoe's was self-imposed; she knew that now. Affluent captives, she and Zoe, of the good life, consumption and security, filled with self-pity. She felt the exercise of an acrid intelligence which had never been turned on anything beyond herself.

'Sol gone?'

'He had a delivery.' Zoe brought the coffee, then sat across from her.

'The miracle of birth?'

'Sol doesn't believe in miracles. Only good luck or bad luck. He spends most of his time now at the track.'

'How's the man from Neiman-Marcus?'

'He's Sol without the white coat.'

'Not fabulous?'

'I keep making things up to care about. They don't last. You know what I mean? I read something the other day. A phrase. It keeps coming back to me. *Suicide of the soul*. I mean, that's how I feel. Nothing matters, you know?'

'Jason matters.'

'Sure. He's my son. I love him. But what can I teach him? How can I teach him anything? I don't *know* anything. I keep asking you – How did I get here? I mean, you're smarter than me. It's like they divided it up when we were little. You were "the smart one". I was "the pretty one". You remember when I chased you with a butcher knife? You locked yourself in our bedroom and I made all those marks on the door – and then when Mama came home we filled in all the marks with white Crayola so she wouldn't find out? I mean, they wanted us to be *perfect*. Like one of daddy's architectural drawings. So why am I a mess? And then I married Sol. He's so perfect, he's not even there. I mean, do you know how I got here?'

'No.'

'Is it different for you?'

'I don't know. I don't know what my life is. I'm trying to find out.'

'You know what I feel like?' Zoe said. 'I feel like a child locked *inside* a toy-store window. My nose is pressed against the glass and I wonder what it would feel like if I lived in the world. You know? I mean, what *is* the world? What do they do out there? Ordinary people. Who do they love? What does it feel like? I mean, how would it be to feel sane and healthy? To not always be on the verge of suicide or feel like I'm losing my mind? You know what I mean?'

'Yes.'

'What happened to us?'

'I don't know.'

'I went to a shrink. You know? I went a dozen times. He didn't say anything. He just sat there. I wouldn't lie down on the couch. I just couldn't. Finally I said my husband doesn't sleep with me. You know what he said? He said: *Why did you pick him?* I never went back. I mean, I know it's supposed to be some kind of childhood trauma. You know? Anyway, I drove back to our old neighborhood. Just last week. The blacks have moved in. A little black boy bouncing a basketball came out of where we used to live. I mean, it's so *tiny*. How the hell did we come out of there believing we were princesses?'

'I don't know, baby.'

'You're smart.'

'No, I'm not. All I know are the obvious things. When I look at it, I know nobody held a gun to my head and said: *Turn over your life.* I handed mine over to Reuben, just like that. Now I'm saying: *I want it back*. And I don't have the slightest idea what I'd do with it.' She patted Zoe's hand. Her own hand was steady. She had a feeling of moving, slowly, away from something, towards something. She loved Zoe. But the motion was away from Zoe. She felt a betrayal in it, a sense of some old broken pact.

'Is that why you're going back to see Burke?'

'I don't know why. Maybe because he made me feel sane.' She remembered how it had felt. She had been nineteen, married to Reuben for two years. Later she had learned the word for it – the ladies' magazine word – unfulfilled. It had felt, to her, as if she were losing her sanity. It had been summer. Reuben had gone to R.O.T.C. camp. She had come back to spend the time in New Orleans. Not looking for an affair, her first affair. Not looking for Burke. Knowing herself too little to know she was looking for anything. She had been nineteen; he had been forty-three. He had gone about the love affair as if it had been an act of nature. It had been.

'His wife died,' Zoe said.

'I know.' Last year the obituary had appeared in the *Times-Picayune*. She remembered reading: 'New Orleans Socialite Dies. Eleanor Corteza Donovan.' The Cortezas had been one of the oldest families in the city. Burke had been born across the river in the Irish channel. It had been one of those matings of tainted new money and respected old family. Burke had been a godless Catholic – steadily married and steadily unfaithful.

'Do you think the two of you might get back together?'

'I don't know.'

'He's rich, isn't he? I mean, that helps. You know? I used to see him around sometimes. In restaurants. I mean he didn't know who I was. I was only seventeen when you – I remember I thought it was fabulous. I mean, he did make all that money bootlegging or something?'

'Rum running,' Mollie said. 'He was vaguely adopted by an old pharmacist in Algiers – Doc. He was about twenty years older than Burke. They used to run whiskey in from the twelve-mile limit. Doc had some kind of powder they used to put in the diesel engine to throw up a crazy smoke screen.'

'That's wonderful. What else?'

'I don't know.'

'He's been all around the world, hasn't he? And didn't he own a gambling casino?'

'In Plaquemines Parish.'

'It's fabulous. I remember I thought he was the most glamorous man in the world. I mean, there you were in that art gallery in the Quarter, and he just walked right up to you and he said – What did he say?'

'I don't know. I don't remember.' All she remembered afterwards years later, were his eyes. The red phone on the wall began to ring. 'Answer it.'

'Do you think it's him?' The phone rang again.

'I don't know. Answer it.'

Zoe tapped across the slate floor in brown satin mules and picked up the phone. 'Hello.' The blue glass eyes shattered into brilliant pieces. Zoe laid the phone on the counter. 'It's for you.' She looked frightened. 'I mean – you won't go away to live in Europe or anything like that?'

Mollie took the phone. 'Yes?'

Raymond's voice came through the wire. 'Mr Donovan's at the Maison de Ville.'

'Thank you.'

'You take care of yourself, Miss Mollie.'

Mollie hung up.

Zoe waited, small and frightened. Mollie stroked Zoe's hair. 'It's going to be alright.'

'Suppose Reuben calls?'

'He won't call.'

She drove Zoe's car, a small red Datsun station wagon. The sun had come out and the sky had turned the color of a jaybird's wing. On the neutral ground of St Charles Avenue, new blades of grass had sprouted and the azaleas were filled with buds. She raced a moss-green rattling trolley towards Audubon Park and the Tulane campus. Going past, she felt youth burst in her chest, an old aching familiar yearning; and she could remember how it had felt, growing up here – the languid pace that matched the humid air, the quiet narrow streets, the determined belief that there was something going on somewhere, someplace else.

She had not found it.

In her dreams, often, she heard the deep toll of a nameless bell. As she entered the Quarter, the clear sound of the Sunday church bells from the St Louis Cathedral filled the rain-washed air around Jackson Square. She drove past the church. Past smartly dressed churchgoers wearing colors as bright as the flowers in a spring garden. Past a covey of small solemn girls in veils and communion dresses and white stockings and white T-strap shoes. She had once envied them. She had been the proper age for communion during World War Two. Those years when adults huddled around cathedral-shaped radios. Those years when her grandmother had cooked for the soldiers – big pots of chicken soup, and *knaidlech*, and grinding and shaping the gefilte fish, and stretching the sheets of strudel dough. Those years when adults talked about 'ovens' and she had imagined Jews roasting like Sabbath chickens, and she had secretly made prayers to Jesus Christ, on her knees, hands clasped, feeling like an image from a stained glass window bargaining for her own survival.

Then her father had gone overseas, and the onionskin V-mail had come twice a week, and her mother got a job in a department store on Canal Street; she grew new breasts and smoked her first cigarette and allowed the afternoon newspaper delivery boy to kiss her on Fridays.

She found a place to park at the French Market. The familiar smell of fish was absent on Sunday. Only one of the fruit and vegetable stalls was open. A row of eggplants caught her eye, smooth-skinned and purple, nestled like huge Elizabeth Taylor jewels. She went inside and ordered coffee and doughnuts at a marble counter. The mirrors were outlined with light bulbs, like an actress' dressing room. The reflected woman in the scarlet wool dress looked as if she knew the terms on which she had decided to live. She remembered the Chinese got married in red.

She walked to the Maison de Ville. It was a narrow building tucked away on a side street, marked by a huge mahogany door and two coachlights, and identified by a small copper plaque. You had to know it was there to find it. Not more than two dozen rooms inside. Not a hotel for tourists. A place for lovers and recluses. At least half of the rooms were let on a year-round basis to people like Tennessee Williams, who returned regularly for rituals of restoration. Not a hotel at all. One of the last remaining authentic pieces of New Orleans.

She came into a small high-ceilinged entrance hall of mixed character, old French overlaid with Victorian – mahogany woodwork, faded wallpaper, a bright crystal chandelier. A wall of small-paned doors looked out on a mildewed courtyard shrubbed with banana plants and untrimmed ivy. She felt as if she belonged here, to this covert private world which yielded to no outer reality.

On her right was a cloakroom. A small, persimmon-faced man nodded at her across the counter. 'He's in two eighteen.' The wizened man knew whom she was looking for, it seemed natural. She felt him watch her climb the winding staircase. She saw herself through his eyes. A lovely dark-haired woman in a scarlet

271

dress. In a small mild way, she understood she was doing it again – seeing herself through a man's eyes, any man's eyes. Yet, somehow, her identity no longer rested in that.

She moved down the hall and stopped in front of Burke's door. On the other side were Burke's eyes. Burke had been the first one. She wondered if she had come looking for Burke, or for some clue to herself. Then the door swung open and he was standing there – the hair gone to Louisiana moss, the body gone to a crude and vigorous stout, the jaw pitted like a sea boulder, and the rest of the face as brown and wrinkled as a much-handled grocery sack. But the eyes were the same, a clear and shocking blue.

'Hello, Miss Scarlett.' The voice was the same. She had once likened it to the roaring sound of a sea shell. A smile broke his jaw, like earth cracking. She felt suddenly awkward. Something turbulent stirred in her chest.

'Hello, Burke.' She came inside. It was a spacious rosy room, light filtering through gauze curtains, a brown marble fireplace. She recognised a red velvet wing chair, the oak sideboard he had carved himself. She wondered if he had brought the massive brass bed. Seventeen years ago, she had spent a summer in the massive brass bed.

'You look fine.' His eyes traveled over her, all the places his hands had once traveled. She remembered how it had been before Burke – the severe denial of her own body. Burke had been the one to set her body free.

'So do you.' She realised he was sixty. He didn't look sixty. Sixty was only five years younger than her father. Something disrupted his face, suddenly, as if he could read her thoughts. He had once been able to read her thoughts.

'How's the old plantation ?'

'Gone with the wind.' She managed a smile.

He crossed to the sideboard. 'What do you drink now ?'

'Vermouth. A little ice.' She sat on a small tapestry sofa. On a glass table was his collection of ivory animals. He had once spent a couple of years in China. She wondered how many places he had been in the last seventeen years. How many women he had known.

'I gave the stuff up myself,' he said. From Burke she had drawn the conclusion that men who drank too much were good in bed. Needy in bed. He brought the vermouth over, then sat in the red velvet chair. She felt awkward. Strange. Still, the sight of him stirred a tenuous rebirth of an old organic bond. She wanted to yield to it.

272

'Whom do we drink to ?' He lifted a glass of red wine.

'Doc,' she said.

'Here's to Doc,' he said. 'Wherever he is.'

'With Churchill,' Mollie said. 'Churchill got Doc out of purgatory just like he got him out of jail.'

Burke grinned. 'You never believed me.'

'Sure I did. Doc was in jail for selling laudanum. Then the British decided to land in Africa in the fall of forty-two. That summer they came through Roosevelt looking for the smoke screen powder the two of you used rum running off the Gulf of Mexico. You bargained Doc out of jail, but Doc refused to give them the formula. They took the two of you to Washington. While the British paced the White House, Doc whipped up enough powder for enough PT boats for the British to land in Africa – in the kitchenette of a suite in the Mayflower Hotel.'

'I'll be damned,' Burke said. 'What else do you remember ?'

'Everything.' A long moment went by. She watched him go back there, back through the torpid New Orleans summer, long slow days and nights filled with lovemaking. Burke had taught her about lovemaking. She wondered if she had always, since then, been searching for Burke – the exotic, the gentile, the outlaw; the man through whom she could break out of the prison of self.

'So do I,' he said.

'What do you remember ?'

'It was your first – love affair. We spent a lot of time in bed and Raymond served us a lot of candlelight dinners. We both came out of it a little better than we went in. That doesn't happen often.'

She picked up a small ivory elephant and cradled it in her palm. She remembered a scar on the small of his back, in the shape of a crescent, from an adolescent gang war. She set the elephant down carefully. She stood up. She went to the window and looked down at the street through the gauze curtains. Outside, a mist had started up again. A horse and carriage clopped by below; a honeymoon couple; only honeymoon couples hired carriages. She heard him rise. She felt him come up behind her. An old remembrance of passion swept through her.

'What do you need ?' He waited. She felt him waiting.

'I don't know. I can't play Scarlett anymore.'

'Have you left him ?'

'Not yet.'

'I read about the bombing –'

'I've got nothing that can stand up to a crisis.'

'The girl I knew could stand up to anything.'

'She's gone.' Mollie turned. 'You taught me. It's no good – you said – unless it comes as naturally as sleep.' She smiled crookedly. She felt tears come to her eyes. 'It's not there anymore, is it?'

'Is it for you?'

She shook her head. 'No.'

'You see? You're still the girl who can stand up to anything.' He looked suddenly strange. Suddenly old. Tired. She heard herself say: *I'd rather you owned me that somebody else owned me.*

Aloud, she said, 'I heard it all in my head. Somewhere – inside of me – I heard it. You'd say, *Eleanor's dead.* You'd say, *We've always been in love, you and me.* You'd say, *Go home and pack up your children – how many are there? Two? Fine. We'll get a house in the country. Maybe in Europe.* You'd say, *We'll live one long summer for the rest of our lives.*'

'I'm sixty and you're beautiful,' he said. 'I wish I had said those things.' He grinned. She felt a terrible sorrow come from him. 'It's the best offer I've had all day.'

'What happened to it? Why isn't it there?'

'Love comes hard at my age,' he said. 'I'm still looking for it. I still hope it'll happen again. We could force it. We could stir around in the ashes and see what we could find. But love requires belief. Innocence. I'm in short supply.' Gently he laid a hand on her cheek. 'You're in trouble. What do you need – ? Money? A place to go? I have contacts in Europe. You were good with that camera. Do you want to work abroad? I'd like to help you. What do you need?'

'I don't know. . . .'

He dropped his hand. 'I don't know what to offer. The times are so goddamned tacky. It's rough on somebody who lived through the twenties, Prohibition, Roosevelt, World War Two – you knew who the good guys were. What I'm saying is, I want to help you. But I don't know what to offer you because I don't know what there is out there worth having anymore.'

'Burke –' She felt the tears spill over. Tears for herself, for Burke; tears for something which had once consumed both of them, and was gone; tears for who they had been, and who they had become.

'Don't cry,' he said. 'The one thing I would have never predicted –' He shook his head. 'I got some faith back. That goddamned Catholic religion. I always hated it. But there's that peasant they made Pope. Pope John. And there's that handful of nuns and priests out there hollering that the church should be for the living and not for the dead. But I can't offer you that. And there's some of those kids out there, with the long hair and the flowers – sometimes I think they're mayflies and sometimes I think it's more profound than that. I don't know. But I'm too old to join them. So are you. All I know is – there's no advice to pass on to anybody else. Maybe if they're stupid. But the bright people? To each his own adventure. Maybe you'll pick up a newspaper sometime and read about a half-drunk white American in Africa, or India – it might be me.' He smiled. 'More likely not.'

'I hope so.'

'Me too.' He gave her his handkerchief. She dabbed at her cheeks, then handed it back. 'Keep it,' he said. 'What else do you need?'

'I don't know. . . . Whatever it is, I guess I'll have to find it myself.'

'You're not a kid anymore.'

'I know.'

'You can never tell,' he said. 'You may turn out to be one hell of a broad.'

Thirty-one

IT WAS a white steepled Baptist church. A glass enclosed sign on the lawn said: ALVIN P. BEDGOOD – PASTOR. SERMON: THE REWARDS OF THIS LIFE AND THE NEXT.

Monk parked the Cadillac in the line of cars across the street, the motor idling, steady and quiet. Reuben laid the loaded rifle on the floor by his feet. The high-noon daylight and the clusters of people just beginning to emerge made him uneasy.

He scanned the faces. Strange and familiar. All bearing the characteristics of common parentage – most of them third and fourth generation, going back to fugitives and indentured servants; most of them grandchildren of men who had fought and lost; landless and proud. He knew they had just heard one of those Calvinist sermons – Alvin P. Bedgood preaching that material goods and worldly success were proof of spiritual goodness; Alvin P. Bedgood preaching that the conditions of the blacks were proof of the black man's sinfulness.

Then he saw him.

Army Jones moved down the steps, through the churchgoers lined up like bright pecking birds on a telephone wire. He looked uncomfortable in a blue suit. The tips of black polished shoes caught the sunlight. 'There he is.'

'Who's that with him?'

'His mother. A widow. Works as credit manager of that tire store down on Lynch.'

'How the hell do you know that?'

'I know every goddamned thing I could learn about him in twenty-four hours.' Reuben watched them. The mother clinging to Army Jones' arm. Coy. Wearing a flowered print dress, a hat with fuchsia poppies, and carrying a shiny white purse as big as a shopping bag. She didn't look like a woman who had given birth to a killer.

'Bastard,' Monk said.

They moved down the sidewalk. They stopped, then crossed the street at the rear of the Cadillac, a few cars behind. Monk adjusted the rear-view mirror.

'They're getting in a pickup.'

'Wait for him to pull out,' Reuben said. 'Then move in after him. Slow.'

In a moment, Reuben heard the sound of the truck, gears grinding; the shadow on the street came next; then the truck moved alongside the Cadillac and stopped abruptly, brakes grating. Reuben froze. The cab of the truck filled in the view from Monk's window – high enough for Army Jones' mother to look down, spot the rifle on the floor. A family moved slowly across the street like a covey of quail. The church bell began to toll, loud and solemn. The truck moved on.

'Did she look down?'

'No.' Monk edged the Cadillac out into the street, let another car move in between, then followed the pickup. 'I don't like this daytime stuff.'

'What the hell do you suggest?' Reuben was tired and irritable. He hadn't slept well. In the other twin bed, last night, Monk had snored like a sawmill. He had lain awake, thinking of Mollie and the cajun doctor, one anger feeding another. Now he knew they were both beginning to feel trapped in the tension of unreleased rage.

'Forget it.' Monk pulled at the flask. 'You want a drink ?'

'No.'

They drove in silence. The Cadillac rolled smoothly down the Sunday streets. They entered the part of town that didn't look like a city – tree-lined streets, old fading houses set back from the curb, a creaking porch swing, an old woman clipping roses.

'It's slowing up,' Monk said.

Ahead, the taillights of the truck blinked on. Then it turned into a driveway alongside a small weather-scalped clapboard house.

'Keep going,' Reuben said. 'Circle the block.'

Monk drove past. Army Jones and his mother were climbing out of the pickup. She had taken her hat off. Her hair was lavender in the March sunlight. Army Jones was coatless. The shirt underneath was stiff and shiny with starch, the sleeves rolled up above the elbow, his tie hanging loose, a thin brown cheroot dangling from the corner of his mouth.

Monk took the block. He slowed as he approached the house for a second time. Army Jones and his mother were just going through the doorway. A black and white cat stretched on the peeling balustrade of the narrow porch.

'What do we do ?' Monk said.

'Circle the block again – slow.'

The car purred around the corner again, then moved past the blue-collar houses with aging Fords and Chevvies parked in the driveways. Reuben realised that the Cadillac was about as inconspicuous as a Roman bishop in full dress.

'We should have taken the truck – this car's a neon sign,' Reuben said.

Monk scowled. 'Who the hell had the idea to track him in broad daylight ?' Monk turned into Jones' street again, moving slowly. 'What do we do now ?'

Reuben took stock of the street. Monk went past an empty weedgrown lot at the corner; then past a couple of clapboard houses; then past the shell of a burned-out structure that looked like it had once been a neighborhood grocery store.

A car came towards them, slowed, pulled into a driveway. A family dressed for church emerged. The woman stopped, stared at the Cadillac. A terrier began to bark crazily and run in circles out into the street.

Monk hit the accelerator and streaked around the corner.

'Goddamnit,' Reuben said. 'Don't do that again. Act natural, for Christ's sake. Act normal. Jesus – pull over to the curb. We've got to think this thing out.'

Monk obeyed. He halted the car, motor idling, his eyes scanning the street. 'What do we do?'

Reuben lit a cigarette. 'I'm trying to think.'

'We can't even see the house from here. While you're thinkin', he could be gettin' away.'

'I figure it's Sunday dinner and a nap. I figure it'll be a couple of hours before he comes out. Maybe even not until dark. If we're lucky.'

'Suppose your figurin's wrong?'

'You do the goddamned thinking then.'

'All we have to do is keep changin' our place. We park on one corner for thirty minutes. Then we park across the street. Then we take it down to the other corner.'

'Why the hell don't you just wave a red flag?'

'Listen – you're the one who was supposed to have it planned out. You got all the information – where the hell to find him, who the hell his mother is. I counted on you. Maybe you're gettin' cold feet. Just let me know. I'll do the goddamned thing myself.'

'Go screw yourself.'

'Fuck off.'

Reuben jerked his head in the direction of an old couple strolling towards them, hanging onto each other for support. 'Let's go. Slow.'

Monk pulled out. 'Where?'

'Drive past that burned-out store again. Let's take a look at it.'

The lock on the dash said three thirty.

The Cadillac was hidden from view by the crumbling walls of the burned-out store.

Behind the wheel, Monk was buried in a copy of *Playboy*.

In the back seat, Reuben's gaze was fixed on the house – an angular view through what had once been the display window.

They spelled each other, watching. Nobody had come in or out. The cat on the balustrade had skulked off an hour ago. Luck was with them – a few cars had passed, that was it. The street was filled with Sunday quiet.

Reuben lit another cigarette. The smoke burned his lungs. Too many cigarettes. His muscles ached from tension and claustrophobia.

The rifle across his knees weighed a ton.

'Turn on the radio. Low.'

Monk reached forward. Low stereo music filled the car.

'Lower ' Reuben said. 'See if you can get the news.'

Monk lowered the sound changed the station. A barely audible voice announced the afternoon news. Reuben kept his eyes on the house. The announcer came on.

'*Local policeman Dudley Campanello has been slain by a member of the black separatist organisation, the African Republic.*'

'Jesus,' Monk said.

'*Akima Oko, a black Milwaukee antipoverty worker, has been arrested and charged with murder.*'

'Black bastard,' Monk said.

'*Early this morning, a combined force of fourteen F.B.I. agents and a dozen Holmesdale policemen surrounded the headquarters of the African Republic in an attempt to serve a warrant on Hoover Stovall, wanted in the robbery-death of a service-station attendant in Jackson, Michigan. In resonse to warnings, the black militants opened fire. Law officers retaliated with rifles and tear gas.*'

Reuben thought about Kornfield. Kornfield had predicted it.

'*The fugitive, Hoover Stovall, has not been found. Critically wounded in the shootout were Brendon Hollyhoke, president of the African Republic, and Clyde Bowden, a local musician. . . .*'

'Clyde Bowden – he's one of your niggers, isn't he ?' Monk said.

'Yes.'

'Goddamned niggers.'

Reuben thought about Clyde. Clyde would be arrested, charged. Anny would appear in his office, ask him to defend Clyde. He killed the image. He didn't need it. He didn't need to be in the middle of anything else. What the hell was he trying to be – a goddamned crusader ?

Screw it.

But it nagged. He had refused to take word to Brendon Hollyhoke for Kornfield. And now he knew the destination of the dynamite he had reclaimed from Buster. And out of all of it, one thing stood out clearly. Last night, while the Kluckers had been holding another damned meeting at the Rawlins' fishing camp, Barksdale was gathering a mixed army to ambush a handful of blacks playing African native.

He kept his eyes on the white clapboard house.

'*. . . the African Republic is a militant organisation formed in Detroit, Michigan, seeking to create a black nation in the South. Earlier this week, they were forced off a plot of farm land outside*

279

Holmesdale in a dispute over payment with the owner, Vernon Powell. . . .'

'Turn it off,' Reuben said.

Monk switched it off.

The quiet came back. Reuben thought about Simmons. When Simmons took office, he had given out an interview in which he pledged: *I'm going to keep this a nice, clean place. The niggers ain't going to run this town, and neither is the Klan.* Simmons had kept half the vow. Monk had known how it would be before he had. He watched the house. Nothing moved. It looked like an ordinary sun-scarred house. Inside, a killer read the Sunday comics. For the last time.

'This shit's just about made up my mind,' Monk said.

'What?'

'I haven't said anything – but I figure, another two years, the kind of money I'm making – I'm going to take the whole damned family, lock, stock, and barrel. I'm going to get the hell out of here.'

'What are you talking about?' Reuben watched the house. Inside, Army Jones was lying down for a nap. His last nap.

'Israel.'

'Israel?'

'Damned right. I'm a builder. They're growing. I've made some inquiries. Open arms, man, open arms.'

'You sound like your papa,' Reuben said. A car went past, cutting his view for a moment. Inside the house, Army Jones dreamed – probably of the girl named Jackie, tattooed on his upper arm. His last dream.

'Shit. My papa doesn't know what Israel is. He still thinks about it like those old Jews in the synagogue. *Fiddler on the Roof.* It's not like that. It's good rough country over there. Man's country. It's maybe what this place used to be like a hundred years ago. A Jew doesn't take any crap over there. Out in the open. Not like us sitting here. Sneaking around. Waiting for some god-damned ignorant jealous redneck – '

'We'll blow his head off,' Reuben said. 'Then it'll be over.'

'I've been thinking about that,' Monk said. 'Maybe it will, and maybe it won't. What the hell are we killing him for? For hating Jews. It was always there, underneath, like a goddamned time bomb. All it's done now is explode. Maybe there'll be a next time. I'm not sticking around for a next time. I'm going to – '

'There won't be any next time.'

'Why the hell not? You grew up here. Like Sheila. *Reform.*

Like gentiles you grew up. You think that makes you –'

'Screw off,' Reuben said.

'I'm not going tomorrow. What the hell's the matter with you?'

'You're a jackass,' Reuben said.

'Why the tell don't you take a nap,' Monk said. 'I'll watch for a while.'

Willie had taken him out to kill the deer.

It was the Christmas he was thirteen, in the woods that had once been bear country, turning the gold and russet and scarlet of delta autumn; and the river jungle had still been wild and thick with cane and gum and pine. And Willie had given him his first drink of whiskey – it had burned his stomach like hellfire.

In the afternoon, they had picked up the trail. Found the tracks, and a rub – the shiny place on a pine where the buck polished his antlers by rubbing against the bark; the bark was scraped away high enough off the ground to see it had been a big one. And near it had been the buck's love trap, the place cleared of grass and leaves where the big buck urinated, then pawed it into the ground to attract a doe.

. . . Mollie had eyes like a doe, too big for her face, black as a well bottom. He tried to remember the color of the cajun doctor's eyes. Blue. They were blue. . . .

The normal range of a buck was about a square mile. Willie had said. They had moved through the wild territory, across the damp earth, as the twilight sounds of the wilderness varmints began. They had camped by the river, Willie making a fire from the ashes soaked in kerosene which he carried in a tobacco tin, oiling his boots by the light of the fire. They had spent the night there, by the river, in woolen underwear and wrapped in blanket rolls, the embers from the fire glowing all night. Then, in the gray dawn, he had opened his eyes, and Willie had been sitting there, staring out through the canebrake across the river.

'I killed me a man once,' Willie had said. 'A Cree. They were the only Indians married niggers, you know. I was your age. Thirteen. Caught him stealin' a chicken. Back then, you weren't a man 'til you killed. I guess it's different now. Maybe it wasn't never right. You been confirmed. If your grandpaw had been alive, he coulda decided. But he ain't. Since it's up to me, I figure a deer'll do for you.'

'I don't know what you mean,' Reuben had said.

'I'll never forget what he looked like, that Cree. Kind of short and squat – come out of the swamp. I bought him a headstone. It didn't seem like anything back then. Like an initiation. Killin' a man. My papa was a southerner in the old tradition. My papa – he had killed a man at thirteen. Your grandpaw – he was different. He did his share, alright, I guess. I used to think, one day, he'd run me off with a shotgun – but he didn't. He didn't need no shotgun. I never understood about Jews. He had that Old Testament strength alright, but he knew how to handle himself. Outstripped the natives, he did. I figure a deer'll do for you.'

That was when Willie had handed him out the whiskey. Along with the rifle. And he had sat there, thinking about how Willie had killed a man, and thinking about killing Willie. Not knowing why he wanted to kill Willie – he liked Willie, but thinking about it anyway, maybe because of Elena, and maybe because of his grandfather, or maybe Willie was the alien. And then it had passed.

And the deer had fallen, like a tree.

And Willie had smeared the blood on his forehead, like the Indians did. Saying: *I figure a deer'll do for you. . . .*

When he opened his eyes, it was dusk. He woke with a start. He had a vague memory of a dream about Mollie. Mollie and the cajun. A dream in which sex became murder. Willie had become the cajun doctor. And Mollie had become Elena. It had gone like that, back and forth. Fear and fury. Somewhere in it, he had heard the clap of a rifle's report.

'What time is it?'

'A quarter to seven,' Monk said. 'I'm starving. What the hell is he doing in there?'

'It's a break. If he doesn't come out until dark, that makes it easier.' Reuben felt his stomach constrict. The outline of the house was beginning to vanish into the twilight.

'Come on out of there, you sonofabitch,' Monk said. The cat prowled up the street and bounded onto the porch. Inside the house, a light went on.

'Why don't we pull out. It's dark enough now.'

Monk started the motor. He edged the Cadillac out and into the curb opposite the house.

Beyond the roofline, the sky had turned purple, darkness falling quickly, the way it did in March. Reuben propped the gun on the ledge of the lowered window. On the porch, the cat was rubbing against the screen and wailing. The door opened. The mother reached out, scooped up the cat, and closed the door again. A yellow porch light went on.

'Sonofabitch –' Monk said.

Reuben felt a cold sweat break. There was still some light left, too much light. The gun leveled, his hand steady. He had never killed a man. Willie had killed a Cree. What man had his grandfather killed? *Initiation*, Willie had said. *I figure a deer'll do for you*. It was imminent now, he could feel it – in a moment, Army Jones would open the door, walk out onto the porch, the rifle would crack, Jones would fall. Like a tree. Or a buck. Willie had smeared the buck's warm blood on his forehead. Why not, after Jones, kill the cajun? Willie had said, *Maybe it wasn't never right. You been confirmed*. The mark of manhood. *I never understood about Jews*.

Reuben focused on the gunsight. It might have been any Sunday, any twilight, any street. It might have been a portion of woods, growing lightless and impenetrable. Willie had taught him patience. And to kill.

Don't spook the buck.

'What time is it?' he whispered.

'Seven,' Monk whispered back.

It would be any moment. March 1968. *It's about time you got initiated, boy*.

It wasn't a buck.

He could see what it was. A man. Framed suddenly in the doorway, the light coming out around him. Reuben felt his heart lurch, begin to pound wildly. Then, suddenly, a strange and foreign word tattooed itself across his brain. *Assassination*.

'There he is.' Monk switched on the motor. Quiet.

There was no daylight left. Reuben peered through the gunsight. The screen door swung open. The wooden door closed. Army Jones moved out onto the porch, beneath the yellow light. Reuben peered through the gunsight. Pulled back the hammer with his thumb. He saw Army Jones was carrying the cat, nestled against a brown leather jacket. Jones stooped. Let go of the cat. The cat bounded off.

'*Now* –' Monk said.

Reuben peered through the gunsight. Army Jones stood up. Pulled a pack of cheroots from the leather jacket. Stuck one in his mouth.

'Now –' Monk said. 'For Christ's sake – shoot.'

It wasn't a buck.

He could see what it was. A man. It had never occurred to him that he could not pull the trigger.

From the past, he heard the rumbling echo of a rifle shot.

The air was silent.

'*Shoot.*'

Reuben peered through the gunsight. He watched Army Jones strike a match. He felt himself freeze. His ears rang with the eerie quiet as he saw Army Jones start down the steps.

A stream of curses poured from Monk as he lurched, grabbed the rifle. Reuben fought back, felt Monk's blow on his shoulder. A harsh, visceral sound ripped – Reuben heard himself shout, '*No, goddamn you – No!*' He felt Monk's second blow, heard the crack of the rifle as it went off, saw Army Jones stagger forward and fall. Reuben lunged at the rifle – heard it go off again, saw the windshield shatter, heard the woman in the house begin to scream.

He swung at Monk. Monk set loose another stream of curses as the Cadillac squealed off, racing, Monk hanging onto the wheel and shouting. 'Goddamn you, goddamn you, yellow bastard! I missed him!' – the Cadillac at full speed – '*You yellow goddamn bastard – all he did was drop and crawl to get our license plate!*'

Thirty-two

THE BLACK RAIN slashed down on Zoe's red umbrella. Mollie crowded next to her as they hurried across the airport parking lot. Somewhere out on Lake Pontchartrain, a baby hurricane raged. Not enough to halt the planes.

'I'm sorry about Burke.'

'It's alright.' She had walked the Quarter, afterwards, in the rain. She hadn't cried for Burke. She had cried for the girl she had been.

The glass door swung open, magically, an electric eye. Zoe shut the umbrella, spraying raindrops. Mollie went through first, stepped on the escalator, Zoe directly behind her. A young pregnant woman and a white-haired gentleman rode up in front. Strangers. She had suddenly become aware of strangers.

'Listen,' Zoe said, 'maybe I'll leave Sol. What do you think? Maybe you and I could get a house together. I mean, I've always been scared. I wouldn't be scared if it was both of us.'

Mollie turned. 'I don't think so, baby.' Zoe wasn't a baby.

Zoe was thirty-four years old. She, Mollie, was thirty-six. It had happened. No longer children. She had suddenly become aware of time.

At the top of the escalator, a clock said a quarter to nine. Her plane left at nine. In an hour, she'd be back in Holmesdale. She knew, later, sometime, she would cry for Burke.

'We'd have alimony,' Zoe said. 'Child support. We could both get jobs. I mean, every single man in the world comes through New Orleans sooner or later. I met a new guy the other day, with IBM. He said he was a customer engineer. What's a customer engineer?'

'A repair man,' Mollie said. Walking together, they crossed the lobby. Past the flower shop. The window was filled with yellow jonquils. 'We can't start all over. Either of us.' The loudspeaker came on, announced a flight to Dallas.

'I don't know what to do,' Zoe said.

The corridor stretched out. A group of long-haired fringe-jacketed kids moved along in front. *Sometimes I think they're mayflies and sometimes I think it's more profound than that.* Mollie's gate appeared, on the left, fifty yards up. She stopped, set the small suitcase at her feet. She looked at Zoe. 'I love you. But I can't tell you what to do.'

'What are you going to do?'

She put her arms around Zoe. Zoe felt warm, like a startled kitten. She held her. 'I don't know.' Then she picked up the bag and ran quickly down the corridor.

The rain slanted across her image in the plane window, black night outside and no sense of motion, only waiting to land. She looked at her watch; in thirty minutes she would land, in her own life, somehow not a child anymore.

It's just like it used to be, her mother had said. A couple of hours ago. Six o'clock dinner. The rain coming down on the roof of the dining room of the Singer apartment. She had been sitting next to Anna, her grandmother, brought in from the Blue Star Home for the Aged. Across the table, Zoe sat next to Jason. Sol had been absent – a delivery. And her mother had said, *It's just like it used to be.*

'How are the children?' her father said.

'Fine.'

'You promised to take pictures.' Edith piled Jason's plate with chicken and rice. Jason sent Zoe a despairing look. Zie removed half of it.

'I will,' Mollie said.

'Don't just *take* pictures, *send* them,' Jacob said.

'Yes, I will.' And the old sense of imprisonment had swept her. But she had been able to see that he owned her mother. She had been able to see he was the first man to own her.

'What about that bombing?' he said. His hair was almost white. He was heavier. He insisted on authority. The authority was meant to express love.

'I don't know.' She heard the rain.

'It's not a good thing,' Edith said nervously. Mollie looked at her mother. Her hair was turning gray. Her face was filled with concern. The anxiety was meant to express love.

'Bombing?' Anna said. 'What kind of bombing?' Almost ninety. The pillow-soft flesh gone to folds, the eyes gone watery and nearly blind, the thin white hair sprinkled like talc. Still the vigor remained, like an old ghost. It occurred to Mollie that no one had ever owned Anna.

'The temple in Holmesdale was bombed, Mother,' Jacob said.

'Ah – wherever we go. I remember in Kiev. You know, Mollie, Kiev? When I was a girl – '

'Kiev's in Russia,' Jacob said to Zoe.

'I know,' Zoe said.

'My papa, he was in the Russian army,' Anna said. 'You know they came and picked them up, as *kinder*. Twelve years old and in the Russian army. Gunstocks he made. But he wouldn't convert. Not on your life. Everything they tried. But he stayed a Jew.'

'We don't run into much anti-Semitism here,' Jacob said.

'Of course not,' Edith said. 'You were on the Beauty Court at Newcomb, Mollie. You never missed out on anything because you were Jewish.'

'My papa got a license to live in Kiev,' Anna said. 'Because he had been in the army. Three fourths of Kiev was illegal.'

'Kiev is in Russia,' Edith said to Jason.

'Avrum and Itsky were in the drayage business,' Anna said. 'You remember, Jacob – Avrum and Itsky? They had no privileges in Kiev. No license. When they got caught, my papa had to go to jail for them.'

'How's Reuben?' Edith said.

'Fine.'

'You're telling us the truth, aren't you?'

'Yes.'

'Eat your dinner, Jason, or leave the table,' Jacob said. The rain kept on, dull and steady.

'There was another brother, Nathan,' Anna said. 'You remember, Jacob – Nathan ? An upholsterer. Tufting. You know, Mollie, tufting ? With buttons ? He worked in the Kiev Conservatory. A beautiful voice he had. The director – a woman – she heard him sing. Arranged for him a gentile passport to study in Moscow. Linsky he sang, in *Eugen Onegin*. He came back with two friends and a typesetter. We hid them all. Pamphlets they made, in the attic. The police used to come, all the time, searching. Always we lived with fear.'

'Please eat, Jason,' Edith said.

'I'm not hungry.' Jason was pale, ephemeral, younger than Phil.

'Leave the table,' Jacob said.

'Leave him alone,' Zoe said.

'Have they called in the Anti-Defamation League ?' Jacob said.

'I don't know.'

'These things should be turned over to the proper authorities.'

'Your father's right,' Edith said.

'Stockings I knitted,' Anna said. 'You know, Zoe – stockings ? The machines were on the windows. The longshoremen, they used to come by and talk to us. I was a good-looking girl back then. In my head I remember everything. How it was. Before your grandpaw, there was a law student. I used to sneak and meet him. Handsome, he was. Such a nice moustache. You know, five hundred dollars his mother wanted just for the nice moustache – '

'You're not eating either, Mollie,' Jacob said.

'I'm not hungry.' She heard herself. She sounded like Jason.

'What's the matter ?' Edith reached over and patted her hand. 'You're not coming down with something, are you ? Maybe I should take your temperature ?'

'No. I'm fine.'

'You look pale. Doesn't she look pale ?'

'I'm fine,' Mollie said. 'I'm just a little tired, that's all.'

'What have you got to be tired about ?' Jacob said.

The plane landed on time. Nine forty-five. It wasn't raining in Holmesdale. The night air was clear and cold. She felt a mild anxiety as she walked through the parking lot towards her station wagon. A sense of something following her. She dismissed it. She was being followed by her life. There had been something good in her life. Burke. It had been worth going back to find that. She went past Monk's truck – it hadn't been parked there when she left. The truck meant Reuben was still in Memphis. She felt

287

relief, disappointment, a new sense of strength which came from motion. She knew she had begun to climb, painfully, blindly, out of some self-imposed pit; to move, painfully, blindly, from some arrested stopping place of her youth. Then, suddenly, she recognised the thing she felt for the first time in years. Hope.

The station wagon was locked. It took her a moment to find the key, unlock it. From somewhere in the parking lot, another car started up abruptly. She looked around. No headlights gleamed. An irrational flicker of fear passed through her – fear of the dark, of the unknown, of being alone and helpless. She saw how it happened, how it got passed on. *Always we lived with fear*, Anna had said. Real fear, which had come out of the reality of deprivation and persecution. Then it got passed on – love and fear inextricably mixed – and the relentless catechism of being special. She climbed behind the wheel. She started the motor, switched on the headlights, and moved towards the parking lot exit. She saw how it had been. Telling Reuben the truth had been her first act of courage – the first, possibly, of her life. Her first step. Going back, without blinders, had been a second step. A start. Now fear rode with her, through the gate and onto the dark, narrow airport road. Fear said: *Where are you going?* I don't know. *What are you going to do?* I don't know. *Who do you think you are?*

The airport road was empty. On both sides the woods hemmed her in – tall dark pines and rustling underbrush – the quiet punctuated by the night sounds of unidentifiable creatures. The fear persisted. A sense of being followed remained with her. Ahead, a dark isolation stretched out – seven miles before she reached the highway. She looked back in the rear-view mirror. The camera equipment obscured the view. She felt the purr of another car, somewhere, but could see no headlights behind her. *I don't give a damn what you do*, Reuben had said, *but you ought to know the F.B.I.'s probably following you around.* The idea had seemed melodramatic, unreal. *They're looking for leverage. I forced them into the bombing case.* The bombing, itself, had seemed melodramatic, unreal. She had gone out to look at the rabbi's house. She had seen the damage, but she had refused the reality. She had removed herself, still clinging to a false and childish sense of immunity. She had not felt truly threatened because she had no emotional stake in her life. More subtle had been an ugly sense of relief, as if the disaster had been the inevitable fulfillment of a secret wish, brimstone, to end her meaningless life.

She had a sudden vision of being followed in New Orleans. Had some trained, professional, invisible man watched her go into the Maison de Ville ? Had he questioned the wizened old man at the desk ? Had he watched through the gauze curtains with binoculars ? And followed her, later, through the Quarter, in the rain ? Was it the F.B.I., or another exercise of her faculty for self-deception ? Did she need to believe it was the F.B.I., and not a detective hired by Reuben ?

She imagined Reuben hiring a detective, planning divorce proceedings, planning to take the children from her. But the vision wouldn't hold. Reuben was an explosive, embattled man. Anger came easy to him, subterfuge came hard. Her own anxiety was being culled from the lonely, woods-lined road. An animal chuckled from the underbrush. She shivered, chastised herself for the self-imposed fear.

Then she looked in the rear-view mirror again. She saw nothing but darkness. Nothing behind her, nothing ahead. She felt her body ease, felt the tension melt.

Then, suddenly, a pair of headlights blinked on in the rear-view mirror – directly on her tail, like a demon bearing down. She fought a harrowing burst of terror as she realised the car had been following her in the darkness, lights off. She pressed the accelerator. The car kept up. Then, abruptly, it swerved out and around her, blinking its headlights on and off – then it moved in again, in front of her headlights and she could see it was a police car. Then it was gone, leaving her shaken. It had happened swift as a streak of lightning – and possibly as accidentally – but she felt it was a signal; she felt something waiting for her, up ahead. The road was narrow. To turn around, she would have to stop, back up, take several turns to manipulate the wagon in the other direction. She kept going. An even pace. Her eyes searching the road by the beam of her headlights – a light fog hanging low on the ground. She saw nothing. Heard nothing, beyond the sounds of the woods. She rolled up her window. Her heart hammered high in her chest. Then she sensed it, knew she was approaching it, whatever it was – could make out, by her headlights, the shape of the police car on her left, just ahead.

Some instinct took over. Some instinct flattened the accelerator. The wagon veered to the right, roared forward in a torrent of speed. She held onto the wheel. Then she heard a sound, like the crack of a whip. The window directly behind her split and shattered.

The wagon leapt forward. She kept going. The wagon flew. The sound repeated itself. She heard something slam against the rear of the wagon. The sound of tearing metal. She hung on to the wheel. The wagon hurled itself down the stretch of dark road towards the intersection with the highway. She fought hysteria. *Someone had taken a shot at her. Two shots.*

She ran the red light at the intersection, and plunged headlong into the highway, swerving to avoid an oncoming car. She looked back. A series of headlights blinked behind her, ongoing highway traffic. Tears streamed down her cheeks. She willed herself to quit shaking. The wagon carried her down the highway at a dizzying speed. The highway was neon lit. The lights whizzed past. Headlights moved ahead, behind. Someone had taken two shots at her. *Who? Why?* The sound of tearing metal replayed itself. She gripped the wheel. She kept her eyes on the highway. Finally, the Morningside exit appeared. The wagon rushed down the ramp, running another red light. The Williamsburg was lit, light coming through the panes of the bay window. There were cars parked outside. The service station was open, lights blazing. The wagon refused to stop. It sped past, down Morningside. She threw several swift glances in the rear-view mirror. No headlights appeared. She streaked to the end of Morningside, tires squealing as she rounded the corner. The house was lit. She headed towards it, then raced up the driveway. At the top of the hill, she halted, cut the ignition and the lights. Then she sat there a moment, trembling and crying. The deep quiet of the woods, and the river beyond, enveloped her. The sound of crickets, the slur of a whippoorwill. Someone had tried to kill her.

She got out of the wagon. The coachlight outside the back door illuminated the car window. It had shattered into a grotesque cobweb – at the center, a small, perfect hole. The flat, sour taste of helplessness caught in her throat. *Someone had tried to kill her.*

Then she heard the sound of a car engine, roaring. A car was speeding past the front of the house towards the corner below. She scurried into the darkness of the shrubbery and looked down. Streaking around the corner, beneath the streetlight, was a long, white ghostlike car – a stranger. The tires squealed as it took the corner, braked at the bottom of the driveway, then swerved and headed up, its blinding headlights sweeping the gardenia bushes. Suddenly the headlights were full upon her.

She ran towards the back door. Behind her, she heard the car screech to a stop. The door was locked. She fumbled in her purse for the key, but it flew from her fingers, landing in the bed of jonquils. Behind her, she heard the car door slam. She realised the coachlight made her a perfect target. She began to run, along the path to the greenhouse, her heels clacking against the brick, her chest roaring with terror. She could hear his footsteps behind her. From the need to scream came silence – shallow, painful bursts of breath· Then the sound that rushed over her was the sound of her own name. He was calling her name. '*Mollie* – ' he shouted. '*Mollie !*'

She stopped, trembling. She heard him call her name again. She felt a crazy jagged laughter threaten. She heard his footsteps. Then the cumbersome silhouette came through the trees, and she fell, sobbing, into Reuben's arms.

He locked and chained the back door.

When he came upstairs, he found Mollie wearing the blue fleece dressing gown, sitting in bed smoking, still trembling. The night sounds of the woods came through. The sound of Syd Kaminsky's car moving off in the distance.

'Is your mother gone ?' Mollie's face was frayed and pale, her eyes still fragmented with shock. He thought about the cajun doctor. He thought about the shots that had nearly killed her. He thought about how it had felt, holding her, out by the green-house.

'Syd picked her up. I told her you caught the flu in New Orleans. We don't need her hysteria.' He sat on the edge of the bed. The white porcelain clock said ten thirty. He could feel the terror still emanating from her. 'I want you to pack up the kids in the morning. Take them down to New Orleans. Stay with Zoe.' He shook a cigarette from his pack, lit it. Then he looked at her. She was crying again.

'It was a police car,' she said.

'You'll be safe in New Orleans. The children will be safe. A few days. A week at the most.'

'No,' she said. 'I'm not running. I'm not running anymore.' The smoke from her cigarette spiraled upwards. He took the cigarette from her trembling fingers and put it out. Her tears kept coming. Under the tears, he felt a grave, innocent courage.

'A week at the most,' he said. 'Until I make sure this thing's over.'

'What "thing" ?'

'They took a couple of shots at you.'

'Who's they ?' she said. 'The police ?' He shook his head. A spasm took her over. 'Don't you understand ? That's the most frightening thing – *not knowing*.' She came into his arms, sobbing against his chest. He felt the familiar shape of her body, torn by terror and need. He held her. The shaking kept on. In the grip of aftershock, she relived the experience. He felt her go through it – held her as she stiffened with fear, then began to tremble again. 'Please – ' she said. '*Please*. Tell me. Tell me the *truth*.'

He looked down at her anguished face. He could see he had no choice. 'I didn't go to Memphis with Monk. We stayed here. We stalked a man named Army Jones.'

She pulled away. She stared at him. 'What do you mean ? What are you talking about ?'

'The man who did the bombing,' he said. 'Tonight, at seven o'clock, he walked out of his mother's house. I had a rifle aimed at his head. I couldn't shoot. I don't know why. Monk grabbed the rifle – fired twice. I tried to stop him. He missed. I was hoping Jones hadn't got the license number. I thought I could cover my tracks by getting rid of my car – took it down to Dick Duggan's and traded it, tonight. But he got the number – there's a cop involved with them. He must have tracked down the plates, done some detective work to find you – maybe as simple as calling the house. They found you. They shot at you. Retaliation.'

He watched her absorb it. He saw the trembling cease, begin again. She crossed her arms and began to caress her shoulders as if a cold wind had blown through the bedroom. 'You went out today – to kill someone ?'

'Yes.' He met her eyes. He felt her thoughts. Nineteen years. Between them, they had nearly done everything. Love, hate, adultery, murder. Everything became nothing.

'I'm glad – you couldn't.'

'You don't know what you're talking about.' It had been no moral decision. Something had broken loose. Killing a man had turned out to be different from killing a buck. At the crucial moment, something had turned him to stone – something irrevocable, from which there was no going back. Monk had pulled the trigger. *Goddamn you, goddamn you, yellow bastard.* There had been no way to explain to Monk the thing he didn't understand himself. In harsh anger, he had left Monk at the Ramada Inn.

Quietly, he filled her in on Barksdale, the F.B.I., Justin, the Rawlins brothers. He watched the fear travel her face, watched her fight the new burst of panic. When he finished, a long silence went by.

'What are you going to do ?'

'Whatever I have to,' he said. 'I don't know now. But I want

292

you and the children out of here. I don't want you in danger. Take the children to New Orleans until it's over.'

She turned her face. She cried softly into the pillow. Finally she turned back, her face drawn. 'No,' she said. 'I have to stay here.'

'That won't make it any easier,' he said. 'It'll make it harder. I'd have to worry about Joe and Phil.'

'I'll send the children. But I have to stay here.'

'Why?'

The tears flooded back silently. 'I don't know why.'

He stood up. 'Get some sleep. Don't think about it anymore.' He switched off the lamp. Darkness swallowed the room. An owl hooted off in the woods.

'Where are you going?'

'Get some sleep. Don't think about it. I'll be up for a while.'

In the kitchen, he plugged in a pot of coffee and took stock of the refrigerator. He hadn't eaten since the brunch he and Monk had shared before heading out to Army Jones' church. He closed his eyes a moment. If felt like the longest day of his life. Why hadn't he been able to shoot? Why had he tried to stop Monk? What was happening to him? The simple supports of what had once been his everyday life had been pulled out from under him, and now he could no longer count on what he believed he knew of himself. The conditioning of the society that had spawned him had come up against that part of his soul tied to a deeper past. He had been ruled by a part of his being to which he had no access.

Frieda had roasted a chicken. The carcass still sported some white meat and a drumstick. He pulled off the drumstick and went to work on it. There were other questions. Had the incident been reported to Simmons? M. K. Taylor was actively involved with the Klan. Was Simmons? His instincts told him not actively – not beyond a policy of laissez-faire. The place where Simmons and Barksdale met. Laissez-faire.

He finished off the drumstick. There were other questions. Was tonight a warning, or the first step in a concentrated campaign to be mounted by the Klan against him. Would they go after Mollie again? Would they go after Joe or Phil? The F.B.I. report had led him to believe they constituted only a handful. Now he believed they were everywhere.

He went outside and opened the trunk of the new white Cadillac. The samovar glittered beside the box of his grandfather's

293

papers. He had transferred all of it. He brought the shotgun inside, chained up the door again. Then he picked up the phone.
The big brass pocket watch on the kitchen wall said eleven o'clock.
He remembered Simmons had been up since dawn. Ambushing
Africans. He dialed the home number. Simmons came on, dull,
groggy, and irritable. Reuben imagined a girl beside him. A
waitress. Simmons liked waitresses. Two of his wives had been
waitresses. Dumb, with knockers.

'What the hell is it?'

'It's Reuben. Somebody took a couple of shots at my wife
tonight. About an hour ago. On the new airport road.'

'I'll be damned. Who was it?'

'Who the hell do you think?' A brief silence passed. Then
Simmons came back with a question.

'Did she see who it was?'

'Try M. K. Taylor,' Reuben said. A swift silence went by. He
felt Simmons bristle, grow wary. He had always thought of
Simmons as an overfed skunk – a white streak of integrity running
down his back. In the past week, he had learned the white streak
was something else. Ambition and self-protection. Simmons
played to his local audience. Ambush a black enclave and feed
the fears that insured his power. But don't make waves in the
status quo.

'I run a clean force,' Simmons said.

'Maybe you need a new goddamned broom.'

'I'll tell you how I feel about them Klan bastards,' Simmons
said. 'Just for the record. If I got a report that somebody shot at
one of them Klan bastards, I wouldn't even look for the man who
did it.'

Reuben felt his stomach turn over. He had a quick vision of
arrest, jail, being tried – assault with a deadly weapon. Simmons
was offering him a blatant exchange. *You lay off Taylor – I'll lay
off of you.* Why was Simmons protecting Taylor? How much
leverage did Simmons have? He cursed Monk. He cursed himself. He cursed Simmons.

'I want a cop out here tonight,' Reuben said.

'Good idea,' Simmons said.

'Bo Garrison.' He had known Bo Garrison's father in Maryville. He had helped Bo's wife once on an insurance claim. 'I
want Bo Garrison out here walking this beat.'

'He's a good man,' Simmons said. 'All my men are good men.'
Reuben hung up.

Screw Simmons. A wave of exhausted anger swept him. Then

he remembered that M. K. Taylor would take the stand in the Higgins case, tomorrow afternoon. His territory. The courtroom.

He'd cut Taylor's balls off.

The need for immediate action still rankled. He thought about Barksdale. He picked up the receiver again, then stopped. A stray, irrelevant piece of information popped into his head. Hoover's mother, like Army Jones' mother, had been a Calvinist. Where had he read that? Why had it come into his head now? Because his senses were still working – making equations between Army Jones and Hoover – telling him not to deal with Barksdale from weakness. It was likely Barksdale knew about the failed attempt on Army Jones. It was likely Barksdale even knew about the retaliatory attempt on Mollie. A phone call, tonight, would put Barksdale back into the role of father. Justin was a funnel. He'd use Justin – let Barksdale come back to him. He still had an ace card. Fifty grand. Another wave of fatigue washed through him. He no longer trusted Justin. He had alienated Monk. He felt alone. He felt himself steeped in an old and classic wish. For a man – or a woman – he could trust.

He realised the receiver was still in his hand. Screw Simmons. Screw Barksdale. Justin. All of them. He dialed information and asked for the number of the Holmesdale Hospital downtown. He got the hospital on the line and asked about Clyde Bowden. He was switched to the charity ward. He identified himself, then inquired about Clyde Bowden's condition.

The doctor on the other end said, 'Two bullet wounds in the left hip. But he's in good shape.'

'Can he be moved?'

'Physically, yes – but we need authority to do it.'

'Have him moved to Sinai,' Reuben said. 'I'll take the responsibility and the bills.'

He hung up, feeling better.

He poured a cup of coffee and carried it over to the table. Yesterday's mail was lying there. He toyed with it. He lit a cigarette, swallowed some coffee, then picked up the letters. On top were three bills. The fourth envelope had been addressed in big, neat handwriting to Mr Reuben Buchman. At the bottom of the envelope, it had been marked: PERSONAL.

He opened it.

There was no salutation. The letter was neatly written in sharp bold strokes.

Last Saturday you invaded my house. You came to ask questions. Because you think a black woman is shit. Because you think a white skin entitles you to do anything.

I never fucked a white man. I never fucked John Higgins. Buster Jackson would have killed any son-of-a-bitch who tried.

Buster was a man. You tell your wife. You tell your friends. Buster Jackson was nobody's *nigger*.

Eula Williams

He folded the letter and put it back in its envelope. He laid it on the table. Then he went through the rest of the mail. More bills. At the bottom was a telegram. He opened it. It began:

THE GOVERNOR AND HIS WIFE REQUEST THE PRESENCE OF MR AND MRS REUBEN BUCHMAN . . .

He realised Olive had telegraphed the invitations. A wire was class, and a wire made up for short notice.

. . . ON THURSDAY NIGHT, IN HONOR OF ISADORE RABIN, INDUSTRIALIST . . .

The last line read:

BLACK TIE.

Thirty-three

MONDAY rained again. Through the guest-room window, Reuben could see Bo Garrison in a black slicker walking the grounds. The grass had turned a bright shade of new green overnight. The season was changing. Reuben took it as an omen. He needed all the omens he could get.

He telephoned Jack Schraft to come by and take a look at Mollie. The sight of Jack kicked off an instant vision of the cajun doctor, every detail, down to the name tag. Last night Mollie had said, *I have to stay here.* Why ? *I don't know why.*

He leveled with Jack about the shooting attempt. To Leila and the children he sold the lie of the flu bug picked up in New Orleans. Jack prescribed rest, then left. Leila cooked breakfast. Reuben told Joe and Phil the policeman was there because of the bombing. Leila left the kitchen, crying. The boys rode to school in

296

Bo Garrison's police car. Arrangements were made for Bo to go home, get some sleep, pick the children up from school.

He left everything in an uneasy state of truce.

He stopped at the Williamsburg, swallowed a hurried cup of coffee, checked out Frieda. Monk didn't show up. By the time he reached the office, Justin was gone.

'All day,' Olive said. 'He's with the governor. Making arrangements for the Rabin do.' She pulled a typed sheet from her desk. 'You never gave me your invitation list. See if there's anybody you want added to this. I can send the wire out this morning.'

'Dr Jean Aucoin,' Reuben said. 'Call Sinai and get his address.'

'I never heard of him.'

'He's physician to the king of Arabia.'

'Is that true? That's not true.' Olive stabbed her head with a hairpin. 'Kornfield's secretary called. She put Higgins on the nine o'clock plane to Atlanta. The connecting flight gets him in at one twenty. Do you want me to pick him up?'

'Send Luanne,' he said.

In between appointments, he spent a hard, full morning finishing preparations for the Higgins case. Every hour, on the hour, he called home. He heard from Jake Gorman, John Abrahmson, and Harris. He reassured all of them. He didn't hear from Barksdale. Twice, he caught himself staring at Mollie's portrait.

By two o'clock it had quit raining. Luanne came back without John Tyler Higgins. He telephoned Kornfield. He was told by a secretary that Kornfield wasn't 'available.' He cursed Kornfield's secretary for lying and hung up. He drove to the Holmesdale Hotel, went up to the Hunt Club, ordered a Scotch and a club sandwich. Floyd Rawlins wasn't on duty, daytime. By a quarter to three, he was on his way to the courthouse. Not for Kornfield and not for John Tyler Higgins. For M. K. Taylor. If he didn't show, it might look as if they had scared him off. He didn't scare and he didn't break.

By the time he had his car parked, he had conditioned himself for the next few hours – the adaptation he had learned in twenty years of practice: how to shelve his own life, his own concerns, how to put everything out of his mind except the case at hand. He had trained himself, like an athlete. Once he entered the courtroom, there was nothing beyond the courtroom. Only the match at hand, to be played at the peak of his powers – to be won, at any cost.

On his way in, he saluted Moses.

It was a few minutes before three when he stationed himself at the counsel table in the fan-shaped courtroom. Without Justin. He could hardly remember the last case he had tried without Justin. Without Higgins. The show would begin without him. Whether the show continued, without him, was up to the judge. Legally, the charge could be tried with the defendant *in absentia*. The few moments left became priming time – time for the witnesses to be ushered into their cubbyholes, time for the lawyer and D.A. to make last minute notes. In some trials, these moments had the air of opening night, surprise and drama. This afternoon had the air of efficiency, a task. Reuben knew they had stacked what they could stack. A closed courtroom, no spectators, implying secrecy and evil. It was meant to be a railroad job and the tracks had been oiled. But there was always the human element that could throw the switch.

He threw a glance at Paul Griffith, D.A., on the other side of the courtroom, going over his notes. He and Paul and Justin had been classmates at Ole Miss. Paul had once had a shock of black hair, twenty fewer pounds, and a pretty cheerleader wife who had been Caroline's best friend. Just before the last election, Paul had divorced the cheerleader. Caroline – out of misguided loyalty – had actively campaigned against him. None of it helped in court.

The jury box was empty. He had drawn the counsel table closest to the jury box, his first piece of luck. He could watch them, feel what they were feeling, remind them he was there, imply they shared a common interest in justice. Higgins, guilty of civil rights activities, would be tried for homosexuality. Two inflammable issues. Some combination of men, in a jury room later, would make their decision emotionally – emotions repressed or expressed. There were lawyers who thought of a trial as a chess game, the jury as pawns. He wasn't one of them. From twelve men came good and evil, the predictable and the unexpected.

Then he became suddenly ware of the personal element, still there, to be battled. With the absence of Higgins, it felt like his trial: his own possible defeat, his own possible victory, his own imaginary audience – Mollie and Barksdale and Simmons and the rest. It interfered with the real preliminary battle, which was to keep Higgins' absence from validating the assumption of guilt which already pervaded the air of the courtroom.

The sheriff's gavel thumped. A black-robed judge entered. The courtroom stood as Judge Walter Alexander took his seat at the bench. He was a small man in his late fifties who looked less like a judge than any man Reuben knew. Rumor had it Alexander perched on a pillow, legs dangling, to reach the bench. He had eyes like a fly, bulging and iridescent, magnified by thick glasses. But his scrupulous fairness was legendary. Not chosen to aid Higgins. Chosen because, when Walter Alexander presided, court errors had to be found with a magnifying glass. Alexander as judge was a gamble on a verdict of guilty – afterwards, the chances of getting reversal on the basis of error would be about the same as catching pneumonia in hell. But it worked both ways. If he freed Higgins, there'd be no errors to get Higgins' ass at a later date.

The bailiff rose from the box in front of the judge and announced the state's charges against John Tyler Higgins. Contributing to the delinquency of a minor. Unnatural acts. Then Judge Alexander's bulging eyes fastened themselves on the counsel table. 'Is the defendant present ?'

Reuben rose. 'If it please the court – ' He paused. Alexander waited. Griffith waited. Reuben felt it was pointless – the plea for postponement on the grounds of the defendant's absence. He went through it anyway. Paul Griffith objected, right from the text-book, learned in the same class at Ole Miss, three seats behind Reuben. The defendant had broken bail, left the state, had been properly served, had proper counsel. The charge wasn't a felony, and could be tried without him.

'Can counsel give good reason why the defendant has not appeared ?' Alexander's voice had the toneless authority of a referee committed to neither side.

'No sir,' Reuben said.

'Motion denied.'

'If it please the court – defendant is absent because he was advised by the American Civil Liberties Union that he wouldn't get a fair trial down here. I've been unable to contact defendant in order to advise him otherwise.' It was a deliberate move. Reuben knew it wouldn't work, but knew, also, it would serve him well later.

'Motion denied,' Alexander said. 'Trial will continue.'

Reuben sat down, watched the bailiff call the veniremen to their feet. Three dozen men, of assorted shapes, sizes, and dress, rose at the rear of the courtroom. The bailiff swore them in. Reuben watched their faces – most of them serious, intent, a little frightened, a little awed by the possibility of power. The first twelve names were drawn and called. As each man filed past, took his seat in the jury box, Reuben checked off his name. James Sandifer had garnered the minimal information on each possible juror – age, occupation, marital status. The rest of his own evaluation would be made on intuition and questioning.

He kept his eyes on the jury as Alexander asked the standard questions. Were they citizens? Poll taxes paid? Had any of them ever been convicted of a felony? The men looked ill at ease as heads nodded negatively. Then a silence fell. Reuben watched Griffith.

'Jury accepted,' Griffith said. No peremptory challenges. No questions. Reuben saw the jury react. Griffith's acceptance looked like an act of blanket trust. Reuben knew it wasn't. Reuben knew that Griffith was gambling; for his purposes, any sampling of Mississippians would do. It was the same soulless view propounded by the A.C.L.U. Contempt for the southern heart.

Reuben rose. He approached the jury box. He scanned the twelve faces. Given a dollar, he had always bet seventy cents on the southern heart. He realised, in the past ten days, his own odds had dropped. Fifty-fifty. Six of the jurors would have to go. Which six? He worded his question carefully.

'Do any of you belong to any organisation of any kind – whether it has three members, or three million members – that has taken an active stand on one side or the other of the race issue – the black and white race issue? Or do you actively support such with time, money, or any other form of efforts?'

He felt the charged question run through the jury box. His intuition tabulated reactions. The flushing, the squirming, the looking at the ceiling. He had said *on one side or the other of the race issue*. He had made the question acceptable. As simple to admit to as possible. Three men reluctantly raised their hands. Reuben faced the bench. 'I ask that these men be excused for cause.'

Griffith rose. 'The question is irrelevant to the charge.'

'Your Honor,' Reuben said, 'a man is entitled to a trial by a jury with an open mind. Necessarily the jury will be exposed to witnesses' evaluation of the defendant's character – pro and con. Given certain facts of the defendant's history, I feel the question is highly pertinent in terms of obtaining a jury with an open mind.'

He watched Alexander remember that in the background was the A.C.L.U. – the audience he had established earlier; the audience who would, later, pore over the record. He watched his ploy pay off.

'The jurors may be excused,' Alexander said. 'Any veniremen who cannot give an acceptable answer to defense counsel's question may refrain from coming forward, if their names are called.'

The three men rose. Reuben memorised their faces and the

names he had checked. Three out of twelve had admitted to an active stand on the race issue. How many of the three were actually Klan members ? Maybe one. Which one ? He'd check all three of them out, later.

The bailiff called three more names. The men filled in the empty seats. Reuben examined the newcomers. Carefully, he put together his second question.

'Are any of you emotionally affected by the idea of a white man and a black woman working together ?' He felt a murmur run through the jury box. He saw Griffith grimace, but keep silent. Two men raised their hands.

'Excused.' Alexander repeated the instruction to the veniremen. The bailiff called two more names. The men came down the aisle and filled the two empty seats.

Reuben moved back to the counsel table and checked his notes. He scrached the five men who had left, and made crosses by the names of those who had taken their places. Then he scanned the roll call by age and occupation. There was a butcher, a foreman at Bell Telephone, an Internal Revenue man, a handicraft merchant, the owner of a lumber company. A road builder, an insurance salesman. A realtor, a peach grower, a superintendent at Holmesdale Sand Co. A highway department employee and an executive at an advertising agency. No professional men – which was fine; professional men competed, felt they knew as much as judge or lawyer. Nine married, one divorced, two bachelors. The ages ranged from twenty-three to forty-seven. Nobody old enough to play sage in the jury room. He had three peremptory challenges – no way to use them except Russian roulette. He made a tactical decision. Griffith had accepted them all immediately. If he continued to hound them with questions or used arbitrary peremptories, he'd come through as a suspicious and insecure bastard.

'Jury accepted.'

'Accepted,' Griffith said.

Reuben watched Alexander lean forward, address the jury. 'Do any of you know anyone involved in this case ?' Heads shook. 'Have you formed any opinion as to the guilt or innocence of this accused ?' Reuben watched the heads shake again. More easily now. 'Are any of you related by blood or marriage to any of the lawyers ? Have you had any business dealings with defendant's counsel, or state's counsel ?' The twelve heads shook negatively. 'Can you, and will you, try the case solely and alone on the evidence and the law ? – and arrive at a verdict solely and alone on evidence introduced in this courtroom and the law that will come to you at the conclusion of all the evidence in the form of written instructions from the court ? – and on these two things only, do your best to arrive at a just and honest verdict ?'

Reuben watched the twelve heads nod in variations of agreement. An irrational burst of hostility flooded him. He believed in juries, he seduced and cajoled juries. Never had he felt so totally hostile towards a jury. He knew it was misplaced anger. He couldn't pinpoint the source.

Alexander banged the gravel. 'When we return, I shall instruct the jury, and counsels will be prepared for opening statements. Court dismissed for a fifteen-minute recess.'

Reuben sat still, fending his anger. He watched Alexander leave. He watched the remaining veniremen leave. The jury filed out. Griffith left for the coffee machine in the hall. His watch said ten till four. Court would reconvene, go on until five thirty, the time it was usually dismissed except in instances when the jury was out. The courtroom had emptied. He realised he was watching the double mahogany doors, that he had clung to the hope Higgins might still show. Now he knew Higgins wouldn't. He knew this trial would be totally dependent on him – his craft, his talent, his passion. *If anybody can do it, you can do it,* Kornfield had once said. Then he knew where his anger was coming from.

He got up and went down the aisle, and through the double mahogany doors into the corridor. At the end of the hall, he slammed the phone booth door closed and put in a credit card call to Kornfield's home. In a moment Kornfield answered, the drama and piety and self-ordained authority traveling through the wire.

'The trial began an hour ago,' Reuben said.

'How's it going ?'

'Where the hell is Higgins ?'

'He missed his connection in Atlanta.'

'You're a goddamned liar.'

'You don't need Higgins.'

'You lying sonofabitch – you never intended to send Higgins back here, did you ? ?'

'Two bombings in less than a week . . . How could I subject him to the possibility of that kind of danger ?'

'If you weren't going to send Higgins, why the hell lay the case on me ? Why the hell not send an A.C.L.U. lawyer down ? I'll tell you why. Because you knew goddamned well a Yankee lawyer didn't have a prayer without a defendant. But I might – I just might. So why the hell not use Buchman's ass ? Isn't that it ? Why the hell not ? You people think you're so goddamned holy you can

302

use anybody. Is that what you call being a "liberal"? – *using* people? You knew goddamned well I wouldn't have touched this case if you had told me Higgins wasn't going to show.'

'I had no choice.'

'I'll see you in hell!'

He slammed the receiver.

He lit a cigarette. The booth filled up with smoke. He let the smoke out, called home. Mollie answered. Bo Garrison had picked up the children. An awkward, ugly silence went by.

'How's the trial going?' she said.

'Fine.'

There was nothing else to say.

He hung up.

He was breathing heavily, like a long-distance runner.

His watch said four.

He'd go back to the courtroom and ask to be relieved of the case. What the hell did he need it for?

M. K. Taylor's bulldog face flashed across his brain. Eula Williams followed. *Higgins was framed*, he had said to Eula. *I believe in justice.* Maybe he had, ten days ago.

Did he now? Hadn't he gone out with Monk to kill Army Jones because he no longer believed in law or justice? Then why hadn't he pulled the trigger? Why, at the last minute, had he tried to stop Monk? Because the last thing left to him had been the law? the courtroom? Because everybody and everything had betrayed him, except that?

Even Eula Williams had lied. *I never fucked John Higgins.* So what? Did that make it any less a frame? Kornfield had used him. So what? Was it any less a frame?

So what? A minor frame. Nothing. It wasn't a felony. What the hell was a misdemeanor? A verdict of guilty brought a five-hundred-dollar fine and six months in jail. What the hell was six months? He thought about Higgins in a Mississippi jail. He thought about Higgins – tall and rambling, that head of white-blond hair, a known civil rights activist. If Higgins got out of a Mississippi jail alive, it wouldn't be in one piece. If the cops like M. K. Taylor didn't get him, the inmates would.

Kornfield had known him. Kornfield had known he would fight.

He cursed Kornfield.

He cursed whatever it was in his own nature that had kept him from pulling the trigger yesterday, that would make him go back to the courtroom today; whatever the source, he cursed it, then felt the anger shifting, like a river, flowing into and becoming the energy of battle.

He came out of the phone booth. His watch gave him sixty seconds to get back to his place at the counsel table. In his head, he was already there. Griffith would begin the opening speeches. He'd come next. Then the prosecution would present its first witness. The day would end in the prosecution's territory – that's what the jurors would sleep on. He debated his tactics. Engage in an overlong jury speech? Hang onto the jury until five thirty by the southerner's inbred love of rhetoric and drama? He knew how to do that. Or make it short and pointed, then make damn sure court recessed at the end of a devastating cross-examination?

He stopped just outside the doors and made his decision. A long opening speech diluted the value of the closing argument. You couldn't do the same acrobatics twice for the same jury. He'd have to take his chances on the cross.

A flashbulb blew up in his face. A reporter grinned at him. 'Have you got a statement?'

'No statement.'

He pushed the doors and went through. The jury was settling down. Griffith was back at his station. He was halfway down the aisle when he realised his own counsel table was no longer empty. Justin sat there, scribbling, making notes. He felt his chest contract. Hundreds of times he had Justin had shared a counsel table. More times than not, they had come out with a victory. A team. The team had been split. What the hell was Justin doing here?

The court rose. Justin rose. Reuben got to the counsel table and slid in beside Justin. Alexander entered, took his place. The gavel rapped. 'What are you doing here?' Reuben said.

'*Court is in session.*'

Justin sat down, silently slid the list of jurors across. He had circled a name. *Roland Owen.* 'This one's going to give you trouble.'

Reuben looked at the statistics. *Peach grower. Age: 44. Married. Five children.*

'What kind of trouble?'

'Peach grower, my ass,' Justin said. 'He's a dirt farmer. Backs up to Vernon Powell's land. He's a hater. It's too late to get him off, but you ought to know what you're dealing with.' Justin's face creased, familiar, intense, zeroed in on the task at hand. Beyond Justin, the jurors shuffled to their feet. Alexander leaned forward, began to instruct them.

'I am instructing you now that an indictment is no evidence

against the accused. You will not regard it as such. The defendant is presumed innocent and the burden is on the state to prove the defendant's guilt from the evidence, beyond a shadow of a doubt.'

'Since when do you give a damn about this case?' Reuben said.

'I give a damn about you. Where are the rest of your notes?'

Reuben pushed his briefcase over. Justin gave him a quick but unmistakable look of affection and trust. *I give a damn about you.* Why the declaration of loyalty? Why now? He watched Justin remove the typed notes Kornfield had sent, the report from the Cleveland Delinquent Home. Justin began to read with total concentration as Griffith got up, came slowly past the counsel table, and stopped in front of the jury box.

Reuben turned his attention to Griffith, watched him take the beat of a good actor, then flash a grin of male camaraderie, like a lingerie salesman – engaging the jury in the chauvinist compact of men making sexual comparisons in a locker-room shower. The subliminal message came through loud and clear: *We, here, are all Men – no doubt about that.* It was a wicked alliance. The southern tradition of manhood was deeply tied to domination of the blacks. Reuben knew the unspoken corollary would come later: *Any southern man who takes up with niggers is a fag.*

'Gentlemen of the jury . . . the state will prove to you that the defendant *in absentia*, John Tyler Higgins III, did willfully and knowingly aid and abet the truancy and delinquency of said minor, Thomas Petry Hampstead. That the defendant *in absentia*, John Tyler Higgins III, did willfully and knowingly seduce and coerce said minor Thomas Petry Hampstead into unnatural sexual intercourse. This testimony will be given to you by witnesses and affidavits which will prove that John Tyler Higgins III, defendant *in absentia*, is *guilty beyond a reasonable doubt* of the charges brought against him by the sovereign state of Mississippi. I ask that you listen carefully to the evidence, then make your decision according to the dictates of your own conscience.' Griffith paused, flashed the message again, the grin, the alliance. A simple, disarming speech and demeanor. Then he began to walk quietly back to his counsel table.

Reuben watched the jury. Twelve pair of eyes followed Griffith's back. Griffith had chosen to underplay – the reverse tactic of easy authority, which made the jury come to him.

'Sonofabitch – ' Reuben looked at Justin, still reading, but having missed nothing. Justin looked up, grinned.

'He can hook them but he can't hold them.' Justin slid the

papers back into the briefcase. Reuben could feel the professional team-work beginning to take hold.

'Why the hell not?'

'Because there's two of us and only one of him. We'll do what we always do. I'll open. You close.'

'How the hell can you make an opening speech without any preparation?'

'All I'm going to do is get them ready for you.'

'*Why?*'

'Defense counsel will proceed,' Alexander said.

Quickly Justin rose and moved towards the jury. Reuben watched him. As if it were any goddamned case, all the old co-ordination working between them; the ability to read each other's minds in court; the method they always used: Justin reassured, he came in afterwards, with force.

'May it please the court . . . gentlemen of the jury . . . ' Justin began. Reuben watched him pause, let his eyes sweep the faces. Justin called a few names. 'Mr Owen . . . Mr Thompson . . . Mr Turner . . . you are about to judge another human being. It's a grave responsibility. I'm sure you know that. . . . ' Justin paused again, appeared to be searching for his next words – the deliberate look of a man searching his own soul, and so expecting no less from those he faced. It was Justin at his best – nothing withheld, no ambivalences. ' "Judge not lest he be judged," ' Justin quoted. 'Yet the law says we must. We who are committed to a civilised society take on the responsibility of the angels. And so we must judge well and fairly – as we would, ourselves, be judged. . . . '

Reuben watched the jurors respond, lean forward. It was a musical composition, Justin as maestro, the overture of respon-sibility, sensibility. The old sense of pride swept him.

' . . . To the indictment, the defendant has entered a plea of *not guilty*. His absence, today, is not an admission of guilt. It is – if anything – an admission of fear. You may well ask – if we are not afraid to judge him, why then is he afraid to be judged?'

It was a daring question. The one, Reuben knew, Griffith had counted on them to avoid. Justin had thrown it out, now, into the open. The jury waited for the answer.

' . . . It is a fellow southerner we try here today,' Justin said. 'A fellow southerner who has become afraid because the Yankee has done its brainwashing; because the Yankee has set about to con-vince him that we are not true and honest men, capable of con-ducting a true and honest trial. For more than a hundred years, the Yankee has been trying to prove to the world that a southerner is a corrupt and unjust human being – we all know that. For more than a hundred years, the Yankee has tried to tell us how to run our lives – for more than a hundred years, the Yankee has blasphemed our basic nature. Together, today, we will *prove the Yankee wrong* – as we have *always* proven him wrong!'

The loss of war, the trauma of defeat, the ghosts of carpetbag government, came as called. The unfailing device of the common enemy united Justin with the jurors. Reuben knew he couldn't have done it better, could not have done it as well. He could feel it begin to work – the thing that worked between them in the courtroom. Separate strengths became one man, one mind, one strategy, one goal.

' . . . A frightened defendant is not a guilty defendant. An innocent man who is frightened should be released, not condemned,' Justin said. 'This is the finest state in the union, composed of the finest men, capable of the finest justice. *Together, we will prove that – here, today.*' Justin paused. He leaned towards the jury, holding onto the rail. 'My honorable colleague has asked you to listen to the evidence. My honorable colleague has asked you to judge according to your conscience – whether the evidence does or *does not prove beyond a reasonable doubt* that John Tyler Higgins is guilty. I ask you one more thing. I asked you to remember that John Tyler Higgins is an innocent citizen of our sovereign state of Mississippi – and fair and honest justice, meted out by fair and honest men, can do none other than find the defendant not guilty.'

Reuben watched Justin finish, stand still, let his final words echo. Then Justin flashed the quick smile of a gentleman, a salute, at the jury. Reuben cast a glance at Griffith. His face had sagged visibly. Griffith had tried to establish a shabby locker-room alliance before a football game. Justin had called a jury of honorable men to war against the Yankee. It was a preliminary victory, and Griffith knew it.

Justin turned, approached the bench. It was working. Like clockwork. Reuben knew what was coming. 'Your Honor – defense counsel requests a continuance until tomorrow morning.'

Alexander frowned. 'On what grounds?'

'Counsel would like to point out that time will not permit full development of prosecution's first witness – plus full development of defense counsel's cross-examination.'

'Request granted. Court dismissed until nine o'clock tomorrow morning.'

'Let's take a ride,' Justin said.

Thirty-four

JUSTIN DROVE. He headed south on the highway in the five o'clock traffic.

In the passenger seat, Reuben sat quietly, smoking, waiting in the pact of silence that was mysterious yet not uncomfortable. He understood that what he felt was the absence of something, the absence of Justin's caution. He understood he had never been with Justin without sensing the protective glass cage. Now the wind through the car as it streaked down the highway – nothing between them but simple quiet, and air. It felt strange and extraordinary. He wondered what had happened. Was Justin in trouble ? Was it Caroline ? Was it Barksdale ? What ? And why ? He had a sense of some genuine, naked emotion burgeoning in Justin, just beneath the surface – a perception as startling as watching a feeling across a face on Mount Rushmore. He wondered if his senses were being tricked by his own old needs.

No. He knew he had felt it. Justin had come in, backed him up, done a brilliant manipulation of the jury – a case Justin had gone on record against, an issue for which Justin had contempt. But Reuben had felt in it a new kind of personal commitment, the kind he had been asking for, for fifteen years. *If you're in it, I'm in it too. Whatever it is.* Was it possible that today, after fifteen years, Justin had simply laid it, as a gift, on the counsel table ?

No. He didn't trust it. Shifts in character, in old relationships, came slow and hard. There had been no signs. If anything, the arrows of the past week had pointed in the opposite direction – a split in the fabric that had never truly been woven into anything beyond the mating of separate talents into an economic bargain.

Justin pulled off the highway onto the road that led to the reservoir. The late sunlight made prisms of raindrops still clinging to the pines. A net of entangled vines climbed a wild plum laden with buds. The road was a chronicle of progress, invading the wilderness.

Up ahead, the reservoir gleamed. The dam had carnivorised the land, to become the receptacle that protected rich delta lands from flood. Reuben remembered that Justin's father had been instrumental in bringing the political solution to reality. Justin's father had been elected lieutenant governor because of the reservoir.

The car turned into the road that circled the dam, moving away from the area of cabins and docked boats. Reuben wondered if Justin came here often. He wondered if Justin came here the way he went back to the land in Maryville. Men lived by symbols. The earth shaped a man for arrogance and will and pride, and each man renewed his contact in his own way. Reuben felt suddenly uneasy. Was he accompanying Justin to some old private ritual? Why? What had changed the thing between them? He felt a deep mistrust of his own perceptions, though a glance at Justin's profile confirmed all of them.

The road curved and narrowed, the dam stretched out on one side, the forest on the other. Suddenly, a clearing appeared. Justin pulled into it. The car came to a halt.

'Why don't we walk?' The first words Justin had spoken.

'Sure.'

Reuben fell in beside Justin. They began to walk along the reservoir road. The cabins were no longer visible. The water had begun to turn the brooding colors of a Mississippi sunset. The improbability of kinship hovered, took on a sense of reality. Something nibbled at the edges of Reuben's consciousness, but wouldn't take shape.

'You did a damn good job today.'

'We're partners.' Justin's words weren't token. Reuben could feel the emotion stirring behind them. He searched for an explanation. It wouldn't come.

The silence came back. They walked to the sound of their own footsteps, the sound of the water sloshing against the concrete basin. Then Justin stopped. Reuben saw Justin's eyes sweep the reservoir. 'Most of the people in this country don't belong anywhere. We're lucky. We have roots.'

'Damned right.' Reuben felt the uneasiness wash through him again.

'My father envisioned this reservoir. First he saw it in his mind, then he got it built. That was the kind of man he was. He saw what this state could be – and he made it happen. He stood for the best of the South. The way we do – you and me.'

'Damned right.' Reuben said. An invisible mirror caught him. He could see the two of them reflected in the expanse of light hanging over the reservoir – and the ghost of the thing that had caused this to happen, but would not make itself known.

'I was a kid when my father died. I loved him. He didn't live to be governor. I'm going to do that – for him. It's for him. I wanted you to know that. Everything he didn't get to do, I'm going to do for him. Everything he wanted to see this state become, I'm going to make it become; *we're* going to make it become. It's a special place. I know it's going to have to change. Transition's inevitable. But there's nothing here to be ashamed of now. Look at the rest of the country – no one's got roots, except us. We have a soil. We have a code. That's what my father stood for.' Justin turned. He looked at Reuben. Reuben saw his face was open, trusting, charged with feeling. 'I never knew, before, what you stood for,' Justin said. 'It's always made a distance – much as there's been between us. I always felt you were of the South – but not of the South. I used to wonder if it was because you were a Jew – but it wasn't that. The code of the South is no different from the Old Testament code – an eye for an eye, a tooth for a tooth, the settlement of justice, with honor, personal honor. You know what I'm talking about.'

A silence fell. *You know what I'm talking about*. What? Why not say it? Suddenly Reuben knew. Justin had learned of the attempt on Army Jones. How? From Simmons? Not likely. More likely from Barksdale. The simple facts – that it had been the navy blue Cadillac, that a shot had been fired. Justin's assumption was that he, Reuben, had fired the shot. That he, Reuben, had been true to the code of the South – the code that claimed the earth brings forth the necessity to defend simple rights. The code of fundamental justice. Twenty-five years ago, Willie had tried to tell him – the bar mitzvah of the South was to master the tools of violence; not for the sake of violence itself, but in order to commit to a code of honor that demands that a man, a single man, be ready to fight with his life to protect his land, his wife, his niggers, his domain. The thing that would make him a southerner.

They walked again in silence. He could feel Justin waiting. How many times, in fifteen years, had he yearned for this kind of kinship? How many times had he wished for the end of the barriers?

It felt hollow. Fraudulent. He had not pulled the trigger. Had not been able to. Had tried, even, to stop Monk.

Yet he heard himself say, 'Yes. I know what you're talking about.'

Justin stopped. The expanse of the reservoir spread out behind him. For the moment they became two men alone in the universe.

'It's the thing I could never get you to see about the law,' Justin said. 'To you, the law was always holy. To me, the law was to serve what's best for the state – what's best for the time, the place, the particular disposition of a special community. And we are a special community. That's why they can't legislate for us in Washington. That's why we can't accept that. They keep making laws for cities. We're still rural here. Any place where people are close to the land – peasant or aristocracy, it doesn't matter which – there's the ancient code that prevails. Sure, we've got the Ingalls shipyard on the coast, and the paper plant in Moss Point, and with a little luck we'll get Rabin to Claymont. But we're not an industrial state, and we're never going to make the mistakes the North has made. The land comes first down here. And the only men capable of making the changes this state has to make are the men who love it, who understand it, who are committed to its heritage. You and me,' Justin said. 'We're going to do it together.'

Together, Justin said. Reuben heard it. Reuben saw love and affection take over Justin's face. Justin had never felt safe enough with him before. Now Justin felt safe. Justin offered him the pact of blood brothers – committed to the same land, the same code.

The moment had been a long time coming.

In it was the end of loneliness, yearning, alienation. In it was the promise of Justin's company, the fellowship of the daring and the courageous from the past. In it was the completion of a lifetime's vision. Reuben felt yesterday's reactions fade, grow ephemeral. He was no longer sure he had tried to wrest the gun from Monk's hands. That impulse was gone, lost to him, no longer important. What he saw, suddenly, was a brilliant, authentic vision of how it might be. Two men who loved and trusted each other, two men who saw eye to eye, taking over the state, changing the state. A mark on the land.

He heard his own voice, his true voice, as heavy with emotion as Justin's had been. He met Justin's eyes, and said, 'Yes.'

'How the *hell*,' Justin said, 'did you ever let Roland Owen get past you on the jury?'

Thirty-five

AT NINE A.M., Roland Owen's face was a piece of scrub land burned out by the sun – impassive, half-closed eyes, one long bony forefinger stroking the bridge of his nose, signs Reuben recognised: a mind already made up. Justin had been right about that.

From the rest of the jury, newly filed in, came an unmistakable estimate of starting-gate odds. Eighty-twenty. Stacked against him. He had known from the beginning it would be a difficult case – but he had counted on Higgins, sitting next to him; had counted on the reality of Higgins' presence; had counted on being able to make the jury see Higgins as an acceptable human being instead of the vague, perverted man who would be created by the prosecution. Higgins' absence had changed the odds. Kornfield had made his decision, hadn't leveled, had used him, had left him with a stacked deck. The difficulty of creating a real person from thin air was insurmountable. Beyond that, absence implied guilt – or, at least, cowardice. The gamble for acquittal rested now on only two things – blasting Taylor's testimony to hell, and his own persuasiveness in the courtroom.

The court rose as Alexander came in. Reuben looked at his watch. He figured two hours until Taylor. He figured Taylor as witness number three. Griffith, like any good prosecutor, would build his show to a climax. Reuben figured the opening witness would be the least – the optometrist from Sears, Roebuck who'd identify a photograph of John Tyler Higgins as the man who had paid twenty-eight dollars for a pair of eyeglasses for the minor Thomas Petry Hampstead, also identified by photograph. An absent defendant, a dead victim. Kornfield had screwed Higgins' chances. Hampstead, who had been sent back to the Cleveland Delinquent Home, had died from concussions received when he leaped two stories onto a concrete yard while trying to escape. It would take a small miracle to pull off an acquittal. The small miracle had appeared this morning. An envelope on his desk – inside, everything he needed to know about Taylor. *Where'd this come from?* he had said. Justin had smiled. *A gift – from Barksdale.*

'Court is in session,' Alexander said.

Reuben sat down, removed the notes from his briefcase. Ten days ago he had taken this case – a moral position, another payment on his debt to Lea. Because Higgins had been a maverick and Lea had been a maverick, and he had believed in the right of two people to save themselves and each other from a hostile society, even temporarily. In the past ten days, moral decisions and old love affairs had become moot and obsolete. In the past twenty-four hours, everything had promised to become one piece. The relationship with Justin had turned suddenly. The truth of it was, he had never trusted Justin either. Now Justin had opened up, maybe they could build. Justin would become lieutenant governor, then governor – maybe even a damned good governor. Maybe he, Reuben, would have a say in the way the state went. Maybe. Last night he had telephoned Barksdale. Ahead, tonight, was another meeting with the Rawlins brothers. And this morning, the brown envelope had appeared on his desk. As if Justin and Barksdale, both, believed he had gone through some final, crucial rite of passage, and had come into membership of the elite, the power holders; and so what he needed, appeared – a detailed map of M. K. Taylor's soul, garnered by Barksdale. Before this morning, he had counted on showing Taylor as heavily prejudiced; with luck, reveal him as a Klansman. Now he could go as far as he wanted to go. When he finished with Taylor, there'd be nothing left for vultures.

The optometrist took the stand.

Reuben's notes said Hampstead was a runaway from the Cleveland Delinquent Home, where he had been incarcerated for truancy, theft, vandalism. Papa Hampstead was a religious fanatic who believed in the immolation of others; Mama Hampstead came through as a depressed hysteric. The conditions of the Cleveland Delinquent Home were bad, but less bad than the beatings and deprivations Hampstead had suffered in his own home – one of which had robbed him of most of the sight in his left eye – doled out under Papa's banner of moral righteousness.

The optometrist identified both photographs, gave the testimony Reuben expected.

Then Reuben laid out his cross. One point. He established that Hampstead had been the victim of an old eye injury. Alexander refused to permit speculation as to how the injury occurred, but admitted the professional opinion that the injury was at least five years old. Which meant that Hampstead, since the age of eleven, had lived with handicapped eyesight, without eyeglasses. Childhood mistreatment implied. Later, he'd remind the jury. *Is kindness a crime? Is it a crime to help a handicapped child? A pair of eyeglasses is hardly an instrument of seduction.*

'No more questions.'

As he took his seat, the air of preordained outcome permeated the courtroom. He cursed Kornfield again, cursed all men like Kornfield – those who called Mississippi a closed society and then set about to prove it. What the hell did Kornfield know about the bond between a man's soul and a piece of earth? What the hell did Kornfield know about men like Justin? men like himself? A swift cognizance flashed of having been swept, not by Justin, but by his own needs. What the hell did he need? His own birthright. What the hell did any man need? To belong to a place that belonged to him. A time would come when men like M. K. Taylor and Floyd Rawlins and Army Jones would no longer find a viable existence in this state. Beginning today. With this trial. Beginning with the moment M. K. Taylor took the stand.

Dr Alton Barnswell came next.

Black and shiny as a newly polished boot, he took a seat in the witness chair with the wary dignity of a Sunday parson in the middle of the week. The bailiff administered the oath. Out of Barnswell came a remarkable voice, the kind that touched off memories of old radio, rainy days, and the power of one's own imagination.

Reuben's notes said Higgins had picked Hampstead up on the road on January second. Had found him close to pneumonia and half starved.

He knew Griffith would now establish that it was Dr Alton Barnswell who had treated Hampstead with penicillin shots for pneumonia; that Hampstead had been brought in as a patient by Higgins. The implication would be unmistakable – obviously a white man consulting a black doctor in the state of Mississippi did so from a need for secrecy. He wondered if Griffith would be shrewd enough to stop there. It was Reuben who had questioned the jurors on their attitude towards the race issue; he wondered if Griffith would leave that to the power of twelve imaginations, with the assurance that any racial material which entered the record would do so through the defense counsel, not the prosecution. How could he mitigate Griffith's damaging implication of furtiveness, clandestine consultation, except by establishing fraternisation with blacks as part of Higgin's normal life-style?

He decided he couldn't. He decided on the strategy of asking Barnswell only one question.

He scanned the jury. Roland Owen looked like a cadaver awakened to a roast goose dinner. He could see how it would be. Alexander would be scrupulously fair. Griffith would refrain from bringing out Higgins' civil rights activities, and even the fact that Eula Williams had been Higgins' hygienist. Griffith knew he didn't need a cannon to shoot a fly off the wall – the absence of the defendant had put the case in his corner.

Griffith stopped exactly where he had predicted. 'Your witness.'

Reuben rose. 'Dr Barnswell. Prosecution failed to establish your credentials as a physician. Would you give them to the court, please.'

The credentials rolled out in that extraordinary voice. They included Holmesdale College for Negroes, a medical school in Vermont, internship in the U.S. Army, twenty years of general practice.

Later, he'd remind the jury: *Is it a crime to save a child's life with penicillin – whether administered by a qualified white hand or black hand?*

It would help, but not much. Barnswell was black, Higgins was white – he could count on the jury to remember that.

He looked over the notes on his carefully planned defense. They wouldn't make up for Higgins' absence. He'd present the reports from the Cleveland Delinquent Home which cast doubt on Hampstead's character, labeled him as incorrigible. He'd present the social worker's report, labeling Hampstead's word as untrustworthy. The boy was dead – he couldn't go too far with the character malignment of an underage corpse. He'd present the old newspaper clippings of Higgins' heroics when he saved the two boys from drowning. Then he'd offer his one and only witness, Dr Whitfield from Webster, who would testify for Higgins' mother as to her son's character throughout childhood and early adulthood. After that, he'd introduce Elizabeth Higgins' box of artifacts from Higgins' childhood – and by pushing his luck, he'd get Alexander to allow Dr Whitfield to testify to the absence of anything in the box which pointed to early homosexual tendencies.

None of it would tip the scales.

The only thing that might turn it was a complete and total discrediting of M. K. Taylor's testimony. 'Thank you. No more questions.' And his own closing speech to the jury. *This is a very special place. The South. We who were born here grow up with an understanding of its requirements and its rewards. Molded by our*

315

*place of birth, we become our own kind, we are committed to our own
kind, we trust our own kind, we help our own kind.*

But what of the stranger?

*What we have here today is a simple matter, but a profound
one. What we have here is a man who dared to help a stranger. A
southerner who helped a Yankee. An older man who helped a boy.
A healthy man who helped a sick child. What are we to make of
that? Are we to make it into something evil? Or are we to understand it as the thing it was – an act of Christian charity?*

It was a damned good speech. He had written it last night, late,
in the study at home. He had planned how to deliver it – haltingly,
as if he were searching the juror's faces and finding his words
there. *Would you have done less?* Under any other circumstances,
it was the kind of speech that would bring in a certain victory.

Not today. Not unless he took Taylor's ass apart first.

The bailiff called, 'Sergeant Maynard K. Taylor to the stand.'

There were ways to kill a man without a gun.

He watched M. K. Taylor swagger up the aisle, wearing the uniform and holster that gave authority to madness, wearing a bulldog mask vain with fundamental ignorance. Member of the
animal pack that leveled guns at women. At Mollie. His wife.
Still his wife, until that was over – no target for hoodlums.
Yesterday afternoon she had gone with Bo Garrison to the airport,
put the children on the plane for New Orleans to stay with Zoe.
He had made her a silent promise. One of the sonofabitches would
get his, today.

He watched M. K. Taylor raise his right hand and begin the
oath of truth. A man incapable of truth. Capable of almost anything else.

That was the thing Simmons understood.

The missing link between Simmons and Taylor had fallen into
place this morning, the clue provided in Barksdale's gift.

' . . . the whole truth, so help me God,' Taylor said. The voice
as glutinous as seaweed.

In the notes had been dates, times, places – Simmons was
making it with Taylor's wife.

. . . Last night, late, he had heard Mollie come down the hall;
had heard her open the door to the guest room, had felt her come
across the room and stand beside his bed in the darkness. Through
closed eyelids, he had been able to see her – knew her that well,
knew her not at all. He had feigned sleep. After a while, she had
gone away. . . .

A man making it with another man's wife had a built-in edge on that man. He could see how it worked. Simmons with a need for an edge over Taylor, because Taylor represented more than a single man. Reuben had put himself in Simmons' place. Like the head of any operation, Simmons had to be aware of the factions, had to handle all of them. In the police department, there were the job holders, the oddballs, the good guys like Bo Garrison. Simmons could handle those. But what about the fourth faction – the Klan – volatile and seeking power ? How would Simmons handle that ?

Taylor began to read Hampstead's confession aloud:

' " . . . I started out from Cleveland right after Christmas. I was going to hitch to Atlantic City, but it gold cold. I got sick. I got dropped off seven miles outside of Holmesdale on January second. Mr Higgins, he picked me up. I said I didn't have no money so he took me to his house. He lived at 8256 Trevor Court. . . . " '

He had figured how Simmons would handle it by putting himself in Simmons' place if he were Simmons, with Simmons' ambitions. He'd set up a relationship that was neat, workable – leave them room to operate, but insure his own control. Since the spokesman for that faction was Taylor, he'd say, in effect, to Taylor : *If you play within the limits – don't expose yourself or force my hand – your group can do whatever the hell it wants to do, I don't want to know about it. But if you make a move to take over the department, or get us into the headlines, I'll throw you the hell out.*

' " . . . the house had two bedrooms, a living room, and a kitchen. He lived by himself except for three cats. He said students came to stay with him in the summertime. . . . We ate supper. Then we got in his car and drove to some man's house but the man wasn't there. It was a fifty-five Ford. I wanted to drive but he said no. He took me to this colored doctor's house who shot me some penicillin and a paper for medicine. The medicine cost seven dollars at the drugstore. Mr Higgins paid. After that, we went back to his house. I slept in Mr Higgins' bed – he said he would feel better if he had somebody to sleep with. We went to bed about eleven thirty and slept until ten in the morning. Then he rubbed on my chest, and rubbed on my leg, and took my peter and messed around with it about five or ten minutes. Then I got in a different bed in the other room because he made me upset and nervous. . . . " '

Simmons was shrewd, a manipulator, a power seeker. Beyond making his statement of authority, Simmons would go looking for secret leverage. Taylor's wife. Available – according to Barksdale's notes – because Taylor didn't sleep with his wife; the impotence of a man turned on by sadomasochistic sex. There were dates, times, places. So it was Simmons in bed with Taylor's wife. Because, in bed, Simmons could find out anything he wanted to know about Taylor. In bed, Simmons could feed anything he wanted to feed to Taylor. In bed, Simmons had probably discovered what Barksdale's notes had revealed. That Taylor had once been an Alabama prison guard; that Taylor had resigned, with commendations, laudatory letters; that the facts of Taylor's resignation had to do with being seized and gang-raped by a group of angry prisoners.

' " . . . that afternoon Mr Higgins took me to get another penicillin shot to the same colored doctor. Then he went out with some man who came in from the North. When they came back I stood in my room all the time the man was there. The next day I got my hair cut in the barbershop near the Jitney Jungle. Then Mr Higgins took me to Sears, Roebuck where a man looked at my eyes for eyeglasses. He bought me some clothes. Two pair of pants, two shirts, some T-shirts. All I had was what I had on. That night we went to a reading at a colored college. I don't read too good. Mr Higgins, he helped me. That night he asked me to sleep with him again. I didn't want to, but there was a knife on the bookshelf and I saw it and got scared. He laid his head on my chest. Then he took his peter in my mouth and reached a climax. I rolled over on my side. I started to doze off. He had relations by my rectum. . . . " '

Reuben made a note. The key he'd been looking for – how to get to Taylor's personal derangement within the limitations of court procedure. Taylor had just given it to him.

' " . . . We went to the restaurant at the Ramada Inn for breakfast. When we came back, Mr Higgins ran some papers off on a machine. I went with him to carry them to Greenborough. I stood in the car. He went into a house and stood a couple hours and came out. He gave me seven dollars. I spent it on cigarettes and other things. That night I slept with Mr Higgins again. I didn't want to, but I saw the knife again. He took his peter in my mouth and reached a climax again. The next day we picked up the eyeglasses from Sears, Roebuck. Mr Higgins paid twenty-one dollars for the glasses. . . . " '

The confession droned on, more of the same – Taylor working to maintain a clinical tone as the shabby chronicle continued, finally came to an end.

Then Griffith approached the witness box.

Reuben checked his notes once more. According to the tapes,

Higgins readily admitted to 'taking and harboring said minor child from returning or communicating with his parents,' and also admitted to keeping 'said minor child in clothing, food, shelter, and medical attention.' Higgins swore, however, there had been no seduction, no unnatural acts. Only a failed attempt to politicise a boy who couldn't read, and the moral dilemma of whether or not to send Hampstead back to the conditions from which he had run in the first place. The dilemma had been resolved by Taylor, who arrested Higgins while he and Hampstead were inbibing two ice cream sodas in a local drive-in. Higgins insisted that Hampstead had been coerced into a fraudulent confession, then packed back to Cleveland where he subsequently died.

Griffith began his questioning. Taylor's version of the circumstances of arrest agreed with Higgins' in the matter of place – 'Woody's' – and the matter of ice cream sodas – 'chocolate.' Taylor claimed to have been driving past when he 'realised somethin' funny was goin' on.' Reuben looked at the jury. In a society of people with double lives, pornography was always a going business. Today it was free. Taylor claimed to have spotted Higgins making 'improper advances' to Hampstead – a circumspect way of saying there was no need to spell it out, having just read the confession. It was also, Reuben saw, a shrewd way of titillating twelve Victorian imaginations. Reuben watched the jury respond, become a squadron of authorised peeping toms – watched the body tension, glazed eyes, flat expressions that accompanied hypocrisy, a concern for appearances, silent convention. The courtroom became a place where women were supposed to be delicate, men virile, proper citizens of a puritanical village permeated by the dank air of a men's room in a railroad station on a rainy Saturday night.

'No more questions,' Griffith said. 'Your witness.'

Reuben rose, moved slowly towards the witness box, giving Taylor time to remember his fist the night of the first bombing. Giving Taylor time to sense the presence of an oncoming second blow. Giving Taylor time to wonder how this bastard Jew was going to go about it.

Professionally. With no overt anger. Quietly. On a matter of principle.

He reached the box and stood still a moment, fixing his gaze on Taylor, letting Taylor see he knew him for what he was – a hollow, obsessive man – a twisted man who needed strange gratifications. Letting Taylor see he knew Taylor was counting on the jury, counting on the aggressiveness of any animal towards the deviant of its own species: ask any man to draw a spook and he will draw a distorted human being. He gave Taylor that moment to wonder how it would feel to have the jury turn on him.

'I believe, Sergeant Taylor, that you told Mr Griffith that the confession you read to the jury was obtained by yourself. Is that correct?'

'That's right.'

'Was there anyone present besides yourself when the confession was obtained?'

'Nobody.' Taylor was making it clear he was going to say as little as possible.

'And the confession was given, without duress, of the prisoner's own free will?'

'That's right,' Taylor said. The bulldog face colored imperceptibly with memories of a rubber hose. There were other memories buried. Reuben believed Taylor's aberrations sprang from some source deeper than the trauma of an Alabama prison rape. And Taylor had company – a klavern of men. Rawlins. Jones. Others.

'And what you have read to this court is an exact replica of the words of Thomas Petry Hampstead?'

'That's right.'

'With nothing altered or changed?'

'Nothing.'

'Not a word? Not a phrase? Nothing?'

'Nothing,' Taylor said.

'Objection,' Griffith said. 'Counsel is badgering the witness.'

'I call the court's attention to two phrases in the aforesaid confession,' Reuben said. 'The first phrase occurs in the context: "he took his peter in my mouth and *reached a climax*." The second occurs: "he had *relations by my rectum*." I ask the court reporter to check my memory.'

'Correct.'

'I ask the court's permission to ask Sergeant Taylor if these were the exact phrases used by Thomas Petry Hampstead.'

'Counsel may continue the line of questioning,' Alexander said. 'Witness will answer the question.'

'That's what he said,' Taylor said belligerently.

'I call the court's attention to the fact that this is a boy who cannot read, who says he cannot read in the course of this same confession. This is a boy who used only simple terms in the course of this confession. This is a boy who used *stood* for *stayed*, who says *he took his peter in my mouth* – a boy obviously lacking in the fundamental usage of words. I suggest to Sergeant Taylor that this same boy would not be likely to use sophisticated phraseology like *reached a climax* or *relations by rectum*.' He turned to Taylor. 'I repeat the question. Did Thomas Petry Hampstead, in fact, use these words?'

A glimmering of sweat popped on Taylor's forehead. He threw a quick, angry look at Griffith. Griffith leapt to his feet.

'Objection. Defense counsel is badgering the witness over phraseology incorporated out of respect to the jury.'

'Your Honor,' Reuben said. 'I suggest counsel for the prosecution is attempting to answer for the witness.'

Alexander banged the gavel. 'Witness will answer the question.'

'It was respect to the jury,' Taylor said.

'So *relations by rectum* was your own phrase?'

'It was respect to the jury,' Taylor repeated stubbornly.

'Can you tell us Hampstead's actual words? Do you remember them? What did he say? Did he say nothing? Did he say *buggered*? What did he say?' He watched Taylor freeze, turn pale, trying to suppress the memory, the need for revenge on the Alabama prisoners. He watched Taylor understand that he knew.

'It was respect to the jury,' Taylor repeated. The voice had gone shrill. His knuckles turned white as he clutched the arms of the witness chair.

'I should like to remind you, Sergeant Taylor, that out of respect to this same jury, you took an oath today. You are, in fact, appearing in this courtroom under two oaths – the oath of truth and the oath of impartial service you took when you put on that uniform. I should like to remind you of your police oath. *I do solemnly swear to preserve the peace, to protect and serve the citizens of this community, fairly, and with honor, and without personal interests or prejudices.* I challenge your integrity on both oaths.'

'Objection,' Griffith shouted. 'Defense counsel has no right to cast aspersions on witness' professional ability.'

'Your Honor,' Reuben said. 'We've got a fine police force here in Holmesdale. Most of them are honorable men.' Deliberately, he isolated Taylor from the rest of the police department. 'Chief Simmons, in fact, is a good friend of mine. But witness' appearance in court, under two oaths, is asking the court to accept him as an honorable, truthful, and impartial witness. Witness has already admitted to one lie. I suggest that a uniform is not necessarily a mark of unblemished character.' He cast a quick look at Taylor. Terror and hatred flared in Taylor's eyes.

'Objection sustained,' Alexander said. 'Witness is not on trial.'

Reuben took a beat. Then he spun, quickly. In a staccato tone, he asked, 'Do you belong to any organisation of any kind – whether it had three members, or three million members – that has taken an active stand on one side or the other of the race issue – the black and white race issue – or actively support such with time, money, or any other form of efforts ?'

'Objection. Irrelevant,' Griffith shouted.

'If it please the court – the relevance of the question has been established in the questioning of the jury,' Reuben argued. He kept his eyes on Taylor, like pins on a moth. Taylor squirmed, flushed. His sweat-soaked brow gleamed.

'Your Honor,' Griffith said, 'counsel for the prosecution has presented no material of a racial nature. Defense counsel's question is irrelevant.'

'Your Honor, witness is in uniform. Witness testifies under the oath of impartial service. Credibility of witness' testimony is dependent on credibility of witness' character under oath.' Reuben could feel Taylor's animosity and fear, live radiations he struggled, vainly, to suppress. The bulldog jaw clamped tight, the mouth vanished.

'Witness will answer the question,' Alexander directed.

Reuben watched Taylor struggle with the trap. A *no* might open him up to a perjury charge. A *yes* and Simmons bounced him.

'No,' Taylor said. The gamble of a trapped man.

Reuben smiled. He knew Taylor would remember the smile, live with it, have nightmares about it. 'Perhaps you might tell the court your work record,' Reuben said. 'I believe you were on Alabama prison guard. Is that correct ?' Reuben watched the blood rush to Taylor's face, then recede, leaving him drained and ashen. No answer came from him.

'Objection.' Griffith rose. 'Witness is not on trial.'

'Your Honor, I asked Dr Barnswell his qualifications, his experience. Witness was arresting officer. Witness was the only officer present during Hampstead's confession. The prosecution has not established the predicate of experience, or qualified the witness in any manner beyond the fact that he wears a uniform.'

'Objection overruled,' Alexander said.

Quietly, Reuben said to Taylor, 'Were you an Alabama prison guard ?' Another moment went by. Taylor's eyes glazed. Reuben could feel every muscle in Taylor strained to the breaking point.

'Yes.'

Reuben glanced at the jury, read the shared conviction that civilisation was dependent upon careful restriction of property, power, sexual gratification. If he pushed Taylor, each juror would disown his own bag of private, secret, human deviances by disowning Taylor.

He looked at Taylor. He knew that of the two hundred million people in the United States, more than twenty-five million had engaged in some kind of homosexual activity – Taylor couldn't be expected to know that. Reuben knew that no man became a homosexual without the complicity of his mother, that no man became impotent without the complicity of his wife – Taylor couldn't be expected to know that. He read Taylor's face – rageful, terror-stricken, alone.

Without mercy, he pushed. 'Did you – or did you not – resign from that position under circumstances of a sexual nature?'

Taylor's face collapsed. His breathing came heavily, in painful snorts.

'*Objection!*' Griffith shouted.

'Your Honor, I respectfully remind the court that this is a trial of a sexual nature. It has been established that witness substituted his own terms for Hampstead's word *buggered*. The sexual nature of a man, the personal experiences of a man in this highly charged area of life, have bearing on the quality and veracity of his testimony. I respectfully submit to the court that if a man is impotent, or if a man has been involved in homosexual activities, through his consent or otherwise, that these incidents have a bearing –'

Alexander rapped the gavel angrily.

Reuben looked back at Taylor – slumped into the witness chair, his hand sliding away from his empty holster to cover his groin, silent tears streaming down his face.

Reuben looked at the jury, sitting quietly, aligned with Taylor. His own savagery had taken precedence over buried fantasies of guilt and prurience. He saw it on their faces.

He had pushed too far.

'No more questions,' he said.

Thirty-six

AT EIGHT P.M. when he left the courtroom, the jury was still out.

He stopped in the corridor phone booth, called home, told Mollie he'd be late, but not where he was going. Their pact had turned into an unspoken agreement to stick to the truth, after the fact. He hung up, stopped long enough to light a cigarette and check the ten grand in an envelope in his breast pocket. Then he went the rest of the way down the corridor, empty, newsmen gone, nobody to give a damn about the verdict.

Outside it had turned cold again. The statue of Moses was lit in the darkness. He came down the courthouse steps reminding himself that nobody ever knew what the hell a jury would do. But he knew what the jury would do. He had gone for a bloodletting, alienated the jury – not because they refused to participate in another man's slaughter, but because they needed their symbols intact. The American flag shouldn't be left to droop in the mud, and cops didn't cry.

It was behind him – the first time in his life he had ever left the courtroom with a jury still out. The truth of it was, Higgins no longer mattered.

Ten minutes later, he parked in the lot of the Holmesdale Hotel, went through the lobby, and took the elevator to the top floor. On the other side of the tufted leather door of the Hunt Club he found a sprinkling of well-dressed people having dinner, Barksdale waiting at a corner table, Floyd Rawlins nowhere in sight. The band was out for an intermission. He made his way across the polished empty floor to the carpeted area of tables where Barksdale waited.

'How'd the trial go ?' Barksdale looked human. Not, anymore, like a cautious, temporary ally. Not, anymore, like a landlord taking issue with a recalcitrant tenant. The bombing had become shared property.

Reuben took a seat. 'The jury's still out. They'll bring in a guilty.'

'It's an old historical tradition. The Marquis de Sade was accused of sodomy with his valet. He left the country, was tried *in absentia*, found guilty, and burned in effigy.' Barksdale smiled. 'Sade – required reading for all custodians of morality.' The ambience was easy, friendly, like the banter of old comrades before a battle. The pledge, and acceptance, had been made this morning, when he accepted Barksdale's file on Taylor's sex life. And now the Army Jones incident hung in the air unspoken. Reuben felt Barksdale's tacit agreement to leave it.

'What happens now?'

'Room ten fourteen. One floor down. One of my men took the room this morning.'

'Where the hell's our boy?'

Barksdale threw a quick glance around the room. Sharp, trained eyes that missed nothing. 'My guess is there's somebody here he doesn't want to see. My guess is – that pair over there.'

Reuben looked at the two men on the other side of the room. 'Kluckers?'

'I'd say so.'

The waiter appeared. Barksdale ordered a martini, a small steak. Reuben ordered a Scotch, a small steak. The waiter left.

'What do we do?'

'We eat dinner. We wait,' Barksdale said. 'Rawlins was here when I came in. Those two men came in right afterwards – he vanished. Maybe he's hiding out in the kitchen, maybe he's gone. If he doesn't show tonight, he'll show another night. His brother's in a bind, don't forget that.'

'Bastards.'

'Stool pigeons. The problem here is, we're not dealing with racketeers, drug dealers, nothing as simple as that. These are stoolies betraying their *cause*.'

Barksdale paused as the drinks appeared. The band started up, a scratchy, sentimental version of 'Moon River.' A girl in a black sequined dress climbed on the piano and began to sing. Syd Kaminsky's old remark came back to Reuben. *It's still 1945 around here.*

'Emotionally, the Rawlins brothers are believers,' Barksdale continued. 'It's the same problem we have with Communist stoolies, or peaceniks. We're not dealing with a believer who's decided to stool because he doesn't believe anymore. The Rawlins brothers haven't had a change of heart – they've decided to stool because they're caught in a bind.'

'What are you telling me?'

'I'm telling you to be patient, to be careful. We can't count on a straight stoolie. It's a different psychology. We have to wait out their fears, their guilts – their fantasies. It's hard for them emotionally to do what they're doing, so they try to dream up a way to serve two masters at the same time. Wherever Rawlins is right now, he's trying to convince himself that when it's over, his old friends will congratulate him – they'll say: you're really not a stoolie, you really helped us in the long run. You have to understand that Floyd Rawlins will eventually show. But it may turn out to be like one of those booby-trapped bombs in Vietnam – you think you've discovered one and in dismantling that one, you set off another one, underneath.'

Reuben swallowed some Scotch. He knew Barksdale was right. Waiting, patience, caution were not among his natural gifts. 'Moon River' went into another chorus. The girl climbed down from the piano and tried to embrace the audience. Nobody paid any attention. The black waiter came back with the steaks.

'Telephone for Mr Buchman.'

Barksdale nodded. Reuben rose, crossed to the end of the bar, and picked up the phone. The nearest patron was six bar stools down. Through the glass pane of the kitchen door, he could see Floyd Rawlins hanging on to the receiver of a bright red telephone, his back to him, near a white tiled counter where a piece of raw chateaubriand was laid out.

'Buchman,' he said.

'You leave now,' Floyd said. 'Me and Elmos'll come later.'

'We just got dinner,' Reuben said. 'Fifteen minutes.'

There was a long pause. Through the glass, he saw Floyd scratch the back of his head. 'What's the room?'

'Ten fourteen.'

Reuben watched Floyd's back. Floyd hung up, stared at the phone, then picked it up again and dialed hurriedly. A waiter came through the door, carrying a tray. Reuben picked up his own receiver, asked for an outside line, and dialed the courthouse. The bailiff answered. The jury was still out. He reminded himself he didn't give a damn about Higgins. Habit died hard. When he looked through the glass again, Floyd Rawlins wasn't in sight.

He came back to the table, finished off the Scotch. 'Fifteen minutes,' he said. 'Floyd hung up, then made another phone call.'

'Elmos.' Barksdale cut into his steak. 'In a phone booth in the lobby.'

Barksdale turned the key, went in first. Reuben followed. Barksdale closed the door, latched it, crossed to the window and pulled the blind. 'Turn on the light.'

Reuben flicked the wall switch. Light flooded the usual hotel room – twin beds, fake French provincial. One of those innocuous places where newspaper-headline murders occurred. He had made an attempt on Army Jones – shot and missed. A retaliatory attempt had been made on Mollie – shot and missed. Maybe they considered it even, and maybe not. How did he know tonight wouldn't be an attempt to get him ? How much protection had Barksdale arranged ? He was swept by the tension and discomfort of being in another man's hands.

Barksdale shut off two of the lamps. The last one burned dim, unobtrusive. Then Barksdale pulled the chair from a squat-legged desk and turned it around. 'You sit here.'

'Any reason ?'

'It's the spot that's most fully covered.'

'Who's covering it ? From where ?' A knock sounded suddenly, harsh, imperative.

'I'll get it. Sit down.' Barksdale crossed the room, cracked the door. Reuben lowered himself into the chair. Barksdale looked back, checked the room out, then unlatched the chain.

Elmos came in first, wearing an old leather jacket with plenty of room for a pistol. Exuding a monkeylike hysteria.

Floyd came behind him, halting sullen and suspicious just inside the door. 'It's bugged, ain't it ? You got guys in another room ?'

Barksdale closed, latched the door. 'Check it out. Take your time.' Reuben heard the note of cold authority, had once been on the other end of it, knew what it was designed to achieve, watched it happen to Floyd.

Floyd looked disoriented for a moment. Then he squared off his shoulders, threw an angry look at Reuben, and clumped to the television set. He switched it on. The sound blared. A used-car commercial. 'We'll talk with that.'

Barksdale didn't anwer. Reuben watched him lower himself into a white chair with a cane back, crossing his legs and pressing his fingers together like a patient but intolerant inquisitioner. Floyd lost his bearings again. When he got them back, he settled down on the edge of one of the twin beds, then nodded at Elmos. Elmos tried the other bed, leapt up, sat next to Floyd, leapt up again. 'I don't like it,' Elmos said. 'I don't like it.' He looked frightened to the point of physical pain.

'Sit down,' Floyd said.

'My ulcers – ' Elmos said. 'I gotta get some milk – '

'I said sit down,' Floyd said.

Hugging his stomach, Elmos sat next to Floyd, slightly rocking, as if someone had delivered him a blow. 'I don't like it,' he said. 'I don't like it, I don't like it,' like a litany.

'This is worth more goddamned money than we asked for,' Floyd said. 'It's our goddamned lives. This thing's gotten mean. It ain't simple no more. It don't mean nothin' to them to pick up a goddamned shotgun – '

'What have you got ?' Barksdale said.

Floyd looked at Reuben. 'You got the money ?'

'What have you got ? Reuben said.

'I don't like it,' Floyd said, 'I don't like it.'

On the television set, the trailer from *Gilligan's Island* ended, and the CBS News began. ' . . . *It was announced today that draft deferments for graduate students and occupational deferments have been eliminated by the National Security Council.* . . . '

'We want twenty thousand dollars up front,' Floyd said.

'For what ?' Barksdale said quietly.

Elmos groaned. His face twisted in pain.

'There's another bombing plan,' Floyd said. 'It's gonna take place this week. The night of the governor's ball for that Jew industrialist.'

With an effort of will, Reuben held his reaction intact, held himself still, silent. Barksdale felt it. Barksdale sent him an imperceptible nod. On television, the newsman said, ' . . . *several prominent labor leaders and Administration backers today have resigned from the Americans for Democratic Action after the ADA endorsed the presidential candidacy of Senator Eugene McCarthy.* . . . '

'Where will the bombing take place ?' Barksdale said quietly.

'What about *me* ?' Elmos said. 'What about *Holly* ?' He rocked back and forth, holding his stomach.

'That's right,' Floyd said. 'We gotta get some things straight first. I told you – Elmos has gotta have amnesty on that conspiracy charge.'

'I ain't gonna be put away,' Elmos said. 'I just *ain't*.'

'If Elmos appears as witness after the bombing, we can ask the court for leniency,' Barksdale said.

'He gets up in court – exposes himself as the guy who fingered this – his life ain't worth a damn. What the hell are you tryin' to sell us – goddamned ice in winter ?'

'He's gotta let me take Holly and go to Mexico,' Elmos said. 'I ain't gonna let Papa raise Holly. All Papa wants is to get my girl. He ain't gonna get her – I ain't gonna let him. He's crazy. I don't know what he'll do to her – he's crazy!'

'Shut up,' Floyd said.

'I don't care,' Elmos said. 'I don't care what Papa does to me. He ain't gonna do it to Holly –'

'*Goddamnit, shut up.*'

The newsman on television said, ' . . . *Governor George C. Wallace, former Democratic governor of the state of Alabama, candidate for President on a third-party ticket, told reporters today that, if elected, he will change the so-called civil rights laws which are an attack on property rights, free enterprise, and local government. . . .* '

Barksdale said calmly, 'If you or your brother runs the day after the bombing, you're marked men to the Klan.'

'If we don't run, you grab us and hold us as witnesses. Is that what the hell you think you're gonna do ?'

'I'm gonna run,' Elmos said. 'I'm gonna run and take Holly and if he tries to stop me, I'm gonna tell the whole goddamned thing – the setup and the dealings and the money. My life ain't worth a damn anyway.'

'You shut up,' Floyd said.

'Who's the hit man ?' Reuben said.

Floyd hesitated. Then he looked directly at Reuben. 'Army Jones. Him and somebody else. I don't know who else.'

'Where ?' Barksdale said.

'I don't know yet,' Floyd said. Reuben saw he was hedging.

'Sure you do,' Barksdale said.

'I don't know yet, I tell you.'

'When will you know ?'

'Tomorrow – by tomorrow.'

'We don't buy half information,' Barksdale said evenly.

'Screw you,' Floyd said. 'We don't get no money tonight, you don't get the time and place tomorrow. We want twenty grand tonight. Tomorrow, ten more. The day after the bombing, twenty more. Fifty thousand all together – that's the deal.'

'No deal,' Barksdale said.

'What do you offer ?' Floyd said.

'What about me ? What about Holly ?' Elmos said.

'Ten tonight. Ten tomorrow,' Barksdale said. 'Twenty after the bombing. That's the deal.'

'Goddamnit,' Floyd said, 'we're riskin' our goddamned *lives* and givin' up everything we believe in. The Klan's part of the South – it's always been part of the South, fightin' the South's battle. If it wasn't for Elmos, I wouldn't give you a prayer in hell. All that money the goddamned Jews have got – we're gonna get what we need.' He glared at Reuben. 'You go to your goddamned partner, Woods. Tell him to get the extra ten grand out of his Jew mother in Greenborough. She ain't spent a dime all these years – all that money she got when old man Woods dropped dead, all that money he made outa that reservoir he took my papa's land for. Playin' the organ in the church and actin' like she ain't no Jew. And she ain't spent a dime. Givin' lessons to Elmos' girl, and takin' his money, and talkin' and talkin' – too much damned talkin' she did, and out it came. *I'm a Jew*, she said to Elmos. And cryin'. And sayin' God was punishin' her with loneliness. I'm tellin' you – you tell your partner to go and get the money outa *her*.'

Reuben stared at Floyd, trying to absorb the meaning of Floyd's words.

'No deal,' he said, in a tone as controlled as Barksdale's – refusing to react in front of Floyd or Elmos, in front of Barksdale, refusing to acknowledge the impact of Floyd's statement. But a series of memories flooded him. Justin's bar, behind folding doors, to be hidden from Minna's visits because Minna was a teetotaler, a hard-shelled Baptist. Thanksgiving dinner – Justin saying grace for Minna. On a hospital room wall a plaster Jesus, and Minna in bed saying, *You are both my sons. . . .*

He believed Floyd.

'No deal,' he repeated. Why did he believe Floyd? On what evidence? From instinct? And why – if he did believe Floyd – was he feeling not anger, but an overwhelming sorrow?

'Listen, goddamn you – ' Elmos said, the first time he had spoken directly to anyone but Floyd. 'Maybe you think you're somethin', I guess you think that big house you got and bein' a lawyer, that makes you somethin' big.' He got up, still holding his stomach, and began to pace the room. 'You *ain't* somethin',' he shouted at Reuben. 'You ain't no better than me, and neither is your goddamned partner – you *see* that, goddamn you!'

'Shut up, Elmos – you let me do the talkin'.'

'Goddamnit,' Elmos said, 'me and Justin are the same age, Floyd, you know that, goddamn you, you know that. *He* don't know that.' Elmos faced Reuben again, his face contorted. 'Like my papa worked that land with *his own hands*, we, all of us, did, *our own hands*. Papa used to say, "We're all sons of the South, boys, that's what we are." And right across the fence Justin used to ride with his papa, ridin' the land, and checkin' out the tenants – right on the other side of the goddamned fence. We was the same person, born in the same month, no difference, Papa said, and one day he'll see who you are. The same school we went to, me and

Floyd. We used to beat him up. He never fought back. We never could understand what was the matter with him. What was wrong wasn't *me* at all. It was *him*. All the time it was him. My girl – she takes piano lessons, and that old lady just talks and talks and out it came. He wasn't no son of the South – he was *son of a Jew*, like you. And me and Floyd, we're better'n both of you. Goddamnit, *better'n both of you*.' Elmos stopped, bent over, grabbing his stomach. 'My ulcers – I gotta get some goddamned milk –'

'Shut up,' Floyd said. 'Shut up and sit down.'

Elmos obeyed. The newscaster said, ' . . . *and an open letter, allegedly from the crew of the* PUEBLO, *was received today by President Johnson. The letter reportedly states that the United States must admit the* PUEBLO *violated North Korean waters, must apologise for the act, and tender promises it will not happen again, before the* PUEBLO *crew will be released.* . . . '

'No deal,' Reuben said quietly.

'Take the ten,' Elmos said. 'Take the ten and let's get the hell outa here.' He doubled over, his face stricken.

'What about Mexico? Floyd said. 'What about his kid?'

'By the time you contact me tomorrow with the final details, I'll have an answer on that from Washington,' Barksdale said. He kept his gaze on Floyd. Reuben felt Barksdale avoiding his eyes.

'I don't like it,' Elmos said. 'I told you, Floyd – after we set it up, they're gonna put me away anyhow. The way it is now we ain't got nobody – not him, not our friends, *nobody*.'

'My brother don't know what he's sayin',' Floyd said. 'He's upset. I'm doin' the talkin' and I'm sayin' okay. Ten tonight on account of I told you what night and who's gonna do it. Tomorrow I get back to you with the time and the place – we get ten more. The day after the blowup, me and Elmos, we get twenty thousand.'

'What time tomorrow?' Reuben said.

'I don't know, I can't say.' A muscle twitched at the edge of Floyd's mouth. Reuben knew he was lying again.

'Ten o'clock tomorrow night,' Barksdale said. 'I want the information before then.'

'Okay.'

Reuben pulled out the envelope, held it out. Floyd rose, crossed the room, took the envelope. He stood there, counted the money. Elmos watched him with glazed eyes.

' . . . *a gas tank truck has exploded in Mexico City. Eight killed, seventy injured.* . . . '

Floyd shoved the envelope into the breast pocket of his bouncer's jacket. He jerked his head at Elmos. Elmos got up like a sleep-walker and followed Floyd out.

As the door closed behind them, Reuben felt a leaden depression permeate his bones. He tried to shake it – it wouldn't shake. He knew it had to do with Justin, but not only with Justin – with the dealing, the whole scummy thing; he felt sullied, Justin simply a part of it. He watched Barksdale rise, walk over to the television set, and shut it off. 'That's it,' Barksdale said – not to him.

'Where's the mike ?'

Barksdale fingered a button on his jacket. 'Two men in a car – they got the whole thing.'

'Bastards,' Reuben said. But the anger had lost its edge. It didn't cut through the despondency. He rose, lit a cigarette, went through the door into the hall. After a moment, Barksdale joined him. They walked towards the elevator.

'Do you need a drink ?'

'No. Thanks.' Reuben heard his own voice, dull, some kind of mourning in it.

'The public thinks it's drama. Maybe you did too. Most of the time, it's like it was tonight. Shabby, rotten – I don't like it any more than you do. But it's got to be done. I've been in it a long time. The best of philosophies – if you live long enough – becomes a system of compromises.'

'Forget it.'

The elevator appeared. Barksdale pressed the button. 'I'll handle Simmons. We have to work with him. Policy. Don't worry – it won't get to Taylor, or any of his cohorts.'

'Bastards.' It didn't help.

He drove to Bill Crawford's service station. He let the attendant fill the tank of the new white Cadillac while he used the pay phone inside.

Monk answered.

'I've got to see you,' Reuben said.

'Screw you,' Monk said.

'Meet me for a drink. I need a drink. I need to talk to you.'

'Now ?'

'Now.'

'Screw you.'

'Fuck off,' Reuben said.

'Tomorrow morning,' Monk said. 'I'll meet you at the Williamsburg.' He hung up.

Reuben deposited another dime and dialed the courthouse. The bailiff answered.

'Where's the jury?' Reuben said.

'They came back ten minutes ago.'

'What's the verdict?'

'Guilty,' the bailiff said.

Thirty-seven

THE KITCHEN LIGHT was on when he let himself in the back door. The clock said a quarter to ten.

His tuxedo was hanging with the copper pots, a note pinned to it in Mollie's handwriting: 'Better get a new one before Thursday.'

He hung up his overcoat in the hall closet, swallowed a shot of straight Scotch, then unhooked the tuxedo and went looking for Mollie. He headed for the darkroom which was in the downstairs east wing of the house, designed, in the beginning, as a playroom for the boys. Four years ago, he had turned it into quarters for Frieda right after Jesse died. He had carried his own guilts, and his mother had compounded them, every night radiating the despair and the loneliness that had taken her over. The time had been spent in a silent battle of blame, Mollie playing shrill and reluctant liaison. Frieda had stayed three months. Afterwards, the wing had become a playroom again, and he had turned the bath built for Frieda into a darkroom for Mollie.

The door was closed. He knocked. She didn't answer. She wasn't there. He realised he had needed to find her there, processing film, watching images appear in the pans of solution, hanging the contact sheets to dry. The way it had been. It wasn't.

He carried the tuxedo up the stairs. The house was filled with the empty quiet of the absence of children, and the heaviness of limb he couldn't shake. At the top of the stairs, he stopped, hesitated, then turned right towards the open door of the bedroom. In the doorway, he stopped again. Mollie was wearing a pale yellow sweater, brown jeans, in the wicker plantation chair absorbed in a piece of needlepoint. He remembered the story of the girl who had saved herself from execution by weaving during the day, and ripping through the night.

'What's wrong with it?' he said.

333

She looked up, laid the needlepoint down. He knew she had felt him awake last night. He knew she could now feel his mood, instantly, the obsolete habits of a marriage still operating like an anachronism.

'I'll show you.' She got up. She looked tired, not young, graceful, lovely. He came through the doorway, met her halfway across the sun-yellow carpet. The room felt strange, the wallpaper alien. Her hair smelled faintly of lemon. She took hold of the tuxedo sleeve, turned it over. 'The elbow's frayed – right here. And the seat of the pants is shiny.'

'Nobody'll notice,' he said.

'It looks seedy.'

'Maybe you could sew some leather patches on it.'

'They're not wearing patches on tuxedoes this year.'

He could feel the two of them, skating cautiously on the surface of the ice they had built. 'Alright. I'll get a new one. Tomorrow.'

'I think you should.'

'What about you ? Don't you need a new gown ?'

'No.' She took the tux from him and crossed to the closet and pulled open the mirrored door. Most of his clothes still hung there. She made room for the tux.

'Why don't you get a new one.'

She slid open the other door and pulled out a dress made of soft white fabric, chiffon. 'I was going to wear this one. Don't you think this one will be alright ?'

He remembered it, five hundred dollars worth of gown, last Christmas. Buchman & Woods had hired the entire Hunt Club. Mollie had given him the gold money clip.

'It's fine. It's a pretty dress.' He felt foolish, awkward, immersed in the details of frayed tuxedoes and white chiffon. Minutiae made up the texture of life. Tonight, it was meant to avoid the texture of their lives.

When she turned around, the clumsy silence wrapped both of them. Finally she said, 'Would you like some coffee ?'

'I'd rather have a drink.'

'So would I,' she said.

He made a martini for her, a double Scotch for himself. He carried the drinks into the living room. She had lit a fire. She was sitting on a pillow on the stone hearth, wrapped in a leopard throw, the firelight throwing shadows across her face.

'It's March. Not much time for many more fires.' He handed her the martini. 'Spring in a couple of weeks.'

'You'd better remind Attica to put a screen on the chimney.'

'I will.' Every summer, the birds built nests in the chimney. If they didn't screen the chimney, the first winter fire smoked up the house. He sat in the brown velvet wing chair, swallowed some Scotch. A log crackled – the sound filled the big silent room, whitewashed walls, antiques; they had done it piece by piece, collecting, for nineteen years. The thought struck him that she would take some of it, he would keep some of it – he had an image of the two of them dividing the substance of nineteen years.

'Leila told me the washing machine quit today.'

'I'll send somebody out.'

'I spoke to the boys. They're fine.'

'Good.'

'When do you think they can come back?'

'I don't know.' He heard the silence again.

'How did the trial go?'

'They found him guilty.'

'I'm sorry.'

He echoed Barksdale. 'It's an old historical tradition.' Another silence fell. He swallowed some more Scotch. He felt her looking at him. He knew the mixture of feeling showed on his face – all the feelings he never carried home, never allowed her to see. He finished off his drink.

'I know you don't like to lose. . . . ' She hesitated, frowning. 'Are you alright?' Her eyes took an inventory.

'Of course I'm alright. I didn't expect to win the goddamned case.' He stood up and headed for the bar. He poured himself another Scotch. In the bar mirror, he caught a glimpse of his face. Everything showed. He looked older, tired, profoundly disturbed; a face that was held together by anger and authority – both missing. He saw Elmos' face again, heard the pain and violence that had burst from Elmos. What should have been anger had been alchemised into a deep despondency.

He went back into the living room. Mollie was sitting in the same place, the martini hardly touched. He had an impulse to drop down beside her, on the hearth. The firelight had turned her young again. In the barracks apartment, in law school, a thousand years ago, they had sat cross-legged in front of the fire of a kerosene stove, wrapped in a common dream.

He sat in the wing chair again.

'Reuben – put your drink down. Please.'

'What the hell for?'

'Because your hand is shaking . . . '

'Goddamnit,' he said. 'my hand's not shaking.' He stopped. He saw that it was. He set the drink down, got his hands under control, lit a cigarette.

'I'm sorry,' she said. 'I know I should pretend your hand's not shaking. That's the way it's always been between us. The way everybody around us behaves.'

'I don't know what you're talking about.'

'It's over,' she said. 'I know it's over. I know we can't put the pieces together, ever – the way they were. But I can't help thinking . . . ' She shook her head. 'I mean – how can you know where you are, when you don't know where you've *been*? I've been trying to go back – to the way I grew up, to how it was when we first got married. . . . '

'No postmortems,' he said.

'It's my fault,' she said. 'I look back and I know I didn't know anything – except how to please, to serve – I thought that was the same thing as love. I remember, I never did the housework in front of you. Mopping floors, washing dishes – I did it all behind your back. I thought a woman shouldn't *sweat* in front of a man. I thought that's how it was supposed to be. Do you see what I mean?'

'No.' He picked up the Scotch, downed half of it, set it back down again. He saw his hand was still trembling. He watched her look away from it.

'It doesn't matter,' she said. 'It's my own need to talk about myself, to try to get it clear in my own head. I grew up in a Catholic neighborhood – maybe I'm looking for absolution from you. I know you can't give it to me. I have to find myself by myself. I never questioned anything before. I just played at everything, the way I thought it was supposed to be – like a child. Nothing real. Then, after I had Joe and Phil, I *had* children – I couldn't *be* a child anymore. Then I tried to grow up – behind your back. Like I did the housework behind your back. I did everything that was real to me behind your back. Then I wept because I didn't know you, and you didn't know me. That's how it was. Then, last week, I picked up a club and started to beat at the façade. When the façade collapsed, so did the marriage. . . . ' She tried a wry smile, sad and touching. 'I did it – with my own little hatchet. . . . '

He looked at her, the shadows from the fire playing over her face – suddenly strange to him, new, a little like Lea. He wondered if all female strength came from the urge to destroy. 'Forget it,' he said.

'Like tonight – ' she said, 'I can see your hand shaking. I can feel your depression. But I'm supposed to pretend you're not depressed; or shaky. I'm supposed to ignore it. I can't say: "Can I help you?" I'm only allowed to do whatever I can do to shore you up quietly, behind your back again. To your face, I'm supposed to pretend you're always strong, always in charge, no matter what's going on with you, no matter what I sense you're feeling. . . . There's nothing at stake now, nothing to salvage. We're not married anymore. We're just two human beings in a lot of trouble. Not for your sake – for my own – I'd like to help you. . . . Can I help you, Reuben?'

'I don't know. No. I don't think so.' He felt confused, uncomfortable, vaguely angry – as if he had been attacked. There was the silent law that allowed men and women to live together: distance was necessary to a man, mystery was necessary to a woman. She knew that. What was she doing? At the same time, he felt himself overwhelmed by loneliness and need. He finished off the Scotch. By an act of will, he kept his hand from shaking. 'I don't need any help,' he said.

'I do,' she said. He watched her light a cigarette. He saw her hand was trembling now. He felt suddenly closed in, short of breath.

'What do you need?' he said. 'I've always given you everything you needed – everything you wanted. Haven't I?'

'Yes.'

'What are you talking about?' A shrill ringing began in his ears.

'I want to *know*,' she said. 'I want to know about you – who you are, who you've loved, where you've been. I have to know who I've lived with for nineteen years.'

'For God's sake, Mollie – '

'I know it's over between us. But we don't hate each other. I'm asking you to help me. I've always been afraid of the world, you know that – you've always protected me. Now I have to learn to live out there. I don't know how. I don't know what it's all about. I'm asking you to tell me the truth. I'm sorry. It's not fair. But – I don't have anybody else to ask. . . . '

The ringing in his ears quit. A dead silence spread out around him. Through it, he heard the logs crackling. He realised he had been staring at Mollie.

'I loved you,' he said. 'I've always loved you. I don't love you anymore. I don't trust you anymore. That's the truth of that. I don't know what other kind of truth you want. You want my schedule for the past nineteen years? You want me to say it was all façade for me? It wasn't. Maybe I kept you a child – I thought that was what you wanted. Maybe I pretended to be strong, in charge all the time – I thought that was what you wanted. You were seventeen. You never did any living. Maybe you had to do some living. Maybe you had to go out and find out what other men were like. If you were my client and not my wife, maybe I'd understand it. I don't understand it. I don't want to understand it. I don't hate you. You gave me a lot of good things. Children. A home. What's a man supposed to want from a woman ? . . . You want to know what the world is like ? Men cut each other's throats for a nickel. You should stay south. It's not as bad down here as it is other places, because it's not as crowded down here, and the economic stakes aren't as high down here. This house we live in – it cost seventy thousand dollars to build down here, on three acres that cost fifteen. In New York, you couldn't buy the land to put it on. In California, it'd be more than a quarter million dollars. The more money at stake, the more throats get cut. I know you can't deal with that. I'll give you enough money – I'll always send you enough money. . . . '

The silence came back. Mollie sat still. The fire played over her face. He heard the small sound of her glass as she set it down on the stone.

'You want to know what the rest of the world is like ?' he said. 'It's lonely and it's isolated, and friends are rare, and love is rarer. Everybody betrays everybody sooner or later – they call it survival. You want to know where I've been ? I've been out there. Doing the best I know how to do. I haven't cut too many throats, and I've helped a few victims, and I have my own system of dues I pay for being lucky enough to live in a place I love, and lucky enough to have work to do I care about. What else ? You want to know who I've made love to ? Whoever was around when you weren't, and I was needy. Does that cover it ? No. You want it up to date, don't you ? You want to know where I've been tonight. Alright. I'll tell you. I've been with the bastards who tell me I'm not entitled to what belongs to me. I gave them ten thousand dollars – for information. There's going to be another bombing. You want to know what the world is like ? Stick around, I'll try to get you a ringside seat.'

The silence came back. It rang again. He looked at Mollie. She sat still, not moving, her eyes fixed on him. Another moment went by. The ringing quit. The air grew still. Finally she said, 'Tomorrow – if you don't have time to buy a new tuxedo – I think I can get the shine out of the old one.'

'Alright. Thank you.' He got to his feet. He looked down at her.

338

He watched her wrap the leopard throw more tightly about her shoulders. 'Good night, Mollie.'

She closed her eyes. 'Good night, Reuben.'

Thirty-eight

HE DREAMED about his father. Jesse, carrying the old man's cane, appeared and spoke to him. When he woke, he couldn't remember what Jesse had come to tell him.

The morning was gray, neither sun nor rain – a mist of clouds, and March fog coming up from the Pearl to hang low in the pines. As he came out the back door, Bo Garrison strolled down the path from the greenhouse, swinging his nightstick. He waved, went on. Garrison's blue-uniformed back moved through the trees. After tomorrow night, the need for sentries would be over. In thirty-six hours the bastards would hang themselves.

He passed Attica's car on the road. The car was loaded down with local maids, seven of them plus Leila, all crammed together and sitting on each other's laps. Public transportation had been discontinued the year the freedom riders arrived. Since then, Attica ran a bootleg taxi service for Morningside domestics. Reuben honked. Attica rolled his eyes like a thief. Last month had been another new axle. *No more than five passengers*, Reuben had ordered. *Yessir*, Attica had said, *five, no more'n five*.

When he got to the Williamsburg, Monk's truck wasn't there yet. Last night he had needed to see Monk, had needed to touch base with the old and the simple and the basic. Last night he had been engulfed in despondency – a deep sadness for Justin, who had been revealed as a man who lived by denial, disowning, disclaiming. Last night he had needed to reaffirm, with Monk, the thing they shared – a stubborn, crazy pride in what they were. Instead, he had dreamed of Jesse, carrying his grandfather's cane – had drawn his strength and sustenance from its source; had confirmed his identity in his own way. This morning, he no longer needed Monk for any of that. This morning it was simpler; he needed a friend.

Inside, he found Syd Kaminsky arranging the meat case. The black boy in the white coat was mopping the brick floor.

'Where's my mother?'

Syd washed his hands. The soapsuds curled in the black hair of Syd's forearms, reminding Reuben of Jesse again. 'She's gone to the governor's mansion. They hired us to cater for the Rabin party tomorrow night.'

'Whose idea was that?'

'I thought it was yours,' Syd said. 'Your partner called yesterday. Turns out Rabin's kosher. We're flying chickens in from Memphis.' Syd grinned. 'Haven't located any kosher grits yet.'

'Give her time.'

Syd turned on the slicing machine and began to feed in a slab of corned beef. 'You want some eggs or something?'

'No thanks.' Through the bay window, he saw Monk's truck pull up. The back was filled up with lumber again. With a mild sense of excitement, he watched Monk climb down and head for the door. He poured two cups of coffee and carried them to the corner table. Monk came across the restaurant and sat down opposite him. In the stubborn silence, he could hear the machines grinding away in the kitchen.

'What the hell do you want?' Monk said finally.

'I want to talk to you.'

'Shove it.'

'There's another bombing planned. Tomorrow night. We're setting up an ambush. The local police. The F.B.I. You want in or out?'

'Goddamnit, we've been friends a long time. I *counted* on you. I stuck my goddamned neck out. I don't give a damn what you –' Monk stopped, stared at Reuben. 'What the *hell* did you say?'

'They took a couple of shots at Mollie. Sunday night. She was on her way home from the airport.'

'*Wait* a minute. Start over. What the hell are you – ?'

'I spent ten grand of the money we raised. Last night. I met with two stoolies.'

'What two stoolies?'

'Floyd Rawlins – he's the bouncer at the Hunt Club. His brother Elmos – he was tried with Frank Flowers after those three civil rights workers were murdered. By the way, their father's the one who made the phone calls.'

'Holy shit. I thought you were in court. Goddamnit, it's in the newspaper.'

'I've been in meetings – with Tom Barksdale, F.B.I. agent.

340

With the Rawlins brothers. Last night we met in a room in the Holmesdale Hotel. They laid out the night, the hit man – our friend Jones. By ten o'clock tonight, I'll know the place and the time. Jones'll walk right into an ambush.'

'*Jesus Christ.*'

'You want in or out ?'

'What do you think ? What the hell do you think ? Jesus Christ – we've got 'em. Goddamnit – you did it – we've *got* 'em. What the hell do you think ? I want to be home watching television ?'

'Keep it down.' Reuben looked around for Syd. The slicing machine had quit. Behind the counter, Syd was dividing pastrami into three-ounce portions to be used for sandwiches during lunch.

'Goddamned right,' Monk said.

The black boy came past, carrying the mop and pail, and disappeared into the back. The bell tinkled. A barber from next door laid some change on the counter, spoke to Syd, poured a cup of coffee and left with it.

'No more talk,' Reuben said. 'You go about your usual business today – I'll go about mine. When I get the rest of the information, I'll pass it on to you. Now drink your coffee and split.'

Monk drained his cup, set it down. 'Jesus – I sure owe you an apology.'

'Forget it.'

'You've got balls.'

'I said forget it.' Reuben heard his own irritation.

'Goddamned right.' Monk started to rise, then stopped in mid-air. 'Jesus – I forgot. Papa sent you a package. I've got it in the truck. You want me to go get it ?'

'For Christ's sake, no. Get the hell out of here.'

'Damned right.'

Reuben watched Monk go through the door. Then he lit a cigarette and spent a couple of minutes reading the gourmet labels on the shelves. White Peaches, and Cherries Jubilee, and French Pâté. He knew what he was doing. He was avoiding the office. He was avoiding Justin. He was avoiding the depression that had come from Elmos' outburst about Justin's mother. He knew when he looked into Justin's face again, he would see a small and frightened man. Whatever came later, there would be that irrevocable moment of loss, to be deferred as long as possible.

His coffee was cold.

He got the newspaper from the counter, poured a hot cup of coffee, and came back to the table. A middle-aged woman wearing a tourmaline mink stole and white leather gloves came in and began to complain to Syd about the price of hors d'oeuvres. Reuben swallowed some coffee, burned his tongue, cursed silently. He tried the labels again, then knew he was avoiding something else; knew his irritation at Monk had been irritation at himself. Reluctantly, he recognised the role he had played with Monk. Super-macho. Cops and robbers. He knew himself well enough. When he staged a melodrama, it was meant to obfuscate some portion of reality he didn't want to deal with. He knew his own life well enough. What he refused to deal with came around the corner and hit him in the face. What? It nagged him. Justin, yes. But more than that. Something else. It wouldn't come up.

The woman left. The door closed behind her. Syd called her a cheapskate in Yiddish.

Reuben opened the newspaper, did a quick run-through. On page four, his own photograph looked back at him. He remembered the flashbulb in the corridor outside the courtroom just after he had telephoned Kornfield. The face in the photograph was furious. Underneath was a short and slanted account of the trial, no mention of Taylor. The headline said simply: HIGGINS FOUND GUILTY. It felt like something that had happened two thousand years ago. Then he knew the feeling was another evasion. It had happened yesterday. Something about the photograph or the item was directly related to the churning in his head.

He laid the newspaper down, sipped at the coffee, lit another cigarette. Syd came from behind the counter, poured himself some coffee, brought it over, and took the seat Monk had vacated.

'How's it going?' Syd said.

'Coming along. How about you? You still like it here?'

Syd shrugged. 'I used to think – it beats Poland, it beats Palestine, it beats Chicago. Lately, it's beginning to smell like Warsaw. . . . '

'Not quite,' Reuben said. Syd's face blurred. Reuben saw Elmos Rawlins' face instead, heard the pain and violence that had burst from him. Heard Elmos screaming to claim his landless southern identity; screaming to claim his due for the forebears who had driven out the carpetbagger and heeled the scalawag and restored the South; screaming to prove he was as brave and proud and honorable as Justin. Then, suddenly, in a third ear, he heard Elmos say: *I told you, Floyd – after we set it up, they're gonna put me away anyhow.* And he saw what it was he had let get buried under the cloud of Minna Woods' Jewishness. Now it came back. *After we set it up . . .*

' . . . he was a salesman, religious goods,' Syd was saying. 'He .

342

used to go in and out of Palestine. In 1939, he took us out of Warsaw – I was six years old. He took us to Palestine. In 1940, he went back. Everybody told him not to go. He had a business – he went anyway. That was the last time I saw my father. The Nazis marched into Poland. By the time they took Warsaw, the Russians were trying to stop them. It didn't help my father. We stayed in Palestine another two years. It was rough then – it wasn't Israel until forty-eight. My mother had a sister in Chicago . . . that was rough too. . . . Here, I've got a house with a yard – my little girl can play. I've got a car, a small bank account – I can see a little security. Then this bombing thing. I don't know. . . . Maybe it's not meant for a Jew to put down roots. . . . '

'Bullshit,' Reuben said.

He took the highway to town.

Monk had left the package on the seat of the car. Reuben knew what it was – the old man's journal, translated into English. He shoved it into the glove compartment. He thought: Alright – so it wasn't another bombing scheduled spontaneously by the Klan. So it was a setup. So it was a bombing set up by the Rawlins brothers in order to collect forty grand and save Elmos' neck. So what? What difference did it make?

It led to other questions. Were the Rawlins brothers setting it up on their own – or was Barksdale in charge? Barksdale, giving instructions? Justin had said: *Hoover requires convictions*. Was an entrapment the best insurance Barksdale could get for a later conviction? They had ambushed the African Republic on a trumped-up charge – it wasn't outside their normal operating procedure. Again, what difference did it make? Then he remembered Justin had said something else: *Tell Barksdale you'll pay for convictions – or bodies*.

But he hadn't done that. He had never suggested that bargain to Barksdale. And even if he had, did he give a damn for Army Jones' life? Hell, no.

So what was it? Not the legal question of entrapment – an often-used method of law enforcement, the judicial decisions ambiguous enough to maintain it. He went over the law: the courts usually held that an innocent person may not be trapped into a crime, but, in order to capture a suspect, the police may help him to commit a crime he could otherwise be reasonably supposed to commit. Army Jones had a record of explosives. Legally, a bombing committed by Jones would fall under the heading of reasonable supposition. So it wasn't that. What was it?

The realisation that the bombing was being set up by Floyd and Elmos was a simple and obvious one. Yet – if it was so damned simple and obvious – why hadn't he put the pieces together before? What had he buried under last night's depression over Justin? under this morning's melodrama with Monk.?

It was buried, still, under his own inability to put his finger on the thing that nagged him. It wouldn't come to him.

He came off the highway at Main. He drove three blocks, then parked in front of *Men for Style*, a one-story mock chateau with velvet-lined windows, one headless dummy in each. He went inside and asked to look at tuxedoes. He knew what he was doing. Avoiding Justin.

He was the day's first customer, no one else in the store. He went through an argument with a pinched-face clerk over satin cummerbunds, then finally settled on two tuxes that he carried into the dressing room.

He was working his way into the second tux when he realised what was going through his head was Barksdale's speech on the nature of stoolies with a cause – the intolerable dilemma that accompanied the need to sell out combined with the need to be liked and admired by their own kind. He grew suddenly clammy – the sign of cold fury; his own need for violence came up without any intelligible reason. Kin to the feeling that had provoked him into punching M. K. Taylor the night of the first bombing without intelligible reason. He knew it was close to the surface. Another moment, he'd lay his hands on it.

The clerk parted the curtains. 'How are you coming along, Mr Buchman?'

'Get the devil out of here –'

The clerk paled, fled. Reuben reached for it. It was gone. Whatever it was, he had lost it.

He settled on the second tux – lightweight wool with a grosgrain cummerbund. Then he stood in front of a three-way mirror while a white-haired gentleman from alterations went over him with a piece of chalk, grumbling about the impossibility of delivering the tux by three tomorrow. In the mirror, Reuben watched several men come in, make purchases, depart. His trousers were being marked when the rabbi came through the entrance, headed for one of the glass counters, beckoned to the pinched-face salesman. Harris didn't see him. He watched Harris begin to examine tux shirts, holding several up in front of him before a mirror. The third shirt around, in the mirror, Harris spotted him – then headed across the store, carrying two shirts.

'Do you think the light blue or the yellow ?' Harris said. 'I don't know much about style. What's in style ? I lean to the blue. What do you think ?'

'Yellow,' Reuben said. 'How's Frances ?'

Harris cast an actor's glance at the white-haired gentleman on his knees. 'Oh – she won't make the governor's ball – she's not well enough for that. But you know she's out of the hospital ? Monk tells me our house will be ready in less than a week. I'll hate to leave Jake's – Rosalie has been so kind. Not that I care for all that modern furniture. Did you say the blue one ?'

'Yellow.'

'Ruffled, do you think ?'

'Tucked.'

'Oh yes, of course,' Harris said, 'not too flashy.'

By the City Hall clock, it was after ten when he parked in front of his office. Justin's car was already there. He took a walk to the corner and bought the newspaper he had already read from Glory Christmas. Then he walked like a man on his way to a dreaded errand.

Inside the reception room, Olive and Luanne were both at their desks. Two new clients waited on the Victorian settee. Justin had walked over to the mansion, would be gone all morning. Relieved, he took the first client upstairs with him, concentrated on the interview, then had the second one sent up. He took notes, returned phone calls, immersed himself in work. At the end of the second interview, Olive appeared carrying a brown paper sack. 'A black woman left this for you.'

Inside were four jars of muscadine jelly and a note from Anny thanking him for putting Clyde in the *horsepital*. He lined the jars up on his desk, offered one to Olive.

'Oh no,' Olive said. 'I've been reading about botulism.'

He had lunch, alone, at his desk. He told Olive to take his calls, make sure no one disturbed him. He closed his door, then opened the drapes to the patio. The sun hadn't come out – it looked like it was going to remain gray all day.

He sat at his desk and went back to Barksdale's speech on the nature of stoolies who betrayed a cause they still believed in. It was a generality that became an evasion. He came back to specifics. Floyd and Elmos Rawlins – stoolies. Two specific men. The thing kept gnawing away, insistently, but it wouldn't be forced to the surface by an urgency of will. He was aware of his own circular thinking, felt the clammy thing come back, knew his anger could be lashed to purpose. He imagined Floyd Rawlins on the witness stand, set his shape in the chair on the other side of his desk.

– Did you set up the bombing?

Sure.

– When did you set it up?

Night before last. We had a meeting.

– Who?

Me and my friends.

– And you decided to do it tomorrow night?

That's right.

– Why?

Because we know every Jew'll be in town for the governor's party. We'll hit after it's over.

– Did Barksdale tell you to set it up?

No answer came through.

– Who's the hit man?

Army Jones.

– Where's the target?

No answer came through.

– What's the target?

The door opened, cut through. Rawlins vanished. Reuben looked up, furious, then realised it was Justin.

A moment of silence echoed as Justin crossed the office and took the chair that Floyd Rawlins' image had occupied – looking no smaller than he had been, the same man, the same caution masquerading as dignity, the same reddish hair, squared cheekbones; a mild elation playing around his mouth, and the sparks of some kind of victory coming out of the blue eyes.

'I'm damned sorry about Higgins – we gave it a good try.' Justin's voice seemed to echo. *We.* 'I heard what you did to Taylor – sonofabitch deserves that and more.' *Sonofabitch.*

'Screw him.' Reuben occupied himself with the motions of lighting a cigarette.

'What happened last night? With Barksdale?'

Reuben did a half-turn and back in the swivel chair. He realised he was behaving as if he were guilty of something. What the hell was he guilty of? The knowledge that Justin's heritage was negotiable? Then he realised he wasn't guilty, he was embarrassed – embarrased for Justin. He couldn't look Justin in the eye. 'For ten grand, the Rawlins boys gave us the night and the hit man – tomorrow night, Army Jones. For another ten grand, today, they'll come up with the time and the place. Barksdale's setting up an ambush. That's how it stands.' He turned the chair back, met Justin's eyes.

'I'll be glad when it's over,' Justin said quietly.

'So will I.' Suddenly it came to him that Doan Newberry had not beat him up for the corduroy knickers. Suddenly it came to him as an overlooked but obvious insight – Doan Newberry had beat him up for being a Jew. He had sliced off a piece of Doan Newberry's ear. But Elmos had said about Justin: *We used to beat him up. He never fought back. We never could understand what was the matter with him.* Reuben saw the boy Justin had been – taking his punishment, believing he was being beaten for the secret thing he was, never fighting back because neither man nor boy could defend what he was committed to hide. The sense of sorrow swept him again. Behind it came a keen sense of pride in his own manhood: southern; more of a southerner than Justin – who had taken it upon himself to do the baptismal rites – by Justin's own definition of southern honor: a man who fights for his own inheritance.

'I've been doing some thinking,' Justin said. 'After we had that talk at the reservoir, I've been doing some thinking about how it's going to be for us. As a matter of fact, there's going to be some politicking at the Rabin party. No announcements yet about the lieutenant governor thing – but talk, feeling around by state officials. It's the beginning of it.' He grinned. 'You know, the partner who doesn't go into politics is the one who rakes the money in. Are you going to be able to be diplomatic? You'll have to practice some politicking yourself.'

'Why not?' Reuben said. 'You're the one who comes from a political family. You know the ropes. You know what's got to be done. I'll do whatever you say.' He watched Justin's face. He saw himself running to Justin the night Harris' house had been bombed. The sense of loss hovered, threatened to settle.

'Thanks.' Justin was visibly moved. 'We're a hell of a team now. Nobody's going to be able to beat us now.'

'Damned right.'

'We'll make a formal announcement in a couple of weeks. If the Rabin factory goes over, we can come out as arbiters of progress with one plant under our belt. I've been thinking – maybe we'll announce on your birthday, for luck.'

'Sure.' He thought about the Russian Jew who had died on that same day. For himself, he was proud of it. He watched Justin's face. He wondered how it felt to live that long with the kind of pretense that bred self-contempt. Shabby.

'After that, we'll swing into a full-scale campaign. Pull out all the stops. What do you think?'

'I think . . . maybe, when things settle down . . . after the ball, after the ambush – when it's back to normal – I think we ought to take a couple of days and go fishing . . . you and me.'

'That's a damned good idea.'

'Not play . . . work.' Reuben chose his words carefully. 'I think we ought to go about this campaign the way we go about a case. Rehearse it. Then, one of us take the role of devil's advocate. Me. Ask questions. Like, what are the weaknesses? What are the cases we've handled that might come up? There may be a primary fight – some crusader from left field. I think we'd better find out where we're vulnerable.' He paused, watched Justin's face. For a moment, he wondered if Floyd had been lying. Then he saw Justin pale beneath his freckles. Saw Justin stiffen imperceptibly. He pushed. 'I think we'd better be prepared for whatever may come out, and how to answer it. You're the one who asked me – way back – is everything under your roof so damned pure?'

Justin rose, crossed to the window, and looked out silently. Reuben wondered if Barksdale had said anything to him. He decided not. The information on Minna Woods had probably been on file for years. If it was so. He believed it was. Yet, what could he say? *Why didn't you tell me you were half-Jewish?* And Justin could answer, *A man has the right to claim any religion he chooses.* Then what could he say? *You don't have the right to disown what you are.* Why not?

Justin turned, his face pale. 'That's good thinking.' He hesitated. 'I like your down-to-earth approach.' He took another moment, his eyes fixed steadily on Reuben – maybe a denial, maybe a plea, maybe a pact, maybe none of it. Reuben couldn't read it. Finally Justin said, 'Maybe . . . two days, by ourselves, might be a good thing. . . . '

Reuben read it. Maybe Justin would tell him later; maybe not. Maybe he would find the answers that would allow him to confront Justin; maybe not. For the moment, this moment, it was tabled.

Then Justin was gone.

Reuben laid it to rest.

The remainder of the afternoon, in between appointments and telephone calls, and waiting for Barksdale's call, he continued to grope in the darkness, trying to illuminate the thing that seemed to be paying absolute obedience to some other set of orders. He found himself thinking about the ways of men: men who crawled,

348

and men who stumbled, and men who rose to whatever circumstances demanded – willing to take chances, willing to risk everything.

He had no idea what any of it meant.

He went back to the newspaper photograph. His own face gave him no clues. The accompanying article led back to Taylor – another dead end.

He gave up and went back to work. He was dictating a brief into the machine when Luanne came in. She stopped in front of his desk, timid, awkward, lids lowered, hands clasped behind her back like a four-year-old. He switched off the machine.

'What is it?'

'Olive said I couldn't.' Her cheeks turned the shade of her scarlet stockings.

'Couldn't what?'

'Take my boyfriend to the governor's ball tomorrow night.' She plucked nervously at a curl. 'Olive said not to ask you.'

'Who's your boyfriend?'

'Johnny Campanello – he works in Stevenson's garage. Olive said he's not –'

'Damn right you can. Take the rest of the day and go find yourself a long dress.'

'Oh, *thank* you.'

'How would you like some muscadine jelly?'

At nine o'clock, Reuben sat in the crewel wing chair of his study at home, working his way through his second drink – one eye on the clock, waiting for Barksdale's call and hoping the Scotch would loosen his thinking processes.

No luck.

No mind-blowing clue to identify the source of the anxiety that had persisted and grown through the day. All day his efforts had been futile. All day he had puzzled over each isolated piece, knowing they fit together, but not being able to see how.

He'd go through it all again.

Alright, he thought. Once more. Begin, again, from last night's meeting, and the fact that you missed Elmos' clear statement that the thing was to be a setup. Alright. It's a setup. Who's in charge? Not Elmos. Floyd. So it's a setup by Floyd. Alright. What would you do if you were Floyd? If you were a stoolie with a cause? If you were caught between saving your brother's skin and selling out your comrades? How would you try to cover your bases?

What rationale would you come up with in order to live with yourself?

Reuben leaned his head back, closed his eyes, listened to Floyd's thoughts. *I gotta save Elmos – get Elmos' kid away. What can I do? I don't want to sell out my buddies but I gotta get 'em to plan another bombing. It can't look like a setup. It's got to look like the real thing. Maybe it'll turn out to be the real thing. If they come in with enough dynamite, maybe they'll do it and get away.*

Reuben opened his eyes, swallowed some more Scotch. It was close, but it was off. The ideal solution for Floyd would be to pull some kind of double cross. What kind of double cross clever enough to outsmart Barksdale and Simmons and himself? What kind of setup that might backfire – and still get Elmos off the hook?

None.

He ruled out a double cross.

That left one more possibility. A setup that included revenge.

It came up. It came up as loud and clear and unmistakable as if Floyd Rawlins were in the study. *Why don't we bomb that fuckin' Jew bastard?* He heard Floyd's rationale: *Maybe they'll get his wife, his kids, his house at the least. It ain't a sellout. Get the Jew while we're at it.*

The cold sweat broke. He felt his hands grow clammy, his brow bead with ice.

He saw it. At noon, he had asked: What's the target? He had asked: Where's the target? Justin had interrupted. He had failed to ask: Who's the target?

You, Floyd said.

He saw Floyd – hating him for having to take the money from him; hating him for being the instrument through which Floyd sold out his friends. He heard Floyd – saying to his friends: *Ain't Buchman the leader of the goddamned Jews? Ain't Buchman the man who tried to get Army Jones? Ain't Buchman the man who defended Higgins? Ain't Buchman the man who went after Taylor's ass?*

Why don't we bomb that fuckin' Jew bastard?

He thought about the ways of men: men who crawled, and men who stumbled, and men who rose to whatever circumstances demanded – willing to take chances, willing to risk everything.

Now he knew what it meant.

He was freezing.

He realised the phone was ringing, had been ringing for several moments. He got out of the wing chair and crossed to the desk and picked up the phone.

350

'Buchman,' he said.

'I just made contact,' Barksdale said.

'What time?'

'One thirty in the morning.'

'Where?'

Barksdale hesitated a brief moment. Then he said, 'Your house.'

Book Four

Thirty-nine

HE WORE the new tux.

He wore Mollie, on his arm, in the white chiffon.

It was one square block in the middle of downtown, the garden lit. They climbed the steps of the Grecian mansion and moved through the double doors to be greeted by an ebony butler in red livery and gold epaulets, a prisoner from Parchman.

Reuben remembered that the governor's entire retinue of servants were paroled to the mansion to serve out their sentences, most of them for life. It was an old Mississippi political tradition which went back before Justin's father's time. Justin's childhood black mammy had once plunged a knife into her common-law husband twenty-one times. Paroled servants were mostly murderers, on the theory that thievery was an ongoing trait, while murder was a one-time crime of passion.

Deliberately, Reuben concentrated on such details.

'*Mr and Mrs Reuben Buchman !*'

Reuben guided Mollie beneath the five massive crystal chandeliers which paraded across the high-ceilinged center hall and up a double staircase. Three hundred prisms apiece. Justin had once said that on the first of every month, each prism was taken down by hand, dipped in ammonia, hung back again – a procedure that took a crew of thirty an entire day.

At the top of the stairway, the reception line waited. The governor stood at the head, directly in front of a portrait of Andrew Jackson on an upended horse, rear view. Reuben remembered that a Yankee newsman, having gone through a similar reception line four years ago, had noted in print that the former governor of Mississippi resembled the horse, rear view.

The same governor, who had put in the solid-gold bathroom faucets, backed into an airplane propeller while the engine was going, stood up at Ole Miss to bar James Meredith, and built a schoolroom on the top floor of the mansion so his grand-children wouldn't have to attend integrated schools.

The new governor, by comparison, was Abe Lincoln.

It's a break, Barksdale had said. *They don't know your grounds – you do. There's been that cop out there the last few days – he knows every inch. Between the two of you, we'll know exactly where to stake out men. Offhand, there's the pool area, the greenhouse, all those trees. We can hide fifty men out there at night with no problem at all.*

No problem at all.

The night Harris' house had been bombed and Reuben had punched M. K. Taylor, he had shouted at Simmons: *It ain't you and it ain't your church and it ain't your goddamned grandfather – !*

'How are you, Reuben?'

'Fine, Governor.'

'That was a fine, public-spirited thing you did, taking up your time with that Higgins case. I like to see that kind of public spirit.'

'Thank you, sir.'

Yessir – nobody can say he didn't get a real trial down here. And I'll tell you something else – nobody can see you don't have about the prettiest lady in the place, right there on your arm.'

Don't tell your wife until you leave, Barksdale had said. *The later the better*.

'Thank you, Governor.'

Beside the governor, his wife wore blue-rinsed hair, and long white satin, and one of those faces that maintained its complexion by lending itself to everything and giving itself to nothing.

Reuben paid his dues – a brief required compliment. A wave of irritation swept him. He felt the sharp intolerance of a man about to go into battle.

Be sure to act normal, Barksdale had said. *Whatever your usual manner, stick to it*.

He concentrated on Isadore Rabin, next in line, looking as nervous and beatific as a rabbi's son about to be bar mitzvahed.

Only the god was Mammon, and the pulpit was a factory site in Claymont. And Rabin's predecessors went back to Justin's father's time, when the industrial plan had been enacted in the legislature. The county issued bonds for the building of the factory, which was handed over without cost to the manufacturer who provided machinery and working capital. Besides the free land and free building, the law also provided for suspension of taxes for twenty years and the unwritten bonus of cheap labor. *The Lord our God, the Lord is One.* Reuben wondered how many times tonight Isadore Rabin would be told: Some of my best friends are Yankees.

Beside Rabin, his wife overflowed from the V-neckline of tomato-colored crepe sprinkled with bugle beads. Reuben shook hands, exchanged pleasantries, kept his eyes fixed forcefully on the bridge of her nose job.

Then he moved on to Justin, who gripped his hand, caught and held his eyes.

Barksdale's a pro, Justin had said this morning. *Count on that. He knows what he's doing. Those bastards won't know what hit them.*

Now he saw that everything said and unsaid had already passed between them. He saw that the glow of imminent victory, fulfilled hope – self-contempt and compensatory dreams – had already begun to dominate Justin's face. With an effort, Justin overlaid a look of concern.

'Good luck,' he whispered.

'Same to you,' Reuben said.

He moved on, to Caroline. Caroline was one of that breed of beautiful overripe women cursed with piano legs, hidden tonight by a long black gown embroidered with poppies. The proximity to power had flushed her cheeks, starred her eyes. He had an image of her, ten years from now, running to fat and flirting with junior legislators. He stepped aside and watched Mollie and Caroline exchange the tight, competitive, female smiles of hostility repressed by mutual consent.

You leave with Mollie at fifteen minutes before midnight, Barksdale had said. *By twelve fifteen, we'll have her safely stashed. By twelve fifteen, we'll have you deputised and stationed with a shotgun.*

He looked at his watch. It was eight twenty-five.

Mollie laid an elbow-length white gloved hand on his forearm. He stopped a moment. He knew he was seeing her out of proportion, bigger than life, brighter, lush and memorable – as if a doctor had just said to him: You have twenty-four hours to live.

'What is it?' Her eyes traveled his face.

'Nothing.' They moved down the corridor towards the brightly lit reception room, past an army of liveried servants lining the wall beneath portraits of southern generals.

'Please, Reuben. I know there's something wrong. You feel cold – like ice. I don't want to interfere – but – you said – Is it another bombing? Please tell me.' She stopped. He could see she meant to insist. He had an impulse to hold her.

'I had Olive send an invitation to Jean Aucoin.'

It took a moment. He felt her stiffen against the blow. Finally she said quietly, 'It doesn't matter.'

'I don't give a damn myself,' he said.

The reception room was nearly filled. Three dozen Parchman refugees in starched white coats were passing champagne and his mother's hors d'oeuvres – chopped chicken liver and tiny knishes. By seven this morning, the mansion kitchen had been scrubbed down, the newly purchased cooking utensils installed, and Harris hauled in to make a *brucha*. Everything kosher.

'I'm sorry,' he said tersely.

It's important that you both act perfectly normal. Don't make any scenes or call any attention to yourself.

She turned her head away. 'It doesn't matter.'

'I'll get you some champagne. Would you like some champagne?'

'Thank you.'

'What about some chopped liver?'

'No thanks.'

'Pink champagne or white?'

'White – please.'

He moved through the guests, trying to spot Monk. He saw Harris, in a blue ruffled tux shirt, talking to Jake and Rosalie Gorman. He made a wide berth, kept going. Most of the Jews had already arrived. He recognised judges, businessmen, state senators, political bargainers, all carrying wives in gleaming jewels and newly sprayed hairdos.

He stopped a waiter carrying a silver tray, picked off two glasses of champagne, then headed back towards Mollie. For a moment he didn't see her. Then he spotted her, standing not far from where he had left her, alone, head held high – whatever trepidation she felt hidden under a quiet, gracious beauty. He knew if he did not know her he would wonder who she was, would try to meet her, would have sexual fantasies about her. He knew it was too late for any of that. He imagined himself telling her: *They're going to bomb our hourse. Tonight.* He imagined her response – fear, hysteria, tears.

'Reuben –'

He stopped, turned, saw it was Bill Thatcher who had called his name. 'How are you?'

'Why the hell didn't you tell me you were going for blood?' Thatcher said. Thatcher had appointed him as public defender. Thatcher was telling him he had caught some hell over Higgins.

Reuben grinned. 'I always go for blood in the courtroom.'

'Next time you do me the favor of taking a case, I'll send an undertaker along.'

'No thanks – I carry my own briefcase.'

'I hear you may be doing that.' Thatcher leaned closer, lowered his voice. 'The way it looks tonight – you're not going to have a law partner much longer.'

Reuben smiled. 'I'll be damned.'

'Too early to say, huh?'

'I haven't heard a formal announcement.'

'You tell him I'm behind him.'

'He'll be happy to hear that.'

Thatcher clapped him on the back. 'What about that quail hunt? A bargain's a bargain – you want it set up for Rabin this weekend?'

'Forget the quail hunt,' Reuben said.

'How come?'

'He doesn't know a shotgun from an elephant's ass,' Reuben said. 'What the hell can you expect from a Yankee?'

He picked his way through the crowd, stopping to touch base with judges and legislators. He spoke quickly to Max Nathan, who was sporting Gina dressed like a shimmering mermaid and wearing too much makeup. He nodded at Victor Karp, avoided Harris again, but ran directly into Leo, who had been waiting for him.

'What the hell's going on?' Leo whispered. 'We haven't heard a word from you since the meeting, and Papa found out this morning there's twenty thousand gone from the account.'

'Tell Jake to keep his pants on.'

'What kind of answer is that?'

Reuben felt the anger surface and fix on Leo with a sudden ugly vehemence. 'Goddamn you, *shove it*.' He saw Leo pale. He caught hold of the fury, pushed it back down, felt himself go a bit numb. 'I'm sorry.' Leo was staring at him.

'Papa wants to call another meeting – tomorrow night.'

'Why not?' Reuben forced a frozen smile.

'I'll tell him.'

'You tell him,' Reuben said. 'You tell him he'll know everything he wants to know by tomorrow night.'

He went past Dave Colman with a peremptory nod, greeted the president of Holmesdale Tile, waved at Mickey and Bonnie Gorman, stopped to shake hands with Judge Alexander, spoke quickly to John Abrahmson and his former secretary, who was dressed prim as a missionary in the manner of all ex-mistresses turned wives.

'You lost the damned Higgins case, didn't you?' John said happily. 'I told you – didn't I? – it wouldn't be worth it. All that goddamned trouble for nothin'. One of these days, boy, you're gonna start listenin' to me.'

'Shove it,' Reuben said.

When he reached the spot where Mollie should have been, he found Monk instead, looking like someone who had been told to hold down the lid of a dynamite keg. 'Look at that Gina,' Monk said. Reuben turned. Gina had cornered Judge Alexander and was turning him to pulp. 'Just 'cause she bit the head off a herring, she thinks she's a shark.'

'Where's Mollie?' Reuben handed Monk the glasses of warm champagne, freed his hand to light a cigarette. Over the flame, he saw Jean Aucoin come through the doorway, accompanied by Jack Schraft and his wife.

'She's gone to the powder room with Sheila,' Monk said. 'Goddamned women – like bitches with fire hydrants. They've got to try every new one. Hey – are you okay?'

'Why the hell not?' Reuben watched Aucoin take a glass of champagne from a passing tray, watched him scout the room.

Monk bent towards him, spoke in a husky voice. 'Any change in plans since this afternoon?'

'No.' He watched Jean Aucoin vanish into the crowd.

Monk said, 'Jesus – you've got guts.'

He removed a glass from Monk's hand and downed the champagne. 'So do you.'

'What the hell are friends for?'

Reuben looked at his watch. It was eight forty-five.

Dinner began at nine.

Two by two, they descended the stairs to find two dozen tables set for six – china and silver and flowers and candles – four roving violinists from the Holmesdale Symphony Orchestra, one white-coated black servant for every three guests, and place cards that seated every two Jews with four gentiles.

Reuben watched Jean Aucoin take a seat three tables away. He tried to imagine Mollie in bed with him. The image wouldn't surface. How did one conjure up one's wife in bed with another man? The cajun doctor seemed suddenly moot, unimportant, ludicrous.

He took a seat beside Mollie, leaned close to her ear, and said, 'I shouldn't have invited him.'

'Who?' Mollie said. Then she turned away and flashed a smile at the vice-president of Atlas Aluminum, falling back on her public manner which had always been impeccable – old ladies were always telling him how lucky he was. He had an insane impulse to announce to the table: *My wife's a whore.* At that moment he knew, with certainty, he no longer loved her.

Frieda served a Friday night supper.

The ideal Sabbath of his confirmation lessons with Rabbi Hellman in Greenborough marched past – a glistening table, a festive board, joy, warmth, hospitality, and a dime in the blue box for Israel.

Through the gefilte fish, Atlas Aluminum complained about the cost of labor. His wife asked what the fish was.

'Quenelle de sole,' Mollie said.

Chicken soup came next, accompanied by a discussion on the odds of Wallace's third-party candidacy for President. After that came halves of roasted chicken, potato kugel, green peas. Reuben looked for the candle salad of his childhood – a slice of canned pineapple, a halved banana stuck into the center representing the Sabbath candle, and topped by a bright red cherry representing the flame. It didn't appear. How did one teach black convicts to make salads that looked like candles? He felt himself caught in some kind of liquid landscape. He went a bit numb again. Once or twice, after that, he caught a glimpse of his mother checking things out, although he had expressly forbidden her to show her face in an apron.

Beside him, Mollie remained gracious, pleasant, charming. He had a need to lean over to her, tell her now.

They're going to bomb our house tonight.

The cold sweat trapped him. He excused himself, found the bathroom, stayed there a few minutes smoking a cigarette and staring at the solid-gold faucets.

When he came back, they were serving mandelbrodt, apple studel, and coffee. Atlas Aluminum was discussing Justin, and he could hear the orchestra tuning up in the ballroom across the hall. He looked at his watch again. Ten thirty. Then he looked at Jean Aucoin. The cajun doctor was quietly lifting a diamond earring from the rosy lobe of his dinner companion, Rosalie Gorman.

Someone tapped a glass. At the end of the room, the governor rose. The table held Isadore Rabin and Justin. The violins halted. The conversation faded to a murmur, then became silence.

'We have here tonight a most honorable guest,' the governor said. 'Mr Isadore Rabin.' He paused, allowed some gentle applause. 'You have all met Mr Rabin, you have all welcomed him, you have all gotten to know him here tonight. But – more important – Mr Isadore Rabin has gotten to know us.' He paused again, threw a glance at Rabin, then looked out over his audience. 'Before Mr Rabin came here tonight, he had heard a number of things. He had heard there are many Souths – he had heard there is one South. He had heard we were hospitable – he had heard we were unkind to strangers. He had heard that we, regardless of individual differences, share a common heritage and a peculiar history. He had heard that what remains of that heritage is sometimes quaint and sometimes shocking. And so he came to sift through the contradictions for himself.

'And tonight he has learned that we possess a mind, a way of thinking, that is continuous with our past. He has learned that our roots are in the past, but our eyes are on the future. A tree without a tap root does not survive, and a tree without new branches, new buds, ceases to grow – and we will share, in order to grow. We will share because we are confident, but not placid. Because this is a land not too long ago claimed from wilderness and Indian. Because this a land not too long ago ravaged by war. Because while we claim the splendor of the old, we welcome the splendor of the new. And so we welcome each other, here tonight. And we welcome Ko-Bee Factory, which will be located in Claymont, Mississippi.

'We welcome *progress*.

'We welcome *friendship !*'

The tables rose. The applause swelled. In the room across the hall, the orchestra began.

Reuben moved quickly across the three tables and stopped directly behind Jean Aucoin.

'Let's take a little walk,' he said.

Aucoin turned, grinned. 'What took you so long ?'

He felt no anger. He felt the sense of an unpleasant errand to be done, felt the presence of his own authority, felt the mild relief of action, as he silently walked Aucoin through the front doors and down the steps of the mansion. He said nothing. Aucoin beside him, he rounded the block and headed for the portion of the alley where the garbage cans had been neatly lined up – a calm, clear image of packing Aucoin, neatly, into one of the cans. Without anger. He stopped there. Aucoin waited. The clouds had parted to reveal a quarter moon. From inside, he could hear the music playing, 'Moon River' again; he could hear the sounds of the servants cleaning up in the kitchen; and he could hear the sound of Aucoin's breathing. He seemed to feel nothing.

'Let's get something straight,' he said. 'I don't give a damn who you fuck – but you don't steal from my clients.'

No smart-ass retort came back. A moment went by. Then, silently, Aucoin dug in his pocket and came up with Rosalie's earring. In his open palm, it gleamed through the semidarkness like a tear. Reuben picked it off, pocketed it. The sense of triumph evaded him.

'What else have you got?'

'A gold cigarette case – I took it from a judge named Thatcher.'

'I'll take that too.'

Aucoin shrugged. The cigarette case emerged from the breast pocket of the rented tux, changed hands.

'What else?' Reuben found himself studying Aucoin's face – dark good looks, an insolent mouth, a clear-eyed intelligence.

'There's a necklace, but I don't have it on me. I dropped it in a potted palm.'

'Which potted palm?'

'The one near the door.'

'Is that it?'

'That's tonight's inventory.'

Another moment passed. 'Moon River' quit. Inside, the orchestra went into 'Mac the Knife.' Reuben told himself to walk away. 'You're a doctor.' he said. 'You're too bright for this. What kind of Russian roulette are you playing with your life?'

'Do you know the only thing anybody ever built in the Louisiana bayou country? A leper colony.' Aucoin smiled. 'But why should you give a damn about that? About cajuns, or rednecks, or niggers. We're out and you're in.'

'Listen – I'm going to give you some advice, free of charge. You stick to your stethoscope or you'll wind up in jail.'

'Don't threaten me,' Aucoin said quietly. 'You didn't bring me here to threaten me, and you didn't come after that earring. And you don't give a damn what I do with my life. You're here because you don't know your wife – and you don't want to lose her – and I know more about Mollie than you do.'

The sound of her name coming out of Aucoin's mouth seemed more obscene than the times he had slept with her. Yet Reuben stood still, said nothing, did nothing, froze, against his will, as Aucoin went on.

'I'll tell you about her,' Aucoin said. 'I'll tell you what she said. She said: *I lie in order to survive.* She said: *I live in pieces.* She said:

For most of my life, I've been legally chattel, physically frigid, spiritually dead, and emotionally strung out. She's starved for truth – that's what I know about her. I fell in love with her and she didn't even know what name to call it.' He stopped, turned around, started to walk off. Then, over his shoulder, he said, 'There's one more thing – '

'Get the hell out of here,' Reuben said, 'before I kill you.'

He took a walk around the block. Then he came back inside, went directly to Mrs Rabin and took a turn with her breasts around the floor. After that, he danced with Caroline, he danced with Luanne, he danced with Rosalie Gorman – stopped, picked her earring off the floor and gave it back. The gold cigarette case he left in the potted palm with the necklace. At eleven thirty-five, he went into the kitchen. He found his mother supervising a lot of food on its way into plastic bags. He told her she had done a good job – kissed her on the cheek, watched her look pleased, surprised, concerned, and weary. On his way out, he wondered if he believed he was going to die.

He found Mollie trying to keep up with the 1930's style of Atlas Aluminum. He cut in and said, 'Let's go.' She didn't argue, she didn't acquiesce, she didn't say anything.

They made their good nights.

At eleven forty-five, a liveried convict brought the white Cadillac to the curb.

He pulled away, offered her a cigarette. She took it, lit it. He lit one for himself. He could feel her waiting. He wished fleetingly that he might say: *I killed the sonofabitch.*

'I have to talk to you,' he said.

'Alright.'

He stopped for the red light on Main, took a left, then turned into the highway. He said, 'We're on our way home. You can see that?'

'Yes.'

He put his cigarette out. The highway lights streaked past. 'The reason I have to take you home first is because they may have somebody following us. It's got to look natural, normal. When we get home, we'll go inside, leave the lights on for ten minutes, then turn them all off – like we've gone to sleep. After that there'll be a car waiting behind the greenhouse to get you out of there. An F.B.I. agent will take you to a safe place until it's over.'

From the corner of his eye, he watched her. She sat still. Only her hand moved as she drew on her cigarette, making a small bright ash in the dark. He turned off the highway onto the Morningside exit. As he went past the Williamsburg, he saw Monk was parked, waiting to be picked up and dropped behind the greenhouse.

'Until what's over?'

'They're going to try to bomb our house tonight.'

He halted at a stop sign, looked directly at her, then went on. Softly she said, '*Dear God.*'

'Barksdale and Simmons have had men staked out since nine. When I pull up in the driveway, if you spot any of them, ignore it. Just go into the house as if there's nothing unusual. Can you do that?'

'Yes.'

He slowed down, came around the corner slowly, giving them time to identify him. Then he pulled up into the driveway, to the top of the hill. He saw no sign of anyone. *Barksdale's a pro. He knows what he's doing. Count on that.*

He moved the Cadillac in beside the station wagon, cut the lights and the motor, then said, 'Let's go.' He walked beside Mollie to the back door, got his key in, got the door open. When he had closed it behind them, he said, 'Turn on the entrance hall light. Then go upstairs. Turn on the bedroom lights. Draw the drapes. Get into some jeans and be ready to go. Can you do that?'

'Yes.'

He echoed Barksdale. 'No problem at all.'

'No problem at all,' she echoed.

He watched her leave, watched the hall chandelier flare up. He lit the kitchen. He needed a drink. He poured himself a glass of milk instead. Then he changed his mind again, laced it with Scotch.

He could hear noises outside, rustling, the muted sound of hoarse whispers.

He finished the milk, poured a second glass, laced that with Scotch, then carried it up the stairs.

In the bedroom, the lights were on, the drapes drawn – she was dressed in a black turtleneck sweater and jeans. He realised he had forgotten to tell her to wear black, as camouflage when they headed for the greenhouse. She had figured it out anyway. 'Drink this,' he said. She obeyed while he changed his own clothes. Then he looked at his watch. It was midnight. 'Five minutes,' he said.

She nodded, set the glass down. He saw she was dry-eyed, reaching for strength, some kind of dignity. Her silence made him uncomfortable. A man needed a woman who came apart under fire so he knew where he was, what he had to do.

'Do you want a cigarette?'

She shook her head. Then she crossed the bedroom and opened her end of the mirrored closet and took something from a shelf. When she turned around, he saw it was a package, wrapped in tissue and tied in needlepoint yarn. 'It was going to be for your birthday.' She made a try at a smile. 'One day's as good as another.'

He took the package. He turned his back to the mirrored doors so he wouldn't have to look at the two of them reflected there. When he got the tissue off, he saw she had taken photographs of the children and had them mounted in a Lucite cube. All the seasons were there. Joe and Phil in swimsuits. Joe in his Little League uniform. Phil in the snow.

'Thank you.'

'It's for your office. I thought – the ones you have – they're a couple of years old.'

'Yes. Thank you.' He looked at his watch again. 'We'd better go.' He set the Lucite cube on the dresser. 'Are you ready?'

'Yes.'

'Do you need a coat?'

'No. It's a heavy sweater.'

'Do you need cigarettes?'

'No. I have some.'

'You go downstairs, turn off the lights down there. Wait in the kitchen. In a minute, I'll turn them off up here. I'll meet you.'

He watched her leave. He waited three minutes. Then he shut off the bedroom lamps and went down the stairs in the darkness. She was waiting in the kitchen, near the back door. When he opened it, she touched his arm.

'Reuben – it's going to be alright, isn't it?'

'I don't know,' he said.

Forty

THE TWO of them moved quickly across the grounds in the darkness. The silhouettes of stationed men became visible. Reuben heard a cough. The rough sound of breathing. Two dozen Holmesdale cops, dressed in black, crack shots. No one spoke.

On schedule, the car waited in the gravel drive behind the greenhouse. Mollie climbed in, white-faced and silent. The car backed away, its headlights off, and vanished into the darkness, the tires making no more noise than a rabbit rustling in the underbush.

She'd be alright. For the next few hours, she'd play gin rummy in the F.B.I. office.

Behind him, a voice said, 'Are you ready?'

He turned. The man was wearing black, too groomed and assured to belong to Simmons – whoever he was, he belonged to Barksdale. 'Yes.'

'Follow me, then.'

Quietly, they moved through the darkness. The moon was masked behind a bank of clouds. The night sounds of wind and cicada went on as if there were no figures in that clump of pines, figures there in the children's play area, figures stationed in the rose garden. At dawn, he had walked this way with Bo Garrison. He had stopped to pull a dead twig from a crabapple; had seen the tulip bulbs were showing first green. The anger had come and gone like ocean waves. In the trunk of his car, two shells were missing from his old hunting rifle, the blasts Monk had fired at Army Jones. He had loaded it with the hope he would not need it, with the fear he could not fire it, with the wish to slaughter. Those feelings, all of them, seemed to have belonged to someone else. He felt only the snow, the immediacy.

'This way,' the agent said.

They began to climb the embankment at the rear of the rose garden. It was the upwards sloping portion of grounds that Attica had left to grow wild with ivy and honeysuckle. At the top of the embankment, the land leveled off again to the spot where Mollie had once talked about building a gazebo with a view of the river, but Monk had pronounced the place too inaccessible for construction. They reached the top. Then the agent pointed. It took him a moment to make it out – in that exact clearing, as if a crane had lowered it from the heavens, a small black sedan was hidden by underbrush.

He found Barksdale inside listening to a voice crackling through the radio equipment. '*The Rawlins brothers have just come out of their father's house. . . . They appear to be arguing. . . . Now they're getting in the car. Floyd is behind the wheel. He's turned on the headlights, but they don't seem to be going anywhere. . . . The argument seems to be continuing. . . . Okay . . . here we go. They're pulling out. . . . We'll get back to you. . . .*'

'Excuse me,' Barksdale said. He switched a knob. 'Did you get that ?'

'*Damned right.*' It was Simmons' voice.

'How's your view of the road ?'

'*Clear as day.*'

'Over and out.' Barksdale turned to Reuben. 'Jones is being tailed too. He left his mother's house a few minutes ago. We'll see where the hell they're all going. Are you alright ?'

'Yes.'

Barksdale handed him a pair of binoculars. Reuben aimed them at the road, turned to daylight by infrared.

'Simmons' command post is over there – on the other side of the road where that ridge rises – '

Reuben aimed the binoculars at the spot, saw nothing.

'We're both tuned to the same radio reports and to ground walkie-talkies,' Barksdale said. 'There's a searchlight system to light up the area, flares in case he takes off through the woods. You remember Floyd's reports – ?'

'Yes.' According to Floyd, Jones planned to use twenty-eight sticks of dynamite with a timing device. Place the bomb in the garage – scheduled to be placed about one thirty, and timed to explode about four thirty a.m. Reuben handed the binoculars back.

'Navy Intelligence flew in a three-man demolition squad this afternoon. They're here, all the equipment – they'll disarm the bomb. I've got a fire truck stationed less than a quarter mile away. They can be here in half a minute.'

The radio crackled. Barksdale threw a switch. A voice came through. '*Car Four. Following Army Jones. Heading south on the highway towards Claymont. Driving light blue Ford sedan, license R41-783, Rose County. No one else in the car. We're keeping him in sight. Any instructions ?*'

'Maintain surveillance,' Barksdale said. He flicked a switch. Into the radio, he said, 'Car One – where are the Rawlinses?'

'*Moving south on the highway. Looks like they're headed for Claymont.*'

'Car Four is following Army Jones, also headed for Claymont, probably headed for rendezvous. Radio Car Four, switch tails. Over and out.' He looked at Reuben. 'Any questions?'

'No.' Reuben reached for a cigarette.

'No cigarettes,' Barksdale said. The radio signaled. Barksdale switched on.

'*Car Four. Jones' light blue sedan pulling off onto dirt road. Have sighted old barn. A number of cars parked in vicinity. Searching for spot to conceal car. One of us will take a look on foot.*'

'No heroics,' Barksdale said. 'Over and out.'

Simmons came in. '*Bastards are havin' a meetin'.*'

Barksdale looked at his watch. 'A short one.'

'*Goddamned sonsofbitches –*' The radio went dead.

Barksdale turned to Reuben. 'I've got a half-dozen agents on the property, but we're going to leave it mainly to Simmons. A local arrest will serve as more of a warning to the rest – and Simmons is the best witness we can have in a local court.'

The radio came in. '*Car One. Rawlins brothers pulling off highway at site of old barn. Am in contact with Car Four. Will switch tails when they come out.*'

'Fine,' Barksdale said. He picked up the binoculars and surveyed the road. 'Take a look at that.'

Reuben aimed the binoculars in the direction Barksdale indicated. He saw a car – in it a couple of teen-agers, necking.

Barksdale turned a knob. 'Chief Simmons – there's a car parked about sixty yards down the road, a couple of kids. Get one of your men on the walkie-talkie and tell him to get rid of them.'

'*Damned right,*' Simmons said.

On the seat, a walkie-talkie beeped. Barksdale picked it up, pushed a button. A voice came in. '*Sergeant Kirk here, Holmesdale police, I've got a deputy named Levitt, post number seven. He's lookin' for Buchman.*'

'Buchman's here – at command post A,' Barksdale said. He shut off the walkie-talkie, picked up the binoculars and fastened them on the road again. 'Simmons has sent one of the squad cars after those kids. We've got four squad cars located in strategic positions, ready to go.' He handed the binoculars to Reuben.

Through the glasses, Reuben saw the squad car approach the lovers, pull alongside. After a moment, the car pulled off. The squad car made a U-turn, headed back to its hiding place.

The size and scope of the operation was staggering.

Reuben fastened the binoculars on his house. It loomed dark and quiet. A couple of squirrels chased each other across the slate roof. The wind rustled the pines. Simmons came on the radio again, cursing.

'The hardest part is the waiting,' Barksdale said.

Reuben held out the binoculars.

'Keep them.' Barksdale opened the glove compartment, brought out a second pair.

Reuben surveyed the road and the grounds again, focused on the men stationed in pairs, threes, some at points he and Bo Garrison had laid out, some at points that hadn't occurred to them.

Then he saw Monk, carrying a shotgun and climbing the embankment of ivy and honeysuckle, on his way up. It didn't take much to read Monk's face: *What the hell are you doing? Are you going to come down here like the rest of us?' Or are you going to sit up there like God?*

'I'm going down.'

'This is for your own protection,' Barksdale said.

Reuben removed his binoculars, saw that Barksdale had his own fastened on Monk. 'It's my house,' Reuben said quietly.

The radio crackled. *'Car Four. Seven cars already at barn. Eighth just arriving. Got license number. Any instructions?'*

'No. Fine,' Barksdale said. The radio fell silent.

Out in the darkness, a branch cracked underfoot. Reuben opened the door, climbed out.

'I'd prefer that you wouldn't,' Barksdale said.

'Sorry.'

Reuben moved out into the darkness, stopped, located Monk with the infrared binoculars, then headed for him.

'Where the hell have you been?' Monk was wearing a badge.

'Let's go,' Reuben said.

Quickly, they moved down the embankment and through the grounds, past several coveys of men.

Then they crossed the pavement of the driveway and ducked into the garage.

Reuben removed the pistol from the glove compartment, then opened the trunk and took out his hunting rifle.

'Tomorrow, goddamnit, you come and get the samovar.' He closed the trunk. 'Where's your post?'

Monk nodded at the row of gardenia bushes that lined the driveway. 'The fourth one up from the street.'

Reuben darted across the driveway, behind Monk, past two men with shotguns stationed behind the woodpile.

Hidden behind one of Attica's prize gardenia bushes, he found a cop in a black shirt wearing a two-gun holster, carrying a shotgun, and holding a talk box.

'Sergeant Kirk,' Monk said.

Reuben shook hands. Kirk handed him a badge. He pinned it on, crouched down beside Monk. He could hear Monk's breathing – short, heavy bursts like a penned bull. The crazy memory that flashed through his mind was twenty-five years old – the fraternity house on Audubon Street in New Orleans, and the theatrical candlelit ceremony that had declared them blood brothers.

Reuben turned around, trained the binoculars back up the embankment, located the position of the hidden car. He couldn't see Barksdale, but he knew Barksdale had glasses trained on him. He turned back to Monk. 'The bastards are holding a meeting in an old barn out on the highway. We've got cars following Jones, the Rawlinses – radioing in.'

'Lay back,' Kirk said.

Monk extracted a flask, began to uncap it.

'No liquor,' Kirk said.

A couple of minutes went by, long and still, except for a light wind in the pines and the sound of the Pearl River lapping at the canebrake a half mile on the other side of the road.

Through the binoculars, Reuben watched a rat scurry around the rim of the wishing well. In the playground area, a swing creaked. A branch rustled against the wrought-iron fence that surrounded the swimming pool.

Twenty minutes crawled by. No one spoke.

Then the talk box crackled. Kirk held it to his ear. 'Kirk, here.' He listened. Tension locked the three of them. In a moment, he laid the box down. 'They're coming off the Morningside exit.'

'Who?'

'Jones and two companions.'

'Bastards,' Monk said, under his breath.

'Chief Simmons' orders – no firing unless he says so.'

Reuben kneeled, parted the bushes, leveled the rifle through the leaves, peered through the gunsight. What he saw was Buster's body in a white velvet casket. He felt his heart lodge, grow heavy, his breathing grow shallow. He reached for the binoculars, ready to train them on the road.

Several minutes went by. He looked at his watch. A little after one. A half hour before Floyd said it was scheduled.

The sound of a motor came into earshot, moved closer.

Reuben tensed. In a moment, a piece of blue rounded the corner under the streetlight.

Reuben felt the cold sweat break.

The car moved slowly towards the driveway, crawling – then moved past the driveway. It revved a burst of speed, and took off.

'What the hell – ?' Monk said.

'Lay back,' Kirk said.

Another moment went by.

Reuben could see Monk's eyes glittering. A shaft of moonlight cut through the clouds, lit the empty driveway, then vanished instantly.

The box crackled. Kirk picked it up.

A whippoorwill, eerie and ghostlike, called down by the river.

Kirk lowered the box. 'Looks like they were just checkin' out the house.'

'Where are they heading?'

'Back to the highway.'

'Shit,' Monk said.

'We'll get 'em,' Kirk said.

Time crawled.

An owl hooted. A jackrabbit hurtled down the driveway.

The clouds thinned out, a dim moonlight appeared.

Kirk's face looked like a paper sack filled with rocks. Reuben realised he was chewing tobacco.

The talk box remained silent.

The moon receded. Reuben looked at his watch. Another twenty minutes had gone by. Kirk spit a stream of tobacco into the woods.

The box acted up – Kirk grabbed it, listened. Then he looked at Reuben. 'It's for you.'

Reuben held the box to his ear. Barksdale's voice came through.

'*The car is headed back in this direction but Jones isn't in it. They just dropped him off at an all-night hamburger place on the other side of Main. My guess is they've set him down where he'll have an alibi. I thought you ought to know.*'

'Double-crossing bastards,' Reuben said.

'*Jones was shot at on Sunday, by person or persons unknown,*' – there was no change in Barksdale's inflection – '*so he knows he's been under some kind of surveillance. It looks like he's decided not to take any more chances for the moment.*'

370

'Who's in the car?'

'Jones left the meeting with two companions. One we haven't been able to identify. The other we don't know anything about.'

'Whoever the hell they are,' Reuben said, 'I want them.'

'At the speed they're traveling, it's about seven minutes to the Morningside exit,' Barksdale said.

The box went dead. Reuben handed it back to Kirk. He looked at Monk. 'Jones isn't coming to the party.'

'Sonofabitch – who the hell is?'

'I don't know.'

'Kluckers,' Kirk said. 'What else do you have to know.' He shoved a wad of tobacco into his jaw and began to chew.

'They're seven minutes from the Morningside exit.'

'We're ready for 'em,' Kirk said.

The owl let loose again. The wind suddenly died down, leaving a graveyard silence behind.

Time crawled.

Kirk spit another streak of tobacco into the darkness. 'Before she married my paw, my mama was a Catholic. When she was a little girl, they burned a cross in front of her house in Hot Coffee, Mississippi. *What they make out of a cross is a sin,* she used to say. I been waitin' all these years to get a crack at them bastards.'

The box signaled. Kirk listened. When he laid it down, he said, 'Chief Simmons says they're turnin' off the Morningside exit.'

Monk crouched, leveled the shotgun through the bushes. Reuben knelt beside him, felt for the pistol in his pocket. Kirk spit out the tobacco, knelt, put one hand on his pistol.

Reuben looked at his watch. It was one thirty-five.

'Chief Simmons' orders – no firin' unless he says so,' Kirk repeated.

The silence stretched out.

Then, through it, came the faraway sound of a car.

Reuben looked through the gunsight of the hunting rifle. The photographs from the Lucite cube flashed in front of him. Joe in his Little League uniform. Phil sliding down the hill on a cookie sheet in the snow.

A long protracted moment crawled by.

The sound of the car moved closer. Then the car came into view, under the streetlight, cornering slowly, a blob of blue.

It moved into the darkness, became a silhouette, slowed, then stopped at the bottom of the driveway.

Nothing happened. The car sat there. Reuben felt his heart cease to beat.

Finally, the car door swung open.

A man emerged, closed the car door gently. Then he stood beside the car, looking up and down the street, and up at the windows of the house.

Reuben reached for the binoculars, trained them on the man. The man was tall, thin, jug-eared, something familiar about him. He heard Doan Newberry: *Tall, skinny sonofabitch. A lot of curly hair and funny eyes. Women follow him around like flies after a garbage truck.* The description matched one of the photographs in the F.B.I. file Barksdale had turned over. The photograph was a match for the face of the man at the bottom of the driveway: *Gerald Gunston III.* Portions of the psychiatric report ran through his mind. *Paranoid condition . . . grandiosity . . . markedly disturbed.*

Gunston turned around. A package was handed to him through the window by a passenger in the car. A good-sized box. About the size of twenty-eight sticks of dynamite and a timing device.

Reuben laid the binoculars down, aimed the rifle through the bushes, peered at Gunston through the sight.

Gunston began to walk gingerly towards the entrance to the driveway.

'He's carrying a gun,' Kirk whispered.

Reuben felt plunged into an ice bath.

Gunston took another few cautious steps, began to move slowly up the driveway, one eye on the upstairs windows.

The silence rang. Reuben felt his skin stretch taut, his hands grow clammy.

Gunston stopped, looked around, then began to move again. Eighteen gardenia bushes lined the driveway. Gunston moved past the first one, cautiously. Then he quickened his step slightly, moved past the second one, light as a cat. Then he began to stride, in earnest, past the third one.

Through the megaphone, Simmons' voice shouted, *'Halt !'*

Gunston whirled – not six yards away.

Reuben heard the sound of gunfire, saw two brief flashes of light.

Monk cursed, wildly, grabbed his shoulder. 'Sonofabitch – !' Blood oozed from Monk's upper arm. Kirk opened fire. From another direction, a pistol and a shotgun went off.

'*You sonofabitch !*' Reuben fired the rifle – it clicked, nothing happened. He threw it to the ground, then leapt from the bushes, the pistol leveled. He fired directly at Gunston. Gunston spun, dropped the package. A hail of gunfire went off in the glare of daylight as the searchlights came on. Reuben ran towards Gunston. Wounded, bleeding, Gunston took off – agile as an acrobat, darting like a crazy jagged streak of lightning as bullets flew all around him. Reuben fired once more, running. Somebody shouted, '*Get out of the line of fire!*'

He kept going. The sonofabitch kept running, somehow, heading for the car – Reuben not ten feet behind him. Then a figure leaned over to open the car door. Reuben stopped, fired three times. Gunston shouted. The figure slumped over, dropped to the seat, then rolled to the ground, face down.

Reuben stopped. Bathed in cold sweat.

Another hail of gunfire riddled the car. Gunston climbed in. Guns blasted. The bullet-riddled car sped off, leaving the body of his companion behind.

Reuben stared at it. Through glazed eyes he saw what it was, believed he was mistaken, saw there was no mistake. A woman.

Two squad cars came from nowhere, took off after Gunston's car.

Ice made its way down Reuben's spine.

Slowly, numbed, he began to walk the ten feet to the bottom of the driveway. Behind him, he heard someone shout, 'Don't touch it!' He stopped, looked back. He realised they were talking about the bomb.

He began to walk again. When he reached the bottom of the driveway, he saw the woman was lying in a pool of blood. She was wearing a white pleated skirt, a navy-blue sweater, high-heeled pumps. Kirk was standing over her. Several policemen had gathered. Kirk stopped, turned her over. 'She's dead.'

Reuben stared at the woman.

She had a rosy face shaped like a honeydew melon. Her breasts thrust from the navy-blue sweater.

He insists he's black.

'Anybody know who she is?' Kirk said.

Hold out your hands, Phil.

He knew who it was, believed he was mistaken, saw there was no mistake.

Jacqueline Carruthers. Phil's schoolteacher.

He turned away. Slowly, he walked across the road. Slowly, he moved through the trees, his heels crunching on the gravel path which led to the river. The clouds parted. Moonlight filtered down through the pines. After a long time, he reached the sand bar, white as snow in the moonlight. He fell to his knees, bent over the bank, and retched into the Pearl.

Forty-one

THE TWO AGENTS played gin rummy.

The one who had brought her here kept winning. Both of them as mute as the photographs of J. Edgar Hoover and Lyndon B. Johnson on the south wall of the sparsely furnished office. Nothing to distract her eye. Her ears tuned to the slap of the cards, and the whirring of an electric wall clock. Mollie paced, halted, sat, smoked, paced again, felt an eternity crawl by filled with fear, and waiting, and godless prayers. She battled chaos, and suffocation, and violent pangs in her abdomen.

Finally, at nearly four a.m., Barksdale appeared and said quietly, 'It's alright, Mrs Buchman.'

'What happened?'

'There was a gun battle. Of course, we hoped there wouldn't be. However, law and order has been established. Your house is safe. Mr Levitt was slightly wounded – in the shoulder. It's been attended to. He's at home now.'

'Reuben – ? What about Reuben?' She saw a flick of something light Barksdale's eyes – anxiety, anger – she couldn't read it.

'I assure you he's alright,' Barksdale said. 'He's gone through an extreme set of circumstances with a high degree of courage. But he's not a trained police officer. Events may have been upsetting to him. One of my men saw him getting into his car. One of Simmons' men saw him head for the highway. I've dispatched several men to look for him.' Barksdale tried a reassuring smile. Mollie felt it was feigned. 'He's driving that white Cadillac – he can't be too hard to find.'

She had an image of the white Cadillac streaking through the darkness. She had an image of Klan shotguns, somewhere, lying in wait. 'He's in danger, isn't he?'

'I don't think so. No one knows he's gone except us, my men, Simmons' men, and Mr Levitt and Mr Woods, because I checked with them. He's an intelligent man. He's had an emotional reaction, but I don't believe he'd do anything stupid.' Barksdale paused. Mollie felt him waiting for her to confirm his statement. An invisible question mark at the end of it.

'I don't know.' She was close to tears.

'Please don't worry,' Barksdale said. It rang hollow. 'However – for the sake of caution – don't do too much calling around. If you hear from him, let me know. I'll do the same. I'm sure my men will locate him in a very short while.'

She had an image of F.B.I. men fanning out, searching for Reuben.

'You'd better go home, get some sleep. Chief Simmons has left two patrolmen on the grounds – you'll be safe. A story has been released to the press, but we've declared you unavailable for questioning. If you need anything, feel free to call on me.'

'Thank you.'

Barksdale turned to one of the agents. 'Take her home.'

The Cadillac was gone from the garage.

There was a patrolman stationed in front, another in back.

The agent took her inside, waited like a sentry while she turned on some lights, then left.

She put on a pot of coffee.

Then she went upstairs and checked the bedroom. Everything was as they had left it. The Lucite cube with the children's photographs on the dresser. She picked it up, set it down again.

She opened Reuben's closet. His luggage was there. No clothes were missing.

She went down the hall to the guest room. Nothing had been touched since Leila had cleaned the room this morning.

An explosion went off in her head, bright and dark, like fireworks spiraling over water.

She went back to the bedroom, switched off the light, crossed to the window and pulled the drapes open. Then she parted the eyelet curtains and raised the window. A rush of cold damp air blew against her face. *He's an intelligent man. He's had an emotional reaction, but I don't believe he'd do anything stupid.*

I don't know.

Pale moonlight lit the grounds. She could see the silhouette of the patrolman. She could see the debris, broken branches, trampled rose bushes, barren patches of earth, as if a small war had taken place.

She heard a hoarse voice, her own, call, 'Reuben – '

She went into the bathroom, washed her face.

An absurd series of thoughts assailed her reflection. What about the black wallpaper? Men didn't like daisies. Which men? Reuben. Did he like the wallpaper? What about the yellow carpet? Had she ever asked him? What had he defended, out there, tonight? Eyelet curtains. Grace and grandeur. But *they* hadn't destroyed it. Wherever he was, tonight, he was also running from her. Because he and she had needed no one to destroy it. They had done it themselves.

She saw she was crying. She washed her face.

She closed her eyes. She tried to see him – out there, tonight – where he had been, where he was now. His image wouldn't clarify. She saw only the shape of the man who had sheltered her to the point where she had felt herself a changeling, never having been born to anything nor ever chosen anything, dominated by a foolish wish for self-containment. She had never seen him – only herself. Terror gripped her. Remorse followed. Shame broke, without tears.

She went downstairs.

The kitchen clock said a quarter to five. She poured a cup of coffee, carried it to the kitchen table, lit a cigarette, tried to decipher the Reuben she had never seen.

A man.

The fear came up, laid itself out.

Fear of men. Fear of the world which was run by men. Fear. Fear of the monsters who had the power of violence or benevolence, punishment or protection. The adaptation came up, laid itself out. A woman seduced, pacified, lied to, tended to – a monster of her own. If she was clever enough, he didn't turn on her and he protected her from the others.

The bond with Leila – there it was.

I'm sorry, Reuben.

Human warmth was found elsewhere, in the outlaws, in the men who lived outside the immediate power structure she had been taught to perceive as the world. Men like Burke Donovan. Jean Aucoin.

I'm sorry, Reuben.

Who was he, then – the Reuben who had sat at this table, across from her, invisible to her biased, frightened eye?

Where was he?

What had happened to him tonight?

She went upstairs, got her car keys.

As she backed the station wagon down the driveway, the headlights illuminated two broken gardenia bushes, several bullet holes in the trunk of a pine.

She pulled up in Monk's driveway. Through the trees a light gleamed from the kitchen, at the rear of the modern structure made out of concrete angles and big panes of glass. The walk was made out of multicolored pebbles set in concrete. The double doors were two stories high. She rang the bell, heard it echo through the house. In a moment, Monk came to the door, wearing a sling. He said, 'Jesus Christ. Come on in.'

She followed him back to the kitchen – chrome, Lucite, black and white plastic. Sheila, wearing tousled blond curls and a pink negligee, was taking a steak from the charcoal broiler. She looked up, ran across the kitchen and hung onto Mollie, weeping. A portion of Mollie's mind took note of the fact that men were bound by common battles, women by common tears.

'Cut it out, Sheila,' Monk said. 'It's over. It's all okay.' He took a seat at a chrome and glass table and finished off what was left of a drink, awkwardly, holding the glass in his left hand.

Sheila went back to the steak, set the plate down in front of Monk, sat down beside him, and began to cut the meat.

'Have you heard from Reuben ?' Mollie said.

'No.' Monk frowned. 'But I'm telling you – there's nothing to worry about – he's one helluva guy.' The anxiety of Monk's face made his words a lie.

'What happened tonight ?'

'It's all going to be on the seven a.m. news.'

'Please.'

'Hell,' Monk said. 'I'm only doing what I was told. I can't do nothing but confirm what comes out on the news.' He looked at Sheila. 'Tell her. Did I tell you any different ?'

'No.' Sheila forked a piece of steak into Monk's mouth.

'How about a glass of milk, baby.' Monk chewed.

'Please,' Mollie said. 'What happened to Reuben ?'

'You've got one helluva husband,' Monk said. Sheila came back with a glass of milk and tried to hold it to Monk's lips. 'Goddamnit, I can do that myself.' Monk drained the glass. Sheila dabbed at his mouth with a napkin.

'Is he alright ?' Mollie said. 'You know how unpredictable he is. Please. I've got to know what happened.'

'Why the hell don't you sit down ? You want a drink ? You want a glass of milk ? Hell – we'll put you up. Goddamnit – Reuben's a hero. A man like Reuben, you know how it is. It could be another plan. Something secret – you get what I mean ?' Monk was a bad liar. 'What the hell are you worrying about ? He can take care of himself. You want a glass of milk ?'

'No thank you.'

'Jesus Christ,' Monk said, ' – what do you need ? Just tell us what you need. What the hell are friends for ?'

The sun was coming up when she pulled into the garage.

The Cadillac was still gone.

She walked the grounds, looking at the rubble, trying to imagine how it had been, trying to reconstruct what might have happened.

She went inside. She had another cup of coffee, several cigarettes. She tried to decipher Barksdale's anxiety, Monk's anxiety. She imagined Reuben drunk somewhere. She imagined Reuben in an auto accident somewhere. None of it came clear.

A few minutes before seven, she turned on the television set in the children's playroom. She sat in the old rocker that had been relegated there, with the Ping-Pong table, and the tumbling mat, and the toy bins, and the ballet bar she had once put up for herself and never used.

She had rocked Joe in the rocking chair. Phil. Both of them, too old now for rocking.

The farm news was ending.

A commentary on the produce market and the price of eggs. Followed by a commercial for a fattening chemical to be added to hogfeed. A farmer in overalls, a straw hat, said: '*It does everything, friends, except produce three hams to a hindquarter.*' A hog answered: '*We're working on that.*'

The seven a.m. news came on.

'*Early this morning, a bombing attempt was thwarted by the diligence of local police in the Morningside area of Holmesdale. Chief Otis Simmons of the Holmesdale Police Department, who has been staking out possible targets in the area since recent bombings, told reporters that his precautions had paid off.*

'*According to Simmons, the residence of prominent attorney Reuben Buchman, among others, had been patrolled for nearly a week. Last night, about midnight, a patrolman reported a light blue sedan circling the area. Simmons quickly dispatched several men. Later, about one thirty a.m., the sedan pulled up to the driveway, and a man – later identified as Gerald Gunston III of Claymont, Mississippi – got out and began to walk towards the house. According to Simmons, Gunston carried a pistol, and a package – later identified as a bomb made of twenty-nine sticks of dynamite and a timing device.*

'*Simmons shouted the order to "Halt" – but instead of obeying, Gunston shot twice, wounding deputised civilian Milton Levitt of Holmesdale. Officers opened fire from an embankment thirty-five or forty feet away. Gunston dropped the dynamite and fled. Hit and badly wounded, Gunston managed to get back to his car, as officers continued to fire. A woman companion leaned over to open the door for Gunston, and was killed when a bullet struck her spine. The woman has been identified as Jacqueline Carruthers, schoolteacher at Morningside Grammar School.'*

Mollie was stunned, as if someone had staggered her with a blow. The shock robbed her of breath. A photograph of Jacqueline Carruthers was superimposed over the announcer's continuing voice.

'Gunston then sped off in his car, chased by patrolmen, but crashed less than a mile away on Morningside Drive. According to police, Gunston jumped from his car and opened fire with a machine gun, hitting officer Mike Harper in the lung, and seriously wounding a bystander who stepped out on a porch of a nearby house. Gunston then ran behind a house where he tried to climb a fence, hit an electrically charged top stand, and dived into a clump of bushes. Officers opened up at close range with shotguns, and finally dragged Gunston into the yard where a crowd of neighbors had gathered.

'Gunston is now under police guard at Holmesdale Hospital, reportedly in serious condition.

'Funeral arrangements for Jacqueline Carruthers will be made in her home town of Inland, Mississippi.

'Gunston has been identified by the F.B.I. as a member of the White Knights of the Ku Klux Klan.

'Officer Mike Harper has been flown to Memphis, Tennessee, where he will undergo lung surgery.

'Tom Barksdale, chief of the Federal Bureau of Investigation in Holmesdale, told reporters: "The one man who took a strong stand against the Klan, and refused to be intimidated, is the man to whom support and respect is due. The credit goes to Chief Otis Simmons."

'Chief Simmons told reporters: "I hope we showed the whole country that not all people in Mississippi are rednecks, and not all police officers are Klansmen. I hope these people right here send cards and letters to Mike Harper, and realise what kind of police force they've got, and that you can't do anything without leadership." '

The broadcaster's voice carried the rest of the news. She heard Barksdale's voice: *Events may have been upsetting to him.* Phil's teacher – dead. She heard Monk's voice: *Reuben's a hero.* The pieces refused to come together, yet she felt it as something terrible. Then the set moved back into her consciousness, and the weatherman was on, and she realised the phone was ringing.

She ran back to the kitchen, grabbed at it.

Justin's voice said, 'Have you heard from him?'

A wave of dizziness engulfed her. 'No.'

'Do you want me to come there? Do you want me to send Caroline?'

'No. Thank you.' The absence of Justin's usual reticence frightened her.

'Listen –' Justin hesitated. 'He's a complex man. But I know him. He's like – my brother. He's alright. I know he's alright. I want you to believe that.'

'Yes.' Anxiety engulfed her.

'Whatever you need – don't hesitate – you call me?'

'Yes.'

She hung up, closed her eyes, willed a small degree of calm. Then she called Zoe in New Orleans. The facts came out jagged. She asked Zoe to keep the boys away from the television. 'One of them was Phil's teacher – she was killed.' Hysteria threatened, abated. She asked for Zack's phone number.

She woke Zack – asked for Reuben. Her heart had quit beating.

'Hell no, he's not here. It's the middle of the night.'

'Please, Zack – I know Reuben's there. Please.' She felt Zack was lying, knew he would lie for Reuben, hoped he was lying. Then she heard a girl's low giggle in the background, like the sound of running water. She felt her knees buckle.

'He's not here,' Zack said. 'I swear on my mother's *mogen-david*.' Something made Mollie turn. She saw Frieda had come in, had been standing in the kitchen, the blood drained from her face. In her ear, Zack said, 'Mollie – ?'

She hung up.

She looked at Frieda. 'It's alright.' Her voice was like paste.

'I saw the television.' Frieda made a dull, heavy motion of despair.

'It's alright.'

'Nobody told me. Why did nobody tell me? Why didn't you tell me?'

'I didn't know.'

'What kind of a wife are you? What kind of a wife doesn't keep an eye on her husband? What kind of wife has things better to do?' Frieda bit her lip, made an effort to control her anger, then sank into a chair. 'Where is he now? Reuben?' Her fingers moved over her cheeks, trembling.

'I don't know.' Mollie saw Frieda's face was frayed by tension. 'Do you? Have you heard from him?'

Frieda shook her head. 'My son. Your husband. You live long enough, things become the same, over and over. You don't know

380

what I'm talking about ? What are you doing with your life that
you don't know what your husband is doing ?'

'Please – '

'I want you for Reuben. You know that. I've always wanted
you for Reuben. I never told you what to do. I never said – make
him come to you for advice. I never said – learn him. I never said –
what do you do with your time ? I never said. Did I ? Ever ?'

'No.'

Frieda opened her purse, pulled out a handkerchief, dabbed at
her eyes. 'Some women are made to be swallowed up,' she said.
'They want it. They like it. But if a woman is born a *person* – ' She
halted, shook her head again. 'I grew up in the North. But I've
lived down here a long time. Forty years. I came to visit when I
was a girl. I thought they were all barbarians. When I went back
to New York, Jesse came after me. He sat on my doorstep. Ten
days. I was engaged to someone else. A German Jew. Jesse
wouldn't take no. He was wild then. I was a girl. We married. I
know this place. This thing – last night, with a gun – you don't
know what it means. Once a man gets into that, he's lost. An
arrogant bum. My Reuben – I tried to teach him. Not for you, I
said. When he was thirteen, he wanted a shotgun. No, I said.
Jesse taught him anyway, to hunt, without a shotgun. Last night –
a gun. Today – where ? What ? Maybe a woman. He's a *man*,
isn't he ? Like Jesse used to be. Like Joe. They were all like him,
the Litvak, the old man. All of them, the same. They elected him
mayor. People thought he was so great. He was a monster. He was
crude. He ate like an animal. He had black women – ' Frieda blew
her nose, began to weep.

'I'll make you some tea,' Mollie said quietly.

'No. No tea. I'm telling you my life. You have to know – for
Reuben. You don't know Reuben. What's in him. The same that
was in Jesse. Like the old man. When I came down here, I saw
what he was, Joe. I knew I couldn't be like her – Sarah. Joe did
whatever he wanted to do, ran everybody, everything. She never
said a word. I was the outsider – I wouldn't be run, I wouldn't be
blind. I saw Joe had mistresses – white, black, everything. I saw
he had raised Jesse wild – a drinker, a gambler, everything, like
him. All the brothers – they rode the fields together, fought,
hunted, ate at Sarah's table, like Jesse never even had a wife. I
knew when I was pregnant with Reuben I'd have to get Jesse
away from those ways, the hunting and the cotton and the drinking
and the women. So I learned Jesse's need. I learned him – his
weaknesses, his fears, his strengths. I was always one step ahead

of him, without his feeling it. When the old man died, I knew if Jesse got the land, the old ways would stay set in him. The brothers fought. I told Jesse we didn't need that land – we'd make it on our own. We did. There were people who said he became less of a man, but he didn't. He ran the best store in the county. It was the only way – the only way – to have a man who's dedicated to his home, his family.' Frieda's tears began to flow. Her shoulders trembled. She buried her face in her hands. 'But then he died on me, a young man. And I don't know if I did right. I'm a lonely woman. *What does a woman do?*'

'I don't know,' Mollie said.

Forty-two

REUBEN pulled the Cadillac off the edge of the road, cut the headlights, opened the glove compartment, reached for the pistol, then waited in the predawn darkness for the car that had remained a steady distance behind for the last ten minutes.

The headlights came up, lit the road, went past.

Trembling, he consumed a cigarette, taking deep draughts until his lungs burned acrid, waiting to see if the car would return.

It didn't. No cars passed. He dropped the pistol in the pocket of his jacket.

A dry, light feeling of nothingness assailed him.

He switched on the headlights, moved back onto the road, drove a few miles, then pulled off onto the shoulder again. He waited a moment. The road remained dark. Then he got out of the car and crossed the gravel, and went through the broken place in the fence.

He stood there, accustoming his eyes to the darkness, finding the shape of the land newly furrowed, the cotton just planted, barely able to make out the rows in the darkness, though he knew each by heart, by instinct.

He heard a sound. Something moved. A rat as long as his forearm scurried across his foot. He grabbed for the gun and fired at the ground. The shot echoed across the fields. The rat sprinted off. His hand was shaking.

He threw the gun – off, into the darkness – heard it fall.

Then he began to walk, moving across the furrows. The earth was soft and malleable and damp. He stopped, dug his hands in it, rose, began to walk again.

After a while, the first gray threads of dawn broke the sky.

He continued to walk, pressing the soles of his feet against the land that had once been his grandfather's, the land that should have been his father's, the land that might have been his. The dampness chilled him. He found he was still trembling.

Then he heard Willie say: *I killed a man once. A Cree. Back then, you weren't a man 'til you killed.*

A jackrabbit hurled itself across the furrows, leaping, sailing, until it vanished into the woods.

A shudder of revulsion passed through him.

He looked up. The sky was beginning to turn to dawn. The wind was blowing across the field, the smell of wet pine and living earth.

He realised his face was wet with tears.

He looked down. The pistol was lying there.

On the road, a pickup truck rumbled by.

He stopped, picked up the pistol. He went back to the road, looked up and down, climbed into the Cadillac, shut the gun back in the glove compartment.

He began to drive again, throwing glances in the rear-view mirror. The road behind remained empty. The road ahead was straight as a carpenter's rule, the rich black land laid out on either side of the horizon.

A couple of tenant shacks passed, a ribbon of smoke curling from a chimney.

He heard Justin say: *The code of the South is no different from the Old Testament code – an eye for an eye, a tooth for a tooth, the settlement of justice, with honor, personal honor.*

A billboard testified to the virtues of Pine Oil room deodorant.

Another wave of nausea swept him.

When he reached the outskirts of Maryville, the morning light and shadow were just beginning to slant across the rooftops of small, neat houses. He drove past a hound dog sniffing and stirring in the dirt. A squirrel raced along a telephone wire. A mockingbird shrieked.

The Square had the look of a ghost town, emptied of people, his engine echoing in the silent new-dawn street, and the pigeons not yet gathered on the statue of the Confederate soldier.

He stopped. The City Hall doors were locked – the portrait of

383

the old man, next to Bilbo, available by the mechanics of time, not the anxieties of men. An old Dodge coupe came around the corner, slowed. He felt his brow break with cold sweat. He reached for the glove compartment. The car moved on.

He left the Square behind.

His tires rumbled across the wooden bridge that spanned a creek – dry as a bone in summer, but water trickling now, unhurried. He slowed. Felt himself – once – barefoot in the stream, the icy water bitter against his ankles.

On the corner, the old cotton warehouse crumbled, the painted letters that had once read BUCHMAN barely legible.

He turned into the dirt street which ran to a dead end at the porch of his grandfather's house. The Cadillac bumped past the shacks which leaned on one another, on themselves, tilting porches, broken windows, peeling tar paper, the smell of frying hog fat, a handful of chickens pecking around in the dirt. He heard someone shout, 'You'd better get on with it, boy!' An old black man hurried from a house, chased a squawking chicken alongside the car, caught it, skillfully wrung its neck.

He parked in front.

He looked back. A gust of wind blew dirt and leaves along the empty street. From somewhere, a child cried.

Then he heard the rocker creaking, heard the sound of slipper soles slapping against the floor of the porch. He closed his eyes. He saw his grandmother in the rocking chair, saw the harsh barren bones exposed in her face, saw the sharp old eyes blaze to life, heard her say: *You're just like him. Just like Joe.*

Then he heard Willie say: *Like an initiation. Killin' a man.*

His mouth turned bitter, the taste of copper. He fended the nausea.

He opened his eyes. He pulled the glove compartment open, reached for the pistol. It was caught.

He pulled. The pistol emerged, caught in the string of a brown paper package. He loosened the gun, shoved it in his pocket. Then he picked up the package, saw what it was.

He cut the string with a penknife, tore the brown wrapping, stared at the journal. Inside the cover were a few sheets of paper, neatly typed. The wind caught them, scattered them onto the seat.

He picked one up, read:

When the Czar rode through the village on his white horse, Gimpel the Water Carrier refused to remove his cap. Gimpel's eye was taken out with a silver spoon.

I was five years old. Why do I, now, remember one-eyed Gimpel the Water Carrier?

The rain pours and lightning and thunder crack and the Mississippi hurls itself against the levee. The cottonseed is washed away. Reb and Jesse and Itz and Nate aim rifles at the Arkansas levee to keep them from dynamiting to relieve their pressure. I lie with chills and fever. God comes, sometimes wearing the face of Abraham Lincoln, and sometimes the face of Alexander the Third.

I write this for myself, I, Joe Buchman, in the sixtieth year of my life, March, 1927.

Gimpel defied the Czar and lost his right eye. My papa, Yitschok, defied God, and lost his right hand. God and the Czar are the same.

Reuben gathered the rest of the papers, laid them inside the journal, stuffed it into his pocket with the pistol.

A chill grabbed him. He felt disoriented by the meaningless ramblings of malaria. He felt no knowledge of the old man, his grandfather, who had penned those Yiddish sentences, translated by another old man, Monk's father, in the French Quarter of New Orleans. Then he heard Willie say: *Your grandpaw ... he had that Old Testament strength. ...*

He looked at the house.

The old man had bought the house from a Confederate colonel. The house, and the slave quarters with it, had stood steadfast through the Civil War, through the ravages of Reconstruction, through the failures of the depression, through the death of the old man and the loss of the land. It stood. Scarred and weatherbeaten. It stood.

It was his.

He got out of the car and moved up the walk, dirt and weedgrown.

No light dappled the porch. The cables of overgrown fig trees wound around the rusted screen.

Then he heard the rocker groan and creak again, heard the slipper soles hit the porch floor. He climbed the steps, peering into the gloom, able to make out the shape of a woman, too solid for an apparition, and softly singing. She stopped.

'Who's there?' she said.

He pulled the screen door open, stepped onto the porch.

She was in his grandmother's rocking chair, a black ageless face that had seen at least half a century, a rag-tied head, a clean cotton dress, a man's sweater over it, rosy lisle stockings rolled low on her ankles, and the pair of men's slippers slapping against the floor. She said, 'I see it's you. It's good you come.'

'Where's Mr Willie?'

'Mr Willie – he's sleepin',' she said, in that way of answering as ambiguously as possible.

'What are you doing here? Who are you?'

'Mr Willie – he come down the street and he hollered at me – *Sister, you come here !* Then he fell out. Ain't my name – Sister – but I been Sister for ten days now. I'm Callie's oldest girl. She worked for your grandmaw. You remember?'

'What's wrong with Willie?'

'He's bad off.' She started to rock again. 'He ain't worked none since nearly two weeks, since the day they done buried Miss 'lena. Ain't eatin' much, ain't sleepin' much, ain't breathin' too good neither.'

'Why the hell didn't somebody call a doctor?'

'I did that. Called into town on Mr Willie's telephone. Doctor come out, one time, said he was bad off. Said he wouldn't come back without gettin' paid. Mr Willie – he ain't got no money. He said, *Sister, this house got to stay like it always was.* Said – *Sister, you keep it shined up, you tend me – I can't pay you nothin' but you can take anythin' I don't miss.* Said if he didn't miss it, nobody else would neither. Every day I been here, I cleans, I tends to him, then I takes somethin'. I get him up, walk him around – if he can't tell what's gone, I don't need to bring it back. I'm tellin' you so you don't think I been takin' nothin' ain't rightfully mine.' She gestured at the corner of the porch.

He saw an old quilt draped over something, tall and narrow. He crossed the porch, lifted the quilt, looked into a standing cracked mirror framed by acorn carving. The old man looked back at him, distorted. He could see the rocking chair reflected, the back of the head kerchief, and the big dark hands holding on to the wooden arms. The image of the old man broke, became his own, distorted. He felt his skin prickle. Then the anger cracked into luminescent shards, like the looking glass. He dropped the quilt over it. He came back across the porch and stopped in front of her, loomed down over her, feeling a mindless fury. Through clenched teeth, he said, 'You get yourself out of that rockin' chair, Sister –'

She stopped rocking, sent him a stubborn, bewildered gaze. 'Ain't nothin' to tend to 'til he wakes up. I set him a glass and a spoon in there. When he wakes up, he raps the glass – I fix him some breakfast. I –'

386

'You get yourself out of that rockin' chair, and you get yourself down the street, and you get *every damned thing you carried out of this house*. You get it and you bring it back here – every damned thing. Whatever he owes you, I'll pay you. You don't take nothin' from this house – *you bring it all back*. You hear me?'

She shook her head, slowly, not taking her eyes off of him. 'I ain't got it all,' she said. 'I done sold some. I done give some away. I ain't – '

'You buy it back, you get it back, you steal it back – I don't care how you get it.' Reuben plunged his hand into his pocket, pulled out a roll of bills, peeled off a twenty. 'You hear me? I don't care how – every piece. You bring it back here. *Every piece.*'

She stood up. Her eyes turned opaque. She took the twenty-dollar bill. She crossed the porch and opened the screen door, then she stopped. 'What about Mr Willie?'

'*Goddamn Mr Willie.*'

He watched something cross her face, pity, masking contempt, becoming obstinate pride, a refusal to be diminished. 'You ain't nothin' like him,' she said. 'I remember your grandpaw. You ain't nothin' like him.'

The screen door closed behind her. He heard her slippers clap down the steps, scuff across the dirt. From somewhere, a baby cried again. A dog howled. The wind caught the rocking chair, flapping it back and forth.

He crossed the porch. He removed the quilt, dropped it, stared at his image in the cracked glass.

The taste of copper returned, bitter, filling his craw.

He grasped the mirror, lifted it, found it heavier than he expected. He carried it inside. The center hall was dark. He set the mirror at the foot of the stairs, trying to recall where it belonged. He looked up the stairs, nothing of the upstairs used since his grandmother died. Willie and Elena had moved downstairs, the door directly opposite. He turned, crossed the hall, cracked the door, looked in. The dank smell of illness pinched his nostrils. He could make out the shape of Willie, under the quilt, could hear the harsh labored sound of uneven breathing.

He closed the door. It came to him. He remembered the acorn-carved bed in his grandmother's bedroom. Both arms wrapped around the mirror, he carried it up the stairs. The hall was dark, musty, a strip of worn patterned carpet, peeling wallpaper, a parade of doors – the bedrooms once occupied by his father, his father's brothers, Elena, as children. The floor creaked beneath him. He moved awkwardly down the hall, set the mirror down outside his grandfather's door. Then slowly, he pushed it open.

He geared himself for the sight of dust, cobwebs, for the smell of years of disuse.

The room gleamed.

Sister's hand had turned it spotless. Through long, narrow, curtainless windows, light streaked through trees, slanting across squat sturdy pieces of newly polished furniture, across broad planks of newly waxed floor. Light particles danced as the wind blew in, smelling of spring, ruffling the edges of the patchwork quilt on the massive four-poster.

Something cracked in his chest, like a bone breaking.

He lugged the mirror in, set it down in the corner, in the place he remembered it – remembered his grandmother standing in front of it, wearing stiff starched black, dressing to go to Greenborough, for his confirmation. *Are you ready, grandma?* He heard Sarah say: *Come here, boy.* He had stood in front of the mirror. She had draped his grandfather's tallis around his neck. Later, his mother had removed it. *Reform Jews don't wear a tallis, Reuben.*

He stood still. He could hear the staccato rapping of a woodpecker directly outside. The faint sound of a woman's angry voice, chastising a child. The street beginning to come alive, morning.

Then a measured silence engulfed him. His body felt suddenly bruised, encompassed by small pains – bleak, as if his ribs had been broken, and and had detached himself, and what he felt was the fore-shadowing of a pain to come.

Slowly, he moved to the bed, sat on the edge of it. Something jutted against his hip. He removed the pistol, stared at it, then laid it on the marble-topped table. Then he removed the journal, the typed sheaf of papers, laid them beside the pistol. Then he lay down.

He stared at the ceiling.

He wept.

Forty-three

Did you think I would not know it was *You?* – again? You come here wearing Lincoln's face. I don't give a damn for Lincoln's face. I never set out to be a savior for anybody. I – Joe Buchman – chose this place. Against *Your* will. I am in Egypt. It is mine.

You make the river rise.

The rains and blizzards of thirty-one states flow through the Mississippi to the sea. I know *Your* tricks. The malaria. And on the streets, not even on Sundays, the Baptists gather to carry on about predestination – those who believe on the day a man is born, it is all written out, beginning, middle, and end.

For myself, I, Joe Buchman, believe in my own indestructibility.

I copy it down. On the day of my birth, the scribe has written:

East of Petrograd, and east of Moscow, and east of Kiev, close to the banks of the River Bug which winds in from Poland through the Ukraine to the Black Sea – Josef Buchman is born. First child, male child, of Yitschok, the red-bearded giant, wagon driver, bootlegger, Litvak from Minsk – himself son of a Lithuanian maker of corn whiskey who died in the Polish uprising.

Snow falls onto narrow streets, fills the stalls of the marketplace, covers the rooftops of the small Ukrainian village in the Pale of the Settlement. In the countryside, a peasant beds down on a dirt floor, with goats and cows and children, mumbling a prayer of gratitude for the debt of government bonds he cannot pay off in a lifetime, communal rights to his small plot of land; grateful because emancipation has brought him one thing more than his right to starve: He is better than a Jew.

In the house of Yitschok, the curtains are drawn and the shutters are bolted to keep out the temperature which has dropped below zero, and to keep out the moonlight with its dangers of spirits, and to keep out the menace of Lilith, first wife of Adam, who brings harm to new-born children.

All through the sixth night, following his birth, a minyan of ten bearded men, wearing caftans and skullcaps and unclipped earlocks, surround the bed of mother and child, and pray for their protection from the Evil Eye.

On the following morning, the guests gather. Mazeltov, Nicholas the Tyrant has been dead for fifteen years. Gezundt. Alexander II has lifted the military restrictions on children. A good time to be born, the best of times. God is on his way to forgiving. Have not the revolutionaries in Petrograd subsided? Who can recall the last retaliatory pogrom?

The infant, Josef, is taken from his mother's feather bed, and placed in the arms of the sandak who occupies the chair of Elijah, facing east, which is the direction of Jerusalem. A piece of cotton is dipped in vodka and placed between the infant's lips. Then the mohel performs the severing of the foreskin, the price paid to God. The rabbi says: 'And as he has entered into this Covenant, may he enter into marriage and good deeds.'

They tell me I, Joe Buchman, urinate in the Rabbi's face.

I know *Your* tricks.

I have been frightened before. Not for me to whine and beg and doven and crawl on my belly.

I am a man.

Where would I have been – by *Your* will? Murdered – like my sister, Gittel? Dead – like my brother, Isaiah? Out of fear become a pious man – like my papa?

You **have taken *Your* retribution. Three sons who are stupid and grasping and cowardly. A daughter who loves a goy. They are *Yours*. I give them back to *You*. Except for Jesse. *You* sent, for Jesse, a strong stubborn woman who turns him against me. But I will win. She carries Jesse's child. She is a good strong vessel for Jesse's seed, which is my seed. The rest are *Yours*. That child will be mine.**

I copy it down. On the day of Gittel's birth, the scribe has written:

A girl, without ceremony, is born to the house of Yitschok, the wagon driver, the bootlegger. The wife of Yitschok, Lenya, recites the woman's Sabbath prayer over the candles – her hands fluttering like the wings of bad luck swallows, in her voice the note of mourning *as familiar as the weekday taste of black bread and herring. After-wards, she begins to put away the best of the chicken feathers for what will be the pillows and feather bed of Gittel's dowry.*

They tell me, on that day, I am carried to cheder, kicking and screaming in the belfer's arms. They tell me I, Joe Buchman, strike the melamed with his own stick.

Why do *You* look at Lincoln's pocket watch?

I will live another twenty years. Against *Your* will. As it was with everything.

I am a man.

Before you took away my papa's hand – he said to me: *Josef – there are two things that stir the heart of a man. Land that belongs to him, and a woman who doesn't.*

I copy it down. On the day of Isaiah's birth, the scribe has written:

In the month of Elul, when from the synagogue come the notes of the shofar, the child Isaiah is born, backwards, and in pain. His name is changed to Nosen to fool the Evil One. Sheets, bearing messages, are hung around his mother's bed. Yitschok engages ten batlanim to fast and offer prayers. On the third evening, Yitschok goes with Josef, his oldest son of seven years, from house to house, calling the villagers to a special synagogue service at dawn to pray for Isaiah's life. And late that night, they stretch cords in the snow of the cemetery around the graves of the virtuous dead.

But Isaiah dies before dawn.

They tell me, at dawn, I follow my papa to the synagogue where the villagers have gathered to pray for Isaiah. They tell me I, Joe Buchman, remove my boots, follow my papa inside, up to the Holy Ark, where I, like Yitschok, raise my right hand and curse God.

I am, afterwards, like my papa, called *The Litvak.*

I lie here. Chills and fever. The river rises. I say to *You:* This is my land. These are my fields. This is my home. Mississippi. I have made it mine. Against *Your* will. As Sarah is mine. Against *Your* will. I took what I wanted. I, Joe Buchman. Against the laws of God, and sometimes against the laws of men. What would *You* have for me?

Poverty? Pogroms? A marriage without love?

* * *

Reuben sat up. His head reeled. Blindly, he laid the pages down on the marble-topped table, then found himself looking into the dark eye of the pistol. He saw the tattoo on Army Jones' arm: JACKIE; saw Jacqueline Carruthers, alive; dead; felt no rest from the sleep which had brought dreams of the dead: his grandfather, his father, his grandmother, Elena, Lea, Buster – each of them filing past; dismal; silent.

What had he read?

His grandfather's voice had filled the room – now it escaped him. A deafness seemed to have fallen on his ears.

He stood up. His limbs felt weak. Driven by a need for activity, he found himself circling the room, past midmorning shadows of jasmine and crape myrtle falling across the polished planks of the floor.

He stopped, found himself standing in front of the cracked mirror – in his distorted reflection, some kind of truth.

He felt the need to bolt.

An arid desolation swept him.

The River Rises. He felt he could hear it. He saw the room darken, heard the thunder, saw lightning crack, felt the beginning of cracks in the levee of his psyche, felt the weight of a dark and swirling river, insistent, ready to wash over what he knew of his life.

He left the room.

He moved down the dark and narrow stairs, left the old man behind. The living room was dark, the shades drawn, the oil painting of the shack and the cotton field hanging in shadow. A mouse scuttled from the overstuffed sofa, eagle-head arms, eagle-clawed feet.

He stopped at the piano, let his eyes roam over the photographs on the draped brocade shawl, saw himself, a child, with long curls that Frieda had refused to cut.

In the corner cabinet, he found the bourbon and the crystal glasses. He poured himself a stiff drink, swallowed it down, felt the liquor collide with dread, and hysteria, and yearning.

He felt a painful groping that threatened to go beyond the limits of blood and history.

He poured another drink.

Then he heard a tinkling sound, like a cowbell in a pasture.

Carrying the glass, he moved out into the hall, opened the front door. The fig vines obscured his view, but he could hear the sound of a group of black children kicking a ball around in the dust. *'How come you do that – nigger –'* one of them shouted.

He left the front door open, moved back down the hall, the sound of the children's shouting following behind him. Then he located the sound, coming from Willie's room, knew what it was – Willie tapping a glass with a spoon.

He opened Willie's door, left it open, let the air blow in. He swallowed some bourbon, then moved to the bed. Willie stopped tapping. Willie's face had turned rawboned, the color of parchment, his forehead beaded with sweat. He said, 'Hello, Willie.'

An attempt at a smile creased Willie's face like old tissue. He said, 'I'll be damned.' A draft blew in, filled with old memories.

'How are you?'

'Not too good.'

'You look fine.'

'You're a liar. I taught you how to be a pretty damned good hunter, but I never could teach you to lie any good.'

'What's the trouble?'

'I got the chills, and the fever.'

'What's the doctor's number?'

Willie put his hand on the phone, beside his bed. 'Won't do no good.'

'Don't worry about the money.'

'Won't do no good,' Willie repeated. 'He cursed me. He don't want me livin' in this house. He knows I ain't got nowhere to go.'

'What are you talking about?'

'Him.' Willie shivered, wrapped the blankets tighter around him. The reddish hair was damp, plastered. Reuben could hear his teeth chattering. The smell of death came from him. 'Long as Elena was alive, he let me alone. Ain't been nobody here since the funeral – but him and me.'

'Who?'

'You know who. I sent Sister up there to clean out his room – but it didn't do no good. He's winnin'. He's been waitin' all these years. He never forgave me.' Willie's eyes rolled back in his head.

'Listen – let me fix you some breakfast.'

'You got a cigarette?'

'Sure.' Reuben set the bourbon down, shook out a cigarette, held the flame to it for Willie.

'Where's Sister?'

'She'll be back later.'

'He ran her off – didn't he?'

Reuben picked up the bourbon, swallowed some. 'I don't believe in ghosts.'

Willie shook his head. 'I ain't got the heart to fight him. I done it to him. I was young. I was wrong. He's right. I ain't got no business in this house. Sister keeps on tellin' me it's the melancholy. It ain't the melancholy. It's the malaria. I ain't never had the malaria. It's him. You know how Elena was – not a woman to keep a man's bed warm. I miss her alright, but it ain't that, It's him.' Willie stopped, dragged on the cigarette, began to cough. Reuben took the cigarette from him, put it out. A look of terror crossed Willie's face. The coughing stopped. A chill took him over, rattled his body. Finally it subsided. 'He brought you back here,' Willie said. 'He means for me to tell you. I ain't gonna do it. I can't.'

'Tell me what?'

'What are you doin' here?' Willie said.

'I came to see about you.'

'You're a liar. I know you. I know you better than anybody. I know your face. I never could teach you to lie any good.' Willie scrutinised his face.

Reuben heard himself say, 'I killed someone.'

A silence fell. The draft sent a series of small electric shocks through his body. He finished the bourbon. His hand was shaking.

'That's how he brought you back,' Willie said.

'I'll fix you some breakfast.'

The river rages.
I fight the chills. I will not die. I defy *Your* will.
I hear him.
Why do I, now, from outside my window, hear the song of the Ukrainian night watchman?
I hear him:

'Friends . . . enemies, listen to me!
Who is here? It is only me, a lonely night watchman.
Flown from me is the peace of the night.
Sleep, numbing sleep, comes creeping through my bones.
Am I, like you, a man?
Or an image cast in stone?'

They tell me it is the quinine which makes for this madness. It is not the quinine. They say when a man is dying, his life moves again in front of him. I am not dying. Why, then, do I see my life?

Why do I remember the Narodnik?
I swim in the River Bug, my twelfth year. He comes to

the river bank – a Jew dressed as a peasant, come to organise the peasants against the Czar. Through the gorod of Kominetz Podolsk, spreading his slogan: *To the people.* He says to me: *The will of the people is more important than the will of God.* A week later, they carry his body through the village.

Why do *You* sit there wearing Lincoln's beard? The rain has washed away the cottonseed. I will plant again. I will not die. I will not whine and lie and beat my breast. I am a man. As my papa was once a man – before You took away his hand.

I remember.
It is my thirteenth year. It is January, 1881. I ride in my papa's sled. The River Bug is frozen solid, sliced by the tracks of skates and sled runners, the ferry moored to the pier. In the back of my papa's sled are six gallons of vodka to be traded to the peasant Serge Trubitsky for six live geese to be later slaughtered by the shohet. In the curve of the bank is a black hole which Gimpel has cut into the ice. The small stretch of beach where I have watched the women do their summer scrubbing is empty.

The moon rises. A cold piece of ice. We enter the forest. I sit next to my papa like a man. The wind howls, carries the sound of wolves. We move through the forest.

The Land clears. Peasants' cottages squat to their windowsills in snow. Stands of barren cherry trees are locked in ice, lined up like Cossacks. My papa sighs. He says: '*The farther a man gets from the earth, Josef, the more of a slave he becomes.*'

I remember.
The sled stops at an inn. A weathered Russian sign flaps in the wind. I am left alone, in the snow. I climb from the sled. I peer through the lighted window. I see peasants gathered at rough tables, two roaring fireplaces. At a bar a Muhzik plays a balalaika. I see a boy my own age. His face is wise, not ignorant like my own. I wonder how it would be to have a different God. Then I see my papa. He calls out to someone who is hidden in the shadows of the bar. It is a woman – not pale and fragile like my mother – but full and round, wearing her own thick, light-colored hair, wearing a pale blue shawl. She is laughing. My papa

embraces her, without shame. My heart begins to beat. I feel pain. She whispers in his ear. He laughs, shakes his head. She leans towards him. Her shawl falls away. Her dress is cut low. I see her breasts. She thrusts a small muslin bag into his hand.

I remember.

At the house of Serge Trubitsky, papa exchanges the vodka for six live geese, each wrapped in muslin. Then the sled moves through the snow. I am quiet. My papa gives me the muslin bag. It is filled with raisins. He says: *'Through windows, Josef, a man does not learn about life.'* I am quiet. He says: *'This is not a Jewish thing I tell you. Only in Gon Aden will the soul be settled. On earth, a man's flesh cries out for the earth. On earth, a man's flesh cries out for a woman of the earth. There is an animal in man that will not wait for heaven.'* I am quiet. He says: *'God is in Gon Aden, it is easy for Him.'* He says: *'There are two sights that stir the heart of a man. Land that belongs to him – and a woman who doesn't.'*

I am quiet. I eat the raisins.

Finally, I say: *'I am closer to you, Papa, than to God.'*

I remember.

The sled enters the forest. I remember. Coming through the trees, their eyes glittering like candles, is the pack of wolves. Papa whips the horse. I throw them a goose. They stop to tear at it. The sled speeds through the snow. The wolves come after us. I throw another goose. A few stop. The rest continue after us. I throw another goose. And then another. When all the geese are gone, one wolf still follows the sled. He leaps. He lands on the sled, teeth bared. My papa fights him. His jaws open. He snarls. My papa shoves his gloved hand down into the throat of the wolf. The wolf struggles, choking to death on my father's hand. Finally, there is silence. The wolf falls limp. My papa removes his hand. It is a bloody, tangled mass.

I remember.

The limb is buried, with prayers, in the cemetery plot which will, in the future, receive the rest of my papa's body. It is a week he does not speak. When he finally speaks, he says: *'God willing, so be it.'*

He has lost.

You have won.

You beat my papa. But *You* will not beat me. The river
rises. The malaria grips me. I know every one of *Your*
tricks. Like Rachel. *You* sent me Rachel – the way, later,
You sent me the boll weevil. Sometimes *You* send a wolf,
and sometimes a beautiful woman. I was young then. How
was I to know when I married Rachel that *You* had sent a
plague upon me?

A splitting pain roared in Reuben's head.

He moved in a blind cloud, through shades of dark, laid the
papers down on the sink, heard the sound of them, like the
funereal rustle of black silk and old women's petticoats, and the
sense of danger that makes an animal bolt through the woods.

The water in the pot was boiling on the hot plate, set on his
grandmother's old wood stove, the water making a sound like the
humming of bees.

He poured in the instant grits, stirred, watched the water suck
them into a cyclonic rage. At the back of his neck, he felt a pain as
sharp and as quick as a razor cut. A fluid terror washed through
him.

He turned off the grits, spooned them into a plate, set the plate
on the tray with the cup of instant coffee.

His footsteps echoed across the tile floor.

He knew what he had to do. Find Sister. Get out of here.

Then he heard the sound of the television spilling out into the
hall, from Willie's room.

Forty-four

WILLIE had turned the set on.

A distorted version of last night's events flickered on the screen,
gleaned from some other version of reality. The details of time and
place were accurate. Then a film clip of Simmons talked about a
series of stake-outs, ongoing police precautions, invented surveillance – all covering the tracks of entrapment. Then, a photograph of Jacqueline Carruthers filled the screen, and over it, a

newscaster said, '*It has been established that the bullet that killed Jacqueline Carruthers came from the gun of Patrolman Mike Harper, who lies, even now, in a Memphis hospital, undergoing a serious operation for a lung wound received in the line of duty.*'

'Did you kill her?' Willie's question came from his own knowledge of official violence and its techniques of camouflage. Reuben looked at Willie, who had somehow gotten himself up, dressed in his patrolman's uniform, had pinned on the badge, was sitting in a chair. 'Was it her?'

'Yes.'

The announcer's voice continued. '*In Miss Carruthers' purse, a twenty-five-caliber loaded Belgian-type pistol was found, along with identification cards indicating membership in the Original Knights of the Ku Klux Klan, and the United Klans of America. Police and F.B.I. agents, after a search of the schoolteacher's home, uncovered literature from hate organisations, and instructions on how to make bombs.*'

'The old man woulda been proud of you,' Willie said.

The nausea came back, settled high in Reuben's throat.

The newscaster said, '*While commendations arrive from around the country, an opposing viewpoint has been expressed by Dean Leland Goss, an active spokesman for states' rights in Mississippi. Goss released the following statement to reporters:*

' "*Jacqueline Carruthers was a wonderful Christian patriot, who tried to teach her students true Americanism and firm Christianity. We do not know the real circumstances of her death, but indications are that this terrible occurrence was a stupid, bloodthirsty act by incompetent police, undoubtedly under the direction of the F.B.I.*" '

Reuben went into Willie's bathroom and retched again.

When he came out, Willie had turned off the television. Willie said, 'It ain't in your nature, that's all. But a man has to fight – even if it goes against his nature.'

He saw Willie had started trembling again, the beads of sweat had come back. Willie looked frail, thin, the uniform hung slack like a castoff on a scarecrow, the badge glimmering in the dim light like the last of Willie's soul shining through. Reuben could feel the shadows of death settling in. 'Eat your grits.'

'I got to talk to you,' Willie said.

'I'm going to find Sister.'

He left the house. The sun was almost overhead, muted by a thin set of moistureless clouds. The children, playing ball, had vanished. A couple of chickens pecked along beside him, as he walked the length of the street to the warehouse, in a fogged state, feeling like a casualty in some battle barely begun.

When he reached the crumbling warehouse that had once held his grandfather's cotton, he turned, looked back down the street. Something caught in his throat, a sound, silent, the cry of the survivor. He looked at the one lone tree he had climbed as a child, an oak, thick-trunked and nearly leafless with dying roots, but still spreading its gnarled arms. A black man shuffled past, tipped a cap, nodded, a familiar face, like a mud-caked mule. From somewhere, somebody began to play a mouth organ, soft and awkward. Then he saw the three black women sitting on a porch, talking in low slurred voices, a swing lurching back and forth, a piece of laughter – the sounds pressed against his brain. Then he saw that two of them were old, like Sister, but one was young, ripe, a memory of Eula Williams.

He came back down the street, stopped in front of the porch, addressing himself to the old one on the swing. 'Where's Sister?'

The old one smiled, nearly toothless, bobbed her head, then said, 'I couldn't be tellin' you,' in that mixture of mistrust, and treachery, and generosity that he recognised as survival.

Then the young one said, 'She don't know,' in a mellifluous voice, sitting on the top step, raising her arms, and grasping the back of her head, and arching her body in an extravagant pull of flesh and bone, as if she could smell the violence in him, the blood of the newly slain, and silently telling him he had finally done it, killed, but hadn't laid a black woman – offering him the completion of his identity, the actualisation of his destiny. He had a sense of her laid out, a warm, dark, swelling body, in his grandfather's bed – the consummation, the final fatality. And afterwards, the diminished suffering, the loss of isolation, the irrevocable evidence of the thing he had been born to, and his deep, abiding commitment to it; like the blood streaming from the body of Jacqueline Carruthers – his semen streaming from her, his place claimed, assured forever.

He heard himself say, 'If you see Sister – tell her I'm lookin' for her.'

'Who you be?' the old woman said.

The young one giggled.

Forty-five

The rain continues. The river continues to rise. Jesse comes to tell me that streams have begun to trickle through the water-soaked bank. The men work through the night by the light of kerosene torches, fifteen hundred on the levee, black, white, even the convicts have been brought in to haul the gunny sacks.

And *You* sit there silent.
As if *You* have not sent the raging river, and the malaria, and all of it.
As if *You* had not sent everything.

It was *You* who sent my papa to Count Valkonsky to exchange the secrets of corn brandy for a pistol – Lithuanian oak, charred and made into pegs, his own papa's secret. It was *You* who sent us both to the river bank, my papa with his right sleeve pinned up, teaching me to shoot – with each shot naming to me every angel and his place in heaven. Saying: '*God has His will.*'

I copy it down, on that day, as the scribe has written it:

On the eve of Purim, a Polish student named Ignacy Grinevitsky throws a bomb at a carriage traveling along the Catherine Canal. An hour later, Alexander II, mortally wounded, is carried to the palace. There, surrounded by Alexander III, by Maria Feodorovna – mother of Nicholas – and by Princess Yuriesvskaya – his former mistress and new bride – Alexander II dies.

From St Petersburg come rumors of the Sacred League, led by Pobedonostsev, the Czar's adviser, claiming that the Jews are the source of the assassination. From other villages come stories of Jews set upon by hooligans known as The Barefoot Brigade.

In the morning the sound of the clamor of hooves comes first to our village, rising from far off like the rumble of thunder. Then, like a thick black cloud, the ruffians hurtle into our village, swooping down upon the poor dwellings with torches.

Terrified Jews, hidden in cellars and lofts, are routed out and attacked.

*Moishe, the blacksmith, his beard and caftan on fire, runs scream-
ing down the streets until a knife is plunged into his back, with a deep
guttural cry of Hep! Hep! Juden Herais!*

*Four hooligans enter the house of Reb Yakob and cut open the
head of his wife. His youngest son, who has been hiding under the bed,
crawls out and kisses her dead body, and is killed on the spot.*

*At the house of Gorenstein, three are killed – one, his head broken
into halves like a peach; the youngest daughter assaulted, then
wounded, left deaf.*

*In the house of Hoffman, both he and his wife are taken outside –
his wife stripped and forced to dance naked. Then two men assault her
while he is forced to look on. No one escapes.*

*In the house of Yitschok – three ruffians enter after setting fire to
the wagon outside. The girl, Gittel, is assaulted and murdered. The
feathers of her dowry, scattered and bloody, drift down over everything. Yitschok, swinging a meat cleaver with his one hand, kills two
men. Josef, the son, crawls to the floorboard beneath which a pistol is
hidden, rises, shoots the last ruffian in the stomach, dead.*

*Behind the looters come peasants, with sleds, to gather up the
things the pillagers will leave behind.*

The pigs of the peasants will eat the corpses of neighbors.

My papa says: '*God has His will.*'

I learn Count Valkonsky's distillery. I learn to germinate
the barley, to dry it, to kiln it and grind it, to add the mash
to produce the wort, to pitch it with yeast to produce the
wash, which will be distilled five times, then aged in the
charred Lithuanian oak barrels. I learn it well. The village
falls upon hard times. The May Laws declare all Jewish
contracts illegal, confine all Jews to the towns of the Pale,
subject them to police harassment and bribery. But my
papa and I – we smell of yeast and kopeks. And Zelda, who
is the mother of Rachel and Sarah says: 'Love is better
with bread.'

You send me Rachel.

I am drunk for my wedding. Rachel wears small braids
with a sugar cube at the base of each, for a sweet life. Like
the honey which was smeared on the cover of my first
book at cheder, the sugar is a lie.

It is our wedding night. I light the lamp. Rachel says:
'Even the mice must not see – it is against God.' She ex-
tinguishes the lamp. She weeps.

She wears layers of garments, prescribed by law. I

command her to remove them. She says: 'A woman must wear something – it is against God.'

I say: 'You are wearing your wedding ring – is that not enough?' She weeps.

She says: 'What kind of man are you? – against God.'

She has beautiful dark hair. I forbid her the woman's wig. At the *mikvah*, they shave her head. She says: 'It is for God.' For the week of her menstrual period and for the week afterwards, she occupies a separate bedroom. She says: 'It is for God. Half of the month I must belong to you and half to God.

I say: '*Let God find his own woman!*'

Rachel is with child.

I take the train from the railway station of Gven into Vinitza. I am drunk. I walk the streets. I go to a house of women. There is a woman with light thick hair like the peasant woman at the inn. . . .

I go often, after that, to Vinitza.

One night, I return at dawn. Rachel has gone to her parents' house. I find Sarah in my house. Everything has been turned upside down. Her eyes are blazing. She says: 'I will not be married to Mottel, son of Reb Yakob. I came here tonight to find enough money to take me to Moscow.'

I say: 'The only Jewish women allowed in Moscow are those with yellow cards – prostitutes.'

She says: 'I will get a yellow card, then. When I have enough money for passage – I will go to America.'

I am quiet. I know I am drunk, still, but it is not the vodka which burns my blood. Finally I say: 'We will go to America. You and me and Rachel – we will all go to America.'

I see she is shaking. She says: 'Why?'

It is not the vodka. I say: 'I will have you. Against God and against man, I swear it. I will have you.'

She is quiet. Then she says: '*Yes.*'

Jesse comes to tell me the rain grows worse. The river is turgid, frothing with scum, rising still.

I look at Jesse. He is my youngest son – more a man than any of the rest. The one I love the best.

I have told him.

There is time.

* * *

Reuben felt himself fill with a desperate need to cry. But he could hear only the sound of his own racking breathing.

He set the diary beside the old man's bed. He rose. He tried to clear his head. Outside the windows, the evening shadows had brought a light rain. He tried to remember where the day had gone. He had read, drunk, fallen into heavy bursts of dreamless sleep. He had sent for the doctor who had arrived during the afternoon – had put Willie to sleep with a shot, had predicted that Willie would not last through another day. How many hours ago? He couldn't remember.

He emptied the crystal decanter, swallowed what was left of the bourbon.

Then he heard the sound of a crash echo up the stairs, followed by another, and the sound of scruffling.

He hurried downstairs and into Willie's room, dark except for a streak of light coming out of the bathroom – Willie, up, dressed in the uniform, thrashing around and knocking things over, and crying out, '*He's come*. He's come to get me. The old man's after me!'

Reuben grabbed Willie by the shoulders and held on until the thrashing quit. 'C'mon, Willie. There're no ghosts here. . . . '

'He's after me,' Willie said. But he allowed himself to be led to the bed and lowered. The light from the bathroom streaked across his face, bathed in sweat. 'You gotta listen. He's after me. I tore it up. I tore up his *will*.'

'There wasn't no will,' Reuben said gently. 'C'mon – there wasn't no will, and there's no such thing as ghosts.'

Trembling tore through Willie's bones. 'I'm tellin' you – five days after the flood – and that convict showed up with his body. It was me at the river, and the convict come to get his fifty dollars for the old man's body. Still wearin' that tuxedo from the weddin' – and I went through his pockets, and there it was – all wrapped in an oilskin packet. I read it – everything left to Jesse. I always liked Jesse. But I hated that old man. You can understand why I hated him. So I tore it up. Me – Methodist Willie – I tore it up. And now he's come to get me – ' The trembling ceased. Tears streamed down Willie's face.

'He ain't gonna get you,' Reuben said gently.

'Now you hate me, don't you?' Willie said. 'I tried to make it up to you. I taught you everything he woulda wanted you to know. I taught you to shoot, didn't I? I gave you your first drink of whiskey. I never said nothin' bad to you about him. I used to tell myself – I gave you somethin' better'n land – somebody to look up to. The livin' – they always make a misstep – but the dead can be what you want 'em to be. And now you know what I done – and you hate me, don't you?'

'It don't matter anymore,' Reuben said. 'It don't mean nothin' anymore.'

Willie's body rattled. His teeth chattered. Then the chill subsided. 'I got a bottle in the nightstand,' Willie said. 'Could you pour me a drink?'

'Sure.'

'You don't hate me?'

'No.'

'Maybe we could have a drink,' Willie said. 'One drink?'

I have the need to tell my life to Jesse.

I say: 'I came across an ocean.'

I say: 'I gave all my money to Rachel and her unborn child.'

I say: 'We live in a ghetto, Sarah and me. We speak no English. I work as night watchman in a sweatshop. My payment is the rags that are left on the floor which I am allowed to sell. I am arrested for peddling without a license.'

I say: 'With Sarah, I join a colony of Jews on its way to Louisiana. It is part of a back to the land movement sponsored by Baron de Hirsch. The temperature is 108 degrees. We live in an abandoned plantation house, ten to a room. I learn to grow cotton, corn. We are surrounded by deserted plantations, ignorant Negroes, cut off from the world, plagued by rattlesnakes and mosquitoes and malaria and floods. Most are not fit, by nature, to work the land. We fail.'

I say: 'With Sarah, I come upriver. I find this place. It is mine. It is yours. What is mine is yours. I know I am in Egypt. But it is mine.'

Jesse does not understand. He says: 'Papa – the river rises.'

I know that Jesse cannot see *You*, sitting there with Lincoln's face. The God of My Fathers.

I have no guilt.

What can *You* do to a man without guilt? I have whored with black women, white women. I have killed. I have made and sold whiskey. I have taken land from the weak. I have lived with a woman not my wife for forty years. It was *You*

404

who prepared me to become a foreigner. This place is mine.

I am a man.

I defy *You* one last time.

I say to Jesse: 'Tomorrow we have a wedding. Tomorrow I marry your mother. You find your brothers on the levee. You give them my instructions. Reb will get the Rabbi from Memphis. Itz will get the wine and the vodka and the *chuppah*. Nate will arrange the musicians – I would like a balalaika. You will set tables for everyone in the Baptist church. We will ride in on five white horses. Everything as it should be.'

I say to Jesse: 'It is not the malaria. It is not the quinine. You do as I say.'

I look at Jesse. The son I love.

I know it is time to give him my blessing.

I begin to reach for Jesse – to stroke his cheek – although he is a man. He is my favorite. I begin to reach for him to tell him: I love you. But I do not know what dybbuk possesses me. Instead – my hand strikes him – with all my strength. And I find myself saying: 'I am not afraid. There is nothing I fear. I am not afraid.'

He leaves me.

I am not afraid.

I am not –

The journal ended.

A silence fell, deep and empty, filling the house.

Reuben laid the journal beside the lamp.

The silence extended itself, rang shrill, became nothingness.

He reached for the crystal decanter, saw he had emptied it. Angrily, he began to rummage through the room, looking for whiskey, pulling out the drawers of the acorn-carved dresser, throwing open the doors of an armoire. He found nothing but old clothes, blankets, the smell of the dead rising to pervade the room.

He came barreling downstairs, flung himself through the parlor, rummaged through the corner cabinet – found nothing but glasses, crystal, shattering as he swept the shelves clean.

He came back down the hall. He halted at Willie's door. He remembered the bottle of bourbon from Willie's nightstand. *Could your pour me a drink?*

He opened the door, came across the room, stood by the bed – the bottle of bourbon where he had left it.

Willie was dead.

He grasped the bottle, tilted it, poured the searing liquid down his throat.

Then he fled.

Forty-six

HE RAN.

He ran through the light rain, coming down, making mud out of the street, misting the light coming out of the shacks.

He ran stumbling past the warehouse, and onto the wooden bridge where he stopped, scorched his throat with the liquor, then began to run again – the sound of his feet echoing across the bridge.

A pair of headlights streamed through the rain, heading towards him.

He left the road.

He ran through yards, past barking dogs, continued to run until the houses stopped, and he could see the dark looming shadows of trees standing undisturbed against the sky. He stopped, once more, guzzled the liquor, felt it burn his gut. Then he began to run again, across the open field, towards the stand of trees.

He stumbled, fell, face down against the earth.

There was an explosion in his head, with shafts of light streaking out like the spars of a wheel, and he could feel his face being ground down and down as the lights consumed him into a terrible darkness, and the silence that pervaded the moment of death – and he felt it happening, but could not name it; could not tell if his eyes were open or closed, because the darkness remained. And he could feel himself buried in something dark and wet, face down, the substance oozing against his face, and the feel and the smell of it, familiar, the Mississippi mud.

He dragged himself to a sitting position, waiting for the pain to wash over him; hearing the sound of water somewhere close, and above him – through the pine needles – moonlight coming down with the rain, but not enough to tell him how long he had been lying there, so cold and wet that he could no longer feel it, in the Mississippi mud.

It felt, suddenly, like snow. . . .

It felt like the snow the year he was twelve.

The year he was twelve, he had wanted a shotgun. Jesse had taken him to the old Cosgrove plantation and taught him how to kill squirrels without a shotgun. *A Buchman's got to know how to survive on the land.* . . .

And now it came back to him. He had tripped, fallen – dropped the dead squirrels in the snow.

The rest of it came back.

The lucid sight of his father's face as Jesse had stopped in the snow beside him. The strange feel of his father's hand as Jesse had reached out and stroked his cheek. The strange sound of his father's voice, saying, *I ain't got much to give you, boy.* . . . Stroking his cheek. And sudden tears in Jesse's eyes.

He could hear Jesse saying, *I know there's gotta be another way for a man to go. Some way that ain't like I used to be.* . . . *Some way that ain't like I've come to be now.* . . . Jesse, shaking his head and saying, *But I can't find it.* . . . Saying, *I love your mama. She's always sayin' – you don't owe nothin' to nobody, Jesse Buchman, that's a man. But that don't seem enought for a man. There's another way. Maybe you'll find it.* . . .

Stroking his cheek. And tears in Jesse's eyes.

I love you, boy. . . .

And Jesse had held him in a suffocating embrace. . . .

The moment he had put out of his mind for thirty years. The moment he had construed as his father's weakness. The moment in time when he had disowned his father.

From somewhere, through the rain, he heard a man crying.

MARYVILLE, 12 MILES

Mollie's headlights swept the sign, moved swiftly on, the station wagon flying awkwardly, at top speed, down the flat white high-way – Willie's terse, strained telephone voice echoing: *He needs you. That woman – on the television – he killed her.*

No.

She knew that much. He was not a killer. She knew that much.

What did she know? Nothing.

What did she know of the bombing? Of the events that pre-ceded it? Of the events as they happened? Nothing. What did she know of the man she now sped towards ? Who he was, what he had done, how he felt about her ? Nothing.

She had stopped to think about none of it, had responded simply at some primitive level. She could not call it love, had no names to give it – only the names no longer applicable, no longer fear, or sham, or self-concern.

He needs you – Willie's voice, not Reuben's.

She reached the outskirts of Maryville.

She came into town, moving past the darkened small-lawned houses misted by rain.

Then she began to hear something – like the strange, discordant tolling of a bell, clanging through the two a.m. quiet, disturbing the night.

She came through the Square, past the City Hall, unable to decipher the direction from which the sound came, confused by the deceptiveness of night sound, but hearing that it had become louder, more strident, constant, eerie – moving with her as she sped down the street which led to the wooden bridge – and was struck, suddenly, by the irrational feeling that the sound had to do with Reuben, somehow, whatever it was, wherever it was.

At the warehouse, she turned into the dirt street.

With relief, she saw the white Cadillac parked at the end, in front of the house – knew then that, whatever the bell was – it had nothing to do with Reuben.

She parked behind the Cadillac, climbed out, ran through the rain to the steps, entered the porch. The sound of the bell filled the air, constant, ripping. She began to bang on the door, calling for Reuben, calling for Willie. But the house remained dark, silent. From somewhere down the street, a light went on. She heard someone shout, 'Who's that bell goin' for out there ?'

She came down the steps, stood in the rain, looked down the street. The street remained empty. The bell kept on.

Then she knew what it was. The sound of the bell.

When she reached the cemetery, her headlights splashed his figure, through the rain. Like an apparition against the iron cemetery fence, and the headstones rising behind him, and pulling on the old fire bell, drunk and crying and muddy, his face contorted by pain, become one with the shattering sound of the bell, and shouting something she could not hear.

She climbed out, and began to run towards him. In a moment, she was close enough to hear the sound of his voice, but she could not make out the thing he was shouting.

She ran to him.

He pushed her away – no recognition in his eyes, consumed by the act of pulling the bell rope, grown threadbare, the rain and the tears and the mud streaking his face, the bell clanging across the graveyard, and the sound of his drunken voice, shouting, '*Enough ! Enough !*'

Shouting, '*Enough of dying !*'

Forty-seven

HE WOKE in the old man's bed.

He turned his head. He was not surprised to find Mollie, sitting in a chair in front of the window, against the light. He could see that the rain had quit – sunshine streamed past her – and, outside, the woodpecker had gone back to work on the tree.

'Willie. What about Willie ?'

'I called this morning. They came – and took his body. You'll have to make the funeral arrangements. I – I didn't think you'd want me to do that.'

He had an image of her, dealing with all of it, quietly, with a strength he had never seen. 'What time is it ?'

'Noon.'

He sat up, realised he was naked, saw she had bathed him. She said nothing. He got out of bed, moved past her into the bathroom.

When he came out, Mollie had his clothes laid across the bed, somehow had gotten them cleaned and pressed, another piece of quiet strength. Then he saw she was standing by the table, and looking down at the pistol, and he saw she knew. She turned, looked at him silently. He knew what she wanted. She wanted him to say it wasn't true. He thought about years of compliance to the dead, and it had not been love. And he knew compliance to the needs of the living was not love either.

He said, 'Yes.'

Her face paled.

He got into his trousers, pulled on the sweater.

Mollie walked to the window and looked out. He could hear the voices of black children, the barking of a dog. He came up behind her.

He looked down at the street. Beneath the window, a half-dozen black boys were kicking a ball in the dirt. One of them shouted, '*How come you do that, nigger ?*'

Mollie turned. He saw the girl was gone from her. He knew he would miss it.

He looked at her for a long moment. He felt tears spring to his eyes. He felt an urge to stroke her cheek. As Jesse had done to him. Felt an urge to say: *There's another way. We'll find it. I don't know what it is – but I know we'll find it.*

He knew it would not be that simple.

'Go home,' he said.

He made the arrangements for Willie's funeral.

He closed all the windows.

He closed the door to the old man's room.

He came down the stairs, slowly, went into the parlor, and picked up the photograph of his father as a young man on horseback, in the cotton fields.

When he came back into the hall, he heard the sound of his grandmother's rocker creaking on the porch – heard the sound of someone singing softly.

When he came out onto the porch, he saw it was littered with stuff – broken candelabra, and old picture frames, and chipped dishes, a hatrack, an umbrella stand, an old hunting jacket – everything in a pile. And Sister, sitting in his grandmother's rocker.

'I brung it all back. All of it. What you want me to do with it ?'

He hesitated. He went over it all once more with his eyes, then came back to Sister's face. 'Keep it.'

The rocker quit. Her eyes narrowed, trying to read his face, all the years of reading a white man's face coming together in her look. 'What you mean – keep it ?'

'I mean – keep it. You can have it. You can have all of it. All this stuff. Everything in the house. You can have the house. It's yours.'

Fear leaped up in Sister's eyes. She wrapped herself in old sweatered arms, her fingers turning gray. 'What you mean – I can have the house ?'

'Live in it. Everything in it. Whatever you want to do with it. I mean – you can have it. I'm a lawyer – I'll make out the papers, send them to you. What's your name ?'

She began to shake her head back and forth. 'Delphia White.'

'Delphia White. It's yours.' He moved across the porch, and opened the screen door. Sister said, 'Wait a minute.'

He stopped, turned. He saw she looked terrified.

She said, 'What you mean I can have the house?'

'It's your turn,' he said.

He went down the steps. As he moved along the weed-grown walk, he heard the rocker begin to creak again, heard the sound of the slipper soles clap against the porch floor.

As he got in his car, he heard Sister begin to sing again, softly.

'Children go . . . go tell it on the mountain . . .'

He drove off without looking back.

STILETTO
by Harold Robbins

**She was scorchingly,
hopelessly in love — with the Mafia!**

Barbara Lang was New York's top fashion model. Count
Cesare Cardinali was Sicily's most irresistible playboy.
Together, the Count and his girl spawned death where
ever they travelled – death by stiletto.

But Barbara, though blinded by love, could not close her
eyes to the horrors of history's most vicious crime
syndicate. Though passionately in love with Cesare, she
was terrified of the stiletto.

Harold Robbins, author of the world's greatest selling
trilogy – THE DREAM MERCHANTS, THE CARPET-
BAGGERS, THE INHERITORS – has excelled his own
brilliant standards with this action-packed story of a
sultry beauty and her angel of death.

NEW ENGLISH LIBRARY

THE FORTUNATE PILGRIM

by Mario Puzo
author of THE GODFATHER

'Highly charged language, penetrating insights, a mixture
of tenderness and rage . . . a classic.'   —New York Times

 'I began reading Mario Puzo's novel THE FORTUNATE
PILGRIM yesterday afternoon and didn't stop reading
until I had finished it . . . No one I know can create a city
scene with more vivid accuracy.'
                              —*Joseph Heller, author of* Catch 22

 In the neon-lit back streets of New York, in the midst
of the Mafia and the immigrant rat race, Lucia Santa's
family fights to survive. In the great tradition of THE
GODFATHER, Mario Puzo describes the blood-chilling
consequences.

NEW ENGLISH LIBRARY

THE PACT
by Orlando R. Petrocelli

A compelling novel that exposes the power games behind American politics.

At 50, Giacomo 'Jock' Carlona was an established Wall Street financier controlling a multi-million dollar financial empire. His sons' successes in politics had secured the family's status as the premier American-Italian family in the country.

But 'Jock' Carlona was not content.

He was determined to see one of his sons in the White House.

And it was his ruthless determination that was to be his downfall. Unable to prevent a succession of terrible events from taking their course, he was to live to see each of his beloved sons die a violent and premature death.

On sale at newsagents and booksellers everywhere.

NEW ENGLISH LIBRARY

NEL BESTSELLERS

Crime

T013 332	CLOUDS OF WITNESS	*Dorothy L. Sayers*	40p
T016 307	THE UNPLEASANTNESS AT THE BELLONA CLUB	*Dorothy L. Sayers*	40p
T021 548	GAUDY NIGHT	*Dorothy L. Sayers*	40p
T026 698	THE NINE TAILORS	*Dorothy L. Sayers*	50p
T026 671	FIVE RED HERRINGS	*Dorothy L. Sayers*	50p
T015 556	MURDER MUST ADVERTISE	*Dorothy L. Sayers*	40p

Fiction

T018 520	HATTER'S CASTLE	*A. J. Cronin*	75p
T013 944	CRUSADER'S TOMB	*A. J. Cronin*	60p
T013 936	THE JUDAS TREE	*A. J. Cronin*	50p
T015 386	THE NORTHERN LIGHT	*A. J. Cronin*	50p
T026 213	THE CITADEL	*A. J. Cronin*	80p
T027 112	BEYOND THIS PLACE	*A. J. Cronin*	60p
T016 609	KEYS OF THE KINGDOM	*A. J. Cronin*	50p
T027 201	THE STARS LOOK DOWN	*A. J. Cronin*	90p
T018 539	A SONG OF SIXPENCE	*A. J. Cronin*	50p
T001 288	THE TROUBLE WITH LAZY ETHEL	*Ernest K. Gann*	30p
T003 922	IN THE COMPANY OF EAGLES	*Ernest K. Gann*	30p
T023 001	WILDERNESS BOY	*Stephen Harper*	35p
T017 524	MAGGIE D	*Adam Kennedy*	60p
T022 390	A HERO OF OUR TIME	*Mikhail Lermontov*	45p
T025 691	SIR, YOU BASTARD	*G. F. Newman*	40p
T022 536	THE HARRAD EXPERIMENT	*Robert H. Rimmer*	50p
T022 994	THE DREAM MERCHANTS	*Harold Robbins*	95p
T023 303	THE PIRATE	*Harold Robbins*	95p
T022 968	THE CARPETBAGGERS	*Harold Robbins*	£1.00
T016 560	WHERE LOVE HAS GONE	*Harold Robbins*	75p
T023 958	THE ADVENTURERS	*Harold Robbins*	£1.00
T025 241	THE INHERITORS	*Harold Robbins*	90p
T025 276	STILETTO	*Harold Robbins*	50p
T025 268	NEVER LEAVE ME	*Harold Robbins*	50p
T025 292	NEVER LOVE A STRANGER	*Harold Robbins*	90p
T022 226	A STONE FOR DANNY FISHER	*Harold Robbins*	80p
T025 284	79 PARK AVENUE	*Harold Robbins*	75p
T025 187	THE BETSY	*Harold Robbins*	80p
T020 894	RICH MAN, POOR MAN	*Irwin Shaw*	90p

Historical

T022 196	KNIGHT WITH ARMOUR	*Alfred Duggan*	50p
T022 250	THE LADY FOR RANSOM	*Alfred Duggan*	50p
T015 297	COUNT BOHEMOND	*Alfred Duggan*	50p
T017 958	FOUNDING FATHERS	*Alfred Duggan*	50p
T017 753	WINTER QUARTERS	*Alfred Duggan*	50p
T021 297	FAMILY FAVOURITES	*Alfred Duggan*	50p
T022 625	LEOPARDS AND LILIES	*Alfred Duggan*	60p
T019 624	THE LITTLE EMPERORS	*Alfred Duggan*	50p
T020 126	THREE'S COMPANY	*Alfred Duggan*	50p
T021 300	FOX 10: BOARDERS AWAY	*Adam Hardy*	35p

Science Fiction

T016 900	STRANGER IN A STRANGE LAND	*Robert Heinlein*	75p
T020 797	STAR BEAST	*Robert Heinlein*	35p
T017 451	I WILL FEAR NO EVIL	*Robert Heinlein*	80p
T026 817	THE HEAVEN MAKERS	*Frank Herbert*	35p
T027 279	DUNE	*Frank Herbert*	90p
T022 854	DUNE MESSIAH	*Frank Herbert*	60p
T023 974	THE GREEN BRAIN	*Frank Herbert*	35p
T012 859	QUEST FOR THE FUTURE	*A. E. Van Vogt*	35p

NEL P.O. BOX 11, FALMOUTH, CORNWALL.

For U.K. & Eire: customers should include to cover postage, 15p for the first book plus 5p per copy for each additional book ordered, up to a maximum charge of 50p.

For Overseas customers & B.F.P.O.: customers should include to cover postage, 20p for the first book and 10p per copy for each additional book.

Name ....

Address..

....

Title ....
(MAY)